Singer-S‹
of the 1970s

Singer-Songwriters of the 1970s

150+ Profiles

ROBERT MCPARLAND

McFarland & Company, Inc., Publishers
Jefferson, North Carolina

LIBRARY OF CONGRESS CATALOGUING-IN-PUBLICATION DATA

Names: McParland, Robert, author.
Title: Singer-songwriters of the 1970s : 150+ profiles / Robert McParland.
Description: Jefferson, North Carolina : McFarland & Company, Inc.,
Publishers, 2022. | Includes bibliographical references and index.
Identifiers: LCCN 2022034688 | ISBN 9781476686615 (paperback : acid free paper) ∞
ISBN 9781476646435 (ebook)
Subjects: LCSH: Popular music—United States—1971-1980—History and
criticism. | BISAC: MUSIC / History & Criticism
Classification: LCC ML3477 .M43 2022 | DDC 782.4216409/047—dc23/eng/20220720
LC record available at https://lccn.loc.gov/2022034688

BRITISH LIBRARY CATALOGUING DATA ARE AVAILABLE

ISBN (print) 978-1-4766-8661-5
ISBN (ebook) 978-1-4766-4643-5

Front cover: (top, left to right) Joan Armatrading (Eddie Mallin),
Harry Chapin (Elektra), Joni Mitchell (Paul C. Babin),
Bob Dylan (Chris Hakkens), Patti Smith (Klaus Hiltscher) and
Neil Young (Mark Estabrook); bottom images © 2022 Shutterstock

Printed in the United States of America

*McFarland & Company, Inc., Publishers
Box 611, Jefferson, North Carolina 28640
www.mcfarlandpub.com*

Table of Contents

Preface:
Art and the Courage
to Create

It takes courage to write, to paint, to sing, or to dance; it is an act of courage to put oneself or one's ideas newborn into the world. In his 1950 Nobel Prize speech author William Faulkner claimed that the writer "must teach himself that the basest of all things is to be afraid; and, teaching himself that, forget it forever, leaving no room in his workshop for anything but the old verities and truths of the heart [...]."[1] Paul Tillich, a theologian, called this "the courage to be oneself." It takes courage to live, he would say, courage to recognize that "the uniqueness of one's individuality lies in its creative possibilities."[2] This book is intended as a resource for you. It is an encyclopedic volume of a sort, an A-Z of singer-songwriters of the 1970s, an era sometimes called the age of the singer-songwriter. Hopefully, it will be a source of information for you. These are individuals who had the courage to put their ideas, their music, their dreams, and their social criticism into form. While I have included some interpretations of their work, the listener with "the courage to be oneself" may have a different view. That diversity of opinion is welcome. I hope that you will listen to these singer-songwriters and respond to them with your own sense of what they say to you.

Sometimes I feel that everyone has a song. People who make music have a special means to express and share this. This book is written in the spirit and belief that songs fill our culture and touch our lives and that they are meant to be shared. Some people create songs. Others interpret and sing them. And that is very good. Songs, while most often written by individuals, become the songs of the people, sources of cultural memory, or triggers to personal memory. They are like the tea and madeleine crackers in Marcel Proust's *À la recherche du temps perdu* (*Remembrance of Things Past*) that stir a memory. The song remembers when, as Hugh Prestwood once wrote for Trisha Yearwood back in 1993.

Okay, so right now I hope that you realize that you can dive into this book anywhere at all. It does not have to be read consecutively A through Z. You can skip this preface too. Just find your favorite 1970s singer-songwriters and offer your own interpretations of their music. Listen to their recordings. Download them or seek them on YouTube. Pull out the CDs, or dust off the old albums. Be patient with the production—or the lack of it, and with the various styles of these singer-songwriters. Make what you will of this long list, these thumbnail identifications of more than 150 singer-songwriters of the 1970s.

Some years ago, when we were leaving the Clearwater Festival, a day of music up along the Hudson River, we saw a man picking up wrappers from the ground, clearing a little portion of the field of some paper waste that had been tossed there. As he rose to stand, we noticed that the man was Pete Seeger. He greeted us and we said hello to him. That simple act of taking care of that little bit of earth spoke volumes. Pete Seeger was a man who lived his commitments. He was also a resource for the singer songwriters who followed the path he charted with his songs, his travels, and his commitments. This overview of singer songwriters of the 1970s is dedicated to him. It is with thanks that I also wish to recognize the role of recently retired editor David Alff and the people at McFarland for their work on this volume and their care with my previous books on popular music.

Recently, I have had the occasion to sit in with people from the Folk Project in northern New Jersey "virtually" on Zoom. This great group of people is one of several gatherings of people in different locations across the United States who have kept community alive with song during a time of covid. I extend my thanks to them—and to the conscientious songwriters I meet with in a Thursday evening songwriting group. They have the courage to create and the joy to sing. A gathering of people in music is a ballast, a salve, and an affirmation of life against any anxiety or pain in contemporary society. It is the voice and heart that the singer-songwriter expresses that is lifted up, listened to, and appreciated by these people. It is truly a gift to hear their voices and their interpretations of songs and to share in their spirit of hope.

The psychologist Rollo May in *The Meaning of Anxiety* (1950) pointed out that what is needed from each of us to confront anxiety is "that particular kind of courage necessary for the creative act."[3] That includes courage and creativity in our work lives, our family lives, and our role as citizens. In 1950, May wrote that every citizen realizes "that anxiety is a pervasive and profound phenomenon of the middle of the Twentieth Century."[4] His comments ring equally true in these first decades of the 21st century. May asked, "Shall we feel our foundations shaking and withdraw into anxiety and panic? Or shall we seize the courage necessary to preserve our sensitivity, awareness, and responsibility in the face of radical change?"[5] Rollo May's answer is: practice art and practice courage. For from its etymological root in the French word *Coeur* that courage to create arises from the human heart.

The courageous life, Paul Tillich asserted, displays "enthusiasm for the universe."[6] This individual knows "courage has revealing power" and "participates in the power of being which prevails against non-being."[7] The singer-songwriter expresses the courage to face things as they are, or as the theologian Paul Tillich put it: the strength to encounter the weight of non-being, or the melancholic strains of life, while maintaining a faith that one may indeed be touched, inspired, seized by a force greater than oneself.[8] "He who is grasped by this power is able to affirm himself because he knows that he is affirmed by the power of being itself."[9] I begin then this exploration of these 1970s singer-songwriters with a trust in that power.

Art holds an important place in our culture, even as much of it is turned into entertainment, or marketed commercially to sell units and gain profits. Art is important because it is an expression of the human spirit. Art reveals the depth dimension of things, significances which are hidden in the people and things of everyday life. This is what singer-songwriters are so adept in bringing out. Through art, as through all cultural forms, one can read the depth content of a cultural period. Modern art, for example, says something about modernity. Kandinsky's expressionist color and Klee's childlike forms, Stravinsky's neo-classicism, or Schoenberg's atonality, each say something about the early 20th century. Singer-songwriters say something about the 1970s—or the movement of folk, pop, and rock music through the 1960s into the 1970s.

A work of art expresses an aliveness of being. As a work of human hands, it expresses and embodies a relation of self to world. It may shatter preconceptions, or it may bring hope. The art of the singer-songwriter reflects our lives and reveals a depth dimension of reality which might not otherwise be apparent. Art expresses the depth content of reality. Through its eloquence, it grasps us. That eloquence—musical and lyrical—is one of the attractions of the singer-songwriters who are recognized in the following pages.

Notes

1. William Faulkner, Nobel Prize speech, December 10, 1950.

2. Paul Tillich, *The Courage to Be*, New Haven: Yale University Press, 1952. p. 117.

3. Rollo May, *The Courage to Create*, New York: Norton, 1975. p. 1.

4. Rollo May, *The Meaning of Anxiety*, New York: Ronald Press, 1950. p.1.

5. Tillich, *The Courage to Be*, p.12.

6. Tillich, *The Courage to Be*, p. 121.

7. Tillich, *The Courage to Be*, p. 181.

8. Tillich, *The Courage to Be*, p.141.

9. Tillich, *The Courage to Be*, p. 173.

Introduction

The 1970s marked the cresting of a wave of singer-songwriters that took to the airwaves and concert venues across America. This is the story of about 150 songwriters whose music and lyrics found an audience during those years. Some of them are well-known and others are more obscure. They wrote and sang their own songs. They were musical voices, song-poets, and storytellers during a time when the singer-songwriter phenomenon was in ascendency. This book brings them together in one place with biographical sketches and overviews of their 1970s creativity. This appearance of the singer-songwriter in the 1970s requires a recognition of the emergence of rock music and folk rock, and an awareness of the divergence of country music from folk. This volume explores the work of songwriter-performers, artists who sing their own songs. While these singer-songwriters draw upon many different styles of music, some styles of music, such as rhythm and blues, Motown, jazz, and country music, while included, are not emphasized here. There was tremendous creativity in these genres but this volume only points out a few prominent singer-songwriters in these musical genres. The focus here is primarily on singer-songwriters who can be linked in some way with acoustic folk music traditions. This is a study of their musical art and their contributions as song-poets and storytellers during the decade of the 1970s.

Music always exceeds any labels or categories we may use in attempting to define it. No straight lines make up a life. The roads all have bends, as pop-folksinger Harry Chapin once sang. Likewise, there are circles and bends in the road here. This overview of singer-songwriters attempts to capture one point in time. These artists were part of the soundtrack of the seventies and some of them made an impact within popular culture. Beyond the 1970s many of these artists added further dimensions to their music. In several cases this has been a matter of watching young men and women turn into older men and women across the years. Other singer-songwriters entered the scene in the 1980s and after, adding further to the richness of song we have been blessed with. The styles of singer-songwriters are fluid and evolving. Artists are always creating, changing, and growing. One can describe and characterize someone's music, but the words only point to a sound that must be heard to be appreciated. This book is something like a road map. It is a gathering, an appreciation, a description that intends to encourage further listening.

You will find here a brief description of each singer-songwriter. Following this is a listing of his or her 1970s albums. In several cases, one 1970s album from that singer-songwriter has been given some attention. You will also find mention of significant reissues of recordings. There are also some suggestions regarding what is available for you to see on YouTube. You can also turn to online sources like Spotify for listening to recordings. If you like an artist and the song or album is available for download or in CD or vinyl do purchase it. Artists merit compensation for their work.

To write songs and to then perform and sing them is an act in which a person brings from a deep and personal place matters of the heart, stories of experience, recognitions about relationships, and concerns about life. Singer-songwriters are storytellers in song, painters in sound and words. The songs that they compose and that they sing give voice to our feelings also. Perhaps they reflect our lives. Each song is an imaginative center. Creating a sound, a mood, it offers an idea. Songs take us to new places. They chronicle emotions, musings, perceptions, and they resonate in listeners. In the tight format of a song is a little piece of the world we share. Songwriters find ways to appeal to the heart. In a sense, songs connect us. We each personally experience songs and we interpret them with our lives. They draw us out from our separateness into some collective connection, some recognition that we share in this life, in these evocations of the human story.

This book is a gathering of unique voices. While songwriters often write effectively in collaboration, or for voices other than their own, the singer-songwriter frequently creates an idiosyncratic art: one that is best presented through his or her own voice. The creative artist sometimes must go deep to risk an emotion, to find and release and shape an idea. Upon reworking the material, they send signals and messages to us and we participate in the songs. There may be something personal in the song for us even when the singer-songwriter plays what Ben Yagoda has called a "story of self-consciousness" and songwriters choose "in the course of a song to comment on themselves." The "confessional song," draws our attention like the confessions of Jean-Jacques Rousseau or St. Augustine, to an intimate ache in the heart. The love song becomes public—not merely as a form of self-indulgence but as a communication of life that stakes a universal claim.

The 1970s was a time when the full album had become the fullest expression and representation of a singer-songwriter's art. Consequently, the emphasis here is on albums more than on hit singles. Songwriters of public visibility and lasting influence are generally given more attention here than the decade's one-hit wonders. However, an effort has been made to be inclusive of lesser-known singer-songwriters and to include some major figures across the rock, pop, country, R&B/soul, and folk genres.

We might call some of these singer-songwriters song-poets. Song lyrics and poetry engage imagery, line, narrative, rhythm and rhyme. They articulate ideas through direct address or through a created speaker. There is an investment of imagination, a reach for creative flow and vision, and a resolve to claim an authentic voice. Even so, the art of poetry may be distinguished from the lyricist's craft. Song lyrics are made for music. The music, the arrangement, the production, and the performance are all part of the song. Song structure, the market, and the sound and zeitgeist of the moment may all contribute to the shape of the song. Yet it is the voice and the style of the singer-songwriter, the themes that interest that artist, that we will explore here.

A Brief History

Let's begin with a look in the rear-view mirror at some of the roads that led to the 1970s singer-songwriter. These are the creative pathways of folk music, country, rock and roll, and the blues. Along the road are the folk songs: borrowings of melodies and adaptations of lyrics by dozens of folksingers. There are work-songs, love ballads, patriotic songs and broadsides, sea shanties, downhome Appalachian songs, ballads transported from the British Isles, regional American folk songs and black gospel spirituals and the Mississippi Delta blues and more. This music branches out in a hundred directions. The folk troubadours tapped into this material and spread across the country with it. John and Alan Lomax gathered, catalogued, and initiated recordings. A creative exchange from American blues to early rock and roll occurred in Britain and in North America. The folk and folk-rock tradition builds upon the legacy of Woody Guthrie: his many songs, his travels with Pete Seeger, his commentary on workers and dreamers and this land that was made for you and me. It gathers in the British and Irish ballads, tunes going back many years. It draws upon the 12-bar blues, songs of lament and tenacity that transform pain into observations, notes of sorrow, or wry humor. The singer-songwriters of the 1970s developed their own sounds with their ears close to the radio or the record player, listening to the music of Elvis Presley, Chuck Berry, Buddy Holly, Little Richard and other rock and roll of the mid–1950s through early 1960s. They listened to The Beatles and the British invasion bands of the 1960s. They listened to country, or to jazz, as well as to Bob Dylan and the passionate protest song, the surrealistic lyrics of *Blonde on Blonde*, and the plugged-in electric sounds of *Highway 61 Revisited*.

In the 1950s the voices of popular folk music included Woody Guthrie, The Weavers, the Kingston Trio, Pete Seeger, Big Bill Broonzy, Lead Belly, Josh White, John Jacob Niles, Lee Hays, Jean Ritchie, Odetta, Ewan McColl, Oscar Brand, Burl Ives, Tom Paxton, Rosalie Sorrels, Harry Belafonte and others. In 1950 The Weavers played at the Village Vanguard, signed with agent Harold Leventhal, and could be heard on Decca Records. Regional folk festivals grew around the United States, Canada, and in Britain. Ewan McColl was one of the central forces gathering the music of the British Isles. In 1954, the Weavers were blacklisted by McCarthyites in the House Un-American Activities Committee (HUAC) and were charged with having communist sympathies. They returned into public view in December 1955 at a Carnegie Hall concert.

By the early 1960s, folk music, always concerned with the working man and woman, connected with the Civil Rights movement and brought the civil rights anthem "We Shall Overcome." Popular radio airplay brought "Tom Dooley," "If I Had a Hammer," "Kisses Sweeter Than Wine." Izzy Young's Folk City and Folklore Center in Greenwich Village was a hub for the expanding Greenwich Village scene of the 1960s. To the area around Bleecker, Minetta, MacDougal, and West 4th, Bob Dylan arrived in 1962. The Village scene included Fred Neil, Dave Van Ronk, Richie Havens, Eric Andersen, Peter Yarrow, Mark Spoelstra, Happy Traum, and others. Those inclined toward the blues listened to the Rev. Gary Davis and others listened to the social justice concerns of Phil Ochs. Another folk scene centered in Cambridge at Club 47 (Passim since 1969), with Joan Baez, Tom Rush, Eric Von Schmidt, Geoff and Maria Muldaur, Carolyn Hester, Taj Mahal, Bill Staines, Bob Franke and many others. The West Coast scene in San Francisco drew heavily upon the blues and folk also. In Los Angeles, the folk club The Troubadour was at the center of the development of what would soon become folk-rock. Chicago was a center for the blues, rock and roll beginnings, and its own folksingers who emerged in the late 1960s and 1970s like John Prine, Steve Goodman, Art Thieme, Bonnie Koloc, the Holsteins, Jim Post, and Milwaukee's Larry Penn.

A connection with country music was also present in the work of some folk-based singer-songwriters. The music of Appalachia and the American South brought important strands of American music. The songwriting of Hank Williams, the music of Jimmie Rodgers, bluegrass, and the blues of the deep south were all creative influences. In 1954, country singer-songwriter Johnny Cash released "I Walk the Line" on Sun Records. The story-songs and the sounds of country music would have an impact on singer-songwriters and on West coast folk-rock in the late 1960s and 1970s.

The music of the singer-songwriters is eclectic and draws upon many sources. The power of the blues winds throughout folk and early rock music. Country music, rich with stories, crosses over and joins with folk and pop. The Tin Pan Alley tradition of pop song embraced the musical theater and lay behind hits written in the Brill Building. The so-called "race records" of the 1920s through 1940s brought African American voices, some quite exploited, and some forgotten. Call it all grist for the mill. Music is music whatever container or record bin it was placed in.

The baby boom teen consumer culture embraced rock and roll in the mid–1950s. Folk music arose amid the crooning of Pat Boone, clean cut vocalists named Bobby, trios in turtleneck sweaters, a Beat movement that favored jazz over folk, and Chubby Checker doing the Twist in the early 1960s. In 1959, the Grammy Awards placed the Kingston Trio's "Tom Dooley" in the country and western category. A folk music category followed in the 1960s, as folk increasingly grew in commercial music sales. Yet, "folk" ranged from calypso to bluegrass and from labor songs to protest songs. It was a grassroots music. As record companies awakened to see a receptive market for Harry Belafonte's *Calypso* (1956) and The Kingston Trio's debut on Capitol Records (June 1958) folk was no longer the last thing on their minds. Bob Dylan was "discovered" and recorded by John Hammond for Columbia Records. The Clancy Brothers sang of Ireland. Peter, Paul, and Mary gave new voice to "The Hammer Song" by Lee Hays and Pete Seeger. The folk traditionalists, however, were not entirely ready for the next phase.

Recorded in three sessions from November 20–22, 1961, Bob Dylan's first album release in 1962 caught the attention of a growing audience of listeners. Greenwich Village had become the epicenter of the folk singer-songwriter tribe who played at Gerde's Folk City, Café Wha?, The Bitter End, Night Owl, Purple Onion. It became home to Dave Van Ronk, Ramblin' Jack Elliott, Richie Havens, Fred Neil, Peter Yarrow, a comedian named Noel Paul Stookey, and others. *The Freewheelin' Bob Dylan* pictured Dylan with Suzi Rotolo walking down a street in Greenwich Village. Civil rights protest entered the folk song in a more public fashion. Perhaps some answer was blowing in the wind. Singer Bob Gibson brought to the Newport Folk Festival a surprise guest, Joan Baez, who soon lit up the folk world.

In 1964 the British Invasion bands came to America: The Beatles, The Rolling Stones, The Animals, The Yardbirds, The Who, The Kinks, and Herman's Hermits appeared on the screen, on record, and in the consciousness of the young record buying public. Rock music converged with folk as Bob Dylan's songs were covered by The Byrds and by The Turtles. Bob Dylan brought The Band and electricity to the Newport Folk Festival in July 1965 and was called "Judas" in Manchester in 1966 by someone yelling from the crowd. Electric guitar and a steady pulse were added to Paul Simon's "The Sound of Silence" for Simon and Garfunkel's second album. The times were a-changin' and so was the sound of an era.

Folk rock emerged in the mid–1960s in America with the sound of The Byrds, the Jefferson Airplane, and other bands. In Britain, it appeared in the music of Fairport Convention, Steeleye Span, and Pentangle. Folk-rock could be heard in Bob Dylan's "Like a Rolling Stone," Buffalo Springfield's "For What It's Worth," and The Turtles cover of Dylan's "It Ain't Me Babe." Sometimes it bore inflections of country music. The Animals had a hit with the folk/blues song "House of New Orleans" (The House of the Rising Sun). The Hollies and Herman's Hermits drew upon the British folk tradition for their pop songs.

The Byrds, the premier band of American folk-rock emerged from Los Angeles in 1965 on the strength of their cover version of Bob Dylan's "Mr. Tambourine Man." Their characteristic sound came from the electric 12-string guitar of Roger McGuinn and the vocal harmonies of the other members: Gene Clark, David Crosby, Chris Hillman, and Mike Clark. Roger McGuinn, born 'Jim,' was a folksinger. He played at The Gate of Horn in Chicago. Alex Hasilow of The Limelighters heard him and invited him to join the group as an instrumentalist. McGuinn went on to play backup for the Chad Mitchell Trio, a clean-cut group that built upon the success of The Kingston Trio. McGuinn also accompanied vocalist Bobby Darin. After a solo show at The Troubadour in Los Angeles, McGuinn was approached by Gene Clark. Gene and his brother were putting together a band. McGuinn joined them and Crosby and mandolin player Chris Hillman. They called themselves The Beefeaters, did a gig at a bowling alley, and recorded a demo, later to be transformed into their album as The Byrds, *Preflyte*. The members of The Byrds were all born between 1941 and 1943. Their sound combines their folk influences with their listening to The Beatles and other bands. The Byrds took Beatle-like harmonies and embellished them in four-part harmony. The ringing chimes of McGuinn's guitar joined those harmonies on Pete Seeger's "Turn, Turn, Turn," Bob Dylan's "Chimes of Freedom" and "My Back Pages," and their own songs like "Eight Miles High," a melodic daydream, likely drug-induced, about flying high. The Byrds came down somewhere in cowboy country in 1967.

The Byrds underwent several musical changes. McGuinn and Hillman each moved through country phases and a space-cowboy phase. Hillman became a consummate bluegrass player, joined with John David Souther and Richie Furay for a record in the 1970s and later led the Desert Rose Band. McGuinn went through a period of religious seeking and returned to his roots as a solo folksinger. In 1990, he released *Back from*

Rio, a folk-rock album recorded with Tom Petty and others. David Crosby, essentially given a severance deal and tossed out of The Byrds, went on to be a member of Crosby, Stills, Nash and Young.

The wide and varied palette of American folk-rock music was created by several other groups. The Band were Canadians who chose to live in the Catskills around Woodstock, New York. The Big Pink was the house where they lived. Bob Dylan, staying in Woodstock, wrote songs and played them with The Band and those songs were collected as *The Basement Tapes*. The group entered around Arkansas drummer and singer Levon Helm and the songwriting of Robbie Robertson. With Rick Danko (bass) Richard Manuel (piano) and Garth Hudson (organ) they had traveled across Canada as a backup band for Ronnie Hawkins, a rock singer. The Band had ragged harmonies, sometimes nasal vocals, and a country flair. Songs like "The Weight" had a gospel feeling. John Hammond, Jr., a blues guitarist introduced them to New York City audiences in the mid–1960s. Their first album came out years later, in 1968. The songs were a blend of folk, gospel, country, blues, and rock. They were perhaps best known for their collaboration with Bob Dylan and their singles "The Weight," "Up on Cripple Creek," and their version of "The Night They Drove Old Dixie Down."

Buffalo Springfield was the seedbed for several singer-songwriters: Stephen Stills, Neil Young, Richie Furay, and Jim Messina. Bruce Palmer and Dewey Martin comprised their rhythm section. Their best-known song was "For What It's Worth" by Stephen Stills. With their second album they moved further toward a rock sound of the period. Jesse Colin Young and the Youngbloods encouraged everyone to try to love one another. The Mamas and the Papas sang about "California Dreaming," and John Sebastian and The Lovin' Spoonful created their own brand of folk/pop. John Fogerty wrote some of his strongest songs while he was the central voice of his band Creedence Clearwater Revival. The eclectic blend of blues, rock, folk, and southern delta imagery could also be categorized an expression of folk-rock.

The Jefferson Airplane were at the center of the San Francisco scene. They drew upon the blues and folk music and merged this with rock and developed their popular singles "Somebody to Love" and "White Rabbit." Paul Kantner was probably the closest thing they had to a singer-songwriter, although he worked in a collaborative band context. Vocalists Grace Slick and Martin Balin were at the center of their sound, even as the band went through changes. Hot Tuna emerged from the blues orientation of Jorma Kaukonen and Jack Casady. San Francisco was home to The Grateful Dead, Janis Joplin and Big Brother and the Holding Company, Moby Grape, Quicksilver Messenger Service, Blue Cheer, and set the stage for the Steve Miller Band, Santana, and others which would gain further notoriety in the 1970s.

Interactions in Los Angeles fostered further development of folk rock. Laurel Canyon and the Troubadour folk club served as incubators and resources for some of those connections. Among the musicians that played and met at The Troubadour, some of whom lived in Laurel Canyon at one time or another, were: The Mamas and the Papas, Crosby, Stills and Nash, Joni Mitchell, Linda Ronstadt, Andrew Gold, Jackson Browne, Warren Zevon, Don Henley and Glenn Frey and The Eagles, and J.D. Souther. Vocal harmonies were a key feature of The Mamas and the Papas, CSN, and the Eagles' emergence in the early 1970s.

Of course, popular music expanded well beyond folk and folk rock. Singer-songwriters drew out a wealth of pop songs that incorporated influences from rhythm and blues, musical theater, jazz, country and other musical styles. Songwriters like Carole King wrote pop hits for vocal groups. Berry Gordy's Motown reshaped the R&B/soul landscape. The songwriter was generally not also the performer of these songs: at least not until the mid- to late 1960s. Of course, some of the singer-songwriters were recording and performing as part of groups or duos. (Simon and Garfunkel, David Crosby with the Byrds, Graham Nash with the Hollies, Stephen Stills, Richie Furay, and Jim Messina with Buffalo Springfield, John Denver in the Chad Mitchell Trio are some examples.) In the early 1970s, songwriters like Jimmy Webb, Carole King, Neil Diamond and others would increasingly be heard singing and performing their own songs.

The brilliant pop songwriting of Carole King, with Gerry Goffin and on her own, lay behind some of the pop-song hits of the 1960s. Carole King's *Tapestry* would be at the center of the singer-songwriter movement of the early 1970s. Carole Klein came from Brooklyn into a world of the Brill Building that included Barry Mann and Cynthia Weill, Jerry Lieber and Mike Stoller, John Kander and Fred Ebb, Ellie Greenwich and Jeff Barry, and others who extended the tradition of Tin Pan Alley, the musical theater, and pop song craftsmanship. Neil Sedaka, Sonny Bono, David Gates, and Laura Nyro are among those who can be associated with this nexus. Neil Diamond, who was among these songwriters scored hits with The Monkees ("I'm a Believer") and began a singer-songwriter career on Bang Records. The collaborative songwriting of the 1960s included the songwriting team of Burt Bacharach and Hal David ("Walk on By," "The Look of Love," "Alfie," "Raindrops Keep Falling on My Head"). In this world the piano was the primary instrument rather than the guitar, which was so central to folk. (Obviously, piano, guitar, and the drums were all essential to rock.) Singer-songwriters like Randy Newman, Laura Nyro, Elton John, and Billy Joel all entered the 1970s as pianist-composers. David

Gates was a capable string arranger. Randy Newman wrote for film and television. Todd Rundgren emerged with the Naz from the Philadelphia soul sound. Stevie Wonder, Curtis Mayfield, Teddy Pendergrass, and Marvin Gaye were creative talents transforming soul and Motown. In 1970, there was the iconoclastic Frank Zappa, the first recordings of David Bowie, and there were the Beatles—John Lennon, Paul McCartney, and George Harrison—after The Beatles: rich in song and ever innovative.

The story of the singer-songwriter expanded in 1970, as Paul McCartney played all the instruments and sang everything on his solo album, Paul Simon departed from Art Garfunkel, and Elton John and others began to appear on record. Singer-songwriters like Laura Nyro and Hoyt Axton wrote hits for vocal groups like Three Dog Night. James Taylor, Joni Mitchell and others brought their audiences into thoughtful meditations. Record companies like Elektra/Asylum, Columbia, Warner, and RCA distributed them and made them household names. Singer-songwriters (Elton John, John Denver, Don McLean, Neil Young, Van Morrison, Carly Simon, Paul Simon, Jim Croce, Cat Stevens, Jackson Browne, James Taylor, Neil Young, Johnny Cash, Stevie Wonder, Eric Clapton, Marvin Gaye, David Bowie, Paul McCartney with Wings, George Harrison, David Gates with Bread) were among the bestselling artists of the decade. This is an account of those years of accomplishment.

* * *

How might we summarize this look back at the era of the singer-songwriter? How did it come to be? The era of the singer-songwriter, in popular and commercial terms, crested in the early 1970s. Its antecedents were the folk music revival, the growth and development of rock music, the energy of soul/R&B and Motown, the gradual movement of country music toward pop music. It was fueled by the songwriting and prominence of The Beatles, the rise of Bob Dylan from folk-protest singer to band infused folk-rock poet, and the emergence of a generation of listeners and record buyers who experienced the cultural currents of "the sixties." The singer-songwriter coincided with the concept album and FM radio, a cultural quest for authenticity, a new context for recording that included companies like Elektra, which signed many singer-songwriters, or Columbia Records and other companies who smartly followed this trend.

There was an eclectic crossover of musical styles on radio in the early to mid–1970s. Several singer-songwriters of the 1970s moved across these genres. The intersections of rock, folk, blues, country, and elements from jazz were already happening years before this. The folk music revival had come in the late 1950s and early 1960s with the voices of Pete Seeger and

The Weavers and the Kingston Trio. It grew with Joan Baez, emerging from Club 47 in Cambridge, and with Bob Dylan imitating and extending the work of Woody Guthrie as he played in Greenwich Village at Folk City and other clubs. There was Dave Van Ronk and Ramblin' Jack Elliott. There was Phil Ochs asserting his political folksongs and Dylan's "Blowing in the Wind" sung by the trio of Peter, Paul, and Mary. The sounds of The Beatles and British Invasion bands like The Rolling Stones, The Animals, The Kinks, The Who, and the lighter pop sounds of Herman's Hermits, The Hollies, and others met with their American copies. The Byrds merged Bob Dylan's folk songs like "Mr. Tambourine Man" with electric guitars and Dylan and the Band did so also. Even Simon and Garfunkel got into the act with drums and electric guitar on "The Sounds of Silence." Motown music filled the air with Diana Ross and the Supremes, the Shirelles, Martha and the Vandellas, Smokey Robinson and the Miracles, little Stevie Wonder, and the tunes of the songwriting team of Holland-Dozier-Holland. Tin Pan Alley met folk and R&B and pop and issued forth from the Brill Building in New York from songwriters like Carole King and Gerry Goffin, Neil Diamond, and others. In San Francisco a counterculture was born, embracing rock, the blues, folk, Beat poetry, and a politics seeking change. From the Troubadour in Los Angeles and from Laurel Canyon came the mix that included the Mamas and the Papas, the Turtles, Buffalo Springfield with Neil Young, Stephen Stills, and Richie Furay, and the later trio of Crosby, Stills, and Nash, Jackson Browne, Linda Ronstadt, The Eagles, and British pop singer-songwriter Elton John. In Boston, Folksinger Tom Rush recorded *The Circle Game* (1968) with songs by Joni Mitchell, James Taylor, and Jackson Browne. The new singer-songwriters began to gain further attention.

So, who was this lone individual with a guitar in her hands or sitting at a piano? Who was this young singer with his "heart on his sleeve" and why did his personal songs of life and love or critiques of culture matter? For across the years some of those songs and the voices of some of those singer-songwriters have had wide cultural impact. They have created a legacy, a soundtrack that is more than quaint nostalgia and PBS specials. To revisit their songs and stories is to experience music, to enter into perspectives, and to allow them to stir feelings in us. We can affirm the value of their lives, their commitments, and their art: the insight of a Bob Dylan or Neil Young, the painterly vision and soaring voice of a Joni Mitchell, the energy of a Harry Chapin dedicated to alleviating world hunger. Listen to the songs of the 1970s and one can hear the youth of John Denver reborn in his twenty-seventh year, Jackson Browne out walking on these days, Cat Stevens urging the world to get on that peace train. In 1970, Laura Nyro leans intently over her piano, long hair dangling down. Elton John has not yet adopted costumes. Bruce Springsteen is still playing in clubs at the Jersey shore. It is a foundational period, this era of the singer-songwriter: a time of reflection in which the words in songs mattered a great deal. They were unmistakably, indissolubly linked with the music, the sounds and soul and life of the times. The spirit of those songs and voices still lives among us today.

Popular music evokes the past. Even if you were not alive there and then you can get a sense of the times by listening to its music. In *Popular Music History* (April 2007) Andy Bennett called the 1970s "The Forgotten Decade." It was hardly that. He investigates why some of this music has not been investigated "by music theorists." He concludes that "rock" may be a misnomer for a broad, eclectic field of music. Indeed, "eclectic" is a word that characterizes 1970s popular music. Turn on a radio in the early 1970s and one would hear R&B-soul-Motown, country, rock played side by side on the same station. In August 1970 Jimi Hendrix played his last concert. The early years of the decade were mottled with a sense of losses, even as the spirit of second wave feminism emerged and calls for an end to a painful overseas war continued. The singer-songwriter gauged the personal and the public dimensions of life in the early 1970s. With the singer songwriter the 1970s brought to popular music introspection, melody, poetics, documentary, social critique, and personal reflection.

There is memory in these songs. Andy Bennett wrote with Susan Jannssen on "Popular Music, Cultural Memory and Heritage" (December 2015, *Popular Music and Society* [39.1]). They pointed out that this edition of the journal had the goal of providing reflections on how popular music had become an "object of memory," "a focus for contemporary renditions of history and cultural heritage." They added: "Pop music's links to and evocation of the past have been evident for several years." This volume seeks to point out those links.

The 1970s was called "the age of narcissism" by Christopher Lasch. However, that term does not recognize the exceptions. Rock music critic Greil Marcus, in the *New York Times*, diagnosed the mid–1970s from a rock music-popular culture perspective. Bruce J. Schulman wrote about an ideological shift in *The Seventies: The Great Shift in American Culture, Society and Politics*. (New York: Free Press, 2001 rpt. New York: Da Capo 2002) He pointed out the growth of the Southern Sun Belt and "public spirituality." The *Contemporary Review*'s (September 2008) Barnett Singer of Ontario, in his article "American Culture and Its Influence," observed that some people are comforted by "the old suits and dresses and slower and more ponderous ways" they see on television reruns (358). Nostalgia books are popular in the 1970s, he pointed out. Don McLean's "American Pie" dealt with a sense of cultural exhaustion and "need to regain a warmer fuzzier past" (357). He proceeded to diagnose American culture as one of loquacity and haste, lacking historical sense. British critic David Hepworth argued in *Never a Dull Moment: 1971 The Year that Rock Exploded* that 1971 represents the year in which many influential albums sprung to life, "more than any year before or since." This includes the work of rock bands, R&B-soul performers, and the singer-songwriters.

This gathering of singer-songwriters is necessarily selective. There were in the 1970s dozens of music-creators across a variety of different genres, just as there is today. Some of those who are mentioned here are included because they made some impact and had some influence or public visibility. However, some singer-songwriters here are less familiar. Some were not commercially successful. Others had fatefully short careers. There is a brief capsule overview of these singer-songwriters. More space is given to those who made greater cultural impact. While some artists carry over from the 1960s, it was necessary to stop at 1979 and not include artists whose first recordings emerged in 1980 or 1981.

A singer-songwriter is someone who writes and performs his or her own songs. If one's image of the singer-songwriter is of a solo artist with a guitar or one singing at a piano what about when they play with bands? Bruce Springsteen and Bob Seger, for example, led bands but were also significant singer-songwriters. The folk, acoustic pop, and folk-rock medium seems to be at the center of the singer-songwriter phenomenon. Ought country artists who write songs to be included? Some extraordinary soul/R&B pop creators? Which ones? And what about popular rock songwriter-musicians of the 1970s like Ray Davies (a songwriter too closely associated with The Kinks and not yet solo), Peter Frampton, T. Rex (Marc Bolan), Frank Zappa, Edgar Winter, Eric Clapton, David Bowie, or one-hit wonders? Where to draw the line?

Singer-songwriters often perform with other musicians, supporting bands, or other guest-artists. Performing songwriters like Bruce Springsteen and Bob Seger worked in the 1970s principally with bands in which they played a central role. They were each the boss of the band, as it were. More than this, Springsteen did eventually perform solo at many events. Seger had a solo album before he gathered his band. Their songwriting argues for their inclusion with singer-songwriters. It draws upon folk and rock and soul roots and upon storytelling. Alice Cooper, Peter Frampton, Edgar Winter, Suzi Quatro? They created songs or instrumentals and were at the center of bands. Yet, their image and songs do not suggest the image of the singer-songwriter. That remains the image cast by *Newsweek*'s 1970 feature article on James Taylor: the sometimes introspective, acoustic-based, story-telling troubadour.

In the 1970s our family, during summertime, would occasionally go to a relative's backyard pool party. The older cousins were obviously steeped in 1960s–1970s recordings like The Moody Blues. In the finished basement of the house, where our elders were having drinks, I found and played some of those records. One non-descript recording was from one of their friends: a tune recorded on vinyl and pressed at a local studio. It was called "I Almost Forgot." I have forgotten who wrote and sang that tune. However, it suggested to me that I could someday record my songs—and that dozens of people have done just that. If I have forgotten or overlooked anyone here, my apologies. There is just such immense creativity and so many heartfelt songs all around us. I hope that this gathering of notes on the artistry of some singer-songwriters will encourage and assist you in your listening.

Singer-Songwriter
Profiles

Eric Andersen

Eric Andersen was one of the leading voices of the Vanguard Records recordings of 1960s folk singer-songwriters. The company distributed records by the Weavers, Joan Baez, Ian and Sylvia, Buffy St. Marie, Mimi and Richard Farina, and Chicago blues players. He was the writer of "Violets of Dawn" and "Come to My Bedside." Eric Andersen's song "Thirsty Boots" was covered by Judy Collins, Bob Dylan, and John Denver. He experimented with songwriting in open tunings. Andersen was for many years a folk music performer in Greenwich Village during the folk music revival there. He recorded six albums with Vanguard records and a couple with Warner Brothers before 1970. He has performed and recorded across the years and has sometimes lived in Europe. Andersen is a capable writer, a song-poet, who has explored many dimensions of love and relationship across some 25 albums.

Blue River, 1972

In 1972, Eric Andersen, a mainstay of the 1960s Greenwich Village folk music circuit went to Nashville to record *Blue River*, an album with a contemplative focus that gathered up some blues shadows. Andersen's folk-roots and his poetic quest for song join melody and lyrics as if they are inseparable. Writing is flow, exploration, reaching for the new, following that river. Andersen's vocals work on a level of tone and feeling with calm, low-key arrangements. Joni Mitchell accompanies him vocally on the title track. David Bromberg adds acoustic guitar and dobro. Norbert Putnam, the album's producer, plays bass. The Jordanaires are also among the background vocalists.

The album opens with "Is It Really Love at All," which is perhaps one of the most thoughtful and tuneful songs on the album. The tempo shifts on "Pearl's Good Time Blues," with a tip of the hat to The Band's "Rag Mama Rag." The song "More Often Than Not" by David Wiffen has a strong folk structure and a bit of forward pulse and tempo. It is the only song on this album not written by Andersen. There is an ache on "Sheila," a request for help that suggests hard times, imprisonment, or a helping hand for freedom from the trap of drugs. Amid the neat structure and gospel of "Round the Bend" is a call to Jesus for assistance. And if Jesus won't bring salvation, then might he please send a friend who has been through the struggle. "Wind and Sand" is melodic, tuneful. The Nashville studio session musician support seems to emphasize simplicity and sympathy. There is a tender but tough focus to this album, and something like the confessional song which would be popularized by James Taylor. Yet, Andersen seems to run deep like the blue river, establishing a clean sound for a record that speaks of struggle and of feeling. As an album, *Blue River* may be the central one in Eric Andersen's catalog. However, his later innovations and writing are also admirable. Master tapes of recordings that were to comprise an album *Stages* were misplaced and were only located years later.

Blue River (1972), *Be True to You* (1975), *Sweet Surprise* (1976).

Joan Armatrading

British singer Joan Armatrading was a singer-songwriter who drew listener attention in the mid–1970s with her sure vocals and thoughtful songs. As one of the few black female singers on the folk-circuit she had a lasting impact on future artists like Tracy Chapman. At first working with lyricist Pam Nestor, before 1970, she came to the attention of BBC radio host John Peel. She was heard several times on his show. There were 14 songs on her first release on Cube Records, *Whatever's for Us* (1972) In 1973, her single "Lonely Lady" was released. She recorded *Back to the Night* (1975) on A&M Records and performed alongside a group called The Movies. "Love and Affection" from her album *Joan Armatrading* (1976), produced by Glyn Johns, took off on the charts. Filled with pop and jazz it entered the top twenty on the album charts. *Show Some Emotion* (1977) and *To the Limit* (1978) were jazz influenced recordings. They included "Willow," "Kissin' and a Huggin'," "Down to Zero," and other songs she performed in her concerts. She received wide airplay on British and American radio, made a guest appearance on the popular show *Saturday Night Live* (May 1975), and performed internationally. She would receive several British arts awards and Grammy nominations in the 1980s.

Joan Armatrading (1976)

Joan Armatrading starts her album on acoustic guitar and is joined by piano, drums, and bass. There is a long first line and multi-syllable near-spoken delivery. The song builds into a bridge with the bass, with dynamics, some drum accents. "Down to Zero" features an assertive vocal. The hook is based in the rhyme of feeling and reeling. On "Love and Affection" acoustic guitars and her vocal are up-front. Jimmy Jewell's saxophone enters later. The vocal is gentler, whispery. We hear "really laugh," "really love," "really moves." The phrases seem to be delivered on eighth notes. The three-chord pattern on her Ovation guitar is simple and supportive of the song. Lines become more rhythmic. We hear Armatrading turning R&B and soul. "Join the Boys" begins in Dave Mattack's drums, snare and high-hat. Armatrading fits a lot of words into each line. Several lines are near to spoken word expression. On "Save Me" the word sinking comes as the last word of a line. The world is in motion, and she calls for a lifeline. This is a reflective song. The title comes to us on high notes and longer held open notes. "Help Yourself" begins with her guitar, supported by bass. She insists that one must do things right. The word "time" is held out. But the assertion that you are wasting my time comes to us in quarter notes. "Get Yourself Together" moves into R&B "Shaft"-like production. The contrast here is most in volume and in production style. There is a string arrangement. One expects horns perhaps also. "People" is bassline driven, catchy, up-tempo, with vocal changes. There are energetic guitar leads. On "Somebody Who Loves You" the vocal is bare. There are accent hits from the drums. She doubles her voice gently on the title. There is some light rhythmic pattern in double-time. "Like Fire" begins in a guitar riff. The singer urges someone to stay together with her because that's how it should be. The song is delivered on acoustic guitar. There is a pause, then drums, then the Sade-like vocal that glides over the band. "Tall in the Saddle" is quiet and calms things down. "Say What you Will" is pop standard bluesy. The song expresses disappointment in someone. The electric guitar lead becomes a kind of voice in this one also.

In *Sounds* (1976) Paul Sutcliffe wrote "we need Joan Armatrading." He observed, "There is a new dimension of expressiveness in her lyrics." Glyn Johns produced the Joan Armatrading album. Its "textural effects" were noted by Richard Williams in *Melody Maker*. Williams said that these effects were used with economy and "unerring rightness."

Whatever's for Us (1972), *Back to the Night* (1975), *Joan Armatrading* (1976), *Show Some Emotion* (1977), *To the Limit* (1978).

Hoyt Axton

A country and pop songwriter from Oklahoma, Hoyt Axton's "Joy to the World" and "Never Been to Spain" were hits for the popular vocal group Three Dog Night. Axton came from a musical family. His mother, Mae Boren Axton, was one the co-writers of Elvis Presley's hit "Heartbreak Hotel." Axton's music was primarily based in country blues and folk. His song "Greenback Dollar" (1963) was a hit for The Kingston Trio. (David L. Wolper produced the documentary *The Story of a Folksinger* that year.) He wrote "The Pusher" for Steppenwolf and the novelty song "No, No Song" for Ringo Starr. Axton recorded several of his own solo albums. "Lion in the Winter" and "When the Morning Comes" were duets recorded with Linda Ronstadt. Axton was responsible for writing several later country music singles. He concluded the 1970s with a role in the film *Black Stallion* (1979).

If you look for Hoyt Axton on YouTube you can find live performances of "Joy to the World," including one at Farm Aid in 1985. You may also find "Less Than the Song" brings a warm vocal with guitar. Axton is joined by a gospel-like chorus. Country steel guitar enters later. He repeats the line that tells listeners all your dreams are real. "When the Morning Comes" is country-sounding, but the speaker has a hangover. Drums, with snare out front, electric piano, and female background vocals are heard. Then one of the female vocalists comes forward to join Axton in a duet.

Joy to the World (1971)

"Joy to the World" opens his studio album of that title. "Alice in Wonderland" is next. We hear the familiar hit "Never Been to Spain" and then "The Pusher." "The Pusher" is situated in production that sounds quite late sixties. It was appropriate perhaps for Steppenwolf, who covered the song. He damns the pusher who leaves people with tombstones in their eyes. You can hear a 1968 home demo of the song on YouTube. The 1971 version is brighter but still has the 1968 sound, complete with a scream after the word "die." The side ends with "Ease Your Pain."

Side Two begins with "Have a Nice Day" with dobro and an easy swing tempo, and the acerbic lyric. The narrator of this song is not having the best day. The ballad "Indian Song" tells a family history of a grandmother who kept her part-Cherokee background hidden. There is steel guitar, drums, and a country music treatment. Axton's voice goes deep on the final word of the end of lines. "California Woman" chugs along on harmonica, a bass line, and chords that climb. "Lightning Bar Blues" is a country sound with pulled strings. The singer tells us he doesn't need diamond rings. All he needs is to drink some ripple in the lightning bar. "Farther Along" follows and then we get some "Old Time Religion." As we go further along into "Old Time Religion" we hear a slow gospel reverie, a background hum. Life's evening sun is sinking. The female gospel vocals become more prominent after two verse sections.

Joy to the World (1971), *Country Anthem* (1971), *Less Than the Song* (1973), *Life Machine* (1974), *Southbound* (1975), *Fearless* (1976), *Snow Blind Friend* (1977), *Road Songs* (1978), *Free Sailin'* (1978), *A Rusty Old Halo* (1979).

Elvin Bishop

A blues rock guitarist and a songwriter, Elvin Bishop was a member of the Paul Butterfield Blues Band. With his own band he toured with the Allman Brothers. Elvin Bishop was most familiar to radio listeners for his single "Fooled Around and Fell in Love" (1976). He also recorded the earlier single "Travelin' Shoes" (1975). Much of his 1975s work was played with The Elvin Bishop Group. He also played solo and sat in with blues greats like John Lee Hooker and B.B. King.

Feel It (1970), *Rock My Soul* (1972), *Let It Flow* (1974), *Juke Joint Jump* (1975), *Struttin' My Stuff* (1975), *Hometown Boy Makes Good* (1976), *Hog Heaven* (1978).

Stephen Bishop

The writer of some catchy pop hits, Stephen Bishop has performed with bands and on his own. He is known for his breezy song "On and On" and his hits "Save It for a Rainy Day," which were on his album *Careless* (1976) and the 1980s hit "It Might Be You" (1983). His album *Bish* (1978) included "Everybody Needs Love" and "A Fool at Heart." With "A Fool at Heart" comes a gentle soul-pop. The lyric tells us that a person seeks to find a spark among a million hearts in the dark. The spark turns into a spotlight. Bishop also created film songs. His songs have been recorded by more than two dozen major pop music artists.

Stephen Bishop is known for his breezy melodic pop song singles. He sings "It Might Be You" (All of My Life). The light pop of "On and On," shuffles along brightly. On a YouTube video of Bishop at the Ventura Theatre (April 5, 2020) he performs the song in good voice and good form.

Bish (1978)

He begins his album with "If I Only Had a Brain" (Harold Arlen/Yip Harburg) from *The Wizard of Oz*. On "Lookin' for the Right One," a single from *Bish* (1978) the singer laments that he has been unlucky, and he is trying to find the right one. The vocal is gentle and the orchestration sound serious. Somewhere in the city must be the right one. Will she ever come along some day? "I've Never Known a Nite Like This," a single from the *Bish* album, points to a Harlem jazz setting into which saxophone enters. The king of swing plays hard to get. This jumps to jazz and climbs to a chorus. "Vagabond from Heaven" begins in church with a Phantom of the Opera–like organ and then dives into funk and a walking bassline. An electric guitar punches into this up-tempo pop. We hear Bishop's vocal at one minute into the song and this narrator sings of reading the Bible every morning. On YouTube Bishop provides some brief snippets of his songs in a medley.

Careless (1976), *Bish* (1978).

Rory Block

Blues player Rory Block drew upon the Delta blues, listening closely to Mississippi John Hurt and now legendary players like Robert Johnson. Her name Rory is a knick-name derived from her given name Aurora. Her father was a sandal maker and store owner in Greenwich Village, and she took in the folk scene there. At 26, her songs were blues songs about identity and dreams. Intoxication was filled with blues guitar and some piano. Ariel Swartly in *Rolling Stone* (February 23, 1978) called her record "habit forming." She eventually recorded several more albums on Rounder Records.

Rory Block (1975)

Oh, she can play! A slide guitar is put to good use. One sets aside one of four fingers on the left hand to do this. Rory Block plays the blues with vigor and soul. "Lovin' of Your Life" gets the full treatment. You can "Let Bygone Be Bygones" and ask "What Do You Do with a Memory" in those first few songs. She sings "I Love My Car" and she certainly does have "Nimble Fingers." On YouTube is "Canned Heat: The Early Years, 1975–1976." This starts with a higher voice, couched in reverb. In "Crying Games" her vocal is forward, with percussion behind her acoustic guitar. Rory Block is Live at the Sheldon, a St. Louis concert. This is a fifteen-minute video which she opens with a Son House tune on slide guitar. She dives into these songs with blues passion and a guitar groove.

Rory Block (1975), *Rory Block* ("I'm In Love") (1976), *Intoxication* (1977), *You're the One* (1979).

David Blue

A participant in the Greenwich Village folk extension of the folk revival in the 1960s, David Blue was an artist of great expectations who came to little commercially in the 1970s. Appearing as S. David Cohen he released "Me" (1970) on Reprise Records. Then there were four recordings on Asylum Records, none of which broke commercially. He joined Bob Dylan's Rolling Thunder review in 1975. David Blue had a heart attack while jogging in Central Park in Manhattan. He was 41. David Blue never quite reached the commercial appeal that Elektra had hoped for him. However, his folk roots can be clearly heard.

On YouTube you can find *David Blue, Live in Sweden*, 1972. He is introduced in Swedish by a woman and enters solo with guitar, wearing black. He is interviewed by a Swedish man in a white jumpsuit before his next song which he plays on piano. Blue tells him that his songs are personal, and they discuss the topic of loneliness. The video is filmed nicely. YouTube videos also include a Unicorn Café performance from 1970 and singles of "Outlaw Man" and "House of Changing Faces." "True to You," sung live on radio with Jackson Browne, has a country sound. There is a two CD repackaging of four albums *23 Days of September* from the late 1960s and three from the 1970s: *Stories, Nice Baby Angel*, and *Cupid's Arrow* on Cherry Red Records.

Me (1970), *Stories* (1972), *Nice Baby and Angel* (1973), *Com'n Back for More* (1975), *Cupid's Arrow* (1976).

Gordon Bok

Folksinger Gordon Bok is a Maine artist with a baritone singing voice who is a folklorist, a collector of traditional folk songs, and a songwriter. The coast of Maine, a world of boats, fishermen, and waves, appears in some of his songs. He played for years as a member of the Bok Muir Trickett trip. Carol Rohl has provided harp and vocals. Noel Paul Stookey produced his first album on Verve Records in 1965. In the 1970s. Bok created several albums in the folk-music genre.

A Tune for November (1970)

The rich baritone vocals and acoustic guitar are at this album's center. "A Tune for November" opens with a strong voice of breadth and depth that sings of fishing and hauling down the sail. One is transported to the coast of Maine. A pretty girl was bothered by the cold winds and the man's house was warm. Our attention also turns to the hills of the "Isle of Haut," in a song that feels like it spilled forth from Scottish ballads and the British Isles. "Duna" is quieter and gentle. The singer tells us of when he was a lad and how he is weary of the sea wind. There are the little stars of Duna that call him home. "Handsome Cabin Boy" is played on a 12-string guitar in 3/4 time.

A Tune for November (1970), *Peter Kagan and the Wind* (1971), *Seal Djirils Hymn* (1972), *Cold as a Dog and the Wild Northwest* (1973), *Clearwater* (1974), *Bay of Fundy* (1975), *Clearwater II* (1977), *Another Land Made of Water* (1979).

Jay Bolotin

While he lacked much media attention Jay Bolotin wrote intriguing songs delivered in a bit of a southern drawl. His songs were rich in imagery. He was from Kentucky and was somewhat influenced by John Jacob Niles. One might think of some of his work as consisting of folk-based expressionistic art songs. This may be partly because he also seeks form as a sculptor. There was "No One Seems to Notice That It's Raining." Kris Kristofferson liked his songwriting and was supportive. Dan Fogelberg recorded his song "Hard to Go Down Easy." On one of his first albums Dan Fogelberg worked with bassist/producer Norbert Putnam in Nashville. He was working with producer David Briggs at the time Bolotin was developing demos and he played on some of them. So did Putnam and notable guitarist Reggie Young. Among Bolotin's talents are work in visual art, in woodcuts and sculpture, and in film. In some earlier songs Appalachian country-folk meets with the blues. His first album appeared before 1970 and the second, recorded in New York in 1970, was held back. He was much appreciated by other songwriters. A few recordings were developed in Nashville, but little that was commercial became of them. He moved to Cincinnati in 1980.

Jay Bolotin (1970)

"Hard to Go Down Easy" is centered by the song's chorus. A guitar riff opens this tune. Three lines beginning with "It's hard" focus the chorus. We hear the l's of lose a lover. The word autumn rides on the melody line. A female vocal accompanies Bolotin. "Dear Father" begins in guitar with arpeggio fingerpicking. The vocal is low, haunting. (Ezechiel with a violin is called a "friend.") "Pretty Burmah" opens on a picked guitar and voice singing of walking with the wind. The lyrics encourages us to look, watch, and listen as a rainbow and a summer's dream come to us. "For the Love of a Summer's Evening" is more up-tempo and leans toward bluegrass and country. "No One Seems to Notice That It's Raining" is one of the album's finest songs. We hear that the sailors are all in port. The ladies await them with flowers. The song brings one to a thoughtful and meditative place. The vocal is set forward over the acoustic guitar. On "Winter Woman" the guitar is fingerpicked in a folk-country style and drums and bass are set back in the mix. We hear that the day was cold when he met her around the bend of a country road. The song focuses on the woman who is said to have a hold on his soul. "I'm Not Asking You" goes into a full strum. The lyric starts on the title and the sound of this song may evoke a bit of Bob Dylan's *Nashville Skyline*. The singer tells the person he is addressing that he will not ask that person to be on a merry-go-round but to be in his life.

Jay Bolotin (1970).

David Bowie

Singer-songwriter? Certainly, one of the most creative and influential rock music creators of the 1970s, David Bowie remade his sound and his image over several times. His fluid identity shifted across a variety of albums and compelling performances. In November 1971, RCA Records released *Hunky Dory* (1971), with the single "Changes." (And the "ch-ch-ch-changes" listeners heard in the hook.) *Hunky Dory* was an album that some executives at RCA did not especially like. However, it started the string of hits that brought David Bowie to the center of public attention. In January 1972, some fourteen concert dates were set for February and March. Bowie's management, led by Dennis Katz, sought to develop publicity for Bowie in the United States. During this time, Bowie's band, led by guitarist Mick Ronson, was becoming the Spiders from Mars. Their act was artifice, cosmetics, and costuming; it was intended to be theatrical. Ziggy Stardust is an expression of Bowie's creativity and the malleability of the artist. Re-released in 1972, the single about Major Tom became a popular hit and a signature song for Bowie. The listener is immediately drawn into reflection upon humanity's ventures to outer space. In March 1972, "Starman" was the first single from *The Rise and Fall of Ziggy Stardust and the Spiders from Mars* (1972). "Five Years" begins the recording ominously with a note of world crisis, the news that the world has only five years of existence left. In "Starman" the narrator is a child who sees a UFO. He tells his friends, and he contacts the Starman. At the center of the record are the songs "Ziggy Stardust," "Suffragette City," and the record's closer "Rock 'n' Roll Suicide." Underlying this recording is a critique of art and the recording industry, of creation, construction, and manufacture. Bowie appears to reflect upon his own constructed image and upon the ways in which the industry and society creates pop stars. We hear about Ziggy who played guitar.

Aladdin Sane (1974) focuses on sanity and madness with its title, which may be read as "A lad insane." This album starts with "Watch the

Man" with Mike Garson on piano, playing dissonant runs and arpeggios. The *Alladdin Sane* cover shows Bowie with a mannequin look with his one eye that sees clearly and his other eye that was injured. Of the dark eye, Marc Spitz says that "in myth and legend, it implies mystic powers." The dilated eye looks inward and the other looks outward. Spitz calls this "dual vision," a capacity to see the spiritual world. Camille Paglia suggests that this is a Homeric image, "a mysterious Nefertiti look" that reflects a "hallucinatory part of his imagination."

David Bowie's *Diamond Dogs* (1974) emerged from his reading of George Orwell's *1984*. The album produced the song "Rebel, Rebel." Beyond the rock riff on that song, Bowie began to move in a soul/funk direction. For many months, Bowie imagined a musical based upon Orwell's novel. Sonia Orwell, who had disliked the 1955 film adaptation of the novel, rejected any adaptations into other media and refused to allow rights for a musical. Bowie wrote "We Are the Dead," "Big Brother," and the "1984/Dodo" theme with Ken Scott producing and his band, the "Spiders from Mars," accompanying him. On "1984" and "Dodo," which were linked, one hears cinematic scoring and the incorporation of fragments of reference to the novel. "Dodo" at first is focused on Winston and Julia, the would-be lovers of *1984*. It then turns to the character of Mr. Parsons, their neighbor who was betrayed by his own child. Bowie's science fiction interests inform the project, along with his rejection of conformity and totalitarianism. "Young Americans," "Fame," and "Golden Years" were hits that moved in a soul music direction.

The Man Who Sold the World (1970), *Hunky Dory* (1971), *The Rise and Fall of Ziggy Stardust and the Spiders from Mars* (1972), *Pinups* (1973), *Diamond Dogs* (1974), *Young Americans* (1975), *Station to Station* (1976), *Low* (1977), *Heroes* (1977), *Lodger* (1979).

Randall Bramblett

Only two recorded albums came from Randall Bramblett in the 1970s: *That Other Mile* (1975) and *Light of the Night* (1976). However, he remained a session player for years afterward. There was southern rock, funk, and blues on those recordings. He played keyboards, saxophone, and guitar. He was involved in recording sessions with Gregg Allman. He also played with a band known as Sea Level. In 1970 there was "Light of the Night." Randall Bramlett toured with the band Traffic. He recorded in New Orleans. John Swenson in *Rolling Stone* (May 20, 1976) commented on his "subtle songwriting." He is noted for his lyrics and his vocal support of other artists. He has worked alongside the Allman Brothers, Traffic, Elvin Bishop, Bonnie Raitt, and others.

That Other Mile (1975)
Light of the Night (1976)

Bramblett begins "Rocket" with a soul/R&B sound on keyboard with a funk wah-wah in the bass. He tells someone that he woke up on the wrong side of town. "Another Shining Morning" opens on piano chords. The lyric delivered in a raspy vocal acknowledges that people can't see the future. As the vocal lifts, there is the dream of a better world. On a recent performance of "Pine Needle Fire" he is on a Hammond organ, live at Tweed Studios. You can read about Bramblett in an article by Steve Wildsmith (November 16, 2020) *https://www.thetiesthatbindus.org/serenity-for-randall-bramblett-means-watering-the-roots-of-his-sobreity.*

Jackson Browne

Before his first album emerged, Jackson Browne had been writing songs for many years, singing them at the Troubadour and at small folk clubs. His father Clyde (Jack) Browne had played piano for Django Rinehardt while in Europe and took music jobs around Los Angeles. Jackson Browne gravitated toward folk music and the blues and songwriting. The songs of Bob Dylan, Joan Baez, and the Byrds drew him toward the folk clubs. He became acquainted with the Nitty Gritty Dirt Band, and he played a solo gig at the Paradox. He signed with Nina Music, the publishing company for the new Elektra Records label. Nico recorded three of his songs on her album *Chelsea Girl*. Songs were recorded by Tom Rush, Steve Noonan. Jackson Browne spent some time at The Troubadour in Los Angeles, where he met Linda Ronstadt, J.D. Souther, her backup band members Glenn Frey and Don Henley that would later become The Eagles. David Crosby, among others, took an interest in Browne's music. Jackson Browne eventually was signed to a record contract by David Geffen. Russ Kunkel (drums) and Leland Sklar (bass) would provide the rhythm section that supported the first album.

Jackson Browne's first album was self-titled. However, it appeared in a brown sleeve with a canvas bag with the words "Saturate for Using" stamped on it and most of the record buying public decided that that must be the name of the album. The record was most filled with the kind of introspective, lyric-laden mellow folk-rock you would expect from early Jackson Browne records. "Doctor My Eyes" was targeted as the single and it reached the top ten on the charts in May 1972. "Rock Me on the Water" followed in August 1972. He held back "These Days." Browne worked with producer Denny Cordell, who had worked with Joe Cocker. "Jamaica Say You Will" was also fashioned as a single. Browne appeared to aim for a universal narrative voice in his songs, rather than the more "confessional" tone James Taylor was introducing listeners to at this time. *Rolling Stone* concluded that Jackson Browne's debut album was to be ranked among the best of the singer-songwriters, with Neil Young's *After the Gold Rush* and Van Morrison's *Astral Weeks* (Bud Scoppa, *Rolling Stone*). After Jackson Browne's album, The Eagles joined the Asylum roster, recording and releasing their recordings. "Rock Me on the Water" was recorded by Johnny Rivers and by Linda Ronstadt, "Jamaica You Will" was recorded by the Nitty Gritty Dirt Band.

Jackson Browne opened for Laura Nyro's tour to support her third album. In late 1971, Browne appeared at The Main Point, Bryn Mawr and did a radio interview with Gene Shay in which he previewed some of his song "Take It Easy." He was in Milwaukee November 22 opening for Yes and The Beach Boys. In February and March, of 1972, Jackson Browne opened for Joni Mitchell's shows in the United States and Canada. By May he was in Europe. Contact with members of The Eagles led to Browne's co-write of "Take It Easy" with Glenn Frey. The Eagles recorded and released the song as one of their first singles. He co-wrote "James Dean" and "Doolin' Dalton" with The Eagles and went on a brief tour with America (Dewey Bunnell, Gerry Beckley, Dan Peek).

Jackson Browne's second album, *For Everyman* (1973), was recorded across nine months (Dave Thompson 253). Linda Ronstadt was joined for a recording by the musicians who would become The Eagles: Glenn Frey, Bernie Leadon, Randy Meisner, Don Henley. *For Everyman* brought a selection of Browne's ballads, including "These Days." The album included "Redneck Friend," "Ready or Not," and Browne's version of "Take It Easy." (Gene Shay "previewed" "Take It Easy" on WFFM, notes Dave Thompson.) Background vocals included Glenn Frey, Don Henley, David Crosby, and Bonnie Raitt. Drums were played by Jim Keltner and Russ Kunkel, bass by Leland Sklar, and piano came from Elton John (as Rockaday Johnny) and Craig Doerge. The song "For Everyman" was written with David Crosby in mind. Crosby contributed harmonies to the recording. Anthony De Curtis connected it with "Wooden Ships" and "that escapist thing" about "human possibility," as Crosby once called it in speaking with *Rolling Stone*. Sixties utopian dreams were affected by social and political tensions in America in the early 1970s. David Crosby and Paul Kantner were science fiction readers and created the daydream of escaping on a spaceship to freedom. Jackson Browne wasn't leaving. He was affirming everyman (and woman) in his song.

Within the context of any supposed decline of late 1960s utopian dreams, Browne was maintaining a balance of ideals and introspection. By this time, The Eagles, Linda Ronstadt, Andrew Gold, Warren Zevon, the

Doobie Brothers, and others were said to comprise a "West Coast sound." The artists who emerged from Laurel Canyon, from the days of The Mamas and the Papas and The Turtles to Joni Mitchell, Neil Young, and Crosby, Stills, and Nash were now a central "sound" in the pop music industry.

Late for the Sky (1974)

Bruce Springsteen has called *Late for the Sky* Jackson Browne's "masterpiece." *Rolling Stone* critic Stephen Holden observed in 1974 that *Late for the Sky* was Jackson Browne's most conceptually unified album to date. He pointed out that while there is no lyric sheet to this album the lyrics are at its center. Holden recognized Browne's willingness to deal honestly with his own vulnerability, romantic concerns, and perspectives on life. He commended Jackson Browne's ability to fuse the personal with his public persona. The "melodic style" was called "limited," which seems to be an appropriate indicator of Browne's melodies during this time. They are pleasant but idiosyncratic. In the early 1970s, he tends to repeat phrasing rather than to go many new places melodically. However, the lyrics have more depth than is customary for pop music. Jackson Browne fits in nicely with the desire for "authenticity" during this era. What could be more refreshing in America during the time of Watergate than some honesty?

There is passion and truth in this voice. The production Al Schmitt and Jackson Browne applied on *Late for the Sky* supports the tracks without overwhelming them with sound. We are given plaintive vocals that come wrapped in emotional clarity. The "sky" is somewhat stark, but it is a space of freedom beyond the hard self-assessment in some of these lyrics. There are fountains of sorrow and fountains of light to be found in love. There is the danger of illusion. "Farther On" envisions a paradise. "Late Show" brings us down into a more desolate reality. "The Road and the Sky," a rock tune, becomes apocalyptic with storm clouds up ahead. "To a Dancer" meditates on death and in pondering attempts to affirm life's path ahead. There is a tango-like melody and movement joined by David Lindley playing fiddle. "Walking Slow," a rock song, precedes "Before the Deluge," which brings the album together in a final statement. In the one sense, the song underwrites the declension thesis of the demise of sixties idealism and sounds an epitaph for this. In another sense, there is an affirmation of hope, a turn toward the future. For there is light still within the human heart that can reach the sky. There is a chorus and the fiddle and Jackson Browne's voice asserting that life and hope are sustained in those who live after the deluge.

Listening to this album now, one might wonder what has been lost in

American idealism? There is on this album a sense of some sadness and pains felt on the way to maturity, a shedding of bright-eyed infatuations and replacement of them with realistic loves. A '54 Chevy on the album cover evokes nostalgia while the blue sky spreading out above suggests expansion and a sense of promise. Yet, there is also a sense of approaching twilight. One of the strengths of this album is that Jackson Browne was able to record it with the self-contained unit of his touring band. The band included multi-instrumentalist David Lindley. What Jackson Browne does here is prompt empathy in his listeners.

Jackson Browne. February 1972. Asylum 5051. "Jamaica Say You Will," "A Child in These Hills," "Song for Adam," "Doctor My Eyes," "From Silver Lake," "Something Fine," "Under the Falling Sky," "Looking into You," "Rock Me on the Water," "My Opening Farewell."

Singles: March 1972, "Doctor My Eyes"/ "I'm Looking into You"; August 1972, "Rock Me on the Water"/ "Something Fine."

For Everyman. Asylum, 1973 "Take It Easy," "Our Lady of the Well," "Colors of the Sun," "I Thought I Was a Child," "These Days," "Redneck Friend," "The Times You've Come," "Ready or Not," "Sing My Songs to Me," "For Everyman."

Late for the Sky. Asylum, 1974. The album was recorded by Browne across six weeks with his touring band: David Lindley, Doug Haywood, Jai Winding, Larry Zak. Don Henley, J.D. Souther, and Dan Fogelberg provided background vocals. Bruce Springsteen, upon inducting Browne into the Rock Hall of Fame, called this album Browne's "masterpiece." "Late for the Sky," "Fountain of Sorrow," "Farther On," "The Late Show," "The Road and the Sky," "For a Dancer," "Walking Slow," "Before the Deluge."

The Pretender. Asylum, 1976. Produced by Jon Landau. "The Fuse," "Your Bright Baby Blues," "Linda Palomba," "Here Come Those Tears Again," "The Only Child," "Daddy's Tune," "Sleep's Dark and Silent Gate," "The Pretender."

Running on Empty. Asylum, December 1977. Mixing live and studio tracks. "Running on Empty," "The Road," "Rosie," "You Love the Thunder," "Cocaine," "Shaky Town," "Love Needs a Heart," "Nothing but Time," "The Load Out," "Stay."

Tim Buckley

Another tragic figure, Tim Buckley died of a drug overdose in 1975 after being given heroin by a "friend." He became a folk music fixture in Los Angeles in the mid- to late 1960s. He wrote songs with Larry Beckett, who joined him in a group with bassist Jim Fielder. They played at Los

Angeles folk clubs. Buckley ended that decade with the largely folk-based recording *Blue Afternoon* (1969). However, much of his folk music audience appeared to turn away from the more rock and psychedelic music he produced in the early 1970s. Tim Buckley recorded five albums between 1970 and 1974: *Lorca* (1970), *Starsailor* (1971), *Greetings from L.A.* (1972), and *Sefronia* (1973), and *Look at the Fool* (1974). His work on *Starsailor* introduced jazz sounds and included "Song to the Siren."

Lorca (1970)

Tim Buckley was sure to alienate any folk audience with *Lorca*. The album begins on keyboards from which long spacey tones bring us into an atmosphere. The vocal begins wordlessly with oh-ah … and a dreary descending bassline brings it down. The word sun is extended on the "n." And sing in smile and wind is a drug trip with a woman's voice running through your veins and blood. This begins to sound like the phantom of the opera playing on an organ behind the keyboard and drowning voice. The organ sound pumps up front with sometimes dissonant runs and the guitar slides down to hell as the phantom plays eerie organ in the distance.

At about ten minutes the song is slow jazz. Somehow fluttering vibrato becomes a fashion on this record. The vocal is drawn out as are the strings but this may cause a listener to focus on the drifting singing. At about 17:48 into this album some light percussion and acoustic guitar sets a nice pattern. A talk with his woman late last night brings reassurance that she is sane. He feels a sense of loss when he is away from her. He wants to go to sing his love from the mountains. The mountain and mention of Moses and Jesus suggests some spiritual sense "in this cold world." In the music is a shuffling movement, with light electric guitar and the percussion on congas. "I Had a Talk with My Woman" then flows into "Driftin'." The strings of the guitar, with some chorus effect on it, sounds like they are being tuned lower even as we listen. A slow, pondering lyric follows. One may drift like the singer's dream out on the sea along with the guitar lines. The vocals move into a bluesy treatment, with long held notes and bends. The guitar figure repeats its downward line beneath this. "Nobody Walking" begins with up-tempo chinka-chicka guitar joined by organ and percussion. The vocal treatment over this is a blues. The full album is available on YouTube.

Lorca (1970), *Starsailor* (1971), *Greetings from L.A.* (1972), *Sefronia* (1973), *Look at the Fool* (1974). The Lorca and Starsailor albums are available for you to listen to on YouTube. See Martin Aston, "An Introduction to Tim Buckley in 10 Albums" *https://thevinylfactory.com* (October 18, 2016).

Jimmy Buffett

Humor, novelty, and Margaritaville are Jimmy Buffett: song-writer, performer, writer of short stories. His keynote is play, escape to the islands, beach bum pleasure. You can drink anytime because it's "Five O'Clock Somewhere." There is a "Cheeseburger in Paradise." As the 1970s began there was Buffett's *Down to Earth* (1970). Buffett moved to Key West. *Changes in Latitudes, Changes in Attitudes* (1977) included the song "Margaritaville." That song launched the broad popular reception of Jimmy Buffet, his audience of "Parrotheads," and the familiar persona of a humorist-troubadour.

Down to Earth (1970)

The inimitable wit and storytelling listeners have come to associate with Jimmy Buffett shines through on his debut studio album. However, there are differences in song style listeners may recognize as at variance with most Jimmy Buffett songs. This is folk song based rather than country based and would have little resonance with the Gulf Stream party crowd. However, "Ellis Dee," a portrait of someone who is down and out does have this sound. Of course, his name resembles the name of popular hallucinogenic drug of the time. He needs to get free and so does this album. We hear "The Christian," "Ellis Dee," "The Missionary," "A Mile High in Denver," "The Captain and the Kid." Side Two has six songs: "Captain America," "Ain't He a Genius," "Turnabout," "There's Nothing Soft About Hard Times," "I Can't Be Your Hero Today," "Truckstop Salvation."

The album opens on the chug-chug percussion and guitars on "Christian" with its critique of someone who has forgotten the core of Christianity. "Ain't He a Genius" is an easy listening folk-country sounding song. This is the story of a struggling artist, once ignored and now suddenly noticed and considered "a star." "The Captain and the Kid" is about the speaker's experience of listening to the stories of an older man who sailed and told stories that were rare. "I Can't Be Your Hero Today" is a light, bouncy tune in which the singer tells his partner that he can't be someone's superman. This is Jim Croce's "Lover's Cross" with an up-tempo bounce. He insists he cannot be a soldier come from home from war or be a hero in a relationship that appears to not be working. "Truckstop" is musically out of character for Jimmy Buffett. The lyric has some quirky turns, like a truck with fertilizer ending up in a creek. Other incidents he reports are all on tape.

Down to Earth (1970), *A White Sportscoat and Pink Crustacean* (1973) *Living and Dying in 3/4 Time* (1974), *A1A* (1974), *Havana Daydreamin'*

(1975), *High Cumberland Jubilee* (1976), *Changes in Latitudes, Changes in Attitude* (1977), *Son of a Son of a Sailor* (1978), *Volcano* (1979).

Kate Bush

In 1975, EMI Records got behind the efforts of this then young British singer-songwriter and David Gilmour of Pink Floyd produced her demo. Kate Bush was a precocious talent who created dozens of songs by the time she was seventeen. The label called for the use of session players on her first album, *The Kick Inside* (1978) but she was able to include her brother Paddy on the recording. She accompanied herself on piano. Her song "Wuthering Heights" charted as a single in 1978. *The Kick Inside* sold well in Britain, less so in the United States. Bush was marked as an experimental, unconventional songwriter, whose lyrics and song structures went in creative, unanticipated directions. With *Lionheart* (1979) her record company launched an extensive tour. There was a stage show that involved choreographed dance, set designs, poetry, and Simon Drake's magic. Kate Bush's impact grew during the 1980s. She was later inducted into the Rock and Roll Hall of Fame.

The Kick Inside (1978), *Lionheart* (1979).

Bill Camplin

Milwaukee's troubadour in the 1970s. Bill Camplin's music of the 1970s sounded like it derived from Bob Dylan's influence, as well as other folk music background. He was well-regarded in the Milwaukee area and as a regional artist. Indeed, Camplin is one of those unsung talents of the 1970s and after. Camplin has been a singer-songwriter whose own influence can still be felt in Wisconsin at a folk music series at Café Carpe in Fort Atkinson.

January (1973)

A strummed guitar is joined by a harmonica and the entrance of drums as this album begins. A stark drawing of some shrubs in the snow suggests the bare landscape of the month of January. "Lost" is the first word we hear from the singer's voice. He meets a man, and a conversation begins over a drink. They talk for four hours. This contact between them seems to have been a temporary cure for aloneness. The encounter seems to not end well. We have gone in about 7½ minutes listening to the story. "January" suggests the tick-tock of time, guitars in breezy motion, and the melodic line that comes with that statement that one can't expect to find things. Camplin's tenor vocal is in a slightly higher register than on the previous song and the lyric is thoughtful. After this atmospheric, reflective piece comes the road song "Rover." He uses a lower register of vocal as the song chugs along like train, giving us an up-tempo country-folk sound. The recognition that it's kind of funny repeats several times. It is a bit jarring to go to an old upright piano played surely but simply in chord patterns. Guitars join this, the sound of steel pedal guitar, and drums. "Ain't It Something" is broadly sung and the style is perhaps here for some variety. "The Long One" brings us quietly back to guitar. "If It's in Your Mind" opens with guitar and the title is the first line of the song. The lyric is directed toward a "you." Yet, it sounds like a personal meditation upon flaws. "Seems I've Seen This Night Before" sounds like a country song with steel guitar. This is John Denver–like in style. Camplin here is folksinger semi-country. He sings that if he is given a chair he will sit in the dark. At night, the stars will be shining. By day, the sun will be shining everywhere. He seems to rejoice in that. The song is one of the most pleasant on the album. This is a good folksinger, and the world should hear more Camplin. The full album is available on YouTube. Overall, it is a fine piece of work which brings attention to the art of this Wisconsin singer-songwriter.

January (1973), *Cardboard Box* (1974), *Bill Camplin's Latest Effort/ Still Looking for the Cure* (1976).

Johnny Cash

One of the great stars of country music, Johnny Cash, "the man in black," was a well-respected singer-songwriter and a popular performer. He played at the Grand Ole Opry, in concert halls throughout the world, and at legendary concerts at San Quentin and at Folsom Prison. He had a television show (June 1969 to March 1971), where he featured the Appalachian folksong. Statler Brothers, the Carter Family Singers, and sang with his wife June Carter Cash. He explored his own roots in Scotland and the British Isles, as well as Appalachian folk and country music. He embraced Native American Indian concerns. Cash also sang with Dylan, Kristofferson, and a long list of country performers. He joined Bob Dylan on the *Nashville Skyline* album on "Girl from the North Country." He met with President Richard Nixon in 1972, encouraging prison reform. He was friendly with President Jimmy Carter. As a born-again Christian he became friends with preacher Billy Graham. He advocated for the poor and needy. Johnny Cash appeared in films and several television shows. For example, he provided a fine performance (as fictional singer Tommy

Brown) on the television detective show *Columbo* with Peter Falk. He is remembered by younger audiences through Wakim Phoenix's portrayal of him.

Johnny Cash songs like "I Walk the Line," "Folsom Prison Blues," and "Ring of Fire" all have become memorable standards. "A Boy Named Sue" by Shel Silverstein made people laugh. Other songs made people cry or pray or nod in agreement. Johnny Cash sang of life. His song choices reached out across country, bluegrass, traditional and contemporary folk, and rock. Cash was popular country and folk roots. He sang about American life, relationships, working men, trains, prisons. He was also appreciated in Britain, where he played at the Glastonbury Festival, and in Ireland. At the end of the decade, he independently produced a recording of his gospel songs. He was inducted into the Country Music Hall of Fame in 1980 and spent the mid–1980s with The Highwaymen: Willie Nelson, Waylon Jennings, and Kris Kristofferson.

Hello, I'm Johnny Cash (1970), *Man in Black* (1971), *A Thing Called Love* (1971), *America: 200 Year Salute in Story and Song* (1972), *Johnny Cash's Family Christmas* (1972), *Any Old Wind That Blows* (1973), *Ragged Old Flag* (1974), *The Junkie and the Juicehead Minus Me* (1974), *The Johnny Cash Children's Album* (1975), *Johnny Cash Sings Precious Memories* (1975), *John R. Cash* (1975), *Look at Them Beans* (1975), *One Piece at a Time* (1976), *The Last Gunfighter Ballad* (1977), *The Rambler* (1977), *I Would Like to See You Again* (1978), *Gone Girl* (1978), *Silver* (1979), *A Believer Sings Songs of the Truth* (1979).

Harry Chapin

With his story songs like "Taxi," Harry Chapin became one of Elektra Records top-selling recording artists in 1972. His humanitarian work to fight world hunger involved him in a deep, idealistic commitment throughout his career as a performing songwriter and musician. Harry Chapin thought about what man's life could be worth and put his words and goals into action. His efforts were those of a man committed to humanity as much as those of an artist committed to music and lyrical craft. He may be best remembered for his song "Cats in the Cradle," which became a #1 hit around the time of his birthday in 1974. The song, written with his wife Sandy, tells the story of a too often absent father and his growing boy who returns the favor as a young man. The story turns on the line that the boy had become like his father: a man with little time for anyone else. In a culture guided by a strong work ethic and striving the song lyric landed in the hearts of fathers and sons everywhere. The range of Chapin's observations and the stories which filled his songs was perhaps only exceeded by his perform-ing at concerts with his band and his politically aware social energy. He could indeed make a large concert hall feel like a big living room in which an audience were friends and participants. Harry Chapin wrote "Circle" for the children's show his brother Tom Chapin hosted and he would often end his shows with the audience joining him in the song. His band consisted of bassist John Wallace, a big man with a big vocal range, guitarists Ron Palmer and then Doug Walker, cellist Tim Scott, drummer Howie Fields, and later cellists Mike Masters, Kim Sholes, and Yvonne Cable. The music was orchestrated by his brother, Steve Chapin.

Harry Chapin emerged from folk clubs. He had played folk music with his brothers, done a stint at the Air Force Academy and at Cornell, and developed his skills as a documentary film maker. In 1972, Elektra Records and Columbia Records both wanted Harry Chapin to sign with their label.

Head and Tales (1972) sold one million copies. That year, Chapin played "Taxi" on *The Tonight Show* hosted by Johnny Carson. *Sniper* (1972) features a disturbing fictional account of the Texas Tower shooting from a Freudian-angle and the viewpoint of the crazed shooter. It was dramatic but too long and perhaps too graphic and troubling for airplay. *Short Sto-ries* (1973) brought listeners the story of a disc jockey down on his luck in the song "WOLD" (the call numbers of a radio station). The album also included "Mr. Tanner," a song about an aspiring opera vocalist who dreamed of success, rented a hall for his debut, and ultimately just ended up singing in the rooms of his tailor shop. There was also "Mail Order Annie," a song about a simple woman from the Great Plains, on which Chapin played some harmonica before his guitar and vocal began. *Verities and Bal-derdash* (1974) was one of Chapin's bestselling albums. That success partly rested on the distribution of the hit song "Cats in the Cradle." Also, on the album was "I Wanna Learn a Love Song," based upon memories of guitar lessons he had given to his future wife. A wry, dark humor came forth on "30,000 Pounds of Bananas," about an unfortunate truck driver. "Shooting Star" included a little reverbed musical run at the start that suggested the shooting star: a relationship in which a life burned bright and the partner who shined back some light. In another slightly self-deprecating humorous song Chapin told his listeners that he was essentially a "Six-String Orches-tra." He intentionally flubbed a few notes on his guitar in the process.

Portrait Gallery (1975) followed with "Dreams Go By." Chapin wrote that year the play *The Night That Made America Famous*. *Greatest Stories Live* (1976) sold two million copies. Albums that followed this were *On the Road to Kingdom Come* and *Dance Band on the Titanic* (1977), the live album *Legends Lost and Found* (1978). *Living Room Suite* (1979) and *Sequel*

(1980), with its reprise-rewrite of "Taxi" on Boardwalk Records, complemented Chapin's busy road tours. He spent much of the rest of the decade principally as a concert performer and an activist. His life was cut short in an accident on the Long Island Expressway in July 1981. He was subsequently awarded the Presidential Medal of Honor for his advocacy efforts to fight hunger.

Verities and Balderdash (1974)

Verities and Balderdash was among the most popular of Harry Chapin's studio albums. It contained the hit "Cat's in the Cradle," his most widely known song. "I Wanna Learn of Love Songs" provides an imaginative recollection of meeting his future wife and giving her guitar lessons. The Harry Chapin Band and some effects shine through on "Shooting Star," which precedes the dark comedy of a trucker who has an accident and slides on the bananas he is carrying. "She Sings a Song Without Words" ends the first side. "What Made America Famous" offers a glimpse at America. In "Vacancy" the narrator laments the gaps or vacancies in his life. "Halfway to Heaven" is followed by "Six-String Orchestra," in which Chapin intentionally flubs guitar lines and satirizes his work as a self-contained folk music act. Of course, Chapin did work with a band. This album is best listened to in the context of other Chapin albums. The recent video *Harry Chapin: When in Doubt Do Something* (2021) offers a fine introduction to his life and his work.

Heads and Tales (1972), *Short Stories* (1973), *Verities and Balderdash* (1974), *Portrait Gallery* (1975), *Greatest Stories Live* (1976), *On the Road to Kingdom Come* (1977), *Dance Band on the Titanic* (1977), *Legends Lost and Found* (1978), *Living Room Suite* (1979).

Tom Chapin

Witty songs with clever wordplay, masterful fingerpicking, an embrace of folk music tradition, and a heart for the spirit of childhood characterize the work of Tom Chapin. He is a storyteller and a musician, who hosted the *Make a Wish* show on ABC-TV, played a role in the Broadway musical *Pump Boys and Dinettes*, and lent his support to World Hunger Year organization founded by his brother Harry Chapin and Bill Ayres. He appears on the folk circuit as a solo artist, entertains children with his music, joins brother Steve Chapin for an occasional tribute to Harry Chapin concert, and continues to be on the board of World Hunger Year to help to feed the hungry people of this world. Tom Chapin is a performer who moves effortlessly from the serious song to the comedic. His daughters perform as The Chapin Sisters.

Tom Chapin created one album in the 1970s: *Life is Like That* (1976). He has recorded some two-dozen albums since that time, including several notable children's entertainment recordings.

Tom Chapin's first album included a song written before cell phones, "Long Distance Life." His colleges tour led to a mid-day phone call. On Tom Chapin's first album, his thought that he dreamed he saw his brother at the end of the rainbow is directed toward Harry. The song repeats that one should watch the circle and encourages strength and balance. The song includes what any singer-songwriter might ponder: What is singing this song worth? Who listens? Why does doing this matter? Tom Chapin continues to write witty songs, perform to audience of all ages, and accompanies himself on banjo as well as guitar.

Life Is Like That (1976).

Michael Chapman

English folksinger Michael Chapman was a notable guitar player in the 1970s. He hailed from Leeds in Yorkshire and recorded on Harvest records. He then recorded on Decca/Deram. BBC radio show host John Peel and Charles Shaar Murray both paid much attention to his songs and recordings. *Wrecked Again* included a Memphis blues sound with horns. Strings were arranged for *Savage Amusement* (1978) by Paul Buckminster. Jazz, folk, ragtime, and elements of progressive rock enter his music. An older Michael Chapman, in cap, glasses, t-shirt pullover, was interviewed by Giovanna. This is available on YouTube. He speaks about his 1964 guitar and defines himself as a guitar player who writes songs. He acknowledges that he is not really a singer. He adds that he hates being called a folksinger. His songs tend to be autobiographical, he says. In older videos you can see "Among the Trees" (1975) and songs from *Pleasure of the Street* (1975).

Fully Qualified Survivor (1970), *Window* (1971), *Wrecked Again* (1971), *Millstone Grit* (1973), *Deal Gone Down* (1974), *Pleasure of the Street* (1975), *Savage Amusement* (1976), *The Man Who Hated Mornings* (1977), *Play the Guitar the Easy Way* (1978), *Life on the Ceiling* (1979).

Eric Clapton

Much attention was focused upon Eric Clapton's guitar playing in the 1960s as he played with the Yardbirds, John Mayall and the Blues-breakers, Cream, Blind Faith, Delaney and Bonnie, and eventually his own band Derek and the Dominos in the early 1970s. It was during the 1970s, when despite romantic courtly love longings over Patti Boyd and drug and alcohol issues, he became a singer songwriter and began to create some enduring songs. His song "Layla" was an international hit single. He turned Bob Marley's "I Shot the Sheriff" and J.J. Cale "Cocaine" into radio hit singles. As a solo artist, Clapton recorded several popular albums throughout the 1970s. He contributed to George Harrison's benefit *Concert for Bangladesh*. There were live recordings on *History of Eric Clapton* (Atco/Polydor 1972), *No Reason to Cry* (with Bob Dylan and The Band), and *E.C. Was Here* (1975). One of his songs following that album was "Wonderful Tonight." While Clapton was a significant solo artist through the 1970s, it was also a time that he developed as a songwriter. He is heard playing solo acoustic on recordings like *Unplugged* (1992).

History of Eric Clapton (1973)

This is essentially a greatest hits double-album that offers live performances and studio recordings of Clapton's blues and rock guitar soloing, collaborations with Cream, The Yardbirds, Delaney and Bonnie, Blind Faith, and Derek and the Dominos. The album includes "Layla," which is among the Derek and the Dominos cuts on Side Four. There are two different versions of "Tell the Truth."

Eric Clapton (1971), *History of Eric Clapton* (1972), *461 Ocean Boulevard* (1974), *There's One in Every Crowd* (1975), *Slowhand* (1977), *Backless* (1978). See *Clapton: An Autobiography*. New York: Broadway Books, 2008.

Gene Clark

A member of The Byrds, who in his solo work and on the late 1960s Byrds recordings anticipated country-rock and psychedelic rock. He was the writer of "I'll Feel a Whole Lot Better," "Eight Miles High," "Set You Free This Time." The song "Train Leaves Here This Morning" co-written with Bernie Leadon appeared on The Eagles first album. "Tried So Hard" and "Here Tonight" were on the Flying Burrito Brothers album. *Two Sides of Every Story* combined folk, blues, honky-tonk, and blues. "Past Addresses," "Sister Moon," "Hear the Wind," "Lonely Saturday," and the old traditional song "In the Pines." White Light (1971) included acoustic and slide guitar, some introspective songs, "Because of You" "For a Spanish Guitar," "When My Lover Lies Asleep." Iain Matthews covered "Polly" and "Tried So Hard" on his 1972 and 1974 recordings. Country rock, soul, choral vocals, and folk were brought together on *No Other* (1974). The work of Dillard-Clark in 1969 led to the Flying Burrito Brothers. He joined with Roger McGuinn and Chris Hillman in 1977. Clark's combinations of country and rock preceded Bob Dylan's *Nashville Skyline*.

White Light (1971)

Gene Clark's *White Light* (1970) opens on harmonica. One can hear some Byrds and some Dylan influence here in how the songs are structured. The lyrics provide a portrait. His singing is clear, smooth, and the songs, while a bit wordy, are accessible and well-played and sung. One can hear his central importance to the vocal mix and songwriting that was The Byrds.

The second song, "With Tomorrow," is a simple guitar/vocal and full of folk song. He sings of a relationship that is over that now seems more like dream than reality. The song is reflective. Country up-tempo emerges next, like the late 1960s recordings of The Byrds. The harmonica returns over guitar and bass and drums. There is a tossing of head and a look in the eyes as storm clouds come in. A rainbow breaks through the clouds. The vocalist recalls the relationship. There is organ and light percussion underneath guitars. If he closes his eyes and wishes to think of some place to fly away. The dark clouds can dissipate, and this person's spirit returns to him. In the next song the pleasant vocal is joined with a guitar and with slide guitar. The lyric is again reflective, don't you come down. Let the troubles fade into sunshine. The backing vocals toward the end could be softer, but maybe that's a matter of the mix and of taste.

"Spanish Guitar" provides a beautiful opening to side two. The bells are ringing and singing of ages past. The lyric unfolds with images. Harmonica playing joins this and we are invited to listen to the music, to laugh, to fly like gull over the sea, or to stand in the rain. "Where She's Sleeping" speaks with thoughtful appreciation. The album included his treatment of Bob Dylan's "Tears of Rage." Jesse Edwin Davis produced this album with Chris Ethridge on bass and Michael Utley on organ. Two members of the Steve Miller Band also contributed to the album, multi-instrumentalist Ben Sidran and drummer Gary Millaber.

White Light was reissued by Intervention in 2018. The remastering provides more fullness and texture to the guitars and situates Clark's vocals nicely within the instruments. See *www.analogplanert.com* for radio show material on Gene Clark.

White Light (1971), *Roadmaster* (1973), *No Other* (1974), *Two Sides to Every Story* (1977).

Bruce Cockburn

The Canadian singer-songwriter Bruce Cockburn has created music that extends across folk to jazz to instrumentals. He is often cited for his fine guitar playing and recognized for his songs of conscience and political protest. There is a sense of a poetry of insight and stark brevity in several early Bruce Cockburn songs. One might see the lyrics as poems on the page: concise, abstract, compact. His folk acoustic music also has jazz influences and the grasp of someone who has a sense of classical music composition. *High Winds, White Sky* has a bare black and white wintry cover that suggests the stark and rich power of the songs on this album. Bruce Cockburn played in bands like Esquires, Flying Circus, and 3's a Crowd in the 1960s and then ventured out as a solo artist in the 1970s, beginning with folk venues and the Mariposa Folk Festival in Toronto. He embraced Christianity and Christian themes in 1970 and a commitment to human rights, ecological concerns, and the rights of indigenous people followed. He concluded the 1970s with his album *Dancing in the Dragon's Jaws* (1979). It included the single "Wondering Where the Lions Are." In the 1980s he was writing and recording overtly political songs like "I Wish I Had a Rocket Launcher," addressing policy in Central America. The songs suggest a deep search into the social questions of our time.

See the autobiography Bruce Cockburn with Greg King, *Rumours of Glory*. New York: Harper, 2014.

There is a bare, stark beauty to *High Winds, White Sky* (1971), which was a ten-song album. This Bruce Cockburn recording was reissued in 2003, adding "Totem Pole" and "It's Elephant's World." His singing and guitar work is at the album's center. There is a spiritually intent, almost Zen-like meditative quality to some of this recording. Here are landscapes of mountains and rivers and an inward vista of reflection.

To begin, "Happy Good Morning Blues" may suggest e.e. cummings' little lame balloon man in his poem "Just Spring." But there are a tom cat, a policeman, and good people. The second song, "Let Us Go Laughing," opens on a canoe on the water and a pensive reflection on a day's dry leftover bones. This appears as a stark landscape. There is poetry in the description of ancient stars, branches that appeared tattered, pale moon and sky through which streaks of distant, "lightning" flash without sound.

In few words of "Love Song" there is a stark poetry. The speaker's love is found in the place from which his wonder comes. In that place, which seems a meditative center, is where he is "real." A listener is led toward the chorus of "One Day I Walk." The lyric of "Golden Serpent" is minimalist. The serpent figure seems to be simply how she moves and how the music moves. Birds, smoke, sky, rings of light fill the lyric of the title song. Cockburn writes concisely. We see stars. Winds spin a spider. Ships sail forth. The word "beginning" rings out as he sings. Later, he has gone to a shining mountain to gain insight and to see. The sun dissolves like fire on the horizon.

Bruce Cockburn (1970), *High Winds, White Sky* (1971), *Sunwheel Dance* (1972), *Night Vision* (1973), *Salt, Sun, and Time* (1974), *Joy Will Find a Way* (1975), *In the Falling Dark* (1976), *Further Adventures of* (1978), *Dancing in the Dragons Jaws* (1979).

Leonard Cohen

One must first mention Leonard Cohen's painstaking approach to songwriting, which involved numerous revisions. The familiar often-covered "Hallelujah" has dozens of verses, many more than we usually hear sung on the many cover-recordings of the song. Leonard Cohen was a poet and novelist, and he was this poet-artist before he began writing songs in the 1960s. "Suzanne," recorded by Judy Collins, became a hit single. Other folk music iterations followed. John Hammond signed Cohen to Columbia records. He recorded *Songs of Leonard Cohen* (1967), his first album. Poetry collections and novels like *Beautiful Losers* (1966) were circulating at the same time as this recording. Cohen was interested in the poets Federico Garcia Lorca and William Butler Yeats. He was drawn toward Buddhism. He now wrote less fiction and more songs. He once commented to an interviewer that he stumbled upon song ideas and then got stuck and had to work on them.

Cohen, a Canadian, delivered his songs with a raspy vocal. *Songs from a Room* (1969) further established him as a songwriter. It included the often-covered song "Bird on a Wire." Cohen's *Songs of Love and Fate* (1971) and *New Skin from an Old Ceremony* (1974) were mostly bare recordings, with the voice and lyrics up-front. A live concert recording was produced in 1973. Cohen collaborated with John Lissauer between 1974 and 1975. Some jazz fusion from the band Passenger was brought in by producer Henry Lewy, who had recorded Joni Mitchell. Jennifer Warner and Sharon Robinson sang background vocals. He was teamed up with producer Phil Spector as he began his recording *Death of a Ladies Man* (1977). He produced a volume of poetry with a similar title.

Songs of Love and Hate (1971)

"Avalanche," "Last Year's Man," "Dress Rehearsal Rag," "Diamonds in the Mine," "Love Calls You by Your Name," "Famous Blue Raincoat," "Sing Another Song Boys," "Joan of Arc."

In interviews, Leonard Cohen recalled the time of creating this album as a time of falling apart. Several songs on the album were written earlier. He played at the Isle of Wight Festival on August 30, 1970. Most of the songs were written by then. He performed these songs in his concerts.

"Avalanche" opens with a fluent almost Spanish guitar feel that holds on one chord. The poetry is strong and draws us into the song. Argeggios play and we hear the singer declare that he once stepped into an avalanche. Cohen's distinctive low vocal has a haunting sound and causes a listener to focus. He admonishes the listener to not dress in rags for him. He already wears one's flesh. "Diamonds in the Mine" has bass and guitars jump up the tempo and female vocals join Cohen's voice. The lyric employs parallel structure. There are no letters in the mailbox, or chocolates, and no diamonds in the mine. In "Love Calls You by Name" he tells the interlocutor that he or she thought it could never happen. The guitar is plucked in that same Cohen style: almost flamenco with a holding on the chords. "Dress Rehearsal" is bare, with strings behind the vocal. It has come to this. There are questions.

Soon he is addressing someone and speaking of "Jane" and of a Famous Blue Raincoat. It is four in the morning, and this is reflective, slower with a clear vocal to a pensive 3/4 time rhythm. One's attention goes to the voice and the lyrics. In "Raincoat" a man is writing a letter to a man who has had an affair with his wife. Of course, there is also the raincoat. In "Last Year's Man" the rain falls on him, has a jew's harp and a crayon, and solo guitar accompaniment. A lady his playing with her soldiers in the dark. Her name is Joan of Arc. That is the first mention of this figure. The strings are quiet, occasionally rising from underneath. They come out in the last section in which Cohen is joined by a chorus that sounds like a children's choir. "Joan of Arc" speaks of the fire, the accusations of heresy, and her destiny. Cohen sings that she would have preferred a white wedding dress.

See Anthony Reynolds, *Leonard Cohen: A Remarkable Life*, 2010.

Songs of Love and Fate (1971), *New Skin from an Old Ceremony* (1974), *Death of a Ladies Man* (1977), *Recent Songs* (1979).

Judy Collins

Known for her crystal clear vocals and interpretations of other songwriter's songs, Judy Collins has also written several songs of her own. Folk music traditions and the folk revival lies behind most of what may called the singer-songwriter era of the 1960s through the 1970s. Judy Collins drew from this as one draws water from a well. The beautiful vocal tone of her singing voice was a gift to the writers of these songs. "Both Sides Now" on Collins's album *Wildflowers* (1967) won a Grammy Award and brought her to the attention of a large listening audience. She also sang Mitchell's "Chelsea Morning," "Someday Soon," and "Cook with Honey." *Living* (1971) brought her folk and art songs out on a solo album. *The Best of Judy Collins* (1971) was also released. Her highest charting hit came in

1975 with her recording of Stephen Sondheim's "Sand in the Clowns." Producer Arif Mardin filled out her sound on *Judith* (1975), which contained that song. On *Bread and Roses* (1976) she turned to some political themes, which underscored her activism. She had strained her vocal cords and had to repair and rest. *So Early in the Spring: The First 15 Years* (1977) provided some retrospective on her career to that point.

Judy Collins's song "Open the Door" (1971) was a single. Her other songs include "Easy Times" (1971) and beautifully pensive "Since You Asked" (1967). "Secret Gardens" (1973) was a single. Her songwriting appearing in 1973 also included "Song for Martin" (1973) and "Che" (1973). Collins was mostly an interpreter of songs with a golden, clear singing voice. The compilation album of *The Best of Judy Collins* included "Some Day Soon," her song "Since You Asked," Joni Mitchell's "Both Sides Now" and Leonard Cohen's "Suzanne," and ended with John Lennon's "In My Life" and "Amazing Grace." The album *Judith* (1975) included "Angel Spread Your Wings," "Houses," a dreamy, clear vocal with strong piano accompaniment to "A Song for Duke," the standard "Brother Can You Spare a Dime," Steve Goodman's "City of New Orleans," and her hit with Stephen Sondheim's "Send in the Clowns."

Whales and Nightingales (1970), *Colors of the Day: The Best of Judy Collins* (1972), *True Stories and Other Dreams* (1973), *Judith* (1975), *Bread and Roses* (1976), *So Early in the Spring: The First 5 Years* (1977), *Hard Times for Lovers* (1979). *Living* (1971) was a concert album.

Mike Cooper

An English folk and country-blues guitarist, Mike Cooper came of age in the 1960s listening to Sonny Terry and Brownie McGhee and blues players like Sonny Boy Williamson and John Lee Hooker, who toured England with their music. He and a friend set up a coffeehouse in Reading where musicians like Al Stewart and Bert Jansch performed. Cooper composed blues songs. In the late 1960s he performed with Mississippi Fred McDowell and began recording blues albums. *Trout Steel* (1971), featuring a wide array of musicians, is considered by some critics to be his most enduring album.

Trout Steel (1971)

"That's How," "Sitting Here Watching," "Good Times 2," "A Half Sunday Homage to a Whole Leonardo Da Vinci," "Don't Talk Too Fast," "Trout Steel," "In the Morning," "Hope You See," "Pharoah's March," "Weeping Rose."

This is an uneven album of improvisation and exploration that wanders between folk, or country-folk, and jazz, while ranging from studio work to home recording simplicity. Upon listening to the first song on this recording, the second chord sounds a bit out. The vocal enters, singing that it is so hard to know what she's thinking and that things get lost on the way. Something has been lost on the way here. This is not a good guitar sound. It is tinkly and bare. It sounds like it is played up the neck. The saxophone runs are interesting, sometimes a bit much. This is bare, like a home recording. Next comes "Sitting Here Watching." The guitar in an alternate tuning is more vigorous than on the first cut. There is a more assertive vocal and up-tempo country-folk sound. The runs on the lower strings are stronger than the tinkly guitar leads on the higher strings. "Good Times 2" is upbeat blues jazz with saxophone. It sounds like it was recorded differently. The sound is cleaner, less rough. "I've Got Mine" begins with a pulse. The instrumental builds. There is some piano and bass as the music begins to gain momentum. A fiddle squeals. A flute breaks in. Now we can hear a steady melodic pattern and rhythm. Things get busy. The vocal begins. Low strings respond after the verse is sung. After a brief interlude, the verse repeats and the pulse and riff that the song builds on returns. Why is it too late to change one's mind or leave things behind? Conceptually that makes little sense. The line seems to be thrown in like all the musical surprises along the way. La-la-la. Yet, this is a most interesting piece instrumentally. It is like a forest full of sounds. "Hope to See" begins in a brisk guitar. The vocal sounds like a backwoods traditional country folksinger joined by a fiddler and a hot guitar player. There is more musical energy than lyrical skill on this recording. There is variety but not a great deal of cohesiveness. The album is more like a collection of interesting demos. Jazz and folk musicians contribute their musicianship. The trout does some slippery swimming and swerving on this album. If this is folk music, it is moving in curious directions. Cooper appears to be experimenting, perhaps seeking to find a new voice on this recording.

   Trout Steel (1971), *Places I Know* (1972), *Life and Death in Paradise* (1975).

Elvis Costello

To approach life from interesting angles is one of the marks of a creative songwriter. Elvis Costello (Declan McManus) had that gift. He caught listener's attention as the new wave rock movement generated energy in the mid- to late 1970s. He was playing at London pubs in the mid–1970s. *My Aim Is True* (1977) burst upon the scene with its energy and clever songwriting. *This Year's Model* (1978) was propelled by the Attractions, the band he had assembled after the first album. His recording *Armed Forces* (1979) built upon the response of his growing audience. His song "Oliver's Army" soared up the British charts. He might be described as a trendsetter with his sound and musical approach during this time. Some new life was injected into the realm of the singer-songwriter with new wave-punk. It flew in the face of disco commercialism. It no longer dwelled in mellow acoustic reveries. In some respects, that era was over. The world of 1969–1975 had shifted midway through the 1970s with the sounds of Bruce Springsteen and Billy Joel, growing commercialism, and the marginalization of folk music. Elvis Costello was that bright new voice: literate and iconoclastic. There was wordplay. There were strains of country music and pop-rock. There were signs in Elvis Costello, Rickie Lee Jones, Willie Nile, and others of a turn toward a new phase of the singer-songwriter in a new decade.

My Aim Is True (1977)

Critics appear to agree that there was something melodic and neurotic in Elvis Costello's *My Aim Is True* (1977). There was something raw, uncompromising, and mid–1970s new wave. "Welcome to the Working Week," which opens the record, has a catchy melody, a pop sensibility with razor sharp edge. You can hear "Miracle Man," and "No Dancing" with its percussion and multi-tracked vocals building sound on sound like in a Phil Spector record. "Blame it on Cain" seems to want to go toward country in the vocal treatment. The song is accented by John McFee's guitar, which comes out more forcefully on "Alison," a moody piece that contains the album's title in the lyric. "(The Angels Wanna Wear) My Red Shoes" is pop-rock catchy bright and "Less Than Zero" directs a critique at a fascist. "Watching the Detectives," which ends the Rhino Records re-release, brings pulsing bass and syncopated drumming to Costello's aching whine. An intensity of various emotions moves through this record.

My Aim Is True received a *Rolling Stone* review by Greil Marcus (December 1, 1977). This came alongside a review of *Little Criminals* by Randy Newman. He compared Costello's songs as "intelligent ... elusive" and witty like those of Newman but not ever "timid." Marcus commented that Elvis Costello can sometimes have the new wave rock style and attitude of a Nick Lowe, the album's producer-recording artist, who fostered a punk rock edge at this time. Marcus predicts that Elvis Costello will shake up his peers and make others seem irrelevant.

My Aim is True (1977), *This Year's Model* (1978), *Armed Forces* (1979).

Jim Croce

Folk storyteller, legend maker, singer of working songs, troubadour of the down-and-out, Jim Croce was inducted into the Songwriter Hall of Fame in 1989. Rightfully so. He was one of the premier folk music and blues-based singer songwriters of the early 1970s. Who knows how many more beautiful songs he may have shared with us had his life not ended at the young age of thirty. Croce sang humorous, rollicking portrayals of tough bar room bad guys in "You Don't Mess Around with Jim" and "Bad, Bad Leroy Brown." He created gentle, honest love songs like "Time in a Bottle," "Photographs and Memories," and "I'll Have to Say I Love You in a Song." He sang about loneliness and loss in "Operator." He sang about working at jobs, like in "Working at the Car Wash Blues." There was humor and pathos, love and humanity in his songs.

Looking at his album covers one first notices the moustache and the penetrating gaze in his eyes. Sounding alternatingly like a tough working man, a sensitive romantic poet, or a storyteller in a barroom, Jim Croce was an exceptional singer-songwriter whose life was tragically cut short in an accident while he was on a performing tour. One remarkable thing about Jim Croce is how many lasting songs he wrote while he was in his twenties. He was from an Italian American family in the Philadelphia suburbs, and he attended Villanova, where he majored in psychology. He recorded *Facets* (1966) as a self-produced album. He married Ingrid that year and converted to Judaism. He and Ingrid, as a folk duo, played folk coffeehouses and college gigs. They moved to the Bronx to pursue the music business. They gave up and lived on a farm. Croce played at a steakhouse in Pennsylvania. He drove trucks, did construction work, jotted down ideas gathered from bars, poolrooms, and truck stops along the road. There were songs like "Working at the Car Wash Blues." He met Maury Muehleisen from Trenton in 1970 and Maury could play the guitar beautifully. He was also trained as a classical pianist. Croce sang with his wife Ingrid, and they recorded a folk album for Pickwick Records. Then he met the songwriting team of Terry Cashman and Tommy West, who had been successful as a duo. (Much like Brewer and Shipley, Aztec Two Step, or Seals and Crofts.) Joe Salviolo, who Croce knew in college at Villanova, brought Croce to the attention of Terry Cashman and Tommy West in New York. Cashman and West produced Croce's first album on a major record label. Adrian James (A.J.) Croce, a future blues singer-songwriter, was born in September 1971 and Ingrid Croce stayed home with him while Jim Croce's recording career began. In 1972 he signed a three-record deal with ABC Records.

In 1972, Jim Croce's recording and performing career took off with "You Don't Mess Around with Jim," the clever lament "Operator," and the wistful "Time in a Bottle," which would later become a posthumous #1 single. The story of "Bad, Bad Leroy Brown," grabbed the attention of listeners through radio airplay. It reached #1 in July 1973 and became one of the biggest songs of the year. "Lovers Cross" and "Working at the Car Wash Blues" were recorded to be heard alongside "I Got a Name" on his next album. The up-tempo title song, "I Got a Name" would stand as a final tribute to Croce's songwriting. For the highway he was bending down now was one to eternity. Sadly, Croce and Muehleisen were killed on September 20 in an airplane crash while on tour in Louisiana. Croce had finished recording his album one week before. Jim Croce died at the height of his success in his recording career. New songs had just been released and there was deep sentiment and sure songwriting craft in those songs. With the sentiment generated by news of his death these songs seemed especially poignant, especially his nostalgic "Time in a Bottle," recorded in 1973. The new album, *I Got a Name*, brought his songs "Lover's Cross," "I'll Have to Say I Love You in a Song," and "Workin' in the Car Wash Blues." In his hit song "I Got a Name" he was moving ahead so life would not pass him by.

His greatest hits album, *Photographs and Memories* (1974) followed. The world of Croce's listeners still knows of bittersweet relationships, sad endings and precious memories, car washes and barroom brawls. Dimes in pay phones are now a thing of the past. However, Croce's songs have an enduring quality. A.J. carries on wonderfully, not only with a legacy but with his own creativity and musical talent. And Jim Croce's songs live on, ever available to stir the heart, tickle one with wit, or get the feet tapping.

You Don't Mess Around with Jim (1972), *Life and Times* (1973), *I've Got a Name* (1973), *Photographs and Memories* (1974).

Also see: *The Faces I've Been, Home Recordings: Americana, Down the Highway.*

David Crosby

David Crosby was a member of Crosby, Stills, and Nash at the time that he created his first solo album. Their first recordings catapulted them into the forefront of rock notoriety. Crosby was previously a member of The Byrds. During the 1970s he teamed up with Graham Nash for three albums and many live performances. In the 1970s, Crosby, Stills, and Nash produced *Déjà vu* (1970), *4 Way Street* (1971), *So Far* (1974), and *CSN* (1977).

If I Could Only Remember My Name (1971)

David Crosby's first solo album begins with the sound of an acoustic guitar and a four-note pattern that is repeated three times. The final line reverses this, three notes down to the root note. A rhythmic pattern becomes clear. The word "everybody" is repeated, Crosby's vocal jumps higher, and "Music is Love" becomes a ragged chant from a chorus of singers that sound like they have kicked off their shoes on a beach or joined in a circle in a field at a picnic. The guitar takes on a sitar-like sound as the chorus of voices stumble over each other a bit in communal connection. "Cowboy Movie" immediately chimes out with an electric guitar sound that listeners can hear on "Wooden Ships" and other CSN&Y tunes. To a slow, steady 4/4 Crosby's voice drops from the upper register of the previous song to a strong tenor with a rougher, throatier edge. It is an evocative vocal that sometimes borders on speech and declaration. Drums clearly hold the bottom and punctuate this.

The recording has a live sound. Some guitar leads have the high-pitched sound with some gain and sustain but no overdrive, as if they were emerging from a hollow body guitar through a small Ampex or Peavy amplifier. "Tamalpa High" follows with "Déjà Vu"–like harmonized vocals. These vocal intricacies move into an instrumental of guitars, bass, and drums. By now Crosby has indicated that this will be a listenable journey in which he will leave a good deal of instrumental space. Clearly, Crosby loves to sing and to play and harmonize with vocal lines. "Laughing" opens with acoustic guitar chords. A solo voice comments on a man who said he knew what was going on. This melts into rich harmonies. It's butter on sweetened pancakes. We hear a mellow and reflective, almost meditative track. Crosby's clear vocal comes through amid touches of pedal steel guitar or slide and vocals that sound very CSN&Y. There is a pause, some space (not John Cage silence, but a moment). There is some guitar noodling. At about 1:40 drums enter, and a repeating pattern is established. We have a song "What Are Their Names" which challenges the men that Dylan called the "Master of War" to step out of their anonymity and identify themselves. "Who really runs this land?" Crosby asks. This now becomes a big vocal chorus that sounds like a Jefferson Airplane song, with Grace Slick and Paul Kantner among those who are calling for a peace that is not a lot to ask for. Then the music fades. When music returns it drifts into gentleness and dreaminess with "Traction in the Rain." The strings sound like a hammer dulcimer. (Crosby creates a pattern that is similar to the third cut on his recent *Sky Trails* album, "Drive Out to the Desert.") "Song with No Words" performs vocal gymnastics. It begins with guitar arpeggios and begins to move in harmonized vocals. Voices caress a melody that proceeds in a kind of circular motion. A jazz-like vocal pattern emerges and carries through the song. Crosby begins the next song, "Orleans," a capella. Chorus vocals join Crosby's, thick like in a Gregorian chant. Crosby's vocal joined by acoustic guitar comes to us in French. A picked pattern on the guitar ends the song with harmonics. Again, a sense of chant and reverie follows in the playful wordless vocals that conclude the album.

Crosby's recording brings together Joni Mitchell, Neil Young, Graham Nash, photographer/folk musician Henry Diltz, and members of Jefferson Airplane (Grace Slick, Paul Kantner, Jorma Kaukonen, and Jack Casady) and The Grateful Dead (Phil Lesh, Jerry Garcia, Bill Kreutzman, Mickey Hart). It was dedicated to Christine Hinton and recorded at Wally Heider's studio with Bill Halverson.

If I Could Only Remember My Name (1971).

Rodney Crowell

This country-pop songwriter's first recordings appeared toward the end of the 1970s. His crossover quality appeals to listeners across country and folk. After moving to Nashville in 1972, he had a song, "Bluebird Wine," recorded by Emmylou Harris. He then played in the support band for her. After working with Tony Brown and Vince Gill, he was signed to a contract for his first album. Three albums followed that sold modestly: *Ain't Living Long Like This*, *What Will the Neighbors Say* and *Rodney Crowell*. He was writing songs for other country artists, from Johnny Cash and Roseanne Cash to Jerry Reed, Waylon Jennings, and the Oak Ridge Boys. Crowell's solo career gained traction in the 1980s and 1990s.

Ain't Living Long Like This (1978).

You can hear Rodney Crowell talking about his song "Ain't Living Long Like This." It was written in jail, where he was held for refusing to pay for his dog's leash law violations. He recalls the high school football team in East Texas carousing after their games and recalls his dog Banjo's leash-law violations (www.smarturl.it). See "Ain't Living Long Like This (Track by Track)." Fans have uploaded his album on YouTube, not necessarily with his consent. On YouTube there is a live performance of the song with a band.

Mac Davis

Popular audiences remember Mac Davis for *I Believe in Music* (1971) and *Baby, Don't Get Hooked on Me* (1972), the title songs for which were his highest charting pop singles. Some will recall his television appearances. Mac Davis was from Lubbock, Texas. He became a staff songwriter for

Boots Enterprises, a Nancy Sinatra music company. He was recorded by Sinatra, B.J. Thomas, Elvis Presley. His song "In the Ghetto" was recorded by Elvis Presley and drew much attention. He signed with Columbia Records in 1970. "Watching Scotty Grow" became a #1 country hit for Bobby Goldsboro. In 1974 Mac Davis began a successful television variety program on NBC. He won the Country Music Entertainer of the year Award that year. Davis passed away in 2020.

Song Painter (1970)

Song Painter's strongest song is "In the Ghetto," a deeply affecting song about the plight of a Chicago ghetto youth recorded by Elvis Presley. Mac Davis's album is decidedly Texas-country: a cross between the strong vocals of a pop singer backed by Artie Butler's orchestral arrangements and down-home country boy. Richly produced songs like "Whoever Finds This, I Love You," the album's single, display Mac Davis vocalist-songwriter, while titles like "Uncle Booger" and a series of interspersed humorous song fragments ("Contributing to My Juvenile Delinquency" and "Babies Butts" among them) suggest a quirky southern raconteur and entertainer like Georgia humorist Augustus Longstreet or Mark Twain.

With his other songs, it sounds like Mac Davis is writing for the country-pop market of the early 1970s. "Memories" is a ballad with a broad vocal. The first side ends with an infectious up-tempo honky-tonk romp, "Hello L.A., Bye-Bye Birmingham." Side two opens with the sentimental story of a boy and his father's response to a divorce. This is followed by "Once You Get Used to It" and "You're Good to Me." Interspersed are more song fragments. "Home," "Closest Fever Came," and "Half and Half" round out the album.

Song Painter (1970), *I Believe in Music* (1971), *Baby Don't Get Hooked on Me* (1972), *Mac Davis* (1973), *Stop and Smell the Roses* (1974), *All the Love in the World* (1974), *Burning Thing* (1975), *Forever Lovers* (1976), *Thunder in the Afternoon* (1977), *Fantasy* (1978).

John Denver

John Denver was one of the best-selling pop music artists of the 1970s. With a clear tenor singing voice, a homespun looking appearance, and songs that drew upon folk and country music, John Denver appealed to middle America. He had written "Leaving on a Jet Plane" for Peter, Paul and Mary and worked with the Chad Mitchell Trio in the 1960s. John Henry Deutschendorf by birth, he took on the name Denver from his love of Colorado and the outdoors. He became associated with a back-to-nature hippie environmentalism and with the broad reaches of the American landscape through his hits like "Take Me Home, Country Roads," written with Bill Danoff, and "Rocky Mountain High." To many he sounded like a hopeful voice in a time of some social upheaval.

He was given a guitar at the age of ten by his grandmother. She taught him how to play it. He brought his guitar to school: a somewhat lonely kid whose life was always in motion, from place to place. (His father was an Air Force colonel.) He sang at parties and people liked it and liked him. Like most of them, he liked Elvis.

John Denver became a prolific songwriter and a performer of his own songs. His song catalogue on the computers at ASCAP (American Songwriters, Composers and Publishers) is quite extensive. John Denver performed throughout the United States and in Europe. However, his dreams went beyond those travels. He often said that he would like to be chosen for the United States space program. This desire was perhaps rooted in his early experience. His father was a flier who held aviation records. It was, sadly, this interest that led him to fly an experimental airplane and set out on a faulty flight that led to his demise.

Most of John Denver's flights were emotional and that wide range of emotions moved into his songs and into his relationships. He once said that he ran away from home to play music. He went to Los Angeles, felt alone and scared, and returned home to finish high school. He attended Texas Tech, thinking of becoming an architect. He listened to the records of Joan Baez, Tom Paxton, and Peter, Paul, and Mary. He spent more time playing and listening to music than attending classes. When he left college, people told him that he was making the biggest mistake of his life. Believing in his music, John Denver hit the road. He got a 1953 Chevy, packed up three guitars, and headed for California with about $125 in his pocket. (His parents sent him a little more to sustain him.) It was 1964.

Once in California, he got a job in Los Angeles as a draftsman. He began singing in the Los Angeles area. Randy Sparks, the owner of Leadbetter's, liked what he heard in John Denver's playing and Denver began to play there regularly. He went to Phoenix for a while and learned that the Chad Mitchell trio had just lost Chad Mitchell. They needed a replacement. Pursuing this, he got an audition in New York with Milton Okun, a music arranger who would later become an important figure in his career. He was sent back to Phoenix, with no word of how he had done in the audition. Shortly after he arrived, they called him.

John Denver rehearsed for six days with the Chad Mitchell Trio and then appeared at the Cellar Door, a folk club in Washington, D.C. One night in 1966 he avoided a party and sat in a room, having some beer and salami, and he wrote "Leaving on a Jet Plane." Peter, Paul, and Mary recorded the song for an album in 1967. It was released as a single in 1969 and became a hit. Those years, John Denver was shuffling back and forth between gigs as a solo performer playing at coffeehouses.

Was John Denver's music folk, country, or pop? Perhaps it was all three. At a time when pop radio airplay was quite eclectic, his work-boots jumped across any barriers between those genres. He had been a folk-singer, a pop singer with country leanings. He had been a resident of Colorado, an advocate of space travel, a proponent of health food and holistic living. John Denver became a friend to Ted Turner and his broadcasting system, a television and movie actor (with George Burns in *Oh, God!*), a marijuana smoker, an EST disciple. In the early years, his image was marked by granny glasses and shaggy blonde hair, like a friend Dutch American hippie, or an amiable sheepdog. He seemed to embody all that was back to nature simplicity, a marijuana high, and getting back to the heart and the heartland. In fact, he was criticized for "packaging" nature and was unfavorably compared with Peter Pan and Tom Sawyer by some critics. He shed some of that image as time went on. His voice remained clear, and the reach of his music extended across the world.

John Denver brought to his music a clear, distinctive tenor singing voice, an All-American homespun image of blonde-moppy hair and granny glasses, and a sensibility that seemed right for the times. He was among the best-selling recording artists of the 1970s. He wrote several hundred songs. In several of them he always seemed to be going away from home and wishing to return. ("Leaving on a Jet Plane," famously covered by Peter, Paul, and Mary. Gee it's nice to be home again.) Perhaps a military family childhood of many moves lay behind some of this. He created a string of hits: "Take Me Home Country Roads," "Rocky Mountain High," "Sunshine on My Shoulders," "Calypso," "Annie's Song," "Thank God I'm a Country Boy." He was known for his love of Colorado and his embrace of ecological and humanitarian concerns. He appeared on television specials, Grammy Awards, with the Muppets on children's television, and in the movie *Oh, God!* (1977) with George Burns. John Denver bridged country, folk, and pop. He brought acoustic music, attention to humanitarian causes, and a kind of optimistic attitude to popular music.

Henry John Deutschendorf emerged from folk roots and interactions with the New Christy Minstrels and Chad Mitchell Trio. He recorded with the group the vocal on Eric Andersen's "Violets of Dawn." Then embarking upon his first solo album, *Rhymes and Reasons* (1969), he was produced by Milt Okun who managed the folk group Peter, Paul, and Mary. Two more albums soon followed: *Take Me to Tomorrow* (1970) and *Whose Garden Was This?* (1970). *Poems, Prayers, and Promises* (1971) was his breakthrough album and "Take Me Home Country Roads," written with Bill Danoff and Taffy Nivert, launched his career as a radio-friendly singles singer-songwriter and performer. "Rocky Mountain High" reached similar heights the next year, receiving extensive airplay into 1973.

Greatest Hits (1973)

The John Denver *Greatest Hits* album distributed by RCA Records is a collection of the familiar songs that launched his career and made him one of the most familiar popular singing voices of the 1970s. The recording includes "Take Me Home Country Roads," "Rocky Mountain High," "Sunshine on My Shoulders," "Leaving on a Jet Plane," "Annie's Song," "Poems, Prayers, and Promises." The album cover greets you with sunshine yellow and his ebullient smiling face and granny glasses under a hat that is held steady by his hand. There are revisions in his treatment of "Leaving on a Jet Plane," "Sunshine on My Shoulders," "The Eagle and the Hawk," "Starwood in Aspen," "Poems, Prayers and Promises," and "Rhymes and Reasons." In that sense, this is a "new" album and not just a rehash compilation of previous recordings. Also, about half this album features John Denver hit songs. The other songs here are central to his sets and to defining his interests, concerns, and style. Future songs included his cross-over into country music with "Thank God I'm a Country Boy" and his tribute to Jacques Cousteau and ecological awareness on "Calypso." This album appears to have confirmed and consolidated John Denver's early 1970s rise to the top of the popular music charts.

Rhymes and Reasons (1969), *Take Me to Tomorrow* (1970), *Whose Garden Was This?* (1970), *Poems, Prayers, and Promises* (1971), *Aerie* (1971), *Rocky Mountain High* (1972), *Farewell Andromeda* (1973), *Back Home Again* (1974), *Windsong* (1975), *Rocky Mountain Christmas* (1975), *Spirit* (1976), *I Want to Live* (1977), *John Denver* (1979).

Neil Diamond

One of the most popular singer-songwriter entertainers of the 1970s, Neil Diamond launched out on his career from days of writing songs for other recording artists from the Brill Building in New York: "Sunday and Me" (Jay and the Americans), "I'm a Believer" (The Monkees), "He Ain't Heavy, He's My Brother" (The Hollies), "And the Grass Won't Pay No Mind" (Elvis Presley, Mark Lindsay). When Bang Records signed Neil Diamond to a record deal several of those songs began to be heard in his own voice. One heard "Cherry Cherry" and "Solitary Man." (Of the 1960s albums, two are on Bang Records and three appear on United Artists

[UNI] Records.) In the early 1970s Neil Diamond singles shot up the charts. "Sweet Caroline" and "Holly, Holly" broke out in 1969. Then came "Cracklin' Rosie," "Song Sung Blue," "I Am, I Said," "Play Me," and others.

Longfellow Serenade (1974)

Neil Diamond's *Longfellow Serenade* (1974) is arguably his central studio album of the 1970s. It followed his live double-album *Hot August Night*, which highlighted Neil Diamond as performer at the Greek Theatre in Los Angeles, and his score for *Jonathan Livingston Seagull*. Producer Tom Catalano brings forth Neil Diamond as singer and musical composer. There is a confident depth to Diamond's vocals and a rich quality to Jimmy Haskell's arrangements. This is not the Neil Diamond of Bang records and the Brill Building, or the pop hitmaker of "Sweet Caroline" and "Cracklin' Rosie." This is a more operatic, middle of the road, album-oriented Neil Diamond. The album is melodic, sometimes meditative. It is sung well, but somewhat lyrically thin. Gone is the heat of *Hot August Night*. If Diamond is still a believer, his belief here appears to be in reflection, orchestration, and meaningfulness. "Longfellow Serenade," which reached high on the charts, is indeed an energetic, sweeping, winged flight that opens this recording. The lyric alludes to the New England poet but is not specific to that poet's work. The rich vocal on "I've Been This Way Before" thoughtfully gathers up recognition of a path through life with the meditative strength of "I Am, I Said," but without the angst. "Rosemary's Wine" is beautifully arranged and has appealing dynamic range. The vocal to "Yes, I Will" is open and full and appeals to emotion. "Lady Magdelene" is likewise introspective. There is poignant yearning here. The bright and extroverted "Reggae Strut" is apparently included for musical contrast: a celebratory journey to the Caribbean islands. A critic may claim that the orchestral production is a bit bloated. Yet, this is music with feeling and some ambitious composition that works as an album with a consistent tone throughout. *Longfellow Serenade* is an accomplishment, an album that reaches not for pop singles but for soul.

Taproot Manuscript (1970), *Stones* (1971), *Moods* (1972), *Longfellow Serenade* (1974), *Beautiful Noise* (1976), *I'm Glad You're Here with Me Tonight* (1977), *You Don't Bring Me Flowers* (1978), *September Morn* (1979).

Donovan

The Scottish singer emerged in 1965. Donovan was popular at the end of the 1960s and his music carries over from that decade. He produced the singles "Mellow Yellow," "Sunshine Superman," and "Hurdy-Gurdy Man" all before 1970. His music was folk-based. However, Donovan caught the psychedelia movement mood of 1967–1971 and contributed to it. In 1970, Donovan paused in his work with Mickey Most and only resumed this in 1973 with *Cosmic Wheels*. He played for a while with the band Open Road. He performed in Japan. *HMS Donovan* was a children's album. He opened for the progressive rock band Yes in 1977 concerts.

Donovan's *Open Road* (1970) aimed at a band recording. Fortunately, much of the psychedelia of his late 1960s recordings is gone. *Open Road* has replaced this with folk-rock. "Changes" is bright pop-rock driven by a band with vocal. He encourages listeners to not let changes get you down. The second song, "Song for John" slows it down into a country 4/4 beat that swings a little easy, with vocals and harmonica. We are given the image of country ladies taking them by hand before the song concludes. Then sounds of the ocean come in. "Curry Land" begins rather bare, then is joined by piano, and begins to build. There are some sea-images of a schooner and waves, a merchant that is on his way abroad, a quest for trinkets. The music unwinds like a spool in piano and drums for a moment. We hear that despair has been replaced by military discipline. We hear about a lonely man. Behind it all are high harmony vocals. Next in Joe Bean's Theme we are in Brazil or samba-territory. The breezy Latin American feel on guitar comes with percussion and a whispery vocal begins until the tune reaches the chorus vocals. Then there is a pleasant guitar lead break. There is a leading lady and jasmine in the air. Then with "People Used To" we are pushed back into bouncy folk song, strum and backbeat, and group around a campfire sing-along. This seems too great a stylistic jump. We have the effects of Donovan's Celtic Rock, and rolls of drums, honky-tonk piano, and ay-di-day chorus. "Roots of Oak" provides another strong composition. There is Irish folk, folk/rock, and whimsy. This album seems unique among Donovan records and overall, perhaps one of his best.

Open Road (1971), *HMS Donovan* (1972), *Cosmic Wheels* (1973), *Essence to Essence* (1973), *7 Tease* (1974), *Slow Down World* (1976), *Donovan* (1977).

Nick Drake

The acoustic guitar centered songs have brought a broader listening audience in the time since his troubled young life ended. The more orchestrated tunes are well-matched by the more starkly recorded ones. *Five Leaves Left* (1969), released when he was twenty, introduced listeners to his songs and reflective sensibility. He had moved from his Cambridge studies to London. John Peel on the BBC played his songs. He opened for Fairport Convention. There were bright, gentle arrangements on *Bryter Layter* (1971). The record was produced with string arrangements and saxophone. Drake's songs were not structured like verse-chorus folk songs. *Bryter Layter* was indeed a brighter record than the subsequent *Pink Moon* (1972), which was spare and brooding. *Pink Moon* was developed with recording engineer John Wood. There were 11 songs on an album that runs under ½ hour. Songs are bare and dark with vocal, guitar, and some piano. There is some energy in the guitar playing. It was to be Nick Drake's final musical statement. In 1972 he retired to his family home in the English countryside. Nick Drake's death at the age of 26 was a loss to music and to life. He created beautiful music but suffered from depression and overdosed on anti-depression prescription medication. See the 1998 documentary *A Stranger Among Us* and the 1997 biography by Pat Humphries, *Nick Drake*. London and New York: Bloomsbury, 1997.

Bryter Layter (1972)

The "Introduction" to *Bryter Layter* (1971) sets the tone for this album with acoustic guitar pattern that is joined by sweeping strings. Hazy Jane gives us up-tempo pulse, with horn and strings sound. What happens when the world gets so crowded that you can't look out the window? The music is propulsive, and it rocks and rumbles along with a whispery vocal above it, with plenty of instrumental space. On "At the Chime of a City Clock" an acoustic guitar pattern is joined by drums, and we are given images of the city. Then strings come in on the line in which he introduces the song's title. He will stay indoors and talk with a few neighbors. A city star is not going shine far. There is a saxophone within the pad of strings and guitar, and this breaks free for a while into soloing. The light of the city falls within this breezy jazzy sense of evening. The guitar is moving quickly on "One of These Things First." The piano come in with bass and drums softly underneath. He mentions all the things he could have been. He could have been many things to the person he is speaking to. The music skips along briskly, as if dancing on the piano and guitar.

"Bryter Layter" gives us a beautiful composition with flute floating throughout. In "Fly" he requests a second grace. The speaker reflects upon what has been done, how he has fallen, and what is behind him as clouds drift by. There is an appeal for the person he addresses to ride with him in his streetcar and there is apparently a desire to be free to fly. Next, "Poor Boy" gives a bit of Latin music rhythmic movement in the guitar and a jazz-touch of the piano. Drake's vocal is joined by female background singers singing about the poor boy. A saxophone breaks in and we soon are brought back to the soft vocal reflecting on experience and floating on long vowels, repeating "nobody" at the start of several lines. The piano has its solo, sounding improvisational and free over these rhythms that shimmer beneath. "Northern Sky" moves along gently with reflection and instrumental passages. The speaker is asking questions. He has felt sweet breezes and wondered at the northern sky. The final song, "Sunday," immediately brings back the flute and it rises over the guitar, which begins to establish some phrases that will repeat throughout the composition. This is an instrumental piece that the listener can enjoy as a fitting conclusion to this recording. It is easy to get caught up in this album. If one can get past some sadness that the world lost such a remarkable talent at so young an age, it is altogether possible to just enjoy the musical gifts that he was able to leave with us.

   Bryter Layter (1971), *Pink Moon* (1972).

Bob Dylan

   By 1970 Bob Dylan had brought a lyrical poetry to folk music. With wit and social conscience, he had caught the edge of the folk revival in the early 1960s and stirred audiences with protest songs and social critique ("Blowing in the Wind," "The Times They Are A-Changin'," "Masters of War"). He then injected electric guitar to create folk-rock, enlisting The Band to back him, and he intrigued listeners with his often brilliant and sometimes obscure and surrealistic lyrics ("Like a Rolling Stone," "Visions of Johanna"). The albums were almost legendary: *Highway 61 Revisited, Blonde on Blonde*. A brief period of retreat and rest followed a reported motorcycle accident. *John Wesley Harding* (1967), *Nashville Skyline* (1968) and *New Morning* (1970) brought yet another side of Dylan: thoughtful, country-oriented, sometimes playful. And where did that richly recorded voice come from on "Lay Lady Lay"? In 1970 there was the somewhat forgettable *Self-Portrait* (1970). Then came renewal, *Planet Waves* (1974), the critically acclaimed *Blood on the Tracks* (1975) album, *Desire* (1976), tours in which he interpreted and reinvented his songs. Following the album *Street Legal* (1978), the ever-questing artist embraced born again Christianity and ended the decade with the recording *Slow Train Coming* (1979).

   In many respects, Bob Dylan set the groundwork for the singer-songwriter era. Dylan was a force connecting folk music sensibility with the growing rock music audience. However, in the early 1970s his output seemed to some critics a bit shallow and uncertain. They had come to expect more, given the power of his 1960s songs and performances. Dylan joined George Harrison for the Concert for Bangladesh. Harrison recorded Dylan's "If Not for You" for his *All Things Must Pass* album. Dylan recorded with Leon Russell ("Watching the River Flow," "When I Paint My Masterpiece"). In 1972, he played on Steve Goodman's *Somebody Else's Troubles* album under a pseudonym. He appeared in the film *Pat Garrett and Billy the Kid*, in which Dylan's song "Knocking on Heaven's Door" could be heard. *Planet Waves* (1974) brought the song "Forever Young," which soon became another Dylan classic. The Band created their opus *Before the Flood*, documenting a 1974 tour with Dylan, and Dylan's songs with The Band could be heard on *The Basement Tapes* (1974). Dylan then shed his brief relationship with Asylum Records and his long-term relationship with his wife. His return to Columbia Records set the stage for *Blood on the Tracks*. In *Rolling Stone*, Jon Landau commented that the record was "made with typical shoddiness." However, *Blood on the Tracks* (1975), with its story-songs, is one of Bob Dylan's greatest albums and his central work of the 1970s. *Desire* (1976) brought the lengthy "Hurricane," an assertion that boxer Ruben "Hurricane" Carter was wrongly accused of a murder in Paterson, New Jersey. He collaborated with Jacques Levy on some songs. The Dylan film *Renaldo and Clara* (1975) appeared and soon faded from public attention. Dylan then set forth on a concert tour with the Rolling Thunder Revue. A world-tour followed in 1978, during which a live album, *Bob Dylan at Budokan* (1978–79) was recorded. *Street Legal* (1978) was another strong studio recording. The evangelical phase with which Bob Dylan concluded the decade (*Slow Train Coming*) and his 1980 follow-ups (*Saved, Shot of Love*) has often been commented upon. It may be viewed, perhaps, as a sign of Dylan's passionate art, iconoclasm, and search for depth, truth, faith, and hope.

Blood on the Tracks (1975)

Bob Dylan's *Blood on the Tracks* is arguably his most complete and vital album of the 1970s. It is a lyrically rich album, with story songs, like "Tangled Up in Blue," "Idiot Wind," and "Rosemary and the Jack of Hearts." There are lyrical love songs, break-up songs like "If You See Her Say Hello" written in the middle of a marital breakup. Whereas *Planet Waves* addressed audience and family, offered a prayer that listeners might stay forever young, and was #1 on the rock charts for four weeks, *Blood on the Tracks* was weightier.

"Tangled Up in Blue," opening this record, was Dylan's first single from the album. He creates a story with a narrator who is always heading to another joint, one who is perhaps emotionally tangled yet free like Jack Kerouac on the road. He is lying in bed and then going out wondering if a woman has changed. He seeks a beer in a topless place where the waitress bends down to tie a shoe. He drifts on a fishing boat that leaves Delacroix. In the air is music and there is revolution like out of the 1960s claims of protest and challenges for reform. The woman has frozen up inside. They will meet someday on the avenue. He will keep on, moving forward, tangled up in blue.

"A Simple Twist of Fate" follows with another story. A man and a woman unable to communicate well are in an old hotel. They are passionate but incompatible and she leaves while he is sleeping. It is a hot night and things have been moving with a simple twist of fate. The woman walks alone in the night, hears a saxophone, and drops a coin into the player's tin cup. The man in the hotel room is awakening. He is also blinded by the turn of fate that returns like the title over and over. "You're a Big Girl Now" gets an evocative vocal treatment. It is not quite the reverbed richness of "Lay Lady Lay" but it is a vocal of feeling. A bird sings from a fence and he sings through some tears. "Idiot Wind" follows with a mix of emotions. There is sadness and remorse, invective, and self-recrimination. There is wounded pride. He is caught up in that idiot wind. It is a wonder she knows how to breathe after it all, he exclaims. "You're Gonna Make Me Lonesome When You Go" ends the side with a mellow tune in which the singer expresses his love for the woman he speaks to. He sings that sees her everywhere: in a grassy field, in people he meets. He drifts to a reference to the French poets Paul Verlaine and Arthur Rimbaud. The song floats along lightly with a harmonica melody.

With side two we turn to the blues on "Meet Me in the Morning." Dylan sings that he struggles through barbed wire, or on a sinking ship. The lengthy "Lily, Rosemary, and the Jack of Hearts" unfolds like a movie. There is a story here with several characters. The Jack of Hearts is a rogue who plays on the emotions of the others and escapes the situation. Rosemary kills Big Jim. Lily thinks about her father and about the Jack of Hearts.

"If You See Her Say Hello" is a melodic song that has the ache, longing, and nostalgia of a relationship falling apart. You might see her in Tangier, and she is far away but not gone. When he says that he won't stand in the way this speaks of a kind of surrender to the situation. He speaks to someone who knows her and may be able to speak to her for him. If she thinks he has forgotten her tell her otherwise. It is not so. She can look him up if she has the time. There is resignation in the final statements.

"Shelter from the Storm" rings out with a line of invitation. This may be shelter from the storm of life, a supportive relationship. She is solace and shelter, like an oasis in the wilderness. The crown of thorns and gambling for clothes reminds one of a Christ-figure facing the passion. From the wilderness he comes, formless, unable to turn back the clock to the past. In the final song he recognizes that love draws one in, sometimes breaks, and there is a bucket of tears but also moonbeams.

New Morning (1970), *Self-Portrait* (1971), *The Basement Tapes* (1974), *Planet Waves* (1974), *Blood on the Tracks* (1975), *Desire* (1976), *Street Legal* (1978), *Slow Train Comin'* (1979).

Jonathan Edwards

In 1971, the song "Sunshine" brought some brightness and some protest spirit all rolled into one pop hit from Jonathan Edwards. The singer-songwriter had a folk-pop sound, the name of a Puritan preacher, and a voice for the modern age. "Sunshine" has a catchy melody and an appealing vocal, but it also critiques the contemporary environment. Edwards declares that "he" will be damned if he will follow the wishes of anyone who cannot run his own life. No one will run his. The album *Jonathan Edwards* (1971) followed his days of moving around to play at colleges at small venues and for free once he left his band in 1970. The songs for *Honky-Tonk Stardust Cowboy* (1972) were written at a Massachusetts farm. On *Have a Good Time for Me* (1972) were songs he had written. He had friends join him for a live album, *Lucky Day* (1974). The title song brings a country banjo sound. He also worked during this time on a recording with Emmylou Harris. He then lived in Nova Scotia and then in New Hampshire. He had found the rural "piece of land" he talks about in his song "Lucky Day."

Jonathan Edwards (1971)

For his first solo album Jonathan Edwards had the woods and a lake to sit beside and write songs. "Everybody Knows Her" is an up-tempo start. We then hear violin and then "Cold Snow" on which Stuart Schulman takes a violin solo. "Athens County" is a bluegrass number written with Joe Dolce. "Dusty Morning" is country-folk/rock. "Emma" is a lengthy folk song. "Shanty" ends side one, with piano and harmonica. "Sunshine," his hit, opens side two. On "The King," piano fades down to end and "Don't Cry Blue" with country-bluegrass follows. "Jesse" and "Sometimes" are in a folk vein. The album ends on "Train of Glory" which brings rousing banjo, pedal steel, and harmonica solo.

Jonathan Edwards (1971), *Honky-Tonk Stardust Cowboy* (1972), *Have a Good Time for Me* (1973), *Lucky Day* (1974), *Rockin' Chair* (1976), *Sailboat* (1977).

Walter Egan

A sculptor as well as a singer-songwriter was Walter Egan. Egan's "Magnet and Steel" was his one and only 1970s hit. In 1970, he formed a band in Washington, D.C., at Georgetown University where he was an art major. They disbanded in 1973 and he became a solo performer. His first album was produced by Lindsey Buckingham with Stevie Nicks in 1977. "Magnet and Steel" appeared on his second album, *Not Shy* (1978). He wrote the song "Hearts of Fire," covered by Gram Parsons. Walter Egan concluded the 1970s with a third album, *Hi-Fi* (1979). He would be placed in an easy-listening category by record stores and radio programmers. However, much of his music is pop rock.

Not Shy (1978)

As *Not Shy* opens, "Sweet South Breeze" declares right away that this will be a straight-ahead guitar-rock album. This is three-chord rock and roll with doubled vocals. This is danceable pop with nothing deep. It is bright but shallow. "Magnet and Steel" opens with some nice doo-wop style harmonies and is sung nicely. The adolescent appeal of boy-girl lyrics continues on the third song on which it's fine to find a girlfriend. The Bay City Rollers or a later boy band might have done a better job with this song. It sounds like Stevie Nicks vocals are vibrato trembling in the background. The pop music continues with boy and girl and car songs. Next there is a simple story about a girl in a car on a highway. We hear of moonlight headlights on the highway follow. We get a video of this one on YouTube. Yet, the music seems pedestrian rather than a snappy ride on the highway. A bit stronger Beach Boys harmony might have brought this one out more. Star in the Dust has an up-tempo, chord-based chunkier guitar sound rock and roll. After noting cities of L.A. and New York, the speaker says the star may be in the dust, but it is going to rise. There are some fine guitar sounds and a strong vocal on this cut.

YouTube gives us concert video of "I Wannit," with a band and female vocals and Egan's vocal. This is catchy, simple pop rock. Guitars chime together and the lead guitar breaks out as bass and drums churns underneath. This could be the seventies band The Sweet, with pop and simple lyrics and band and vocalist achieve some dynamics that serve the song well. The song simply says that the singer badly wants to bring back the good times. If that is your interest, this album delightfully underscores that hope. "Make It Alone" is pushed along by rock guitars and a doubled-vocal fills it out nicely. It has a pulse and is bright and the electric guitar sounds add some dimensions to this song. The song expresses a sentiment of believe in yourself and believe in love. "Unloved" is a catchy shuffle, with a reverbed vocal and is sometimes drenched in a background vocal chorus.

Walter Egan still plays out occasionally in small venues. One can respect those efforts, even if the *Not Shy* album is not lyrical Bob Dylan. "Magnet and Steel" still has a pleasant sound, performed alongside a single female vocalist. On a video filmed at a Georgetown University concert, the song is filled out by a band and background singers on another YouTube video. Walter Egan still has a good singing voice, many years later.

Fundamental Roll (1977), *Not Shy* (1978), *Hi-Fi* (1979).

Bill Fay

English recording artist and pianist Bill Fay created his self-titled *Bill Fay* (1970) and *Time of the Last Persecution* (1971) on Deram/Decca Records. The recordings did not sell well, and he was dropped by the company. Fay's music was not heard again until long after his first recording. He did not tour as a singer-songwriter. He took care of an ailing mother. He became a groundskeeper for a park. There were reissues of Fay's recordings in 1998 and in 2005. Wilco has played his song "Be Not So Fearful." Fay recorded his songs on *Life Is People* (2012) and has recently completed *Countless Branches* (2020).

Time of the Last Persecution (1971)

Bill Fay's *Time of the Last Persecution* (1971) was a psychedelic–folk era recording. This album never reached the United States. One hears piano, strings and horn arrangements, social critique balanced with odes to peace, nature, friendship.

"Omega Day" opens this album with a gentle movement of piano and drums. We begin in a bar where attention falls upon one man. Perhaps this is a Christ-figure. The man's climbing rope is broken. The omega day is come. He speaks to the stranger who says that you know me from long ago. We hear the music build with a band with horns behind it. "Don't Let My Marigolds Die" is an appeal with simple guitar accompaniment. Some guitar leads are added on the other channel. The plea from the singer is please, don't take the sun from the sky. At first the vocal shifts slightly off-key. Don't let the rain blow away or take sunshine from the sky. In the city let the grass grow again. There is more sentiment than developed lyric. Piano opens "Release is in the Eye." The song then becomes driven by a full rock band: bass, drums, organ, guitar. Love is in the kitchen. Christ in the bathroom and Satan is in the garden shed. Business is booming. Clouds are over the mountains. A guitar lead and piano get bent and wild.

The title song arrives later, as track twelve. It begins in piano but then builds to an apocalyptic shiver. Standing on the side of the mountain one wonders at the gas masks, the raising of Caesar, and totalitarian powers.

It is the time of the anti–Christ. The music builds into sounds of chaos and dissension. Piano with guitar lead and drum rolls follow. It ends on a peaceful and sweet descending line from the piano.

On later work, in "Garden Song" there is a quiet beginning in a garden. The singer is awaiting the anointing of the rain and the stirring of the sense by frost. Suddenly, there is a build into a saxophone solo. We come back to the restful meditation of people telling the singer something he doesn't know. We also don't know what this is. This song's orchestration becomes rather bloated. A horn announces itself in bright melodic lines. The strings swell and then diminish. We hear of a leader of the chase, a toreador, and a corrupt minister. When the sun goes down it will not again come up. There is a swell of horns and strings and drama. The moon wants to run away amid swirls of strings and horns.

Bill Fay (1970), *Time of the Last Persecution* (1971), *From the Bottom of an Old Grandfather Clock*, demos 1965–1970.

Jose Feliciano

The blind Puerto Rican troubadour, Jose Feliciano, may be heard during the Christmas holidays singing "Feliz Navidad." His recording of "Light My Fire" by the Doors was also a lasting hit. He became well-known in Latin America and then burst upon the scene in the United States and Canada with his recording *Feliciano* (1968). The year 1970 brought his Christmas album and "Feliz Navidad." Feliciano was a television personality and made guest appearances on shows in the 1970s. He created the theme song for the television series *Chico and the Man*. Feliciano drew upon Spanish guitar traditions as well folk music. He is best known as an interpreter of others' songs. However, he also wrote several songs in the 1970s: "Affirmation," "Angela," "Destiny," "Once There Was Love," "Pegao," "Ponte a canta" (with Rudy Perez), the often-covered song "Rain" and "Tale of Maria" (with Janna Merlyn Feliciano), "The Gypsy" (with Betty Cropper), and "Watch It with My Heart." He contributed his guitar playing to John Lennon's *Rock and Roll*, Bill Withers *+Justments*, Joni Mitchell's *Court and Spark*, and recorded "Light My Fire" with Minnie Riperton on *Minnie* (1979), her last studio album. In "The Gypsy" he sang that he was just a gypsy getting paid for the songs that he sang.

Jose Feliciano (Feliz Navidad) (1970), *On Mi Soledad * No Llores Mas* (1970), *That the Spirit Needs* (1971), *Dos Cruces El Jinete* (1972), *Memphis Menu* (1972), *Compartments* (1973), *And the Feeling's Good* (1974), *For My Love ... Mother Music* (1974), *Affirmation* (1975), *Just Wanna Rock n' Roll* (1975), *Angela* (1976), *Sweet Soul Music* (1976).

Dan Fogelberg

The artistic sensibility of Dan Fogelberg weaved through songs rang-ing across folk-rock, country, bluegrass, lyrical ballads, and fiery rock. He had a brilliant way of harmonizing with his own vocals. There was poetry and story, perhaps partly inherited from his mother, and music from the bandleader father to whom he paid tribute in "Leader of the Band." He drew well while in his teens and was recognized by the Scho-lastic Awards while still in school. His first album *Home Free* (1972) came with a self-portrait drawing on the cover. The ballad "To the Morning," while folk music–based also had an expansive classical music quality and clear vocal reaching for the heavens. He sounded like an individual enrapt in the rise of sunshine acknowledging that now there was going to be a day. The album included the gentle and drifty song "Wysteria." Fogelberg had played in the coffeehouse at the University of Illinois and in some other folk clubs. *Souvenirs* (1974), with a photo of Fogelberg on the front, launched out brightly with the backing of manager Irv Azoff, producer Joe Walsh, and members of The Eagles, who sang harmony vocals. Dan Fogel-berg's ballad "The Long Way" featured his soaring voice and an affirma-tion that a hopeful relationship had traveled far. Then "Part of the Plan" cut through with its D-A-G chord movement and bright electric guitar part. These became Fogelberg's first hits. "Souvenirs" looked back on a home far away to which he still had the key. *Captured Angel* (1975) greeted record buyers with the yellow halo brightness of the painted image of an angel in white which seemed to float on the album cover. Its bright, rip-pling guitar sound was captured in Nashville by Fogelberg working with bass player–producer Norbert Putnam. *Netherlands* (1976) brought an orchestrated sound, songs that were almost art songs, and a singing voice that seemed as high as the mountains. *Twin Sons of Different Mothers* (1978), recorded with Tim Weissberg, was an album noted for its musician-ship and crisp audio fidelity. The recording included breezy instrumentals, Brazilian-Latin guitar, and the rousing rock of "Tell It to My Face." *Phoe-nix* (1979) shot out with energetic electric guitar, alternate tuning, driving rhythm. It contained the hit song "Longer."

At the end of the 1970s Dan Fogelberg was composing the songs for the brilliant double-album *The Innocent Age* (1980), which is perhaps Fogel-berg's masterpiece. The album opened with the music and rather meta-physical lyrics of "Nexus" and contained the hit songs "Run for the Roses," "Leader of the Band," and his often-played story song, "Same Auld Lang Syne," set at Christmastime. "The Reach" was a powerful folksong-based tribute to the life of coastal Maine, to which he had turned his attention at the time. Fogelberg appeared to be less comfortable with the fast, industry driven commercial life of Los Angeles than the peace of the Colorado Mountains or coastal Maine. There was also a marked sensitivity to some of the songs. For example, the poignant title song of *Windows and Walls* (1984) depicted an elderly woman dealing with loneliness as the clock of time keeps ticking. Fogelberg's roots were of the Midwest. Hailing from Peoria, he sang his tribute on "Illinois." The folk-troubadour elements in his music always grounded his reach into rock, his semi-classical instrumentals, and his explorations of other musical styles. *High Country Snows* (1985) explored bluegrass roots with some fine bluegrass musicians. Some influential popular music artists have waited for years to be recognized by the Rock and Roll Hall of Fame. Dan Fogelberg, as of this writing, is one of the most deserving of being inducted.

Taken as a unit, Dan Fogelberg's albums of the 1970s are clearly within the singer-songwriter context of the period. *Home Free* (1972) is imbued with a bright, simple beauty. *Souvenirs* (1974) produced with Joe Walsh, broke free into popular circulation with "Part of the Plan," "The Long Way," the gritty and up-tempo "As the Raven Flies," and Fogelberg's harmonies joining his own lead vocals along with the singing of Glenn Frey and Don Henley of The Eagles. *Captured Angel* (1975) explored a bright sound aided by Norbert Putnam's production. *Netherlands* (1977) and *Twin Sons* (1978) both reached for a sublime beauty inspired by the Colorado mountain landscape.

Home Free (1972), *Souvenirs* (1974), *Captured Angel* (1975), *Netherlands* (1977), *Twin Sons of Different Mothers* (1978), *The Phoenix* (1979), *Innocent Age* (1980). Jean Fogelberg has documented Dan Fogelberg's final year beautifully on a website. One might hope for a book.

John Fogerty

Creedence Clearwater Revival charged up late 1960s music with dreams of southern bayous and rolling rivers, anti-war critique, bad moons rising, hallucinatory looks out the back door, and driving E7 chords. John Fogerty was the band's voice and center, creating most of the music and most of the lyrics. Tom Fogerty, Doug Clifford and Stu Cook capably supported the band's straightforward rock sound. "Proud Mary," "Bad Moon Rising," "Fortunate Son," "Green River," "Down on the Corner," "Who'll Stop the Rain" were songs with infectious rhythms.

After rejecting recordings of their performance of Woodstock, Creedence Clearwater Revival arrived in the early 1970s intact. However, that soon began to change. Fogerty headed out on his own. He was hampered by business claims to his songs. He created an album of country-sounding material that he said was by the Blue Ridge Rangers. It was entirely by Fogerty. He followed with another recording in 1974. He was able to put his own name on a recording two years later. *John Fogerty* (1976) included the single "Rockin' All Over the World." His planned next album *Hoodoo* (1977) had a song called "Magic" on it that was released as a single. However, there was little magic on the rest of the record and Fogerty scrapped it. It was never released. Fogerty took a break from the business and from recording until the mid–1980s release of *Centerfield* (1985). Fogerty told interviewer Paul Zollo that he often writes songs beginning with a riff on guitar (Zollo 708). That seems obvious from his catalog both with Creedence and in his solo work. A single chord or a riff pattern played with a rhythmic pulse can set one of his songs in motion.

John Fogerty (1976). See the compilation *John Fogerty: Wrote a Song for Everyone* (May 28, 2013). Also see John Fogerty and Jimmy McDonough, *Fortunate Son: My Life, My Music*. Boston and New York: Little Brown, 2016. *Finding Fogerty: Interdisciplinary Readings of John Fogerty*, ed. Thomas M. Kitts. Lanham: Lexington, 2012. Thomas M. Kitts, *John Fogerty: An American Son*. New York and London: Routledge, 2016.

Steve Forbert

Every few years in the 1970s along would come another young singer-songwriter who would be touted as Dylan-like and was invested with great hopes. One of these was Steve Forbert. Toward the tail end of the decade, he flared up like a brief comet, shooting into airplay, an album, and a tour. *Alive on Arrival* (1978) had about it a sense of the early Dylan and the record earned widespread praise.

Forbert is from a large family in Meridian, Mississippi. He started playing guitar at the age of eleven and played with rock bands in high school and through college. He moved to New York with his guitar and songs and began to play at folk music spots. At CBGB's, a central hub of the emerging punk–new wave scene, Forbert met Danny Fields, a Ramones manager, and Linda Stein of Sire records. He was eventually signed by Epic records, which is part of the Columbia Records group. Forbert toured with Joan Armatrading, Southside Johnny and the Asbury Jukes, Dave Van Ronk, and McGuinn, Hillman, and Clark of The Byrds. In 1979, the record *Jackrabbit Slim* utilized Nashville studio musicians and Muscle Shoals rhythm section players. Forbert's follow-up, *Little Stevie Orbit*, had the single "Get Well Soon" on it. There was a rollicking band support for "Meet Me in the Middle of the Night." That song continues to receive airplay on folk-pop radio and may be Forbert's best known song to date.

Alive on Arrival (1978)

On *Alive on Arrival* (1978) listeners first heard Steve Forbert on the five-minute song "Goin' Down to Laurel." Following this are "Steve Forbert's Midsummer Night's Toast," "Thinkin'," "What Kinda Guy," "It Isn't Gonna Be That Way," "City Cat," "Grand Central Station March 18," "Tonight I Feel So Far Away from Home," "Settle Down," "You Cannot Win If You Do Not Play."

Alive on Arrival (1978), *Jackrabbit Slim* (1979).

Peter Frampton

There was an immensely success solo career curve from *Frampton* through the concert recordings of *Frampton Comes Alive*, which were widely heard in 1976. The Humble Pie guitarist had created four solo albums before that live album went through the stratosphere. Frampton would generally not fit into the singer-songwriter image. He was a lead guitarist, a rock performer surrounded by a band. "Show Me the Way" seemed to be played everywhere one turned. You could hear the novelty voice box. Frampton asked his listeners "Do You Feel Like We Do?" His strongest skill was his guitar playing. He was indeed one of the most popular artists of the decade.

Wind of Change (1972), *Frampton's Camel* (1973), *Something's Happening* (1974), *Frampton* (1975), *Frampton Comes Alive* (1976), *I'm In You* (1977), *Where I Should Be* (1979).

Bob Franke

One of folk music's most respected songwriters, Bob Franke takes time with his songs. Franke expected to attend Episcopal Theological School and ended up as an artist-in-residence at St. Andrew's Episcopal Church, while also creating enduring songs like "Hard Love," "For Real," and "Thanksgiving Eve," among others. He has written songs of social conscience, songs on personal themes, and spiritual reflections. His songs have been recorded by folk music artists John McCutcheon, Claudia Schmidt; Peter, Paul, and Mary; country-crossover artist Kathy Mattea and others. "A Healing in the Night" opens on a theme of what songs can do. He was a principal founder of the Saturday Night in Marblehead Coffeehouse on the Massachusetts coast.

Love Can't Be Bitter All the Time (1976)

"White Water," "A Little at a Time," "401," "Love Can't Be Bitter All the Time," "Memorial," "Light Upon the Way," "What Will You Leave

Me?," "Break Through Angels," "Goodbye," "After the Lights Went Out."

Performances of "For Real" and "Hard Love" are available on YouTube.

The Songs of Bob Franke music score was published in 1992 (Peabody, MA: Telephone Pole Music). *The Songs of Bob Franke* were also collected as a Folk Project Publication, 1992.

Kinky Friedman

From Chicago to the University of Texas came Kinky Friedman. From country satire writer to candidate for the governor of Texas, possibly the only major Jewish singer-songwriter in Nashville, Kinky Friedman was a voice of mischief and rebellion. In 1970 he was assisted with country rock support from Commander Cody. He recorded on ABC records, *Sold American* (1973), *Kinky Friedman* (1974). He toured with Bob Dylan in 1975–76. His songs had titles like "Get Your Biscuits in the Oven and Your Buns in Bed," "Ride 'Em Jewboy," and "How Can I Tell You I Love You When You're Sitting on My Face?" He wrote "We Refuse the Right to Refuse Service to You," the ballad "Western Union Wine," and "They Ain't Making Jews Like Jesus Anymore." He became a fine chess player, spent two years in the Peace Corps, obtained a psychology degree at University of Texas–Austin, and he has written a few books.

Sold American (1973), *Kinky Friedman* (1974), *Lasso from El Paso* (1975), *Silver Jubilee* (1977).

Richie Furay

A solo performer who comes from the bands Buffalo Springfield and Poco might be expected to play in the style of folk-country-rock. However, the Christian commitment of Richie Furay was less expected. *I've Got a Reason* declared this. There was sincerity. There was truth. The high, strong singing voice was up front. The tunes aimed for a kind of pop-rock crossover airplay that never quite happened. His earlier songs, "Kind Woman," "Good to Know" and "Pickin' Up the Pieces," were already known by listeners to Buffalo Springfield and to Poco. He had recently recorded two albums with Southern-Hillman-Furay (1975–1976). So, what were they to make of Furay's new direction? Christian rock embraced Furay's move even though his lyrics were not explicitly gospel oriented. *Dance a Little Light* (1977) maintained that audience. "I Still Have Dreams," the title song of his next album, found its way to radio. His singing was clear and bright, and the song's assertion was hopeful. Even so, he apparently found greater hope in his faith-journey, as he became pastor of Calvary Chapel in Broomfield, Colorado, near Denver.

I've Got a Reason (1976)

Richie Furay's first solo album was a pop album with less post–Poco country-rock tendencies. Following two recordings by the trio of Southern-Hillman-Furay, "I've Got a Reason" was a strong personal statement after his Christian conversion and embrace of ministry. The lyrics underscore this with subtlety. They are not overt gospel lyrics, and they affirm that there is a reason for life and for making music. Furay's strong tenor vocals rise assertively and celebrate life throughout the album. The first three songs are "Look at the Sun," "We'll See," and "Starlight": each of which suggests light and/or vision. "Gettin' Through" and "I've Got a Reason" sound like affirmations. "Mighty Maker" underlines his Christian commitment and tends to acknowledge God as creator while also recognizing the creative spirit. "You're Still the One I Love" comes across as a love song. "Still Rolling Stones" is followed by the longer "Over and Over Again." There is an interesting balance of extroverted energy and inward-looking reflection.

On the opening cut Furay's singing is bright, resonant, and placed up-front. Tom Stipe's keyboards support the song. Stipe co-wrote the opener "Look at the Sun" with Furay and also the closer to this album "Over and Over Again." They also so-wrote "Starlight," and "Gettin' Through." Jay Truax (bass) and John Mehler (drums) fill out the band. Al Perkins and Steve Cropper contributed some guitar. The synthesizer-strings production by Michael Omartian on the songs "Mighty Maker" and "Over and Over" seems a bit overdone. Sometimes simplicity better serves faith and sentiments like this. Furay's strong singing was certainly not in need of being orchestrally propped up. Myrrh Records, a contemporary Christian music label, reissued the album in 1981 and on Wounded Bird in 2003.

I've Got a Reason (1976), *Dance a Little Light* (1978), *I Still Have Dreams* (1979).

David Gates

David Gates was a songwriter of strikingly beautiful melodies and sentiments, a masterful string arranger, and a singer with a distinctive tenor. Gates is best known for his songs "If," "Make It with You,"

"Everything I Own," and "Baby, I'm a Want You," which were radio air-play hits in the early years of the 1970s. Gates also wrote and sang the hits "Aubrey" and "Guitar Man." These songs were performed with Bread, a light pop-rock quartet in which Gates teamed up with James Griffin, drummer Mike Botts, and studio guitarist and keyboard player Larry Knechtel. Robb Royer, one of the group's original members, remained a songwriter collaborating with James Griffin. (They had written lyrics to the Academy Award winning song "For All We Know" with music by Fred Karlin.)

Gates was born in Tulsa, Oklahoma. Surrounded by music as a child, he learned to play piano, violin, and guitar. He played in a band during high school, working for a time with Leon Russell, and doing an opening set for Chuck Berry while in college at the University of Oklahoma. In 1961, he set out for Los Angeles. While there he became a music copyist, studio musician, and arranger-producer. He wrote a song "Popsicles and Icicles" for the Murmaids, which hit the charts in 1964. He wrote "Saturday's Child," which was recorded by The Monkees. Gates arranged the song "Baby, the Rain Must Fall" for Glenn Yarborough. He met and produced Robb Royer and the band Pleasure Fair in 1967. That meeting led to the formation of Bread.

Besides David Gates' work with the band, he recorded two more solo albums during the 1970s on Elektra Records. The albums generally sound like an extension of Gates' work with Bread from 1969 to 1973. Bread's sound owed much to the talents of Gates, who had studied classical violin as a child and to Larry Knechtel's studio chops. Jimmy Griffin contributed songs like "Truckin'" and "Sweet Surrender" that broadened their sound. Mike Botts added to the mix his sharp drumming and good looks. Bread was somewhat country, slightly rock, and also a pretty slick musically trained unit. They reunited for the album *Lost Without Your Love* (1976), which featured the title song which was sung by Gates. David Gates wrote and sang the song "Goodbye Girl" (1978) for a notable film based on a Neil Simon script. Gates retired from the music business to the open spaces of Montana and to his ranch in northern California.

First (1973)

The clarity and range of the singing voice of David Gates may be one of the first things listeners notice. That voice is familiar from the ballads he wrote while with the group Bread: "If," "Everything I Own," "Make It with You." As a composer, he shines on this first solo effort on the larger canvas of his instrumental pieces like "Suite: Clouds, Rain." There are string arrangements, tempo changes, lush productions mixed with pop rock.

This album is essentially Bread (Larry Knechtel and Mike Botts, minus James Griffin) add Larry Carlton (guitar), Russ Kunkel (drums), Jim Horn (horns), Jim Gordon, Louie Shelton, Jimmy Getzoff, and John Guerin. There is a good deal of melody, song structure, musical arrangement. The songs are pleasant but are not likely to be life-changing, since there is little story or lyrical depth. However, the musicality seems to make up for some of this pleasant shallowness of lyrical ideas. Gates here seems less poet and more singer-arranger.

The album opens with David Gates' vocal on his ballad "Sail Around the World." His next song "Sunday Rider" has the characteristic structure, vocal attack, and bite of a Bread pop-rock tune. "(I Use the) Soap" brings us back to bouncy ballad. After the magnum opus of "Suite: Cloud, Rain" Gates again returns to pop-rock form with "Help is on the Way." This is followed by the plaintive "Ann," an affectionate address in the style of his songs like "Aubrey" or "Diary." The song "Do You Believe He's Comin'" turns to gospel in the manner of Southern Baptist. Listeners are treated to "Sight and Sound" and then given the swaying soft pop-rock of "Lorilee." Gates' subsequent album, *Never Let Her Go*, followed in a similar vein: well-produced, light pop-rock sounds mixed with beautifully sung ballads.

"Sail Around the World," "Sunday Rider," "I Use the Soap," "Suite: Clouds, Rain," "Help Is on the Way," "Ann," "Do You Believe He's Comin'?," "Sight and Sound," "Lorilee."

First (1973), *Never Let Her Go* (1975), *Goodbye Girl* (1978).

Marvin Gaye

What's Going On brought social conscience to R&B/soul and pop music in the early 1970s. Berry Gordy at Motown was going to hold the record back. Marvin Gaye insisted. His creativity gave shape to R&B in that period. "I Heard It Through the Grapevine" became a pop standard. "How Sweet It Is (To Be Loved by You)," "Ain't That Peculiar," "All My Life," "Inner City Blues," "What's Going On?" were widely heard recordings. The 1970 single "What's Going On?" dug deeply into the issue of police brutality at an anti-war rally at Berkeley. "Mercy, Mercy Me" ("The Ecology") reflected the environmental movement and lamented that the things that were happening at the present time were not how they used to be.

Marvin Gaye, as singer-songwriter-performer emerged from the group The Marquees. In 1970, Marvin Gaye grasped the edge of social-political statement, as well as the soul and cool of R&B-soul. Motown released *Trouble Man* (1971) with "You're the Man" and *Let's Get*

It On (1973), with the title cut and "Come Get to This." Marvin Gaye went on tour with Diana Ross in 1974–75. They recorded an album together and Marvin Gaye created *I Want You* (1976). The song "Got to Give It Up" (1977) followed, with the song featured in a concert album *Live at the Palladium*. He recorded *Here My Dear* (1978) and continued to perform regularly through the rest of the decade. Before his death in a squabble with his father in 1984, Marvin Gaye was at the center of the pop music world in the R&B-soul genre.

That's the Way Love Is (1970), *What's Going On?* (1971), *Trouble Man* (1972), *Let's Get It On* (1973), *Diana and Marvin* (1973), *I Want You* (1976), *Marvin Gaye Live at the Palladium* (1977), *Here My Dear* (1978).

Andrew Gold

Within the L.A. music scene, Andrew Gold was a multi-instrumentalist who played on many recordings. He was the son of a soprano vocalist and a film composer. Gold became the principal guitarist for Linda Ronstadt. He was a Beatles influenced songwriter and was notable for his guitar stylings. Andrew Gold's cover of "Doo-Wah Diddy" by Jeff Barry/ Ellie Greenwich and his own song "Lonely Boy" (1977) were hits. He wrote "That's Why I Love You" and had a UK hit single with "Never Let Her Slip Away" (1978). His song "Thank You for Being a Friend" (1978) became the theme song for the television show *The Golden Girls*.

Andrew Gold (1975)

It is the guitar-lines and the bright pop vocals of Andrew Gold that stand out on his first album. There is as much of a Beatles influence as L.A. sound here. There are pop harmonies, fine arrangements, guitars that complement all of this with lush lead lines and ambient tone. Critic Stephen Holden heard in his music "variations of early Beatles licks" (December 4, 1975). "A Note from You" and "I'm Coming Home" were melodic pop creations. Linda Ronstadt sings on "Heartache of Heartaches," which has that smooth L.A. country-folk-rock sound Gold contributed to. Gold could play a variety of instruments and had capably supported Linda Ronstadt's recordings. He even had hits with "Lonely Boy" and "Doo-Wah Diddy." So, what happened? Andrew Gold never caught on.

Whirlwind (1980) was Gold's fourth solo effort and was filled with songs he developed in last years of the 1970s. These are guitar-driven rock songs with an edge of new wave late 1970s in them. Brian Garofalo played bass and Mike Botts of Bread was on drums. There was, however, nothing commercial on this record that would sustain Andrew Gold's solo career.

There is now an *Andrew Gold Asylum Years* anthology of six CD on Cherry Red/Esoteric recordings.

Andrew Gold (1975), *What's Wrong with This Picture?* (1976), *All This and Heaven Too* (1978).

Lotti Golden

A writer of confessional songs and counterculture quests, Lotti Golden moved into jazz and soul. She wrote of the East Village in lower Manhattan. From the 1960s into the 1970s, her personal statements appeared on "Motor-Cycle" and "The Space Queen." She explored gender and identity and drug culture. Lotti Golden was listed among the female singer-songwriters featured in a *Newsweek* article in 1969. She also performed solo with an acoustic guitar, wrote as a rock journalist, and became a record producer. Her work as a producer has extended to dance, rap/hip-hop, and R&B.

Motor-Cycle (1969/1970)

Motor-Cycle was released in 1969 and was performed by Lotti Golden throughout 1970. There is some tape buzz on the downloaded YouTube recording. However that soon disappears under the bright jazz-soul arrangements and soaring vocals. The recording starts in drums and the up-tempo title song lives in honky-tonk piano and a bluesy vocal. The production gives this an almost Motown feel. Golden's voice flies energetically along on-top of the music. This soulful-bluesy voice moves seamlessly into the next movement. References to the universe and moving with the sky come out forcefully in a kind of improvisational singing. This swings into jazz-club piano and upright bass and saxophone. One might picture a vocalist in a smoky room, where the voices of people come through. We move back Golden declaring how Michael let her ride the motorcycle. An echoing reverbed bass sustains some notes. Golden's voice floats above these single notes. A band kicks in on the vocal line. She persuades Johnny to meet her there. All this brightness swims into stoned dissolution for a moment. Her mother was an angel, she declaims in Joplin-like energy as bass pulses. Spoken word conversation follows. Outta sight, dig it, she says to a group of people. We are back to roller coaster energy, vocals on the edge of screams. The YouTube recording breaks down here, like a skipped record. A blues vocal follows and then a big band sound. Then we are rolling along on up-tempo piano and drums with some vibraphone in the background. She sings about an East side king who was once cool but he's a lot like Lucifer. The drummer is kicking it out and a horn section joins this. There is jazz with tempo changes all through this recording and much energy and passion in the singing.

Motor-Cycle (1969–1970), *Lotti Golden* (1971).

Bobby Goldsboro

A clear tenor with some vibrato came through on the sentimental hit "Honey" (1968). The speaker misses his love who has passed away and looks out at how the tree in the yard has grown in the years that have gone by. There was a bright country music quality, a television-ready photogenic smile to Bobby Goldsboro. (*The Bobby Goldsboro Show* on television ran from 1973 to 1975.) Goldsboro sang to middle-America of nostalgia and homegrown values. He wrote "With Pen in Hand" (1969), covered by Vikki Carr, Johnny Darrel and Della Reese. He was an interpreter of others' songs and had hits with Bobby Russell's "Honey," Mac Davis's song "Watching Scottie Grow," and Roger Cook and Roger Greenaway's "Hello Summertime" (1974). He wrote the country song "The Cowboy and the Lady" (covered by Dolly Parton, John Denver, and Brenda Lee).

Muddy Mississippi Line (1970), *We Gotta Start Lovin'/Watching Scottie Grow* (1970), *Bobby Goldsboro's Greatest Hits* (1970), *Come Back Home* (1971), *California Wine* (1972), *Brand New Kind of Love* (1973), *Summer* (1973), *10th Year Anniversary Album* (1974), *Hello Summertime* (1974), *Through the Eyes of a Man* (1975), *A Butterfly for Bucky* (1976), *Goldsboro* (1977).

Steve Goodman

He was one of Chicago's luminaries of folk music, with strong songwriting, some dazzling guitar playing, a sense of humor, and an engaging talent for performing to an increasingly strong cult-folk music following. Steve Goodman was the writer of "The City of New Orleans," recorded by Arlo Guthrie. Willie Nelson made a hit country song of it. Some have called it one of the best train songs ever written. In it the singer welcomes America to a good morning and declares that he is a native son. Actually, the next lines suggest that the speaker is the train itself, The City of New Orleans, holding the history of America itself as it makes its journey south. Goodman wrote dozens of songs, many of them delightfully witty. He wrote "You Never Even Called Me by My Name" with John Prine and David Alan Coe's recording of the song became a country music hit. Goodman wrote the humorous "Chicken Cordon Blues," "Would You Like to Learn to Dance" (recorded by Jackie De Shannon), "Lincoln Park

Pirates," and "Go, Cubs Go," which has been played at Chicago Cubs games. Other songs, later covered by Jimmy Buffett, are "Door Number Three," "Woman Going Crazy on Caroline Street," and "Banana Republics." He covered the Michael Smith song, "The Dutchman." Despite dealing with leukemia, Goodman remained as productive as possible in the later years of the 1970s and into the 1980s. He was an artist whose creativity burned brightly and quickly and whose life ended too soon.

Somebody Else's Troubles (1972)

Somebody Else's Troubles (1972) has the qualities of witty lyrics, bright singing, and fine guitar playing that are characteristic of Steve Goodman's music. *New York Times* writer Ian Dove called the album "deceptively casual" while recognizing that it brought together all of Goodman's talents for songwriting and performing his own music. John Prine and Jimmy Buffett are friends who appear in the photo on the album's cover. Bob Dylan played piano as "Robert Milkwood Thomas." The recording opens with Michael Smith's song "The Dutchman," which Goodman made something of a hit in folk music circles. Following "Six Hours Ahead of the Sun" and "Song for David," we get the humorous "Chicken Cordon Blues," which Goodman wrote with Paula Ballan and Tony Mandel. The title song follows. Goodman often made reference to Chicago and does so in "Lincoln Park Pirates." Among the strongest songs on this album is an a capella treatment of the story of a Vietnam widow. "The Ballad of Penny Evans" concludes the album. The April 18, 1976, live performance of this song at the Capitol Theatre in Passaic, New Jersey, is available on YouTube.

The Essential Steve Goodman (1976) is a two-record retrospective with 20 songs from *Steve Goodman* (1971) and *Somebody Else's Troubles* (1972). *No Big Surprise* (1994) is also a double-album overview anthology of his recordings. One record is from studio recordings and the other is live. In the 1970s, Disc jockey Vin Scelsa in New York gathered up his radio sessions with Goodman and assembled the *Easter Tapes*. On YouTube you can see an entertaining Steve Goodman concert at the Capitol Theatre in Passaic, New Jersey.

Gathering at the Earl of Old Town (1970), *Steve Goodman* (1971), *Somebody Else's Troubles* (1972), *Jesse's Jig and Other Favorites* (1975), *Words We Can Dance To* (1976), *Say It in Private* (1977), *High and Outside* (1979).

Henry Gross

The mindset of a few of Henry Gross's songs on the first album appears to be reflective of a Woodstock generation back to the country sensibility. Gross had played Woodstock with Sha Na Na and had recently moved from that group into his solo recording. Terry Cashman and Tommy West were behind the production of this album which drifts along gently on Gross's tenor vocals. After this reflective, folk-acoustic-based first album, he created his "Yellow Album," also titled Henry Gross (1973). (You can hear his song "Simone" from this album on YouTube.) Then there is a shift toward Henry Gross's being plugged into something. The mellow singer-songwriter of the first album seems to sneak in a song on the second side of his record that anticipates the rock character of his later album. The jump to rock is unexpected, but indicative of his direction. The guitar bursts out with some clean overdrive. He could hit some high notes too. The "Yellow Album" brings out a little more of this side of the Brooklyn-born songwriter. His rippling, chord-driven rock appears most obviously on *Plug Me into Something* (1975). *Show Me the Stage* is a "produced" album with some hints of Phil Spector–Brian Wilson Beach Boys production. Radio listeners may remember Henry Gross for his hit song "Shannon," with his vocal reaching above the treble clef staff into the far reaches of falsetto. However, there are many further dimensions to his music than that airy ballad. Henry Gross was a rocker with sky high vocal range, a sense of humor, and songs with some bright pop-rock energy.

Henry Gross (1972), *Henry Gross* (The Yellow Album) (1973), *Plug Me into Something* (1975), *Release* (1976), *All This and World War II* (1975), *Show Me the Stage* (1977), *Love is the Stuff* (1978). Henry Gross albums have been remastered and are available from the artist's website. *Plug Me into Something* can be heard on YouTube. People have also posted the song "Shannon."

Steven Grossman

At twenty-two Steven Grossman recorded *Caravan Tonight* (1976), a recording that was bold at the time because he expressed openly gay themes. Grossman asserted that he was a gay man living in Greenwich Village and playing folk music. Threads of singer-songwriter style reminiscent of Joni Mitchell or Cat Stevens wind through the album. Eric Weissberg plays on the record. Critic Stephen Holden observed, "his communication of intense compassion ... and the purity of Grossman's sensibility" (*Rolling Stone* May 23, 1974). There was only one later album. In 1991, Steven Grossman succumbed to AIDS.

Caravan Tonight (1974).

Arlo Guthrie

Storyteller and folksinger son of Woody Guthrie, Arlo Guthrie wrote clever songs, performed at Woodstock ("Coming in to Los Angelese") and notably performed the story-song "Alice's Restaurant." His songs of social justice are directly in line with his father's famed efforts. He sang Steve Goodman's "City of New Orleans," which is sometimes called the greatest train song ever written.

Washington County (1970)

Washington County includes seven Arlo Guthrie songs (including Introduction), one Woody Guthrie song ("Lay Down Little Doggies"), one Bob Dylan song ("Percy's Song"), and the co-written "Valley to Pray" (Doc Coutsa, John Pilla, Arlo Guthrie), which concludes side one. The full album is available on YouTube.

A piano chord begins the album's "Introduction." The piano is punctuated by some electric guitar. The tune picks up energy and sets a tone for the album. The vocal enters: throaty, nasal, declaring that people are all imagining there is a way. There is an invitation to listen to the song. There is a rollicking piano break. The music picks up energy as "Fence Post Blues" begins. The singer is looking out from the edge of wheat fields and is sitting on a country fence post watching trucks roll by on a country road. Next, he brings things down to an acoustic guitar and melodic instrumental. He wakes up on a snowy morning and beckons to children to "come on." The song draws upon a traditional gospel song lyric framework. It brings to us a rather pretty and gentle folk music with guitars, light bass and drums and strings. The community is encouraged to gather with hope and vision for change and salvation. The notion of wheels in the air suggests the prophetic vision of Ezekiel. The theme of creating peace and a heaven of the earth is contemporary to the period of Woodstock hopes. Bright banjo-driven bluegrass follows on the title cut. It becomes clear that this recording involves various styles. The production shift is considerable to the big chorus-filled gospel of going to the valley to pray. It is recorded as if in a tunnel of reverb and includes voices and some horns.

Flip the record over and Woody Guthrie's "Lay Down Little Doggies" is sung with guitar accompaniment and a couple of background singers. "I Could Be Singing" is produced with piano, bass, gated drums, in that distant reverbed quality, with questions about being sent to war, and hope for a new world coming together. The piano takes us into "If You Would Just Drop By" slow and easy. The song begins with the inquiry of friends and an appeal to someone to visit. This wistful song, piano accompanied, might have an almost Tin Pan Alley quality if it was given to another singer singing it in a smoky lounge. We are brought back to up-tempo folk song with the Bob Dylan song, with its turn to wind and rain refrain and dark images and critique of improper justice. The vocal, bright and sure, treats the lyric focus on social justice with an energy which evokes both Woody Guthrie and Bob Dylan. "I Want to Be Around" concludes with a rousing, rollicking group-chorus.

Washington County (1970), *Hobo's Lullaby* (1972), *Last of the Brooklyn Cowboys* (1973), *Arlo Guthrie* (1974), *Amigo* (1976), *One Night* (1978), *Outlasting the Blues* (1979).

Tim Hardin

"If I Were a Carpenter" is Tim Hardin's best-known and most covered song. He is perhaps more notably an artist of the 1960s, producing six albums during those years. His albums of the 1970s were folk-based. During this period, he was plagued with a heroin addiction. Four of the ten songs on *Bird on a Wire* (1971) are cover songs. The tracks were prepared in advance with other musicians playing on the record, so Hardin would just sing. The title song was from Leonard Cohen. Hardin moved to England and managed to record another two albums. The British session musicians on *Painted Head* (1972) included Peter Frampton. None of the songs were his own. They came from Pete Hamm (Badfinger), Randy Newman, Jesse Winchester, and Willie Dixon. There were a couple of Hardin's songs on *Nine* (1973) which had an electric-folk sound which again included Frampton on guitar.

Bird on a Wire (1971)

Bird on a Wire (1971) seems a bit uneven. The album's title comes from his cover of Leonard Cohen's "Bird on a Wire," which comes first on this recording. This begins slowly with light strings and organ behind arpeggios on guitar. There is contrast between Hardin's tenor and bluesy approach and Cohen's baritone vocals. In comparison with Cohen's version, there is a more of a gospel approach in the singing and musical build here. This treatment points more in the direction of Ray Charles than that of folksinger. On side two we can hear a version of "Georgia on My Mind." Tim Hardin's own songs include "Southern Butterfly," "Soft Summer Breeze," and "If I Knew" and "Hymn" which closes the album. Joe Zawinal, who is on keyboards, provides arrangements on side two. Following *Bird on a Wire*, Tim Hardin moved to England. *Painted Head* was created as he sought methadone treatment for a heroin addiction. All of the ten cuts are covers by other songwriters.

Bird on a Wire (1971), *Painted Head* (1972), *Nine* (1973).

Jack Hardy

New York's principal gatherer and mentor of Fast Folk was folk-singer Jack Hardy. From Greenwich Village came an array of talented singer-songwriters of the 1980s–1990s and into the 21st century. Folk City was still open through the decade. The Bitter End changed its name to The Other End. Kenny's Castaways opened up down the street. Jack Hardy began a songwriting circle at his place and folksingers made that little walk up the stairs to share songs.

Jack Hardy (1971)

As *Jack Hardy* (1971) begins, the guitars are crisp. The vocal is out front and he sounds like an Irish singer. It is harder to get a drum sound. The drums accompanying sound like they have been recorded in a basement. Yet, the playing is capable. The first song is a shuffling lament in which it is difficult to find a good woman. Maybe if the bars were open some Guinness would help along this melancholy to be as smooth and bright as the music is here. The guitar opens the second song with a gentle run. This is joined by a piano and Hardy's vocal singing of loss and a fine lyric that meditates on what love is.

The tempo changes with some guitar playing, including some electric guitar, and a kind of country, or country-imitation. It is hard to match a New York City folksinger with the backyards of Kansas. In today's Kansas, parts remain rural, but there is statewide access to 21st-century technology. Maybe this character is from the 19th century? The song seems like an out of place attempt to create a character, fake a dialect, and to reach for something comic. In the 2020s it does not work very well. "Talk to Me, Babe" while still with a country back-beat and some steel guitar is more conversational. The drums are also better placed within the over-all mix here. The guitars of the next song create an atmosphere for smiles that hide a heart that is broken. The speaker of this song is well-defined. He is a working man talking with someone he has broken up with. He is trying to do his best but feels the break is inevitable. He is caught between wanting to return and feeling that he has to leave. A shift follows with cymbals, broad guitar strums, and drums, and a declaration of the young rover who was insane. Now he is the ".45 caliber" man, recalling how he never stayed home. A fuzzed guitar adds a bridge guitar lead. He continues to recall the past of the family and friends. "I'm Still Dreaming" is an up-tempo shuffle reflection on a relationship. He recalls worn out shoes and blues and a worn dress. This has steel guitar, guitar, and drums that sometimes sound like they are boxes being struck in the garage. The guitar that follows with a meditative vocal brings some wistful beauty, reverie, and romance back to this record. He is bound to love and to stay amid memories of the one he loves. This is one of the more affecting songs on this album. The Irish ballad sounding singer returns on "Kathleen." She is gone and it seems wrong that she is but the song with her name is resonant and reflective. She is a memory in song. However, he can go on. Certainly, Jack Hardy's legacy among folksingers should go on also.

Jack Hardy (1971), Early and Rare 1965–1974 (1974), Mirror of My Madness (1976), The Nameless One (1978).

Roy Harper

This English folk-rock fingerstyle guitarist created 10 live albums and 32 studio recordings across the years. He was from Rusholme, a suburb of Manchester. An influential guitarist, he was commented upon by Jimmy Page (Led Zeppelin) and Ian Anderson (Jethro Tull). Among his strongest 1960s albums was Sophisticated Beggar (1966) on Strike records. Harper did not fit easily into the world of folk music at this time. His guitar-playing was intricate. Circle (1966) preceded a free concert he performed in Hyde Park along with Pink Floyd and Jethro Tull. In 1969 he toured with folksinger Ralph McTell and with Ron Geesin. He met the Norwegian singer Lillebjorn Nilsen, who recorded "On the First Day of April" (1971). Pink Floyd's manager Peter Jenner signed Harper to a contract with Harvest records/EMI. Upon Harper's album Flat Baroque and Berserk (1970) he visited and performed in the United States. Led Zeppelin responded to Harper on "Shake 'Em on Down (Hats Off to Roy Harper)" on Led Zeppelin III (1970). Harper produced Stormcock (1971) with only four songs, largely instrumental. Valentine (1974) followed. Harper sang "Have a Cigar" on Pink Floyd's Wish You Were Here (1974). They were both recording at Abbey Road studios at the same time and Pink Floyd needed a vocalist for the song. Harper was forced to drop a song from his curiously titled next album Bullinamingvase (1977).

Stormcock (1971)

Stormcock (1971) is four songs released at a time when concept albums and prog-rock were emerging. Roy Harper is spacey, iconoclastic, and sharpens his critique against dogmatism, law, and anything that inhibits freedom. "Hors d'oeuvres" begins with simple guitar strum. Rather Syd Barrett drifty acoustic. A judge-jury and a lyric not pinned down in any certain meaning, although there is a critique of the judiciary here. There are a lot of "-ise" rhymes. The backgrounds form a high choir.

"The Same Old Rock" twelve and a half minutes begins with guitars up front with parts on left and right channels. (Jimmy Page is here on guitar also.) The vocal comes in bright over the guitars providing images. Ancient reflections spin across the ancient ways and something shrouds the sun which is setting. Is this a knight figure who is fighting for the promised land? The word consternation would not likely enter a pop tune. Is this a straggler on the edge of time? An esoteric portrait of someone? If one can be more obscure than Dylan at his most obscure here it is. Effects in echo chamber come in later, with his vocal doubled, drenched in reverb. This is a figure of the psychedelic era.

"One Man Rock and Roll Band"—We get more guitar playing at the top of this with a run. The vocal is again produced to wobble within effect. Guitar riffs on lower strings. If you like reverb and psychedelic folk, you may like this. The singer reflects for a while on soldiers, then goes somewhere else. Grandad was a hero, but his name must have been changed to Nero. He claimed that he fought for peace. What he did was kill people in war and get medals.

"Me and My Woman" is 13 minutes long. It begins with the declaration by the singer that he never knew what kind of day it was. Acoustic guitar is prominent. This sounds folk story from the beginning. The voice sounds doubled. There is a sense of almost medieval-early modern troubadour. An organ-strings breaks in. (Then we go back to guitar-vocal: Think of "Nights in White Satin" by Moody Blues.) The vocal and guitar are joined by a distant horn for a while. Then drifting chorale vocals enter for a moment and return later. There is organ, guitar, vocal. Another movement comes with the thought that this is a bright day for living. The singer laments how we fail the children. But where does this go? Darkness is the speaker's lover. The guitar sound may remind you of Led Zeppelin's acoustic work. The voice and atmosphere can be enchanting while the lyric is at times obscure.

Flat Baroque and Berserk (1970), *Stormcock* (1971), *Lifemask* (1973), *Valentine* (1974), *HQ* (1975), *Bullinamingvase* (1977).

George Harrison

George Harrison sought his musical voice alongside John Lennon and Paul McCartney. His quest increasingly became a search for wholeness, with an Eastern mystical religious focus. George Harrison, turning East, wrote songs with titles like "The Inner Light" and "Within You, Without You." He was a guitar player first but with songs like "Something" and "While My Guitar Gently Weeps" he produced a kind of quality that anticipated how he would extend his career and influence beyond The Beatles. The song "I Me Mine" on the *Let It Be* album referred to a dissolving of the ego in his LSD experiences. Through these experiences Harrison came to an understanding of his personal self as an expression of a greater transpersonal collective force, a universal consciousness. In "I Me Mine" he was critical of his own and others' selfish behavior. Harrison wrote in his autobiography that he had come to dislike his ego: "it was a flash of everything false and impermanent" (158). Harrison reflected that despite the depths of mind, spirit, and consciousness, people in the West often fixed their attention upon mundane realties and to live like this was to be like "beggars in a goldmine." (242)

Some of Harrison's most memorable songs seem to have emerged naturally, to have been suggested in a moment of inspiration. "Here Comes the Sun" came to mind while he was strolling with his acoustic guitar through the garden of Eric Clapton's home. "While My Guitar Gently Weeps" began when he was reading the *I Ching, Book of Changes*, which encourages randomness. Following the Eastern concept that all changes and whatever happens is meant to be, the *I Ching* teaches that there is no coincidence. Harrison's eyes fell upon the words "gently weeps" and his beautiful song often covered by other artists began to unfold. (Beatles Anthology 306).

All Things Must Pass was a fitting title for a time when the members of The Beatles went their own ways. Of course, the multi-sided album was a creative milestone for George Harrison and his phrase offers his recognition of the evanescent quality of the process of life. In *Rolling Stone* (January 21, 1971) Ben Gerson wrote that Harrison's music for this record came "pouring out.... It is both an intensely personal statement and a grandiose gesture, a triumph over artistic modesty, even frustration." Gerson called the album an "extravagant expression" of "piety and sacrifice and joy." On that album, "What Is Life?" asks a perennial question and adds the lover's realization—who am I without you?—which may be addressed to a beloved friend, a lover, or the divinity regarded gratefully by the singer.

"My Sweet Lord," a staple of radio airplay in the early 1970s, is George Harrison's best-known post–Beatles song. The lyric to "My Sweet Lord" evokes seeking. The musical pattern may owe much to many other songs besides Ronald Mack's "He's So Fine." Despite Harrison's distinctive guitar lines and apparently earnest intention, he was charged with "unconscious plagiarism" of the Chiffon's "He's So Fine." The song owes more to "Oh, Happy Day" by the Edwin Hawkins Singers which inspired Harrison while he was on tour in Europe with Eric Clapton and Delaney and Bonnie in December 1969. The repetition of the chorus with layered vocals suggests community and harmony. The Hallelujahs became linked with the Maha Mantra and Sanskrit prayer.

The issue of poverty in the new nation of Bangladesh drew Harrison's concern. Several songs from *All Things Must Pass* were performed at The Concert for Bangladesh, which included two concerts on the afternoon and evening of August 1, 1971, at Madison Square Garden in New York City. The first of rock's benefit concerts, the show was intended to bring attention to the plight of the people of Bangladesh following the Bhola cyclone of 1970 and civil strife and poverty in the country. With the support of Ravi Shankar and a host of well-known popular musicians, including Eric Clapton, Bob Dylan, and Ringo Starr, the concert and subsequent album and film raised $12 million in aid. The album won the 1973 Grammy Album of the Year Award.

Living in the Material World (1973)

Harrison's "Give Me Love (Give Me Peace on Earth)" is perhaps the most memorable song on George Harrison's *Living in the Material World* (1973). It is a prayer that rises with his familiar slide guitar lead. Harrison recalled the spontaneity of the song's creation: "Sometimes you open up your mouth and you don't know what you are going to say and whatever comes out is the starting point..." (*Beatles Encyclopedia* 321). There is an approach to songwriting in this: an idea emerges while one is playing, or a word or phrase comes to mind, and the songwriter follows it. *Living in the Material World* owes something to the teaching of A.C. Bhaktivedanta Swami.

All Things Must Pass (1970), *The Concert for Bangladesh* (1971), *Living in the Material World* (1973), *Dark Horse* (1974), *Extra Texture* (1975), *Thirty-Three* (1976), *George Harrison* (1979).

Richie Havens

Richie Havens was best known as a folk-based performer who effectively covered songs written by others. This creative interpreter also wrote a few songs of his own. At Woodstock, his anthem "Freedom" spontaneously unfolded. It became one of his most memorable performances. In August 1969 he was Woodstock's first performer. Upon singing the bluesy spiritual "Motherless Child," which roused the crowd, Havens launched into "Freedom," an edgy declaration that set the tone for the days of music that would follow.

A veteran of the Greenwich Village folk club scene, Havens was a rhythmic guitarist with a fast right hand that created percussive effects on the guitar. His gravelly and assertive vocals became widely heard after Woodstock. *Stonehenge* (1970) appeared on his own record label. Havens covered George Harrison's "Here Comes the Sun" and his version received considerable airplay. The single propelled his album *Alarm Clock* into the top 30 on the album charts. Havens' sound was best captured in live performance. A studio album *The Great Blind Degree* (1971) was followed by *Live on Stage* (1972), which displayed his energy and spontaneity as a performer. *Portfolio* (1973) and *Mixed Bag* (1974) followed.

Through the years, Havens focused on work at home in the Bronx fostering a children's museum for the study of oceanography. He created National Guard, an organization to educate children about the environment. In 1978, as Native American Indians walked from Alcatraz to Washington, D.C., Havens performed on behalf of treaty rights to avoid confiscation of Indian lands. Years later, he could be seen in a Maxwell House coffee commercial and a commercial for Amtrak. Havens sang at the Bill Clinton presidential inaugural. He also played music for Tibetan freedom and regularly coupled his music with concern for human rights. Havens, sadly, is no longer with us. He has left a legacy of many recordings.

Stonehenge (1970)

On *Stonehenge* (1970) we hear "Minstrel from Gault," which Havens co-wrote with Mark Roth and "Ring Around the Moon," co-written with folksinger Greg Brown. Havens performed "I Started a Joke" by Barry Gibb and the Gibb brothers. He sang Bob Dylan's "It's All Over Now, Baby Blue." This first album is filled with many of Haven's songs: "It Could Be the First Day," "There's a Hold in the Future," "Prayer," "Try Little Blues," and the album closer "Shouldn't All the World Be Dancing?" *Alarm Clock* opens with "Here Comes the Sun" and is followed by eight songs written by Havens. Bill Keith and Rick Derringer make appearances.

Stonehenge (1970), *Alarm Clock* (1971), *The Great Blind Degree* (1971), *Live on Stage* (1972), *Portfolio* (1973), *Mixed Bag II* (1974), *Mirage* (1975), *The End of the Beginning* (1977).

John Hiatt

Songwriter John Hiatt, from Indianapolis, settled down in Nashville, signed a publishing deal with Tree Music, and wrote songs. Three Dog Night recorded "Sure as I'm Sittin' Here." Hiatt was not just sitting around. He became a gruff-voiced singer-songwriter in the 1970s recording several albums of his own. *Hanging Around the Observatory* (1974) was his first recording. It was followed by *Overcoats* (1975), another album of fine songs and grumbling baritone. Neither album sold well and Epic, with its focus on commercial profits, dropped Hiatt. He continued to be a prolific songwriter. His folk-country-pop songwriting migrated toward new wave rock in the vein of Elvis Costello. A recording titled *Slug Line* (1979) came out on MCA Records. It was in subsequent years that his catalog of songs began to become a resource for other artists. A wide array of well-known recording artists covered his songs. His own voice was increasingly heard. A listener can recognize in many of Hiatt's songs "the small, telling detail," as Paul Zollo has pointed out (647).

Hanging Around the Observatory (1974)

John Hiatt's vocal delivery is an earnest sometimes nasal grumble, an evocation. His first album is mostly guitar-vocal, keyboards and drums. "Sure as I'm Sitting Here" on *Hanging Around the Observatory* (1974) was recorded by Three Dog Night. On the first side of this album, we hear "Maybe Baby Say You Do," "Whistles in My Ears," "Sure as I'm Sitting Here," "Rose," and "Hanging Around the Observatory." Flip the vinyl LP over and you will hear "Full Moon," "Wild-Eyed Gypsies," "It's Alright with Me," "Little Blue Song for You" and "Ocean."

The up-tempo thrust of the first song is pushed by piano, bass, and drums. We hear the word "baby" repeated, as he asks questions and a guitar lead and energetic organ and piano pumps into the mix. This song, "Full Moon," and "Hanging Around the Observatory" are readily available on YouTube. "Full Moon" begins on acoustic guitar and piano and electric guitar and percussion pick up the tempo. There is a pulse to *Hanging Around the Observatory*. The telescope's mighty eyes are bigger than us. The speaker addresses the professor, who responds with thoughts about space and the earth. We get an old West barroom upright piano. "Sure as I'm Sitting" has a keyboard leading in a breezy soul bit of swing punctuated by staccato chorus that skips along.

There are ten songs on his follow-up, *Overcoats*: "One More Time," "Smiling in the Rain." "I'm Tired of Your Stuff," "Distance," "Down Home," "Overcoats," "I Want Your Love Inside of Me," "I Killed an Ant with My Guitar," "Motorboat to Heaven," "The Lady of the Night." While not commercially successful these albums showed the creative spirit of Hiatt and his peculiarities. These first two recordings were a mix of blues, pop, country, soul, and idiosyncratic vocal style. Hiatt moved toward new wave rock on *Slug Line* (1979) at the end of the decade. See *https://www.trouserpress.com/reviews*

Hanging Around the Observatory (1974), *Overcoats* (1975), *Slug Line* (1979).

Chris Hillman

Songwriter Chris Hillman came from a California home filled with music: vocalists, jazz players, early rock-and-roll. The folk revival and the Kingston Trio, the Weavers, and other roots-oriented folk caught his attention. Bluegrass music was also stirring, and he became interested in the mandolin. He listened to country music and bluegrass. Following his father's death, the Hillman family moved to an apartment in Los Angeles. Some time with a bluegrass band, based in San Diego, followed. They traveled up to Los Angeles to play at The Troubadour. He met his present folk-bluegrass music partner Herb Pedersen in 1963. He became a member of The Byrds, who brought folk into electric folk-rock. He was encouraged to be the group's bass player, although he had never played bass guitar. They listened to The Beatles and began writing songs. They heard Bob Dylan's songs and responded to "Mr. Tambourine Man." They recorded with Terry Melcher producing. Disc-jockey Bob Eubanks played the song regularly, which then caught on nationally. Pete Seeger's "Turn, Turn, Turn," drawn from Ecclesiastes became The Byrds featured song. *Sweetheart of the Rodeo*, the Byrds country-Nashville album, set up Chris Hillman's work with Gram Parsons for The Flying Burrito Brothers. He then played with Manassas, which produced a couple of albums and toured in the U.S. and Europe. Souther, Hillman, Furay followed: three singer-songwriters supported by a band.

In the 1970s, Hillman expressed a broad spectrum of musical styles on his albums. *Slipping Away* (1976) offers the title song, which moves into a shuffle beat and a tasteful soul movement into string harmony vocals with light percussion behind with guitar lines off a hollow body guitar. The one you love is slipping away. With a nicely warm vocal, this is a high point of pop-song creation. Some of the songs for the album were written with Peter Knobler. He brought a band together for the subsequent tour. A second solo album followed. Hillman reunited with his former mates from The Byrds as McGuinn-Clark-Hillman. He took a turn back to folk and bluegrass music. Two albums on Sugar Hill followed in the early 1980s with bluegrass and then an electric recording, *Desert Rose*. The Desert Rose Band emerged from this and Dan Fogelberg's *High Country Snows* concerts. The Desert Rose Band became a popular and very capable bluegrass and country band.

Slippin' Away (1976), *Clear Sailin'* (1977).

Rupert Holmes

Rupert Holmes is the stage name of David Goldstein, a talented playwright and singer-songwriter, who lives up along the Hudson River has created orchestrated story songs, jingles, pop tunes, and theatrical scripts. In the 1970s he recorded a few solo albums. But he is most associated with "Escape (The Piña Colada Song)," in which a separated couple look for romance in the personal ads and are ultimately surprised to find that they have answered each other's ad. Among his accomplishments is *Drood*, his scripting of a production of Charles Dickens's unfinished novel in which the audience selects from a variety of endings.

An album, *The Cuff Links* (1969) with Holmes on piano, was one that Ron Dante had to drop out of because of contractual obligations to The Archies. This recording brought Rupert Holmes' music into the new decade of the 1970s. *Widescreen* (1974) was one of his stronger albums and Barbra Streisand chose some songs from it to record. *Partners in Crime* (1979) included the song that people best remember and won't let Rupert Holmes forget. However, he has no regrets about being a one hit wonder.

Widescreen (1974), *Rupert Holmes* (1975), *Singles* (1976), *Pursuit of Happiness* (1977), *Partners in Crime* (1979).

Catherine Howe

A British actress and singer, Catherine Howe developed some gentle albums in the 1970s. "What a Beautiful Place" is orchestrated. "It Comes with Breezes" features her mezzo-soprano which floats across the accompaniment. Her song "Harry" is available on YouTube. In the video she stands at a microphone and sings to guitar accompaniment while a fiddler sits in the background awaiting his part. "Harry" received the Ivor Novello Award in 1975. "What Are Friends for Anyway?" was a single. She recorded on RCA Records. There was a CBS release in Italy. Howe concluded the decade on Ariola Records. She then "retired" for a time and pursued acting. She later continued singing and performing occasional concerts.

What a Beautiful Place (1971), *My Child* (1971), *When the Sparrow Flies* (1974), *Harry* (1975), *Silent Mother Nature* (1976), *Dragonfly Days* (1979).

Janis Ian

As a young songwriter, Janis Ian (Janis Eddy Fink) recorded "Society's Child" in which peers and mother resisted an inter-racial relationship. Such things were, of course, quite possible in a racially mixed community like East Orange, New Jersey. As Janis Ian, pointed out, these relationships were not acceptable to some people. As a teenager she was living amid a largely African American community. Her song "At Seventeen" appeared on *Between the Lines* (1975). The speaker of this song realized that her appearance was not that of a beauty queen and a self-pitying lament followed. The greater issues of the world were not addressed in this girl's adolescence, but the song was poignant for a teen, perhaps. This hit song was on Janis Ian's most popular album, *Love Is Blind* (1975). *Fly Too High* (1979) was produced by disco producer Giorgio Maroder. In an interview with Paul Zollo, Janis Ian commented that she values music because it "crosses boundaries" (Zollo 312).

Between the Lines (1975), *Love is Blind* (1975), *Fly Too High* (1979).

Bert Jansch

Best known for his musicianship, guitarist Bert Jansch, from Edinburgh, Scotland, brought together jazz, with time signature shifts, with folk of the British Isles and Appalachian folk. His guitar playing was highly regarded and received comments from Jimmy Page and Mike Oldfield, among others. The country folk blues of Big Bill Broonzy and Brownie McGee were among Janch's influences. He developed several records in the 1960s, including recording with John Renbourn and Roy Harper. He moved to London and played with the band Pentangle in the early 1970s. Around 1973–74 he retired to a farm in Wales. *Rare Conundrum* (1977) followed, along with a band also with that name. The album *Avocet* (1979) concluded the decade. He has recorded two dozen studio albums.

Rosemary Lane (1971)

Jansch's *Rosemary Lane* (1971) is filled with songs that dwell in the realm of traditional English folk song balladry. The guitar on the original track of the title song "Rosemary Lane" (1971) comes across more subdued than more recent live versions on YouTube. The vocal is forward in the original recording, and this brings attention to the story within the song. The original album recordings of "Reynardine," with alternate tuned guitar, and "Sylvie" are also available on YouTube. There is a medieval troubadour quality to these songs. Jansch establishes a speaker of each song-story. In each song, the speaker spies a female character who is absorbed in memories or dismayed. On "Reynardine" he sings of overhearing a woman as he was out rambling. We hear her story and his. In "Sylvie" the structure is one which each verse repeats the first two lines and then develops the tale gradually. We are told that Sylvie was walking by the riverside. She was thinking tearily about her lover. A gentleman comes along to whom she tells of her loss. A bright guitar playing fills and enhances this ballad.

On YouTube, you can hear a more recent Bert Jansch's "Rosemary Lane." He played this tune in 2012 on guitar. He sings from a room with music posters on the walls as he sits on a couch. The guitar rings out clearly as he sings us the tale. There is a small live audience whose applause we hear at the end of the song. There is also a 2010 live performance on YouTube, with the guitar up even stronger and the vocal drenched in reverb.

Rosemary Lane (1971), *Moonshine* (1973), *L.A. Turnaround* (1974), *Santa Barbara Honeymoon* (1975), *A Rare Conundrum* (1977), *Avocet* (1978–1979).

Billy Joel

One may think of 1970 Billy Joel as the piano man in a Long Island bar playing songs for a disillusioned bunch long past happy hour imbibing another round of beers. That immense creativity, gritty delivery, and piano talent washes by them like traffic on the Long Island Expressway or waves on the north shore. (Mixed metaphors for a mixed crowd and a mixed bag of songs.) They are the souls of working-class Hicksville, Oyster Bay, and places due west to New York City, all in the mood for a melody. So, why are the tracks for *Cold Spring Harbor* (1971), Billy Joel's debut, speeded up a bit? The album included "She's Got a Way" and "Everybody Loves You Now." The album is listenable despite the slightly speeded up tape. Soon listeners could ask why "Captain Jack," the story of a burdened young man's hard life, was so depressing and invigorating all at the same time. The song caught the interest of CBS executives and joined Joel's single "Piano Man" on his breakthrough album *Piano Man* (1973) ("Piano Man," "You're My Home"). *Streetlife Serenade* (1974) followed his move to Los Angeles with the rousing up-tempo piano and satirical look at the entertainment business in "The Entertainer" (songs cut down to 3:05), the Spanish music sounding "Los Angelenos," and Joel recalling flying east on a plane and drinking champagne during the flight home to the family barbeque.

Billy Joel's masterpiece, *The Stranger* (1977), is one of the most complete and tuneful singer-songwriter albums of the 1970s. Producer Phil Ramone made a difference on this record and contributed to Joel's sound across later years. The album immediately caught listener attention with the piano melody and tuneful whistling intro to "Scenes from an Italian Restaurant," a masterful song on a broad canvas that blended into the hit "Moving Out (Anthony's Song)." The record produced a string of hits: "Just the Way You Are," "Only the Good Die Young," "Moving Out (Anthony's Song)," "She's Always a Woman," and "She's Got a Way." These songs received extensive airplay and launched this album into platinum, as one of the top sellers of the time. Billy Joel became a widely familiar, critically respected, and sought-after performer. He could approach songs with different vocal and musical styles (rock, R&B, ballads) and play a mean piano. His "New York State of Mind" drew upon his appreciation of the work of Ray Charles. *Turnstiles* (1978) gathered a band for songs like "Say Goodbye to Hollywood" and a title that suggested Manhattan, as did *52nd Street* (1978), home of CBS ("My Life," "Big Shot," and "Honesty").

Cold Spring Harbor (1971), *Piano Man* (1972), *Streetlife Serenade* (1974), *The Stranger* (1977), *Turnstiles* (1978), *52nd Street* (1979).

Elton John

The 1970s was an Elton John soundtrack. Turn on a radio and one heard Elton John: "Daniel," "Honky Cat," "Saturday's Alright for Fighting," "Goodbye Yellow Brick Road," "Crocodile Rock," "Bennie and the Jets," "Candle in the Wind," "Philadelphia Freedom." You would have to have lived in a distant jungle or on another planet to have not heard the songs he composed with lyricist Bernie Taupin. This is a case of composer-performer writing with a collaborator. In separate rooms they worked, words and music going back and forth. Elton John then performed the songs with his band. But let's consider him a singer-songwriter and one of the most familiar pop music voices of the decade. Along the way, Elton John transformed from Reginald Dwight into Elton John in the 1960s, a sure artist at the piano at clubs who would play at The Troubadour in 1970. His first commercial release was *Empty Sky* (1969). His second album, *Elton John* (1970), brought "Your Song," the first of a string of dozens of hit songs. There was a live album *17-11-70*. *Madman Across the Water* (1971) included "Levon" and "Tiny Dancer." "Rocket Man" and "Honky Cat" appeared on *Honky Chateau* (1972). *Don't Shoot Me I'm Only the Piano Player* (1973) brought the song hits "Daniel" and "Crocodile Rock." The powerful double-album *Goodbye Yellow Brick Road* (1973) followed ("Yellow Brick Road," "Bennie and the Jets," "Candle in the Wind," "Saturday's Alright for Fighting," "Funeral for a Friend/Love Lies Bleeding"). His first *Greatest Hits* (1974) album sold strongly worldwide. At mid-decade one saw Captain Fantastic adopt glam-rock with color-rimmed glasses and feathers and frills. By the end of the decade, he had become one of the most acclaimed pop music acts on the planet. *Caribou* (1974) was recorded at a ranch of that name ("The Bitch is Back" and "Don't Let the Sun Go Down on Me," which built into a big ballad with an orchestra). He collaborated with John Lennon on a recording of "Lucy in the Sky with Diamonds" and "Whatever Gets You Through the Night" and he sang with Kiki Dee on the pop hit "Don't Go Breaking My Heart" (1976). "Someone Saved My Life Tonight" appeared on *Captain Fantastic and the Brown Dirt Cowboy*. Elton John dissolved his band at this time. However, he pulled in several musicians who brought a rock sound to his next album, *Rock of the Westies*. Both albums went to #1. *A Single Man* (1978) did not include Taupin lyrics; Elton John teamed up with Gary Osbourne. An astounding period of accomplishment seemed to have come to an end—at least temporarily. Elton John flirted with the idea of not performing, but appeared in the U.S., Europe, Israel, and the Soviet Union.

Empty Sky (1969), *Tumbleweed Connection* (1970), *Madman Across the Water* (1971), *Honky Chateau* (1972), *Don't Shoot Me I'm Only the Piano Player* (1973), *Goodbye Yellow Brick Road* (1974), *Greatest Hits* (1974), *Caribou* (1974), *Captain Fantastic and the Brown Dirt Cowboy* (1975), *Rock of the Westies* (1975), *Blue Moves* (1976), *A Single Man* (1978), *Victim of Love* (1979).

Rickie Lee Jones

When pop-jazz singer-songwriter Rickie Lee Jones made her album debut in 1979 "Chuck E's in Love" was heard often. "The singer-songwriter took over the pop craft in music," she told the *Los Angeles Times* (June 13, 2019). On her album jazz met folk, the Beats, a sensibility that sought freedom. There was a relationship with Tom Waits during the years immediately preceding that album. A creative uniqueness of her own is what stands out. "Chuck E's in Love" is probably what most listeners will remember. The era of the music video had begun, and a video accompanied the song. Dr. John, Michael McDonald, and Randy Newman contributed to her album, which included the songs "Youngblood," and "Coolsville." There was Rickie Lee Jones, wearing a white beret, black bra, crouching down for an Annie Liebowitz photo on the cover of *Rolling Stone*. She was a new voice and the 1980s would open the door to many more female singer-songwriters. Rickie Lee Jones received the Grammy Award for Best New Artist. Her second album was *Pirates* (1981).

Rickie Lee Jones (1979).

See the article by Alison Festerstock, "Rickie Lee Jones Settles Down—Sort Of" *Los Angeles Times* (June 13, 2019). *https://www.latimes/entertainment/music/la-et-ms-rickie-lee-jones-kicks-20190610-story.html*. See also Rickie Lee Jones's memoir *Last Chance Texaco: Chronicles of an American Troubadour*. New York: Grove Press, 2021.

Greg Kihn

Working solo with a guitar and with a band, Greg Kihn broke into radio airplay in the mid–1970s. Kihn was supported by the Greg Kihn Band, with bassist Steve Wright. Wright is co-writer on most of the songs. So, it is difficult to fit Kihn easily into the singer-songwriter category. There were no hits in the 1970s. "The Breakup Song" reached the pop charts in 1981 and "Jeopardy" made the pop charts in 1983. One can find "Don't Expect to Be Right" from the first album on YouTube. The song starts in electric guitar with a folk-rock-almost-country sound and the staccato delivery of the title line introducing the chorus seems to abruptly shift the character of the song.

Greg Kihn (1976), *Greg Kihn Again* (1977), *Next of Kihn* (1978), *With the Naked Eye* (1979).

Andy Kim

The one-hit wonder vocalist of "Rock Me Gently," Andy Kim from Canada, was a writer of pop songs. The memorable song starts with a bassline, soon joined by a Hammond organ sound, and his vocals (Sounds like Neil Diamond? Engelbert Humperdinck?). Some female background vocals join him later in the song. Andrew Youakim, of Lebanese background, had written the hit "Sugar, Sugar" (1969) with Jeff Barry and The Archies. He became a solo artist in 1969–1970. Before 1970 he reached the charts with his song "Rainbow Ride" and had a Canadian hit with "Baby, I Love You." Andy Kim began the 1970s with a song on The Monkees' *Changes* album. His 1970s albums, one with United Artists and one Capitol Records with were both titled *Andy Kim*. While the album titles were not clever, his singing voice was appealing, and he was good with stage names. When he ended the decade, he began to change his stage name again, to Longfellow.

Andy Kim (1973), *Andy Kim* (1974).

Carole King

Picture Brooklyn in 1959: apartments bathed in evening sunlight that traces across the sidewalk, up front steps, brick walls, and reflects off the windows. Behind one Carole Klein is at her piano. Up on the roof, peaceful as can be, you look out over Flatbush and Bensonhurst. Families live here, in apartments, or in houses in rows close together with little postage stamp–like square backyards stretching between the garages and the hedges. The D-train takes you from there, over the bridge to Manhattan. Before it turns toward Rockefeller Center, you get out at 42nd Street. It is a fine, clear day, so you begin to take a walk uptown. You pass by the theater where the musical featuring Carole King's life and songs has been playing successfully for years. If you listen and dream back across the years, the Brill building is where Carole King is. Klein to King, Brooklyn to Manhattan: none of that was much of a jump. She was beckoned, led there by a great talent and impulse to write songs. Sitting again at a piano, you can see her working out a tune to shop to the Shirelles. Gerry Goffin has some lyrics: a few words, an idea. They write "One Fine Day" for the Chiffons, "Take Good Care of My Baby" for Bobby Vee, "Up on the Roof" for The Drifters. Are they really going to move to West Orange, New Jersey? To someone in Brooklyn, that is like someone going to the country.

Pleasant Valley Sundays in West Orange meant bigger yards, broader lawns, a place to raise the children. To Goffin it also meant conformity: the kind that folksinger Malvina Reynolds wrote about when she sang of little boxes made of ticky-tacky. If you travel to the Eagle Rock park you can see the New York City skyline. Brooklyn it ain't. So long Brill Building and that human energy of the city sidewalks. King and Goffin are a well-established songwriting team and they have royalties from their songs and a new family to raise. So, they try it out. Goffin writes his song lyric for "Pleasant Valley Sundays" for The Monkees, a tuneful and charmingly contrived made-for-TV take on The Beatles. Carole King sets the music for "Locomotion" (for Little Eva). The Beatles are covering "Chains" in 1964. Herman's Hermits are singing "I'm Into Something Good," first recorded by Earl Jean.

By 1970, life had changed for Carole King. She and Gerry Goffin had divorced in 1968. Carole King moved to Laurel Canyon in Los Angeles. She was clearly musically inspired, swept up in a new streak of songwriting: songs she was writing on her own.

Carole King's *Tapestry* was a high point, one of the benchmarks of the singer-songwriter era of the early 1970s. Turn on most any radio then and her songs were everywhere. Turn on a station that plays that light-FM fare today and inevitably you will hear a Carole King song before the day is through. In the 1970s record buyers saw that image of her on the album cover: barefoot, casual, kicking back in jeans and blouse, sitting by a window with Telemachus, her cat, looking on. Carole King had come out to sing her songs on stage during that time, coaxed by James Taylor and others. King and Taylor both played "You've Got a Friend" and "Up on the Roof" in their sets. It was a time of "easy listening" smash hits, tender ballads saying there would always be a friend through thick and thin. Winter,

Spring, Summer, and Fall Carole King was on the charts lamenting that someone was so far away. In this fast-paced, changing society, why didn't anyone stay in the same place for long? One heard the pulse and rhythm of "Smackwater Jack" and a lively, bluesy world in motion. King was a ubiquitous pop-song angel on the radio and the phonograph.

More than 100 pop songs hits and 25 albums have come from Carole King's creativity and artistry. There have been four Grammy Awards, the Gershwin Prize for Popular Song in 2013, and the Kennedy Center Awards in 2015. She is honored as a member of the Songwriter Hall of Fame.

Writer (1970), *Tapestry* (1971), *Music* (1971), *Rhymes & Reasons* (1972), *Fantasy* (1973), *Wrap Around Joy* (1974), *Really Rosie* (1975), *Thoroughbred* (1976), *Simple Things* (1977), *Welcome Home* (1978), *Touch the Sky* (1979).

Bonnie Koloc

Bonnie Koloc was a mainstay of the Chicago folk scene, the musical home of Art Thieme, Jim Post, Fred Holstein, Steve Goodman, and John Prine. Folk music issued from Earl of Old Town and several folk clubs/restaurants. From working class Iowa, Bonnie Koloc recorded "Roll Me on the Water" on *You're Gonna Love Yourself in the Morning* (1974). Of *Close Up* (1976–77), music critic Robert Cristgau wrote later in his guide to *Rock Albums of the Seventies* (1981) that Koloc's "modest, unmistakable intelligence" truly worked on this record. Following the 1970s she performed as an actress in plays.

After All This Time (1971)

Bonnie Koloc wrote or co-wrote all of the songs on *After All This Time* (1971) her first album of the 1970s, except "Jazz Man" and "Victoria's Morning," which are by Ed Holstein. "Don't Leave Me" opens this recording, with band doing a blues and a passionate Joplinesque performance by Bonnie Koloc. The sound is a bit late 1960s early 1970 psychedelia dated. Kind of like the Jefferson Airplane on a bad trip. Yet, this first cut is interesting and shows some of Bonnie Koloc's vocal strengths.

On "After All This Time" piano gives us a bluesy beginning. Koloc's vocal rides above this reflecting on changes, sometimes gliding toward notes in the sky. The central idea repeated is making it on her own amid the changes. At times she is in a blues bending note that would be right down the center of a piano keyboard. However, her vocal range flies upward as well. Long notes high above the treble clef staff are extended.

This Chicago lady sings beautifully of the "New York City Blues." She addresses someone who is isolated from anyone who knows how she feels. That "you" is "hurting bad" in an empty bed, in an empty room. A well-paced piano is out front of guitar and bass, and a blues harmonica cuts through. Got to go back to Chicago to mend, she sings. In style and delivery, this song may remind one of a Billie Holiday vocal performance. Koloc's vocal instrument is like a soprano sax. "Devil's Nine Questions" moves into a haunting folk music with a lovely vocal, imagery, and a Renaissance musical quality. This is a pensive ballad sung with grace that suggests myth and wonder. Koloc is joined by a band on "Another New Mornin'." The song opens on a hollow body electric guitar, which is on the left channel with drums on the right. While the vocal is strong, the musical production does not really serve it well. It seems distracting after the opening cuts on this album. The production choices here don't enhance the band's sound, which is rather raw. Koloc's voice could have done quite well without the clutter. In contrast, her vocal performance on songs like "Sailing Ship" on her next album *Hold on to Me*, is much cleaner, folk-music centered, and coherent.

After All This Time (1971), *Hold on To Me* (1972), *Bonnie Koloc* (1973), *You're Gonna Love Yourself in the Morning* (1974), *At Her Best* (1976), *Close Up* (1976–77), *Wild and Recluse* (1978).

Kris Kristofferson

Windshield wipers keeping time were the pulse behind "Me and Bobby McGee." There may have been some hard-drinking Saturday nights behind "Sunday Morning Coming Down." One would have to imagine that a ruggedly handsome actor-musician like Kristofferson had someone to help him make it through the night. Who is to say if songs like those come through imagination from some life experiences? Kristofferson has had a varied life as driver, helicopter pilot, janitor, Oxford scholar, teacher, and actor. For this writer of thoughtful, literate lyrics, country music seemed a natural home. He met Tom T. Hall and Johnny Cash and others in Nashville in the 1960s. In 1969, the drinking song "From the Bottle to the Bottom" was recorded by Billy Walker. Kristofferson began the 1970s with the enduring hit song "Sunday Morning Coming Down." "Me and Bobby McGee" was recorded by Janis Joplin. "For the Good Times" was recorded by Ray Price.

Kris Kristofferson released his first solo album in April 1970. He endured some criticisms of the limitations of his singing voice. However, the songs had some impact: "Help Me Make It Through the Night," "Just the Other Side of Nowhere," "Darby's Castle," and "Blame It on the Stones," which opened the record. His second record was *The Silver-Tongued Devil and I* (1971). With "Pilgrim-Chapter 33" he referred to himself as a walking contradiction. There were nine albums between 1972 and 1979. He acted in a lead role in *A Star is Born* and appeared in other films.

"Kris Kristofferson is the New Nashville Sound" Paul Hemphill of the *New York Times* reported on December 6, 1970. "Sunday Morning Coming Down" was high on the charts. He gave his audience the ballad in which he becomes the narrator sitting in a bar with a young maiden that the silver-tongued devil steals away. Fred Foster produced the album on Monument Records. It consisted primarily of Kristofferson's songs and was commercially successful.

Kristofferson (1970), *The Silver-Tongued Devil and I* (1971), *Border Land* (1972), *Jesus Was a Capricorn* (1973), *Spooky Lady's Side-Show* (1974), *Who's to Bless and Who's to Blame* (1975), *Surreal Thing* (1976), *Easter Island* (1978), *Shake Hands with the Devil* (1979).

John Lennon

John Lennon's solo years began with musical experimentation with Yoko Ono. This began with *Unfinished Music, No. 1: Two Virgins, Unfinished Music, No. 2: Life with the Lions* and *The Wedding Album* (1969), all begun while Lennon was still with The Beatles and becoming enmeshed in a heroin addiction. Their peace anthem "Give Peace a Chance" is one of the enduring works of this period. As The Beatles were dissolving, Lennon created the Plastic Ono Band. The album which emerged was, of course, called *John Lennon/Plastic Ono Band* (1970). It was produced by Lennon with Ono and with Phil Spector. The album which followed, *Imagine* (1971) featured the title song "Imagine." For all of that song's enduring emphasis on peace, Lennon was not at peace with Paul McCartney, to whom he wrote "How Do You Sleep?" With *Sometime in New York City* (1972) John Lennon and Yoko Ono returned to activism. This appears to be a period during which Lennon's attention to music slipped along with his marriage, temporarily. He made an extraordinary comeback, however, with *Mind Games* (1973), which included the tuneful, reverbed, and entrancing title cut. *Walls and Bridges* (1974) brought the hits "#9 Dream" and the rollicking up-tempo romp of "Whatever Gets You Through the Night." On *Rock n' Roll* (1975) Lennon chose to revisit rock and roll standards, like "Stand by Me." At this point, John Lennon chose to go into a five-year retirement from recording and performing. It was as he was preparing to release *Double Fantasy* (1980) with a return to some balance and creative renewal that he was assassinated on December 8, 1980, near his home at the Dakota on the West Side of

New York's Central Park. The album included the hits "Watching the Wheels," "Woman," and "(Just Like) Starting Over."

John Lennon/Plastic Ono Band (1970), *Imagine* (1971), *Sometime in New York City* (1972), *Mind Games* (1973), *Walls and Bridges* (1974), *Rock n' Roll* (1975).

Gordon Lightfoot

The 1960s saw Gordon Lightfoot become arguably Canada's greatest traveling folk music minstrel and balladeer. His songs "Early Morning Rain," "For Loving Me," and "Ribbon of Darkness" became folk music standards and popular songs recorded by others. Winter snows, romantic breakups, railroad lines, ships on the Great Lakes: that was Gordon Lightfoot. "Alberta Bound" and "Canadian Railroad Trilogy" accounted for long journeys, and he made many to perform his music. The 1970s brought Lightfoot wide popular acclaim with mainstream hits like the poignant "If You Could Read My Mind" (1970), "Sundown" (1974), which soared to #1, "Carefree Highway" (1974), "Rainy Day People" (1975), and the extraordinary ballad "The Wreck of the Edmund Fitzgerald" (1976), which tells the story of a shipping disaster on the Great Lakes.

In his songs there are a wide range of experiences. There is love in "Beautiful," ache and breakup in "Early Morning Rain" and "If You Could Read My Mind," gritty assertion in "Sundown," freedom of the road in "Carefree Highway," and tribute, lament, and chronicle in "The Wreck of the Edmund Fitzgerald." The sound of Lightfoot's songs throughout is mostly acoustic, driven at times by a small ensemble of bass guitar and drums.

Sit Down Young Stranger (1970)

Gordon Lightfoot began the 1970s with the hit "If You Could Read My Mind," on his *Sit Down Young Stranger* album. "Sit Down Young Stranger" establishes a pattern on a single guitar and voice that repeats throughout. We are focused on a long verse that raises questions for the young stranger. The young stranger, returning home, stands in the doorway but does not know where he belongs. He may have ideals and ideas about the world than are different from the practically minded others around him. Life is not learned in school. The song brings us images of war and of a system they are caught within. This is the album that brings us "If You Could Read My Mind," which is among the finest of breakup songs. "Minstrel of the Dawn" and "Approaching Lavender" have orchestral arrangements by Randy Newman. Kristofferson's "Me and Bobby McGee" had not yet become a hit for Janis Joplin when Lightfoot's cover of the song was recorded. There is a folk music simplicity to this album. Van Dyke Parks and John Sebastian also appear on this album. As Gordon Lightfoot gained more popular attention with songs like "Sundown" and "Carefree Highway" a bit more of pop-music commercial edge entered into the mix.

Sit Down Young Stranger (1970), *Summer Side of Life* (1971), *Don Quixote* (1972), *Old Dan's Records* (1973), *Sundown* (1974), *Cold on the Shoulder* (1975), *Gord's Gold* (1975), *Summertime Drea*m (1976), *Endless Wire* (1978).

Lobo

Perhaps only in the singer-songwriter era could an artist with the stage name of Lobo and a song titled "Me and You and a Dog Named Boo" become a bestselling recording artist. His first album *Lobo* (1971) followed that single. Lobo is Spanish for wolf. His birth name was Roland Kent Lavoie. "I'd Love You to Want Me" was a tuneful three chord folk-pop song that appeared on *A Simple Man* (1972) and shot up the charts as a single. He sounded like a romantic rather than a wolf. On *Calumet* (1973) were more singles: "How Can I Tell Her?," "It Sure Took a Long, Long Time," and "Standing at the End of the Line." He did not write the songs that appeared on *Just a Singer* (1974). *Come with Me* (1976) came next, on the Phillips label. There were no other 1970s albums. The songs "After Glow" (1977), "All I'll Ever Need" (1978), and the single "Where Were You When I Was Falling in Love?" (1970) rounded out the decade for him.

Lobo (1971), *Simple Man* (1972), *Calumet* (1973), *Just a Singer* (1974), *Come with Me* (1976).

Dave Loggins

Perhaps the most fitting lament of a troubadour's life on the road in the 1970s came from Dave Loggins in "Please Come to Boston." In this song, a "rambling" singer of songs urges his lady to please come to Boston. She responds, no, it's time for you to come home to me. After all, L.A. isn't Boston. You're meant for a simpler life at home, not one wandering all over the country singing your songs. You're a country boy from Tennessee at heart and your number one fan is right here at home waiting for you. There really weren't any other hits from Dave Loggins. Maybe that didn't matter. This one plaintive song stayed in the memories of listeners. Dave Loggins wrote "Pieces of April" (1973) for Three Dog Night and songs recorded by several country artists. He is a second cousin of singer-songwriter Kenny Loggins.

Following *David Loggins* (1979) he recorded no further major record releases. The songs he wrote in the 1980s were recorded by other artists.

Personal Belongings (1972), *Apprentice* (1974), *Country Suite* (1976), *One Way Ticket to Paradise* (1977), *David Loggins* (1979).

Kenny Loggins

The solo career of Kenny Loggins as a singer-songwriter was supposed to have started in 1970. However, Jim Messina's role as record producer turned into a collaboration. *Sittin' In* appeared and Loggins and Messina became one of the most popular recording and performing duos of the 1970s. Another six Loggins and Messina albums followed. Kenny Loggins' solo work emerged after 1977. From folksinger of "Danny's Song" and "A Love Song" through country-inflected sounds of *Mother Lode* and the rock and roll of "Your Mama Don't Dance" with Messina, Loggins showed himself to be a flexible and creative musician-songwriter. On *Native Sons* (1976) they drew apart more as solo singer-songwriters playing on the same record. *Celebrate Me Home* (1977) included the single "I Believe in Love." On *Nightwatch* (1978) "Whenever I Call You Friend" was a duet with Stevie Nicks. With Michael McDonald he wrote "What a Fool Believes," a hit for the Doobie Brothers and "This is It." He concluded the decade with his album *Keep the Fire* (1979). In the 1980s he created notable soundtracks for popular films and by 1990 had moved through pop and rock styles ranging from the energetic driving pulse of "Danger Zone" to electronic sounds and vocals on *Vox Humana* (1985) to new age–spiritual sentiments and renewal on *Back to Avalon* (1988) and *Leap of Faith* (1991), and across a variety of other musical expressions.

Celebrate Me Home (1977)

"Lady Luck," "If You Be Wise," "I Believe in Love," "Set It Free," "Why Do People Lie," "Enter My Dream," "I've Got the Melody," "Celebrate Me Home," "Daddy's Back," "You Don't Know Me." There is Kenny Loggins *Celebrate Me Home* video on YouTube.

Celebrate Me Home feels authentic, or at least not bound to a market, a film score, or a performance tour. This was Kenny Loggins official first (finally) after the successful years with Jim Messina. (They had five platinum records and ten pop hits.) Producers Phil Ramone and Bob James could add some slickness and smoothness to this recording. Kenny Loggins followed this album by touring to open concerts for Fleetwood Mac on their *Rumours* tour. Loggins had the ability to sing well, and this was supported by his musical chops. His songwriting had stylistic range and could convey both warmth in his ballads and an energetic brightness in his up-tempo rock and country inflected material or folk-rock songs. This album strikes up a mood and is a melodic journey into a singer-songwriter's dreams. Loggins co-wrote several of these songs with other songwriters, such as Jimmy Webb on "If You Be Wise." "Lady Luck" puts the acoustic guitar out over a bass bottom and joins the main vocal with harmonies. It explores the theme of matters of faith and hope or faithlessness. "I Believe in Love" shows his vocal range and is a joy-filled exclamation. Alan and Marilyn Bergman wrote the lyrics to Kenny Loggins' music. "Set It Free" opens gently on keyboards and builds. He introduces his falsetto on "Why Do People Lie." "Enter My Dream" which opens side two is indeed dreamy, a vague and mellow sounding comment about dreams of love. Patti Austin contributed the song "I've Got the Melody (Deep in My Heart)" and she joined in the vocals on this recording. The album addresses returning home, even as Kenny Loggins was stretching forth on tour on a new leg of his career as a singer-songwriter. For the moment, as he developed this album, he was evidently content and back home. "Daddy's Back" is full of groove and optimism and maybe underlines this return home. "You Don't Know Me" is an Eddy Arnold–Cindy Walker country song of unrequited love recast by Loggins. This album sold strongly in the 1980s when Kenny Loggins produced several film theme songs and other hits.

Celebrate Me Home (1977), *Nightwatch* (1978), *Keep the Fire* (1979).

Nick Lowe

A producer and recording artist at the center of new wave rock in the mid- to late 1970s, Nick Lowe might only loosely be considered a singer-songwriter. After working with Dave Edmunds in the band Rockpile, Nick Lowe created his first single. "So, It Goes" was released on Stiff Records. He worked as a producer for the record company. "I Love the Sound of Breaking Glass" was a single in the UK. "Cruel to Be Kind" was written with Ian Gomm. *Labour of Lust* (1979) is a Rockpile album which is listed as a Nick Lowe album. Nick Lowe had an impact upon the shape and direction of several new wave–punk recordings. He produced Elvis Costello. He spent time with Johnny Cash when Cash was in England.

Jesus of Cool (1978), *Labour of Lust* (1979).

Barry Manilow

Entertainer, arranger, master of the modulating pop ballad, Barry Manilow was one of the top selling pop music artists of the 1970s. He does not fit into the typical image of a singer-songwriter but indeed he wrote songs and performed and sang them with pizzazz. "I Write the Songs," by

Beach Boy Bruce Johnston, is one he did not write. However, songs like "Mandy" and "Could It Be Magic" he did co-write. He was brought into Columbia Records by singer Tony Orlando, who co-wrote "Could It Be Magic." In 1971 Manilow was playing piano at Continental Baths as musical director for Bette Midler. He co-wrote the song "Mandy" with Scott English. He recorded and released the #1 hit "Mandy" on *Barry Manilow II* (1974). It reached #1 in January 1975. This began a series of singles that reached the pop charts throughout the 1970s. Several of these songs were written by others. For example: "Looks Like We Made It" (Richard Kerr/ Will Jennings), "Weekend in New England" (Randy Edelman), "Can't Smile Without You" (Charles Fox/Norman Gimbel).

   Barry Manilow (1973), *Barry Manilow II* (1974), *Trying to Get the Feeling* (1975), *This One's for You* (1976), *Barry Manilow Live* (1977), *Even Now* (1978), *One Voice* (1979).

Bob Marley

   The key figure in reggae music, Bob Marley's reputation grew in the United States, Canada, and Europe in the 1970s. Along with the sprightly energy of reggae, there was a political edge to his lyrics. He brought reggae and ska to the world. Meanwhile, he embraced Jamaican cultural identity. Bob Marley and the Wailers performed widely from the mid–1960s on the strength of the single "One Love/People Get Ready." In the early 1970s, he became a Rastafari, pursuing a spiritual path. He moved to London. After *Catch a Fire* (1973) and *Burnin'* (1973), Bob Marley released material under the band's name, even though they had disbanded. He was writing his own songs, performing his own gigs. In this sense, he was a reggae singer-songwriter. *Natty Dread* (1974) was followed *Rastaman Vibration* (1976). There was an assassination attempt in Jamaica in 1976. He again retreated to his home in London. However, he was dealing with melanoma even as he recorded his album *Exodus* (1978). Following his death in 1981, there was a state funeral in Jamaica. *Legend* (1984), a compilation of Bob Marley's songs, continues to stand as the best-selling reggae album worldwide.

   Natty Dread (1974), *Rastaman Vibration* (1976). *Exodus* (1977–78), *Kaya* (1978), *Survival* (1979). See also *Legend* (1984).

Iain Matthews

   In 1970 Iain Matthews left Fairport Convention and formed a band named Southern Comfort. They recorded Joni Mitchell's song

"Woodstock" in a dreamy sounding easy listening version with vocal harmonies. They recorded *Second Spring* (1970). Iain Matthews first solo album followed, produced by Paul Samwell-Smith. One could hear "Tigers Will Service" and "If You Saw Through My Eyes." There is a pop-rock-country sound on this album. He recorded with Andy Roberts in 1972. *Valley Hi* (1973) was produced by Michael Nesmith, formerly of The Monkees.

Iain Matthews's songs "If You Saw Thro' My Eyes" and "You Couldn't Lose" can be heard on YouTube. The album *If You Saw Thro' My Eyes* (1971) consisted of "Deserts," "Hearts," "Never Ending," "Reno Nevada," "Little Known," "Hinge I," "Hinge II," "Southern Wind," "It Came Without Warning," "You Couldn't Lose."

Second Spring (1970), *If You Saw Thro' My Eyes* (1971), *Valley Hi* (1973), *Journeys from the Gospel Call* (1974), *Go for Broke* (1976), *Hit and Run* (1977), *Siamese Friends* (1979) and *Discreet Repeat* (1979).

Curtis Mayfield

An influential songwriter-performer within the context of R&B-soul, Curtis Mayfield was also an activist who addressed the need for reform in America. He supported the civil rights movement and later promoted black pride. Rhythm and blues and funk filled his music. Socially conscious lyrics filled his songs. In the 1960s "Keep on Pushing" referred to the freedom rides and "People Get Ready" was adopted by the civil rights movement. In 1970, Curtis Mayfield left The Impressions for a solo career. His first album *Curtis* (1970) gave attention to social issues and commented on inner city ghettos. "Superfly," the composition for which he is perhaps best known, was a soundtrack for film. His single "Freddie's Dead" was the first single from the *Superfly* (1972) soundtrack, which is mostly instrumental. Mayfield's high vocal over a funky bass line, wah-wah pedal, and string orchestration stands out in that song. *Back to the World* (1973) expresses anti-war sentiments and responds to the winding down of the Vietnam War. *Claudine* (1974) was completed with Gladys Knight and the Pips. *Sparkle* (1976) was recorded with Aretha Franklin. While Mayfield may not fit easily into the singer-songwriter category, he was an influential force in R&B-soul during the time of the singer-songwriter era. His social concerns intersected with those of the more politically oriented singer-songwriters of the time.

Curtis (1970), *Roots* (1971), *Superfly* (1972), *Back to the World* (1973), *Claudine* (1974), *Sweet Exorcist* (1974), *Got to Find a Way* (1974), *Let's Do It Again* (1975), *There's No Place Like America Today* (1975), *Give Get Take and Have* (1976), *Sparkle* (1976), *Never Say You Can't Survive* (1977), *Short Eyes* (1977), *Do It All Night* (1978), *Heartbeat* (1979).

Paul McCartney

With the exception of his first solo recordings, it is difficult to call Paul McCartney a singer-songwriter. He spent the 1970s with his band Wings. However, no one would dispute McCartney's importance to popular music both with and following The Beatles. Nor can it be said that he does anything less than hold his own on guitar and piano while performing his songs solo.

McCartney (1970), the first solo album by Paul McCartney, is memorable for several reasons. It includes "Maybe I'm Amazed," one of McCartney's finest songs and strongest recorded studio performances. McCartney played every instrument and he recorded all of the vocals on this album, with the exception of some backgrounds from Linda Eastman McCartney. The release of the album at the same time as The Beatles' *Let It Be* soundtrack and McCartney's announcement of the disbanding of the group was controversial. The *Ram* (1971) album featured the tuneful and well-crafted musical arrangement of "Uncle Albert/Admiral Halsey," with its tempo-changes and bright harmonies. The album also included "The Back Seat of My Car." In 1971, McCartney formed the band Wings, including guitarist Denny Laine. The band's first album was *Wild Life* (1971). The single "Hi, Hi, Hi" ruffled some sensibilities with its apparent advocacy of getting high on drugs. "Live and Let Die" provided an energetic theme song for a James Bond film. *Red Rose Speedway* (1973) included the #1 single "My Love" with McCartney's clear and distinctive vocal. *Band on the Run* (1973), arguably the strongest McCartney-Wings album of the 1970s, followed. Along with the title cut, which received extensive radio airplay, was the hit "Jet." McCartney and group received the Grammy for Best Pop Vocal Performance. *Venus and Mars* (1975) contained the hit single "Listen to What the Man Said." The band toured internationally, following *Wings at the Speed of Sound* (1976). This album included the hit "Silly Love Songs" which argued that innocuous love songs were just fine and "Let 'Em In" with somebody knocking at the door and a flute and harmony part that was infectious. The arrangements of these songs were among McCartney and band's finest accomplishments during the decade. *London Town* (1978) had the single "With a Little Luck." As the 1970s wound to a close, Wings finished a disco hit "Goodnight Tonight" and its final studio album *Back to the Egg* (1979). In 1980, Paul McCartney released *McCartney II* (1980), his first solo album since 1972.

Solo: *McCartney* (1970), *Ram* (1971), *McCartney II* (1980). With Wings: *Wild Life* (1971), *Red Rose Speedway* (1973), *Band on the Run* (1973), *Venus and Mars* (1975), *Wings at the Speed of Sound* (1976), *London Town* (1978), *Back to the Egg* (1979).

Don McLean

Don McLean's "American Pie," an 8½ minute anthem of intriguing lyrics and cultural critique set to a romping folk-rock rhythm, launched his career beyond folk-music circles. With continual airplay, "American Pie" topped the charts and was soon followed by the reflective "Vincent," a sensitive and image-filled tribute to the painter Vincent Van Gogh. McLean's first album, *Tapestry*, recorded a couple of years before the album *American Pie*, displayed his keen writing and strong folk-guitar and banjo skills. This album included "Castles in the Air" and the song "And I Love You So," later recorded by Perry Como. Unfortunately, it bore the same title as Carole King's extremely successful recording of that same period. McLean had emerged from New Rochelle, played folk clubs, and made troubadour journeys up and down the Hudson River on Pete Seeger's *Clearwater* sloop. "American Pie" was recorded on May 26, 1971. It was first played in New York on WPLJ-FM and WNEW-FM. Widely circulated on radio throughout the United States, the song reached #1 in January and February of 1972. There is clearly an autobiographical element to the song, but it also captures the spirit of a generation. For all of its upbeat musical energy, the song is a disillusioned nostalgic lament that resembles the declension thesis that "sixties" idealism began to wane in the early 1970s. The lyrics, with their references to Buddy Holly, Elvis Presley, The Beatles, The Rolling Stones, and Bob Dylan were interpreted by disc-jockeys, fans, and critics many times over.

The album *Don McLean* which followed was more introspective, folk-music based, and bore a stark black and white cover with a streak of red for the artist's name. "Dreidel" and "If We Try" had a bit brighter tone to them and served as singles. The comic "On the Amazon" offered wordplay on exotic creatures of the region and McLean included it often in his live performances. *Playin' Favorites* followed as an upbeat tribute to some of his musical influences, including Buddy Holly's "Everyday" and the Scottish folk song "Mountains of Mourne." *Homeless Brother* (1974) stayed in the folk music genre. It brought reflections on the hobo traveler of the album's title and the story of Andrew McCrew, who was embalmed after death and sold to a circus. The Temptations contributed vocals on "Crying in the Chapel." On "La La Love You," Cissy Houston sang background vocals. Hugh McCracken, who also played on Billy Joel's *The Stranger* album, played some guitar. *Prime Time*, with Arista Records, had a four-color cover of McLean gazing up toward an airplane flying off into the wild blue yonder. Several songs are upbeat, but the production overall seems a bit rushed. Or, rather, it is not as finely crafted and complete and rounded-out as producer Joel Dorn and Don McLean's careful work on *Homeless Brother*. *Prime Time* produced the single "It Doesn't Matter Any More." Songs for the album *Chain Lightning* (1978) were recorded before the release of *Prime Time*. Notably, this album featured Don McLean as a singer. His clear and rich singing voice was especially evident on the Roy Orbison song "Crying."

American Pie (1971)

Don McLean's chord-driven "American Pie" invites us to explore how we remember the music. It has a catchy sing-along chorus and despite its length was a huge hit single. While McLean's song is in some respects autobiographical, it aspires to be an American epic that captures an era. It is busy remembering and generating memories. Listeners tried to interpret the lyrics. "Vincent," his sentimental portrait of painter Vincent Van Gogh, was a poetic lyric with a melody that became a classic. "Till Tomorrow" and "Empty Chairs" bring a reflective quality to this album. The album is viewed as a context—a "Crossroads" where roads lead to where we are tight now. The song signifies a generation that is in some way lost: the wonder, passion, and energy of people who met a world of change during the late 1950s and 1960s. What McLean talks about in *American Pie* is within living memory. The folksinger's commitment to American music includes a look at a cultural canvas of America. We say bye, bye, as in farewell, to Miss American Pie. The All-American Chevy seeks the levee but encounters something like T.S. Eliot's wasteland, a dry levee. As in Eliot's poem, snippets of song seek to find a way to remedy this.

McLean did make people "happy for a while." This is the folksinger's public role: for despite it all, there is an assertion against demise. The chorus of "American Pie" may be conceived of as a rousing drinking song, in the manner of an old English or Celtic ballad. Amid the drinking whiskey and rye, the rollicking piano and rhythmic guitar belie the nostalgic, at times pessimistic, lament of the lyrics. A nostalgic sadness returns in the slower sections, where the music takes a breath. But then there we are, back in that energetic chorus again. There is affirmation here, despite the pessimism. However lagging, idealism is not lost. The world may be going to hell but we're going to make music anyway—like the dance band on the

Titanic. Join together with me and raise a toast to the sky. The generation mentioned here may recall Woodstock specifically, or some less definable air of solidarity.

"Empty Chairs" works as a well-played and sung reflective center for the album. It has some of the melodic qualities of McLean's "Castles in the Air" on his *Tapestry* album. There is a confessional tone to "Crossroads." He feels tied up within himself. No one can identify what his malaise is about. However, he recognizes that there is change. The singer proclaims that all roads come together to where he now is. He has gone down those roads, whatever his original plans may have been. "Winterwood" is a breezy folk-tune suggesting a bare woodland in the winter season. With "Everybody Loves Me Baby (What's the Matter with You?)" gives us an up-tempo tune that seems to include some self-critique as well as some criticism of the interlocutor. "Sister Fatima," "The Grave," and the traditional chorus round of "Babylon" offer a somewhat somber ending.

Tapestry (1970), *American Pie* (1971), *Don McLean* (1972), *Playin' Favorites* (1973), *Homeless Brother* (1974), *Prime Time* (1977), *Chain Lightning* (1978).

Ralph McTell

Folksinger Ralph McTell has been most influential in folk music circles in the UK since the 1960s. He is clearly best known for his song "Streets of London," which offers a compassionate response to a landscape of poverty and human need. He has drawn upon the styles of American blues players in his music. He plays guitar, piano, and harmonica. "The Streets of London" was recorded in one take for an album developed in 1968. *You Well-Meaning Brought Me Here* (1971) included "The Ferryman," a song inspired by Hermann Hesse's novel *Siddhartha*. "Streets of London" was also recorded again. McTell played at the Royal Festival Hall and the Isle of Wight Festival. He also played in Belfast and throughout Northern Ireland despite The Troubles. He spent some time with members of Fairport Convention. *Not till Tomorrow* (1972) was followed by tours in 1973, including performing at Royal Albert Hall. Upon releasing his album *Streets* (1976) McTell played at the Montreux Festival. He recorded *Right Side Up* (1976) and ended the year with a Christmas concert in Belfast. He concluded the decade with *Slide Away the Peg* (1970), recorded with Simon Nicol, Dave Pegg, and Richard Thompson.

You Well-Meaning Brought Me Here (1971), *Not till Tomorrow* (1972), *Easy* (1974), *Streets* (1975), *Right Side Up* (1976), *Ralph, Albert, and Sidney* (1977) (live album), *Slide Away the Peg* (1979).

Melanie (Melanie Safka)

She went by her first name professionally, so let's place her here, as Melanie. She is perhaps best known for her song "Brand New Key," a 1971–72 hit. Her family background is Ukrainian on her father's side and Italian on her mother's side. She was born in Astoria, Queens and the family moved to Red Bank, New Jersey. She attended the Academy of Dramatic Arts and played at a coffeehouse in Long Branch and at the Bitter End in Greenwich Village. Her song "Beautiful People" (1969) preceded the 1970s and can be connected with her first recordings on Buddah Records. "Lay Down (Candles in the Rain)" recalls her Woodstock performance during which lights appeared from the crowd in front of her. They were mostly cigarette lighters, but candles are a more romantic thought. She left Buddah Records in 1971 and recorded "Brand New Key" for her own label. The idea came to her after a trip to McDonald's. Roller skates blended with a happy, bright sound. "Ring the Living Bell" and "The Nickel Song," came in 1973. There were many Melanie albums during the 1970s. She also recorded songs on several film soundtracks. Her *Photograph* (1976) album followed and was among those later reissued on CD.

Candles in the Rain (1970), *Leftover Wine* (1970), *Gather Me* (1971), *The Good Book* (1971), *The Four Sides of Melanie* (1972), *Garden in the City* (1972), *Stoneground Words* (1972), *Melanie at Carnegie Hall* (1973), *Madrugada* (1974), *As I See It Now* (1975), *Sunset and Other Beginnings* (1975), *Photograph* (1976), *Phonogenic: Not Just Another Pretty Face* (1978), *Ballroom Streets* (1979).

Steve Miller

The pop-songwriter and blues player Steve Miller is best known for his work with the Steve Miller Band. He was the central singer and songwriter in this band. The prominence of his songs on the pop charts also argues for his inclusion here. Steve Miller did indeed perform solo, primarily as a blues guitarist. He became an important pop-rock writer in the 1970s. It is a stretch to call him a singer-songwriter, since he was rarely heard outside of the context of his band.

Although he was born in Milwaukee, Steve Miller's family moved to Dallas, Texas, where he picked up most of his southern blues and familiarity with country and rockabilly. His focus was the guitar and the blues, and he was encouraged by musicians to pursue this. He studied English literature for a time at the University of Wisconsin. Miller played with Buddy Guy, Muddy Waters, Howlin' Wolf, and Chicago blues players. He went back to Texas and then to San Francisco, where he got involved in the scene that was beginning to ripen there during the mid–1960s. The Steve Miller Band emerged during this period.

In the 1970s, there was a string of hit singles by Steve Miller: "Take the Money and Run," "Fly Like an Eagle," "Rock n' Me," "Jungle Love," "Jet Airliner," "The Joker."

Number 5 (1970), *Rock Love* (1971), *Recall the Beginning* (1972), *The Joker* (1973), *Fly Like an Eagle* (1976), *Book of Dreams* (1977).

Joni Mitchell

Joni Mitchell's precise, thoughtful lyrics abound in specific images. They are swept up in tuneful melodies that run from the purest folk to the most eclectic jazz. As a singer her voice is high and rangy, taking off in scat-like vocal excursions. Words and images spring from her poetic sense of sound of language and the visual art of a painter. When Joni Mitchell sang her songs, it was like little windows of wisdom began to open. The sky was filled with clouds like angel hair and ice cream castles. One could conjure rich imaginative possibilities by looking at life that way. Her listeners went round and round with her in a circle game of life. They were drawn into jazz influences with Charles Mingus. Joni Mitchell had a beautiful way with language, varying line lengths, playing with interesting rhythms. She wrote songs about relationships and personalized experience. "Help me," she sang when falling fast in love, echoing the experience of many of her listeners.

From her youth in Calgary to Alberta, where she was an art student, Joni Mitchell (Roberta Joan Anderson) entered folk music circles, married into the world of the Chad Mitchell Trio, and then began to sing in folk clubs, including in New York City. Her performing debut was at the Mariposa Folk Festival in Toronto. She was signed by Warner Brothers–Reprise. Joni Mitchell moved to Laurel Canyon in Los Angeles. Her first album, produced by David Crosby, was folksy, with high ringing vocals. One side was filled with city songs and the other with country songs. Her second album, *Clouds,* includes her well-known songs "Both Sides Now" and "Chelsea Morning." ("Both Sides Now" first was presented on Gene Shay's folk music radio show in Philadelphia.)

Ladies of the Canyon followed, drawing upon her West coast experience. The album features "For Free" in which she comments on hearing a street musician playing clarinet for free. "Big Yellow Taxi" is one of the earliest pop songs to address environmental concerns. In the hook she asks a question that arises as a recognition. When it's gone is when a person realizes what he or she once had. In this case, one of those things is a natural environment: a paradise that has been paved over for a parking lot. The modern world has come with the big yellow taxi. That hope for a paradise that will not be encroached upon emerges in "Woodstock": Joni Mitchell's anthemic tribute to a festival she could not attend because of her commitment to a television interview in New York. The song, written in a hotel room, caught fire with Stephen Stills' reworking of it for a Crosby, Stills, Nash and Young recording. Her relationship with them continued for several years. While she was living with Graham Nash, he wrote the song "Our House," which was recorded by CSN.

Blue is an album of song-poetry. Some critics have regarded it as a high point in Joni Mitchell's creative work. Here Joni Mitchell brings her folk music into connection with rock. She plays "All I Want" on dulcimer and sets a calypso beat. Her voice rides over her dulcimer playing. James Taylor plays guitar. She wants to be free and alive. "My Old Man" and "Little Green," "California," and "Carey" follow, with contributions from Stephen Stills on bass and guitar.

Court and Spark (1974) was a bright album that was promoted with a wide-ranging tour. The recording had a pop sound. Mitchell's songs became less folk song structured, more open-ended jazz sounding. With her next album, *The Hissing of Summer Lawns* (1975), came a further turn toward jazz. Her seventh studio album opened with "In France They Kiss on Main Street." The painter Henri Rousseau's world of city, music, and drugs was the artistic palette for Mitchell's song. "Jungle Line" involved a sampling of African musicians drumming from Burundi. "Edith and the Kingpin" moves back into jazz with the story of an underworld figure. "Don't Interrupt the Sorrow" drifts in a stream of consciousness flow. "Shades of Scarlett Conquering" provides the story of a southern belle who emerges like a saint from the fire of mystical union. She then imitates Scarlett O'Hara of *Gone with the Wind*, as if she is living in a sentimental movie. Mitchell drew upon the work of jazz composer Charles Mingus. Mingus passed away while in Mexico in January 1979. An acoustic-electric mix of musical fragments appeared soon afterward. Mitchell titled her final album of the decade *Mingus* (1979).

The life and work of Joni Mitchell is presented in *Joni Mitchell: Reckless Daughter* (2017), a fine biography by David Yaffe. Further insights into her work can be discovered in her conversations with Malka Marom in *Joni Mitchell in Her Own Words* (2014).

Blue (1971)

Is Joni Mitchell's *Blue* a wistful longing for adventure or for a return home? Is her weave of songs a reckless dance with sensitivity? There is throughout this album a theme of seeking love, traveling, and seeking home. Listeners may get the impression that this is an album, not merely a collection of songs. These songs flow from one into the next with a well-paced continuity and a balance of dulcimer, piano, guitar, and vocals. There is an emphasis upon personal experience and a call to be fully alive right where one lives. Lyrically, Joni Mitchell's songs are filled with vulnerability, direct address, and imagery. The details of objects and places situate us while her themes are universal. Her vocal flies, careens, cavorts and takes us on a ride of flight. One may hear jazz tendencies in her enjambment of vowels, words that sometimes rush through a line, breaking rhythm or disrupting metrical pattern. Her soprano reaches up over the treble clef, like a delicate bird sky-bound, lifting then diving. The album unfolds as a unity that is focused in tone, storytelling, and musical approach.

"All I Want" begins rhythmically with dulcimer chords, guitar, and the statement that she is on a road traveling. That key word traveling is repeated several times. She addresses a lover that she both loves and hates "some." Rhymes flow in threes: fun, sun, one and sweater, letter, feel better. Mitchell's soprano voice climbs and dives alongside a Latin-inflected guitar part and a bass pulse. She announces hopes for their love. There is a quest for love and laughter and cherishing and affirming life. The rhythms are jagged and bright.

The second cut, "My Old Man," comes to us on piano. There is a chord based folk kind of playing rather than musicianship of classical training. The narrator describes her live-in partner, the mean old daddy she likes. They have no need of a marriage license. We see him as a park singer, a dancer in darkness. We witness walks in the rain and the sunshine of morning. On "My Old Man" we hear a descending line and there is a bending of some blues notes. Vocally, she sustains the open vowels on the end of lines. The melodic dynamics continue in notes up above the staff.

Guitar arpeggios move us into the ballad form of the third song, "Little Green." The guitar sounds as if it the guitarist may be using a capo and playing these patterns up the neck of the instrument. There is a light pickup on this. We are given images of northern lights, perhaps Canada. "Little Green" is a song from 1967, a lyric that appears in a shape or form on the inside jacket of this album. There are northern lights and icicles, a child, and birthday clothes,

On "Carey," we return to the sound of the dulcimer and rhythmic percussion. Stephen Stills' bass propels the song. There are images of travel, a tourist town, the wind in from Africa. We hear the rhythm of an island-calypso and we come down to the Mermaid Café. At the center is the figure of Carey. Maybe he can be mean. Even so, she likes him.

The title song "Blue" concludes side one on atmospheric and reflective chord-based piano patterns. "Blue" feels private, personal, and inward. In "Blue," songs are tattoos. There is the shell in which one hears an echo and there is a melody open and unresolved. It seems to be the only "blue" song on an otherwise bright and rhythmic album. The most arresting image may be the foggy lullaby heard inside a shell. A descending arpeggio brings us to the song's end.

The dulcimer brings us into the chords, high vocals, and tonal brightness on "California." On the word "California," up goes Joni Mitchell's vocal. James Taylor supports this song on guitar and Russ Kunkel moves the song along with bass pedal and high hat on the drums. From the mention of Paris, Spain, and Grecian isles to that of California, the listener travels with the speaker. We see people reading popular magazines. Words get rushed, packed into lines. Percussion pushes the song along, in a bright, wistful, longing for home. There is a sense of wandering, anticipation, celebration. The times seem turbulent and peace is not being given a chance: this may be a commentary on European and American culture from 1968 to 1971.

A strummed guitar opens the next track, up-tempo, "This Flight Tonight." The loneliness of travel comes through "This Flight Tonight," "Blue," and "A Case of You." "On This Flight" brings the view from an airplane, a stream of consciousness lyric. "O Canada" appears within the lyric. The scene is one of lights viewed from an airplane, which is like a falling star over Las Vegas' sands. The flightpath seems to be guided by the stars. Down there is a town. Maybe it is someone's home. The flight and the lyric are consistent with the sense of wandering and drift in this part of the recording.

"River," four minutes long, is self-reflective, a Christmas song. Piano begins in a melody a little like "Jingle Bells" and we are in the Christmas season. Chords support this and the vocal drifts into a quieter reflection. She wishes to skate away on the river. The lyric is directed again to her paramour, telling a story. We are brought to a piano ending.

The lap dulcimer chord pattern returns. "A Case of You" is conversational. The lyric includes dialogue and direct address to an intimate. The singer ponders a time just before their love got lost. She views herself as a painter living in a box of paints. You are in my blood, she says to him, and it is like holy wine. This suggests a sacred aspect to this relationship. The song ends in a chord pattern.

Piano flows through the final song, "The Last Time I Saw Richard." Recalling Richard in 1968 when he was a romantic radical, she remarks on the fall of the romantic and fading hopes. The song tells the story of café days which have dissolved into a middle-class mediocrity of drinking alone at home. The piano concludes the album on a single chord.

Ladies of the Canyon (1970), *Blue* (1971), *For the Roses* (1972), *Court and Spark* (1974), *The Hissing of Summer Lawns* (1975), *Hejira* (1976), *Don Juan's Reckless Daughter* (1977), *Mingus* (1979).

Christy Moore

From County Kildare, Ireland, Christy Moore is a political folksinger and brother of singer-songwriter Luka Bloom. He produced *Paddy on the Road* (1969) and built a songwriting-performing career in the 1970s that involved left-wing liberal Republican views. He formed Planxty for performances and this extended to about 1975. Christy Moore plays a rhythmic guitar that pushes his songs forward. His 1970s albums were *Whatever Tickles Your Fancy* (1974), *The Iron Behind the Velvet* (1975), and *Live in Dublin* (1978). Performances and recordings were filled with political critique songs. "Viva la Quinta" is about Irish recruits fighting against Franco in the Spanish Civil War. He supported the H Block prisoners in their 1978 hunger strike. "Back Home in Derry" is from Bobby Sands, the hunger striker.

Whatever Tickles Your Fancy (1974), *The Iron Behind the Velvet* (1975), *Live in Dublin* (1978).

Tim Moore

Beyond his music, Tim Moore has an interest in social psychology and computer interfaces. In the early 1970s, the quality of his work as a singer-songwriter was clear. His first album, *Tim Moore* (1974), was completed by Moore's double-tracking guitar, vocals, keyboards and bass parts over drum tracks. Both Clive Davis and David Geffen sought to have him record with their companies. The first album was reissued by Asylum Records. Moore's first single was "A Fool Like You" (1973). Eric Andersen and Iain Matthews also recorded "I'm a Fool Like You." Moore's piano-accompanied vocal on "Second Avenue" rises to meet the imagery and sentiment. Art Garfunkel later covered the song. We also hear the single "Charmer," and "Aviation Man" and "I'll Be Your Time," among his other songs. *Behind the Eyes* (1975) album was recorded at Bearsville Studio in Woodstock and included the involvement of Peter Tork. On "A Fool Like You" Donald Fagen provided background vocals. "Rock and Roll Love Letter" (1976) provided a bright pop musical vehicle for the Bay City Rollers. *White Shadows* (1977) was his third album and included Michael McDonald, Jeff Porcaro, Timothy B. Schmitt among the musicians. "In the Middle" (1977) was the single from this album.

Behind the Eyes (1975)

"For the Minute," "Lay Down a Line," "(I Think I Wanna) Possess You," "Now I See," "Rock and Roll Love Letter," "If Somebody Needs It," "The Night We First Sailed Away," "Captain Kidd," "Sweet Navel Lightning," "Bye Bye Man."

"For the Minute" opens in bright piano which is joined by strings. He counsels that while you've been upset, it's just for the minute. Give life a chance. We're only alive for the minute, so embrace life. There is a Paul McCartney meets Gilbert O'Sullivan quality to this song. It is piano driven and grows big with strings and some vocal backgrounds. In "Lay Down a Line" piano streams out and the singer looks for news as he returns to someone. This track sounds like an Elton John song in structure and in manner. Moore's vocal is surrounded by background vocals and then surrounded by orchestration. "Possess You" is soul-pop-rock punctuated by rhythmic piano, drums, chunky bass, and funk rhythm. The band provides a steady pulse and there is a strong and lengthy guitar lead down the center of this song. Later there is an organ solo. Moore's rock voice is accompanied by a big background chorus. "Now I See" also has this 4/4 ballad shuffle and a clear voice over piano and background vocals. "Rock and Roll Love Letter" is an up-tempo pop-rock romp that was recorded by the Bay City Rollers. Each of the first lines is responded to by an instrumental line. It all leads to a chorus. This innocuous pop ditty about a music man's letter to the world ends side one.

The strongest song on side two is arguably the ballad "The Night We First Sailed Away." The piano takes us into a song which suggests an evolution of humanity. There is anthropology in the hunter and wind in the caves. Humanity has evolved like arteries from mother earth. The ape may not evolve enough to achieve a state of grace, but humanity is still hopeful. Yet, are we in a cage that is revolving and can dissolve into tears? The singer declares that our purpose is clear. Bells on the cliffs ring out and we hear the ocean's song as we recall sailing to the sea. The production enlarges. Ultimately, the speaker directs his attention to one who is like Eve in the garden and is perhaps a hope for tomorrow.

"Sweet Navel Lightning" is a rock tune in 4/4 with backbeat, built up with guitar, bass, drums, and backing vocals. The word "sweet" is held out. Mama's a trauma and papa is proper and regretting how she turned out. Ah, but she's so nice, so roll the dice. The guitars and vocals have pop rock written all over them.

Tim Moore (1974), *Second Avenue* (1974), *Behind the Eyes* (1975), *High Contrast* (1979).

Van Morrison

From his time with Them in the 1960s ("Gloria"), Van Morrison emerged as an iconoclastic, spiritually reflective singer-songwriter. He created the often-played "Brown Eyed Girl" in the 1960s, with its sha-la-la hook. "Moondance," from 1970, has become a standard of classic rock and pop radio airplay. Soul and R&B merge in his music with Celtic spirit and with something like an improvisational quest in his performances. This is when a stream of consciousness mode of singing his tunes surfaces. His family roots are Belfast Protestant Irish, and his musical roots are rock and soul. The title of his song "Into the Mystic" describes his spiritual quest. He was described by Greil Marcus and Lester Bangs in *Rolling Stone* (March 17, 1970) as "a consciousness that is visionary in the strongest sense of the word."

Morrison's band Them gave us "Here Comes the Night" and "Gloria" and "Mystic Eyes." Morrison created four singles for Bang Records. "Brown Eyed Girl" went to #10 in 1967. Warner Brothers then signed him, and he brought together a group of jazz musicians; jazz improvisation met with Irish romantic mysticism on *Astral Weeks* (1968). Morrison lived in Woodstock, New York, for a time and brought together a horn section for *Moondance* (1970), his next album. He recorded "Into the Mystic" and so did Johnny Rivers, for whom the song became a hit. Morrison moved to California and *His Band and the Street Choir* followed with the singles "Domino," "Tupelo Honey," and "Wild Night."

Moondance (1970) was a well-crafted album. The free-floating style of *His Band and Street Choir* (1970) included the song "Domino." *Tupelo Honey* (1971) brought the songs "Wild Nights," "Tupelo Honey," and the country closer "Moonshine Whiskey." Morrison sought a free, live sound on this recording, one uninhibited by second and third takes and overdubbing. *St. Dominic's Preview*, which followed, created the improvisational landscape.

By 1973 he had formed an 11-piece group that called themselves the Caledonia Soul Orchestra. For *Veedon Fleece* (1974) drew upon his time in Ireland and created a quite poetic album. For the next couple of years, Morrison took time off to regather, and to listen to music and to life. He re-emerged with the aptly titled *Period of Transition*. *Wavelength*, with its pop sensibility, sold briskly. *Into the Music* (1979) gathered spiritual-religious themes.

Van Morrison once told an interviewer: "I am an inspirational writer" (10). By this he seems to mean that he regards his music as a medium that is inspired and through which he may inspire others. Morrison's music resists categorization as rock and owes much to the blues and gospel. From these traditions he draws inspiration and transforms his work into an inspiration.

Rock critic Lester Bangs observed Morrison's repetitions of single words or phrases. Van Morrison told his interviewer: "I release the words into singing syllables ... signs and phrases." (Miles, Introduction). Dave Marsh asserted that neither Bruce Springsteen, Bob Seger, or Gram Parsons "has yet taken the spiritual basis of rock and rhythm and blues and the blues so far into an almost religious concept" as Van Morrison (25).

St. Dominic's Preview (1972)

With *St. Dominic's Preview* (1972), Van Morrison drifted back to the spirit of *Astral Weeks'* (1968) introspection, innovation, and openness. "Listen to the Lion" and "Almost Independence Day" stretch out across more than ten minutes each. The album's opening cut "Jackie Wilson Said" is a mix of jazz-blues or soul-folk. The song was reworked a few times before recording began. "Gypsy" in double time and triple time evokes the exotic with layered guitars. "I Will Be There" presents daily, material life, as he gathers his clothes. Side One closes on "Listen to the Lion," which was initially going to be on the album *Tupelo Honey*. On Side Two, the title track "St. Dominic's Preview" bring together soul and folk. "Redwood Tree" embraces a sense of nature. On "Almost Independence Day" a Moog synthesizer is used, with a repetition of two chords. There is an image of looking out across the bay of San Francisco. The *Astral Weeks'* emphasis on meditation returns with this composition.

In *The Words and Music of Van Morrison* (Praeger, 2009), Erik Hage writes of this album that "it is one of the strongest albums in the Van Morrison canon." He observes that the recording embodies past signature moves of Van Morrison while opening new horizons with stylistic experimentation. In *Rolling Stone* (August 31, 1972) Stephen Holden observed that the record shows versatility and the "coexistence of two styles." Peter Wrench has written about this album—*St. Dominic's Flashback: Van Morrison's Classic Album, 40 Years On* which is available via Feed-A-Read on Kindle. You may gain some insight into Van Morrison's songwriting through Bob Sarlin's *Turn It Up! (I Can't Hear the Words)* (New York: Coronet, 1975).

There are several more Van Morrison biographies and analyses of his music, lyrics, recordings, and performances: Brian Hinton, *Celtic Crossroads: The Art of Van Morrison*, Sanctuary, 1997; Clinton Heylin, *Can You Feel the Silence: Van Morrison, A New Biography*, Chicago Review Press, 2003; Greil Marcus, *When That Rough God Goes Riding: Listening to Van Morrison*, Public Affairs, 2010; Peter Mills, *Hymns to the Silence: The Words and Music of Van Morrison*, London and New York: Continuum,

2010; Steve Turner, *Van Morrison: Too Late to Stop Now*, Viking Penguin, 1993; Ritchie Yorke, *Van Morrison: Into the Music*, Charisma Books, 1975.

Moondance (1970), *His Band and the Street Choir* (1970), *Tupelo Honey* (1971), *St. Dominic's Preview* (1972), *Hard Nose the Highway* (1973), *Veedon Fleece* (1974), *A Period of Transition* (1977), *Wavelength* (1978), *Into the Music* (1979).

Michael Murphey

In his 1970s incarnation, Michael Martin Murphey was the singer of "Wildfire," a soulful and sentimental hit about a horse lost on a winter night. The album *Blue Sky–Night Thunder* (1976) also included his song "Carolina in the Pines." The record, in a peach-colored cover, was produced by Bob Johnston, who he teamed up with when he was signed by A&M Records in 1971. At that point, while in Texas, he was blending country, rock, blues, and folk. From Nashville to *Cosmic Cowboy Souvenir* (1973) it became clear that he was destined to be mostly a country artist. Yet, he had an urban cowboy redneck persona like Willie Nelson. Middle-America heard a fine voice, clear and rich in tone, plaintively calling for Wildfire. The song told the story of a ghost and a ghost horse. Michael Martin Murphey as he came to be called was recognized as a singer-songwriter whose songs would be recorded by several country artists.

Geronimo's Cadillac (1971), *Cosmic Cowboy Souvenir* (1973), *Michael Murphey* (1974), *Blue Sky–Night Thunder* (1975), *Swans Against the Sun* (1976), *Flowing Free Forever* (1976), *Lone Wolf* (1978); *Peaks, Valleys, Honkey Tonks, and Alleys* (1979).

Elliott Murphy

The energy and rock and roll vitality of Elliott Murphy's first recording is indisputable. "The Last of the Rock Stars" bursts out at you like the flicker of fire from a lighted match. He still plays the song, on an acoustic guitar, as well as when he is joined by a band. He also plays "Drive All Night" and other songs from his back-catalog. That song by Elliott Murphy, a musician from Long Island, was one heard by Bruce Springsteen in Freehold, New Jersey, when he began writing songs about seeing burnt out Chevrolets, Mary leaning on the hood of Dodge, and driving all night. *Aquashow* (1973) blasted out with harmonica and organ, up-tempo rollicking guitar and catchy horns. There was a sure rock attitude running through the songs on this album. One critic said that Bob Dylan met with Scott Fitzgerald's *The Great Gatsby* on Elliott Murphy's songs. He liked Fitzgerald, of course, and he was a wordsmith like Dylan; or he was a rock songwriter who used a lot of words in his songs. There was that similarity also with the early albums of Springsteen: they seemed to want to write books as well as rock down Thunder Road. *Lost Generation* (1975) was produced by Paul Rothchild, who had produced The Doors. *The Night Lights* (1976), *Just a Story from America* (1977). He had guests sitting in on recordings. They included Springsteen, the Long Island singer-songwriter Billy Joel, David Johanssen, the Violent Femmes. He is often joined for performances by guitarist Olivier Durand.

There are several performances by Elliott Murphy in recent years available online. Also see the biography *Elliott Murphy, Hardcore* (2015) by Charles Pitter. In *Rolling Stone* (July 17, 1975).

Aquashow (1973), *Night Lights* (1976), *Just a Story from America* (1977).

Graham Nash

While he is perhaps best known for his work with Crosby, Stills, and Nash, or his contributions as a member of The Hollies, Graham Nash recorded two albums of his own material in the 1970s. He also produced several records by other musicians. Graham Nash's *Song for Beginners* (1971) has a minstrel quality. He was a strong harmonizer with The Hollies and throughout the recordings of Crosby, Stills, and Nash. He also sang in a duo with David Crosby, recorded at Wally Heider's studio in San Francisco.

Songs for Beginners (1971)

Graham Nash's first solo album is song-driven. It is folk music based and tends to be more lyric centered than Crosby's record. The liner notes quip "All Artists Appear Courtesy of Themselves." And guest artists there are: Rita Coolidge, Jerry Garcia, Dave Mason, Joe Yankee, Phil Lesh, saxophonist Dorian Rudnitsky, and the improbably named Seeman Posthuma. Nash appears on the cover in a self-portrait, as if in a mirror in a garden, holding a camera. The album sleeve insert is a sharp black and white photo by Joel Bernstein that shows Nash intently perusing reports on the state of the world in an open newspaper. Bill Halverson was the recording engineer for this album, along with Larry Cox and Russ Gary. Nathaniel Kunkel remixed the tracks in Maui. Nash begins the album with "Military Madness" and concludes with "Chicago."

"Military Madness" is about his father in wartime Britain in the 1940s. Nash traces a bit of his own autobiography and reflects upon how his father's experience of war and his own intersected with how the war affected the country. The song sounds the keynote of social concern about war and peace and the note of nostalgia or memory that winds through this album, along with its wistful romantic feelings. "Military Madness" opens on a full strum of the acoustic guitar and moves along with a bounce. A wah-wah pedal adds its distinctive color and later becomes the sound of a guitar lead.

"Better Days," which follows, is in one sense a hopeful recollection and a meditation on love that has gone away. In the lyric the speaker recognizes a search for love and truth in a strange land. Nash's vocal is front and center and very present above a piano that is then joined by guitar, bass, and a gated drum sound heightened with a touch of reverb. Nash's vocal jumps an octave over a slow march rhythm. There is a tempo change introduced by a piano and this is accompanied by Beatles-like background harmonies. A beautiful saxophone solo breaks in melodically and the song fades on a drum pattern, sax, and background vocals.

"Wounded Bird" brings an acoustic guitar and a quiet, intimate vocal and an ABAB rhyme scheme. The song is addressed to someone who has gone through difficulties. It counsels that a person has to love himself and balance humility with pride. A minstrel image of a wandering hobo or knight who faces danger for the sake of the lady enters the song. The wounded bird could be Crosby, but the personal tone of this song also gives it a universal quality embracing anyone who has been wounded in some way.

"I Used to Be King" may be a self-critique. One can have big dreams and feel like a king but if one builds on sand those illusions can all be swept away. The sand shifts and the dream disintegrates. This is also a love song that asks questions, considers overcoming loss and hurt, and vows to not be heartbroken again. It begins in 3/4 time and then jumps to double-time only to slow back to a steady 3/4. Nash doubles his vocal. Jerry Garcia adds the steel pedal guitar that CSN&Y listeners would also hear on Nash's song "Teach Your Children." The song "Be Yourself" has a chorus "comprised of everyone loose there," say the liner notes. With the strummed acoustic-guitar the folk music quality of Nash's album continues. This song is not the quite the spontaneous sounding hippie fest of Crosby's "Music is Love" but it is similar in its communal spirit. The singer begins by asking what it feels like when drifting aimlessly. There may be a trace of the Biblical in references to a lost savior and the prodigal son's return. The song seems to be about self-awareness and authenticity. It argues against computers or mechanisms that may shut off true vision, or TV broadcasts that may teach lies. There is a call to be true to oneself and set oneself free.

With "Simple Man," Nash speaks of singing songs and playing tunes and addresses someone in a sincere sounding love song. He recognizes a need for her companionship and realizes that alone he might not make it. There is a simple chord-based piano part. Rita Coolidge adds a nice vocal that complements Nash's. Dorian Rudnitsky contributes stirring lines on a fiddle. "Man in the Mirror" beginning in 3/4 time is almost country-sounding. The mirror seems to be a through-line on this album: an image of self-reflection, like the album sleeve cover image. In this song, the singer is walking on a wire, as if he is a performer in a circus. Even living at this height—in a tree, or in the air—does not mean that one is free. The tempo increases and we hear Hollies or Beatles-like harmonies. The title is appropriate: this is a song of self-reflection.

"There's Only One" favors a locked end rhyme. It begins by moving from "-all" to "-ool" (five times each). This is broken up by three short lines that end "on," "one," "in." The song continues with the end rhyme of "-ace" three times followed by the matching off-rhyme "waste" and "taste." A saxophone solo returns and is joined by "ooo" background vocals as the song plays out to the end. "Sleep Song" begins with a simple strum of the guitar and a quiet, intimate vocal that sounds almost like a lullaby. The lyric speaks of the exchange of a kiss and a couple's arms placed around each other. The singer asks if it was all a dream and watches the lover leave, seeing a trace of her disappearing through a doorway. It is as if he has captured the moment in a camera frame and then the image has evaporated. Yet, as the lover vanishes, he makes a promise of a return to that intimacy they knew together. The song slips into a beautiful vocal round.

"Chicago" is the song that declares that we can change the world by attending to the call of justice, by being uniquely individual yet joining in solidarity. (Nash slips in a caustic reference to the "silent majority" of the Nixon years.) "Chicago" opens on drums and organ and moves into an insistent march. Nash's assertive doubled-vocal rises over the top on the chorus. His vocal and the five female backing vocalists singing in unison lift the song to further insistence and an almost jubilant declaration of purpose. People need freedom beyond regulation and freedom is a possibility. We can create that change.

Songs for Beginners (1971), *Wild Tales* (1974).

Willie Nelson

On the road again often at least since the 1970s, Willie Nelson became one of the most visible of the country singer-songwriters. He is perhaps best known for his recordings of his songs "On the Road Again" and "To All the Girls I've Loved Before." He has provided songs for several recording artists, notably "Crazy" for Patsy Cline. There was "Funny How Time Slips Away," "Hello Walls," "Pretty Paper." After a half-dozen albums in the early years of the 1970s, he emerged forcefully into the public eye, with the albums *Shotgun Willie* (1973), *Phases and Stages* (1974), an album about divorce, and *Red-Headed Stranger* (1975). He joined Waylon Jennings, Jessi Colter, Tompall Glaser for *Wanted, The Outlaws* (1975). The outlaw persona was developed to combat the increasing movement of country toward commercial pop that was embraced by artists like Dolly Parton with "Nine to Five." Willie Nelson was among those who sought something closer to country roots. However, he also became widely popular and more relevant in commercial terms. There was *The Troublemaker* (1976), *The Sound of Your Mind* (1976), *To Lefty from Willie* (1977), *Stardust* (1978). He concluded the decade by recording an album of Kris Kristofferson songs and his album *Pretty Paper* (1979). In the 1980s he would be one of the Highwaymen with Johnny Cash, Waylon Jennings, and Kris Kristofferson. See *Willie: An Autobiography*. New York: Simon and Schuster, 1988. *Roll Me Up and Smoke Me When I Die: Musings from the Road*. Foreword by Kinky Friedman. New York: William Morrow, 2008.

Both Sides Now (1970), *Laying My Burdens Down* (1970), *Willie Nelson and Family* (1971), *Yesterday's Wine* (1971), *The Words Don't Fit the Picture* (1972), *The Willie Way* (1973), *Shotgun Willie* (1974), *Phases and Stages* (1975), *The Troublemaker* (1976), *The Sound of Your Mind* (1976), *To Lefty from Willie* (1977), *Stardust* (1978), *Willie Nelson Sings the Songs of Kristofferson* (1979), *Pretty Paper* (1979).

Randy Newman

From pop songs to film scores, across a range of songwriting styles, Randy Newman has composed some of the most familiar music of our time. He has also crossed singing styles on his recordings and contributed lyrical twists of humor and satire. There is in his work the skill of a composer-arranger, the influence of some blues and Ray Charles, some southern drawl, and an unmistakable wittiness. Randy Newman writes songs from the viewpoint of invented characters. He injects irony, social comment, and humor into several of his songs.

Newman has been well-known for writing songs recorded by other artists and for his film scores. There was a long string of recordings of his songs from the 1960s by Petula Clark, Dusty Springfield, the O'Jays, Pat Boone, Jackie De Shannon, Gene Pitney, and many others. "Sail Away"

(1972) and "Short People" (1977) were among his 1970s hits as a solo artist at his piano. As 1970 began, a full album of his songs had been recorded by Harry Nilsson on *Nilsson Sings Newman* (1970). Three Dog Night had a hit with his song "Mama Told Me Not to Come." Randy Newman played piano on recording sessions for other artists. He did the orchestration for Gordon Lightfoot's "If You Could Read My Mind" and the string arrangements on Lightfoot's *Sit Down your Stranger* (1970). His solo album *12 Songs* (1970) appeared. "You Can Leave Your Hat On" (1972) was covered by Three Dog Night and by Joe Cocker. Further solo outings followed. There was a live album in 1971. The *Good Old Boys* (1974) album included "Rednecks," a criticism of racism in the American South and of those who see southerners as racist. He later wrote and sang the memorable theme song "It's a Jungle Out There" for the television series *Monk*. Newman has won or been nominated for many Academy Awards for his film scores.

Sail Away (1972)

Sail Away (1972) became one of Randy Newman's most popular albums of the early 1970s. It underscored Newman's penchant for irony. The title song opens the album. "Lonely at the Top" follows. "He Gives Us All His Love," "Last Night I Had a Dream," "Simon Smith and the Amazing Dancing Bear," and "Old Man." The album's second side opens with "Political Science" and "Burn On," which refers to pollution in the Cuyahoga River which passes Cleveland and caught fire from pollution in 1969. The second album side also includes "You Can Leave Your Hat On." Stephen Holden in *Rolling Stone* called the album confirmation that Newman was the most sophisticated pop art song composer at work in 1972. He regarded "God's Song," which concludes the album as Newman's most "far-reaching" song to date. Spiritual vision is challenged by the pain and suffering in the world. In his review, Holden identified a wide range of resources from which Newman draws, including classical composers like Mahler and Copland to Tin Pan Alley and Great American Songbook composers like George and Ira Gershwin and Jerome Kern, as well as pop, blues, and other styles. Rhino Records reissued the album in 2002.

12 Songs (1970), *Sail Away* (1972), *Good Old Boys* (1974), *Little Criminals* (1977), *Born Again* (1979).

Harry Nilsson

Nilsson Schmilsson (1971) was a top album with a #1 hit single, "Without You," written by Pete Hamm and Tom Evans of Badfinger. Nilsson's own songs filled out most of the albums. "Coconut" was a silly novelty song sung in four different voices. The lime was put in the coconut, and some-one ate it up. And why? Who knows? Who cares? It was dumb and it was fun. "Jump Into the Fire" was another notable song on the album. In 1970, Nilsson had sung a full album of Randy Newman songs, who, as most lis-teners will recognize, is a songwriter who can also write quirky and witty lyrics. Nilsson was born in Brooklyn to parents who were performers in an "aerial ballet." He was a vocalist with a reach of more than two octaves. He recorded a hit with Fred Neil's "Everybody's Talking." The vocal group Three Dog Night turned his song "One" into a hit. On *Harry* (1969) was the song "I Guess the Lord Must Be in New York City." The Beatles once commented that their favorite American band was Harry Nilsson. He had become a Los Angeles–based song writer and a friend of Ringo Starr and John Lennon. Nilsson had been pulling out the stops creatively before that. On his second studio album, *Son of Schmilsson* (1972), while going through a divorce, he directed an expletive toward his wife that would not be played on AM or FM radio. Other lyrics were flippant or bawdy. He and Lennon in a period of drinking indulgence in 1973 ran riotously through some Los Angeles clubs. On *A Little Touch of Schmilsson in the Night* (1973), Nilsson sang with an orchestra. His musical choices and lyrics were less commer-cial at this point. He put out into the world what he felt like putting out.

Nilsson Schmilsson (1971), *Aerial Pandemonium Ballet* (1971), *Son of Schmilsson* (1972), *A Little Touch of Schmilsson in the Night* (1973), *Pussy Cats* (1974), *Duit on Mon Dei* (1975), *Sandman* (1976), *That's the Way It Is* (1976), *Knillssonn* (1977). See Alan Shipton, *Nilsson: The Life of a Singer Songwriter*. New York and Oxford: Oxford University Press, 2015.

Laura Nyro

Laura Nyro at the piano was an exceptional songwriter whose songs were frequently covered by other artists. These ranged from Three Dog Night's hit "Eli's Coming" and Blood, Sweat and Tears' hit "And When I Die" to recordings by The Fifth Dimension and Barbra Streisand. Laura Nyro was born Laura Nigro in the Bronx. Her art grew through her listen-ing to Billie Holiday, Judy Garland, Leontyne Price, and classical orchestra pieces. At home, where she developed her piano and composition skills, she could hear her father playing the trumpet. For a time, she became a street singer, singing in the subways and on street corners. It was as a pop songwriter that she made her mark. In the 1960s, Nyro's song "And When I Die" first went to Peter, Paul, and Mary. With *More Than a New Discov-ery*, Laura Nyro appeared on the Verve Folkways label. She appeared at the Monterey Pop Festival, a long-haired Madonna with loose songs that sounded like bursts of inspiration and the rhythm of the city. The Bronx may seem an unlikely place for a folksinger. Yet, in Laura Nyro the emotion and images of the city came to life in a soulful music that was more pop than folk. Between 1968 and 1970, Nyro's songs included "Stone Soul Picnic," "Sweet Blindness," "Save the Country," "Time and Love," and "Wedding Bell Blues." At nineteen, she was forced into a wedding gown for a publicity photo for that song, her first single. *More Than a New Discovery* is filled with commercially crafted songs. David Geffen began the management of her career in 1968–69. Her album *Eli and the 13th Confession* followed.

Eli and the 13th Confession was recorded across a year. It was released in 1969 and continued in circulation throughout 1970. There is a fresh sound to the record and Nyro appears like the figure in a Renaissance portrait on the album cover. The record opens with the song "Lucky" and the rhythms carry us along. In "Sweet Blindness," a dance song, we take a drink of wine. "Poverty Train" could be riding through the Bronx with someone trapped in a ghetto struggle. "Eli" sparkled as one of the highlights of the album and it was soon recorded by Three Dog Night, one of the most popular vocal groups of the time. In "Timer" Nyro apparently is singing to a lover as she reflects on time, life, and death. "Stoned Soul Picnic" was a fun song recorded by The Fifth Dimension. "The Confession" ends the album. It is a song in which she accompanies herself on piano and sings about how love is miraculous.

New York Tendaberry (1969) is less orchestrated, more subdued. Nyro combines ballads with rock and roll and jazz forms. Her words seem more expressions of emotion than discursive statements. The album is more introspective than her previous record. One hears a growing maturity but also an inward turn. There were concerts at Carnegie Hall in 1969. Nyro's introspective turn continued on *Christmas and the Beads of Sweat* (1970), which included innovative songs with curious titles like "Upstairs by a Chinese Lamp" and "When I Was in Freeport, You Were the Main Drag." Duane Allman played lead guitar on that latter tune and Nyro was accompanied by the Muscle Shoals rhythm section. She recorded Carole King and Gerry Goffin's song "Up on the Roof." She also sang about the Vietnam War, with a voice that lamented its casualties. On this song she becomes a voice that affirms that she loves her country even as Madonnas weep. The word war joins tears for all wars of hell that the Madonnas weep. They become ghostlike. As if at some sacred side-altar at Christmas, they extinguish the candles but are still haunting presences.

In 1970–71, Jackson Browne opened for several Laura Nyro concerts. He was beginning his recording career, upon being signed by Asylum Records. In 1971, Asylum Records anticipated signing Laura Nyro to an album contract. However, she stepped away from that deal. With *Gonna Take a Miracle* (1971), Nyro took a step back to her favorite early rock and roll songs. She drifted away from the music industry after marrying David Bianchini: a marriage that lasted about three years. Nyro's first album on the Verve label was re-released by Columbia Records in 1973 as *The First Songs*. While she remained a bit reclusive, away from the world of rock and the music industry, her songs were often heard covered by other artists in the early years of the 1970s. A collection of Nyro's songs, *Smile* (1976) appeared a few years later. This album was followed by a tour by her with a rock band. The tour produced a live album, *Season of Lights* (1977). Nyro's final album of the decade was *Nested* (1978), after which, with her child, she nested with another break from music.

New York Tendaberry (1969), *Christmas and the Beads of Sweat* (1970), *Gonna Take a Miracle* (1971), *The First Songs* (1973), *Smile* (1976), *Season of Lights* (1977), *Nested* (1978).

Gilbert O'Sullivan

Conversational pop songwriting by Gilbert O'Sullivan brought the tuneful lament "Alone Again (Naturally)" to listeners in 1971. "Alone Again (Naturally)" and Roberta Flack's vocal on Ewan MacColl's "The First Time Ever I Saw Your Face" competed for the #1 spot on the pop charts. The Gilbert O'Sullivan song set a bright, almost cheery melody against a despondent lyric about loss by a speaker who meditated throwing himself off a tower. It was not your typical pop-music song. However, this was a time of eclectic radio airplay, ranging across a variety of musical styles and sentiments. "Nothing Rhymed" (1970) was a hit in the U.K. and #1 in the Netherlands. "We Will," "No Matter How I Try," and "Under the Blanket Go" were all singles that were appreciated by listeners in Western Europe. "Alone Again (Naturally)" made Gilbert O'Sullivan a familiar voice and bestselling artist in the UK, Ireland, the United States, and Canada.

In the sentimental "Claire," the singer wonders about the age difference between himself and the girl he addresses. It is perhaps a meditation upon affection and upon time. The *Back to Front* (1972) singles were top sellers. You could play them on a vinyl record (33 or 45) or on an 8-track. Soon Gilbert O'Sullivan insisted he was a writer not a fighter. "Get Down" (1973) provided another side of Gilbert O'Sullivan with its up-tempo rock pulse. The singer insisted he still wanted her around although she was a bad dog. The album engaged more of a rock and funk sound in contrast with the mellower sounds of his previous recordings. *A Stranger in My Own Back Yard* (1974) followed. The single "I Don't

Love You, But I Think I Like You" was released the next year. *The South-paw* (1977) album resulted in a squabble with Gordon Mills' portion of the song income. The case was found in Gilbert O'Sullivan's favor in 1982. By 1977 the age of singer-songwriters had waned. While R&B and pop-rock were on the charts, disco was emerging, and new wave rock was reacting with minimalist rebellion. Gilbert O'Sullivan's brand of pop songwriting slipped from commercial radio. He continued writing songs and recording beyond 2000 and developed an appreciative following across Europe and in Japan.

Himself (1971), *Back to Front* (1972), *I'm a Writer, Not a Fighter* (1973), *A Stranger in My Own Backyard* (1974), *Greatest Hits* (1976), *The Southpaw* (1977).

Graham Parker

The new wave rock edge of Graham Parker's music emerged in the mid- to later 1970s. It is difficult to separate the British singer-songwriter Graham Parker from his band The Rumour, formed in 1975. *Howlin' Wind* (1976) was a full band effort. It was followed by *Heat Treatment* (1976), which sounded similar. The song "Back to Schooldays" was released in a compilation on Stiff Records. *Stick to Me* (1977) hit the charts in Britain and in Australia. A double-album *Parkerilla* (1978), with three live concert sides, changed the sound a bit with attention to the popular music market in the United States.

Howlin' Wing (1976), *Heat Treatment* (1976), *Stick to Me* (1977), *Parkerilla* (1978).

Van Dyke Parkes

As a budding arranger and producer, Van Dyke Parkes studied with Aaron Copland. He worked as an actor in 1960s film and television. After creating *Song Circle* (1967), mixing pop, ragtime, bluegrass, and other styles, Van Dyke Parkes worked with Brian Wilson and the Beach Boys. In 1970, he launched into the Afro-Caribbean music of Trinidad and Tobago and worked as an arranger and producer. He became the audio-visual director at Warner Brothers Records in 1970. Perhaps he was not yet a singer-songwriter at this time, but he was in the center of popular music's reach into a variety of new areas. With *Discover America* (1974) he gathered up his compositions, which now included calypso. He worked closely with Harry Nilsson, contributing to some of his recordings in the 1970s. He later turned his attention more fully toward film.

Discover America (1974), *Clang of the Yankee Reaper* (1975).

Gram Parsons

Gram Parson was one of the most influential folk-rock/country-rock songwriters of the 1970s. He brought together folk, rock, country, and other genres and styles and can be considered one of the formulators of the folk-rock-country sound. He was a member of The Byrds, following the departure of David Crosby in 1968, and of The Flying Burrito Brothers, in which he joined Chris Hillman. He wrote "Sweetheart of the Rodeo." He influenced country-rock. There was also some drawing upon psychedelic rock. His work also led toward what we now call Americana: a blend of country-folk and pop. *The Gilded Palace of Sin* appeared in 1969. Gram Parsons' solo was at first produced by Terry Melcher. They fell into drug use and made little progress. He joined Emmylou Harris on tour. He joined the 1971 Rolling Stones tour and played the blues with Keith Richards.

In the early 1970s a motorcycle accident sidelined Parsons. *GP* (1973) appeared as a solo album. *GP* has a country sound and includes Emmylou Harris. In the process of developing his next album, he checked in at the Joshua Tree Inn on 29 Palms Highway. He never left. Parsons was dead at the age of 26. (See Patrick Sullivan, "Gram Parsons: The Mysterious Death and Aftermath," *Rolling Stone*, October 25, 1973.) *Grievous Angel* (1974) followed. (See *Gram Parsons: The Solo Years* on Rhino Records.)

GP (1973), *Grievous Angel* (1974).

Dolly Parton

Don't let the big personality or stage and screen credits fool you. Dolly Parton is fundamentally a fine country music songwriter and singer. Her venture into crossover-pop with a touch of R&B with "Here You Come Again" (1977) followed a string of well-crafted country songs emerging from her Tennessee roots. There were duets with Porter Wagoner from 1967 to 1970 and solo recordings in the 1970s of songs like "Coat of Many Colors," "Daddy Was an Old Time Preacher," "Come Back to Me," "Do I Ever Cross Your Mind?" "Apple Jack," "All I Can Do," "Falling Out of Love with Me," "I Will Always Love You," and her signature song "Jolene."

Coat of Many Colors (1971) was nominated for album of the year by the Country Music Association. "My Blue Tears" was the first single from the album. The title song was released next as a single. "Coat of Many Colors" was written while she was on tour with Porter Wagoner. It is available for you to listen to on YouTube. Dolly Parton wrote the song about her mother, who sewed a coat of many different scraps of cloth (see *https://dollyparton.com*). The recordings from this album are available on Sound Cloud.

Dolly Parton's country-pop sound broke out with the hit single "9 to 5," which was released in 1980. This album includes five of her own songs on *9 to 5 and Odd Jobs*. The album has songs by Woody Guthrie, Mel Tillis, Randy Travis. Parton also sang "The House of the Rising Sun." The album stood at #1 on the country charts for ten weeks.

The Fairest of Them All (1970), *Porter Wayne and Dolly Rebecca* (with Porter Wagoner) (1970), *Once More* (with Porter Wagoner) (1970), *Two of a Kind* (with Porter Wagoner) (1971), *The Golden Streets of Glory* (1971), *Joshua* (1971), *Coat of Many Colors* (1971), *The Right Combination • Burning the Midnight Oil* (with Porter Wagoner) (1972), *Touch Your Woman* (1972), *Together Always* (with Porter Wagoner) (1972), *My Favorite Songwriter, Porter Wagoner* (1972), *We Found It* (with Porter Wagoner) (1973), *My Tennessee Mountain Home* (1973), *Love and Music* (with Porter Wagoner) (1973), *Bubbling Over* (1973), *Jolene* (1974), *Porter 'n' Dolly* (with Porter Wagoner) (1974), *Love Is Like a Butterfly* (1974), *The Bargain Store* (1975), *Say Forever You'll Be Mine* (with Porter Wagoner) (1975), *Dolly* (1975), *All I Can Do* (1976), *New Harvest...First Gathering* (1977), *Here You Come Again* (1977), *Heartbreaker* (1978), *Great Balls of Fire* (1979).

Tom Paxton

Folksinger who began performing and recording in the 1960s, Tom Paxton is the writer of "The Last Thing on My Mind," "Whose Garden Was This," "Ramblin' By," "Bottle of Wine" and other folk standards. Tom Paxton has never stopped performing and recording his songs. His songs have been widely recorded by folk music artists. The 1960s was a time of considerable accomplishment with songs in the folk genre. The year 1970 began with his song "Going to the Zoo" appearing on television shows. Seven albums followed before *Heroes* (1978), which included "Phil," a song to Phil Ochs, and a song about anti-apartheid activist Steve Biko. "Let the Sunshine," an ecological song, appeared on *Let the Sunshine* (1979).

How Come the Sun (1970), *Peace Will Come* (1971), *New Songs for Old Friends* (1972), *Children's Song Book* (1973), *Something in My Life* (1975), *Saturday Night* (1976), *New Songs from the Briarpatch* (with Steve Goodman) (1977), *Heroes* (1978), *Let the Sunshine* (1979).

Teddy Pendergrass

While he was with Harold Melvin and the Blue Notes, Teddy Pendergrass was encouraged by producers to come out from behind the drums and sing. He sang "If You Don't Know Me by Now" and "I Miss You" (1972). Harold Melvin, chief vocalist, also seemed to be drawing in most of the group's profits. Teddy Pendergrass left the group in 1976. Leon Huff and Kenny Gamble connected him with Philadelphia International Records. They were at the time writing hits like "Love Train" and "Me and Mrs. Jones." They were significant contributors to his subsequent success. He recorded *Teddy Pendergrass* (1977), *Life is a Song Worth Singing* (1978), and *Teddy* (1979). Listing him as a singer-songwriter is a bit of a stretch. He was primarily a vocalist. His songs were mostly written with co-writers. His songwriting included "Give It to Me" and "Don't Keep Wasting My Time," as well as several other co-written songs. A 1982 accident resulted in paralysis. Some recordings followed, including songs he contributed to creating. A documentary of the life of Teddy Pendergrass, *If You Don't Know Me* (BBC, 2019), appears on Showtime.

Teddy Pendergrass (1977), *Life is a Song Worth Singing* (1978), *Teddy* (1970).

Larry Penn

Milwaukee's folksinger of songs about trucks and trains, working men and women, labor, and the American Midwest is remembered by folk singers and audiences annually. Penn was a civic-minded Teamster, a supporter of labor unions, who sang at labor rallies and at folk clubs, coffeehouses and colleges. He also sang for children. At his wife's suggestion he wrote "I'm A Little Cookie," recognizing the needs of emotionally disturbed children. *Working for a Living* (1976) was his first recording. It was recorded for a small label, Collector Records, run by Joe Glazer, a labor organizer in Silver Spring, Maryland. He retired from his work as a trucker. He joined Rose Tattoo, a group of travelling musicians that also included Bruce "Utah" Phillips.

Working for a Living (1976), reissued on Folkways (1980).

Andy Pratt

Rock and classical music joined together in some orchestrated Andy Pratt compositions. He later moved toward writing Christian gospel songs. Pratt's great grandfather created Pratt Institute, an important college for the arts based in Brooklyn. Clive Davis signed him to a contract with Columbia Records partly on the strength of his demo for "Avenging Annie." At the time, record companies were on the lookout for artists that they could market amid the singer-songwriter trend. He recorded *Records Are Like Life* (1969). His first record of the 1970s was the self-titled album *Andy Pratt* (1973). In *Rolling Stone* (July 1, 1976) Stephen Holden found his work on *Resolution* (1976) "emotionally charged." He observed that Pratt's songs often "require concentration." The song features an energetic piano part. In 1977, Roger Daltrey recorded "Avenging Annie" for an album. Pratt by then had moved in a more experimental direction with his music. *Rolling Stone* commented that Pratt took harmonies a step beyond those of the Beach Boys. Bee Gees producer Arif Mardin was enlisted to pop-up Pratt's 1976 release to make it more commercial. However, while well-regarded by critics, Pratt never quite caught on with a large audience. His musical sense brought some complexity, and his songs became less focused on a commercial market.

Andy Pratt (1973), *Resolution* (1976), *Shiver in the Night* (1977), *Motives* (1979).

John Prine

A perceptive and smart songwriter from Chicago, John Prine navigated across folk music into country music and pop with witty songs that captured contemporary life. His songs in the 1970s ranged from country-pop hits like "Angel from Montgomery" and the poignant recognition of aging and loneliness in "Hello in There" to the wry comedy of "Dear Abby" and "Illegal Smile." So, the mailman-turned-troubadour delivered messages and stories of people's lives and dreams to a public extending far beyond "the city of the big shoulders," as Carl Sandburg once called Chicago. His first album *John Prine* (1971) gathered some of those stories in song. He was backed by studio musicians, including Elvis Presley's rhythm section. He opened with "Illegal Smile," and detailed the struggles of a returning veteran in "Sam Stone," and a nostalgic, elderly narrator in "Hello in There." The song "Paradise," a critique of strip-mining, was also among the recording's high points. Kris Kristofferson, responding to Prine's songs, was supportive of that first recording. He had encouraged Prine to go to New York and sing at The Bitter End, where record executive Jerry Wexler heard him. It was, of course, Prine's lyrics, storytelling, and insight that touched most listeners. *Diamonds in the Rough* (1972) was indeed a rough and straightforward vehicle for the gems that were his songs. The recording used minimal production and leaned toward bluegrass. *Sweet Revenge* (1973) included "Dear Abby" in which a lament culminates in an awkward moment in the back seat of a car with his girlfriend's hair up in curlers and her pants to her knees. Other songs on the album were "Christmas in Prison" and "Grandpa Was a Carpenter." John Prine and Steve Goodman together wrote "You Never Even Called Me by My Name" (1974), a hit for David Allan Coe. *Common Sense* (1975) brought the quirky song "Come Back to Us Barbara Lewis Hare Krishna Beauregard." Steve Goodman produced John Prine's next album, *Bruised Orange* (1976) with the title song and the songs "That's What Makes the World Go Round." And "Sabu Visits the Twin Cities Alone."

 John Prine (1971), *Diamonds in the Rough* (1972), *Sweet Revenge* (1973), *Common Sense* (1975), *Prime Prine: The Best of John Prine* (1976), *Bruised Orange* (1978), *Pink Cadillac* (1979).

 See the John Prine biography by Eddie Huffman, *John Prine in Spite of Himself.* Austin: University of Texas Press, 2017. All of *John Prine* (1971) is available on YouTube.

Gerry Rafferty

 Stealer's Wheel vocalist and solo artist Gerry Rafferty may be best remembered for his song "Baker Street," with its distinctive saxophone hook and searing guitar lead, and "Right Down the Line." The Scottish pop-rock singer's earlier hit with Stealer's Wheel was "Stuck in the Middle with You," a reel-like romp with a bit of a Bob Dylan imitation. The song commented on clowns on his left side and jokers hanging out on the right. This was perhaps in the music industry itself, but it could have been about society at large. Co-writer Joe Egan sang the harmony part. Rafferty performed in a band-context for much of the decade but also recorded singer-songwriter solo albums. *Can I Have My Money Back* (1971) was his first solo album. Stealer's Wheel was formed after that album. *City to City* (1978) was his second solo album and it included "Baker Street." He recorded a third solo effort *Night Owl* (1979). "Mattie's Rag," on *City to City,* concerned a reunion with his daughter and travels from London to Scotland. The songs "Night Owl" and "One Drink Down" mention the alcoholism he struggled with.

 Can I Have My Money Back? (1971), *City to City* (1978), *Night Owl* (1979).

Bonnie Raitt

 The 1970s recordings of Bonnie Raitt were blues-influenced. She became one of the most visible interpreters of folk and country blues. Bonnie Raitt was the daughter of Broadway singer-actor John Raitt. As a child in the Los Angeles area, she was given a Stella guitar as a birthday present. From Los Angeles she went to Cambridge Massachusetts and was involved in the folk club circuit there. In 1970 Bonnie Raitt appeared at the Philadelphia Folk Festival with bluesman Fred McDowell. Her debut album *Bonnie Raitt* (1971) was focused on the blues. In the 1970s listeners could hear "Give It Up or Let Me Go" (1972), "Love Has No Pride" (1972), "Street Lights" (1974) "Sweet Forgiveness" (1977), "Two Lives" (1977), and "The Glow" (1979) among other original songs and blues tunes. "Takin' My Time" followed. Her recordings became increasingly familiar to popular music audiences in the 1980s and 1990s.

Bonnie Raitt (1971), *Give It Up* (1972), *Takin' My Time* (1973), *Street Lights* (1974), *Home Plate* (1976), *Sweet Forgiveness* (1977), *The Glow* (1979).

Willis Alan Ramsey

Creator of a single solo release in the 1970s, Willis Alan Ramsey was a Texas-Americana style folksinger of psychologically probing songs. That sound came from his Birmingham and Dallas background and folk roots. When he was about twenty years old, he recorded his album *Willis Alan Ramsey* (1972). The record included the song "Muskrat Candlelight," which was recorded as "Muskrat Love" by America and the Captain and Tennille. He moved to Great Britain in the 1980s.

Willis Alan Ramsay (1972).

Kenny Rankin

A gentle and fluent jazz voice, Kenny Rankin, as singer was able to create songs like "Peaceful" (a hit for Helen Reddy), and interpret everything from jazz standards to The Beatles. Vocally he could hit some high notes. He played guitar on Bob Dylan's *Bringing It All Back Home* album. He wrote the song "Peaceful" in 1967 and re-recorded it for his *Like a Seed* album. This was a well-paced easy listening album of song interpretations and original compositions. His vocals moved closer to jazz, like a smooth saxophone or clarinet that could move up and down scales with ease. Rankin was friends with comedian George Carlin. His songs were recorded by Peggy Lee, Mel Tormé, Helen Reddy, and Carmen McRae. His music crossed over from folk to jazz and Brazilian rhythms on guitar.

Like a Seed (1972), *Silver Morning* (1974), *Inside* (1975), *The Kenny Rankin Album* (1977).

Terry Reid

A British rock musician, Terry Reid played with bands, in studio, and as a sideman for other artists, as well as solo. His most accomplished work of the 1970s is perhaps his album *River* (1973). His song "Dean," used for a feature film, is one that stands out on that record. Reid's song "Without Expression" was recorded under different titles by The Hollies and by Crosby, Stills, and Nash. Reid performed as an opening act and on tours with The Rolling Stones, Fleetwood Mac, and Jethro Tull. He bowed out of Jimmy Page's plan to create "the new Yardbirds" but suggested Robert Plant and John Bonham, who would become the core of Led Zeppelin. He did not wish to be an artist in the folk-ballad singer-songwriter age, as producer Mickey Most suggested. He went his own way. He produced his own record *River* (1973), including David Lindley. His other 1970s albums were produced by Graham Nash (*Seed of Memory*) and Chris Kimsey (*Rogue Waves*). In the 1980s he played guitar on recordings by Bonnie Raitt, Don Henley, and Jackson Browne.

River (1973), *Seed of Memory* (1975), *Rogue Waves* (1977). *Seed of Memory* is available on YouTube. You might listen also to *The Other Side of the River*.

Kenny Rogers

One of the best-selling country artists of the 1970s and 1980s, Kenny Rogers established his solo career as he moved from his group The First Edition. He became a familiar singing voice on a variety of easy listening pop and country-crossover radio stations. Kenny Rogers does not fit well into the singer-songwriter category. However, he was a prominent interpreter and co-writer of songs who made an impact as a solo artist in the last years of the 1970s. The solo career began with *Love Lifted Me* (1976), *Kenny Rogers* (1977), and *Daytime Friends* (1977). All of those albums sold well on the strength of Rogers's singles. *Every Time Two Fools Collide* (1977) was recorded with Dottie West. The song "Lucille" (1977) by Roger Bolin and Hal Bynum was a hit that established Kenny Rogers at the pinnacle of the pop-country music business. *The Gambler* (1978) was a huge success, with the hit title song by Don Schlitz telling the story of a gambler explaining his techniques of card-playing and how to fold them and hold them. He concluded the decade with another album with Dottie West, which was followed by *Kenny* (1979). From 1976 on, the band Bloodline supported Kenny Rogers on his performing tours. He became a familiar face on television and in some films in the 1980s. Most of the songs that Kenny Rogers wrote were co-written with other songwriters. His hits like "Lucille," "The Gambler," "She Believes in Me" were written by other songwriters. He is credited with "Love Lifted Me." More than a half-dozen artists have covered his song "Sweet Music Man," which was not co-written.

Love Lifted Me (1976), *Kenny Rogers* (1977), *Daytime Friends* (1977), *Every Time Two Fools Collide* (with Dottie West) (1977), *The Gambler* (1978), *Classics* (with Dottie West) (1978), *Kenny* (1979).

Todd Rundgren

Something/Anything? double album released in February 1972, a recording that Todd Rundgren produced and arranged, for which, across three album sides, he wrote all of the songs, played all of the instruments, and sang all of the lead vocals and background vocals. Rundgren was joined by other musicians on the fourth album side. *Something/Anything?* represented a rich palette of musical variety before Rundgren's shift on *A Wizard, True Star* to extended forays into progressive rock. *Something/Anything?* had scored three top 100 singles: "Hello, It's Me," (#5) "I Saw the Light" (#16) and "Couldn't I Just Tell You"(#93). Todd Rundgren had also recorded the sessions with Badfinger that brought "Day After Day" and "Baby Blue" in the autumn of 1971, before he began recording *Something/Anything?*; and then in June 1973 he had produced the Grand Funk album single "We're an American Band" that we continually heard on the radio. Todd Rundgren was also behind the August 1973 New York Dolls' album, a seminal recording for the rock underground. His own music moved across pop, rock, soul, R&B, and other styles.

Something/Anything? (1972)

Todd Rundgren gravitated toward C major 7th, in the middle of the keyboard, as he began writing the songs for *Something/Anything?*. This is a chord that is a little more opened out, more dreamy than the C major. The C chord is a triad with three main tones: the root or tonic C, the E, which is two steps higher, and the octave of the C, which sings out eight tones higher. The C scale is eight notes that are played along the center of a keyboard, or in other positions: no flats, no sharps, all white keys. To this is added a major 7th, which tends to soften the chord. Rundgren's songs emerged as he played keyboard or guitar, moving his hands around in chord patterns.

The drums were one of the songwriter-producer's biggest challenges. To get the right rhythmic structure and to provide a pulse and bottom for the songs he had to start with the drums. He worked without a click track, keeping a sense of the rhythm steady in his mind. He hummed aloud as he played, and he tried to play the song straight through. Most of the drum playing is rudimentary but it is solid and sufficient. His goal was to make the final recording sound like a band was playing. So, he layered the tracks. Rundgren was wise to leave space on his tracks, to not clutter anything as he overdubbed instruments. His arrangements were spontaneous. He did not plan much in advance. Instead, he created the songs and their sound as he went along. Once he had gotten a few overdubbed tracks down, the process moved past the incubation phase and the sound of each song started to become clear.

He worked alone, in his house in Nichols Canyon, with an 8-track recorder. Maybe the name of the street—Astral Drive—served as an inspiration for the more ethereal moments. Maybe not. In any case, he recorded his "Intro" and "Breathless" there by layering keyboards and guitars. The techniques of recording technology—those available in 1971—were all-important in this process and he was not shy about adding effects. He had to work from channel to channel on the recording equipment, setting up his VCS3 synthesizer, running the wires for the guitars and the amplifiers. Like a slightly mad scientist in his laboratory, he conjured his alchemy. *Rolling Stone* would later applaud his command of the studio.

Runt (1971), *Something/Anything?* (1972), *A Wizard, True Star* (1973), *Todd* (1974), *Initiation* (1975), *Faithful* (1976), *Hermit of Mink Hollow* (1978).

Tom Rush

Go back fifty or more years. You are at Club 47 in Cambridge (later known as Passims) and the folksinger on the stage is Tom Rush. He is singing Bob Dylan's "Baby, Let Me Follow You Down." On the wall is a board announcing next week's appearances by Joan Baez, Maria Maldaur, and the Jim Kweskin's Jug Band. Tom Rush signed a two-record deal with Prestige/Fantasy Records in the mid–1960s. Emerging from the 1960s folk revival, Tom Rush's *The Circle Game* (1968), along with Bob Dylan's cultural impact, set the tone for the 1970s singer-songwriters.

One might not think of southern New Hampshire as a land of the blues, unless one means by that winter snow and hills stretching away into a blur of sunshine. Yet, that has been home for Tom Rush, whose *The Circle Game* recording featured the songs of then emerging young talents—James Taylor, Joni Mitchell, and Jackson Browne. One of his finest interpretations was his recording of Joni Mitchell's song "Urge for Going," a beautiful ballad that drifts in reverie across the seasons. During the 1970s, Tom

Rush was busy touring from venue to venue. By the late 1970s, he had set that aside and retired to his farm in New Hampshire.

Tom Rush's compositions are plainspoken songs, by turns romantic and ironic. His performances have been colloquial, with ordinary speech lifted into the folk-sentiment of songs like "Ladies Love Outlaws." Rush has addressed the human condition in wry parody, or with a sense of burden in "Driving Wheel." He has created a concert experience with storytelling between songs, sing-alongs involving the audience, and blues covers like "Drop Down Mama," by Sleepy Joe Estes. In later years, one could see his fingers slipping around the neck of his guitar, not always with the smoothest motion but playing in earnest. Tom Rush's shows became celebratory and perhaps a bit incongruous, with mostly white New England middle-aged baby boomers singing the blues. These folk-fans, now parents and working professionals, passed his music along to their children. From the 1980s into the new century, Tom Rush's folk music audience was growing older and they were still listening with delight and a wistful nostalgia.

The wave of singer-songwriter popularity began to decline after the mid–1970s. R&B soul stayed alive on the radio airwaves, but the lighter sound of folk-pop began to diminish. Popular music took a turn from album-oriented rock to the radio singles of bands like Foreigner, Journey, and REO. The underground of punk and new wave percolated in rebellion against corporate rock and disco. Singer-songwriters had to adapt or reinvent themselves with a rock-edge or be sustained by smaller audiences of their faithful following. Joni Mitchell explored jazz. Billy Joel, Bruce Springsteen, Dan Fogelberg, and others already had a rock edge. Many pure folksingers, like Tom Rush, vanished into the woodwork and returned to the coffeehouses from which their music careers had been born. The renewal of Tom Rush came with an annual Christmas concert in Boston: an event at Symphony Hall that became something of a tradition in the 1980s.

Tom Rush (1970), *Wrong End of the Rainbow* (1970), *Merrimack County* (1971), *Ladies Love Outlaws* (1975), *The Best of Tom Rush* (1976).

John Sebastian

In the 1960s, "Do You Believe in Magic?" (1965) bounced along on a bright, shuffling melody with a question that evoked hope and wonder. Magic could be in a young girl's heart. John Sebastian's song was performed by The Lovin' Spoonful, of which he was a member. As a child he had lived in the heart of the folk music community in Greenwich Village. He attended school in Blairstown, in the northwest of New Jersey.

He played guitar, harmonica, and autoharp. In 1968–69, John Sebastian set music and lyrics to Murray Shisgal's play *Jimmy Shine* which featured actor Dustin Hoffman. John Sebastian's casual appearance at Woodstock in August 1969 is also often recalled. He was an attendee but was allegedly called to the stage during a rain break. *John B. Sebastian* (1970) was released on Reprise/Warner Brothers Records and included vocal contributions by Crosby, Stills, and Nash. For *The Four of Us* (1971) Sebastian enlisted Paul Harris (keyboards), Dallas Taylor (drums), and Kenny Altman (Bass). Harris and Taylor soon became members of Manassas with Stephen Stills. Sebastian released a single titled "Give Us a Break." He used session musicians and welcomed guest appearances on *Tarzana Kid* (1974). Television viewers in the 1970s heard the theme song "Welcome Back" for *Welcome Back Kotter*. It was John Sebastian's principal song hit of the 1970s. An album, *Welcome Back* (1976), immediately followed its wide commercial success.

John B. Sebastian (1970), *The Four of Us* (1971), *Tarzana Kid* (1974), *Welcome Back* (1976).

Bob Seger

While he has been inducted into the Songwriter's Hall of Fame and his catalog includes several highly regarded story-like ballads, Bob Seger generally performed and recorded with The Silver Bullet Band rather than as a solo act. He was, of course, the band's vocalist and most visible member. He also wrote most of their tunes. The "long foreground" that Ralph Waldo Emerson once suggested was behind Walt Whitman could also be applied to Bob Seger. He played for years with Detroit-area rock bands. That is the band-context he dwelled within as he wrote his songs. *Brand New Morning* (1971) was a solo album. He played in a duo that year and into 1972. "Turn the Page" was released in 1973. In 1974 he formed The Silver Bullet Band. The album *Seven* (1974) was their first record release and *Beautiful Loser* (1975) was their second. His familiar hit songs followed: "Night Moves," "Turn the Page," "Against the Wind," "Hollywood Nights." Sung in a bright while gravelly rock voice, the songs told tales of youthful romance, life on the road, and overcoming adversity. Seger and the Band produced *Live Bullet* (1976), which critic Dave Marsh regarded as "one of the best live albums ever made." *Night Moves* (1977) was Seger's major commercial breakthrough album, featuring the singles "Night Moves," "Rock and Roll Never Forgets" and "Main Street." The man with the raspy voice had become a pop singles creator. *Stranger in Town* (1978) brought "Still the Same" and "Hollywood Nights," "We've Got Tonight" (covered by Kenny Rogers and Sheena Easton), and "Old Time Rock and Roll" (by George Jackson/Thomas E. Jones with a lyric rewrite by Seger). He wrote The Eagles' single "Heartache Tonight" with Glenn Frey and his songs for *Against the Wind* (1980).

Mongrel (1970), *Brand New Morning* (1971), *Smokin' O.P.'s* (1972), *Back in '72* (1973), *Seven* (1974), *Beautiful Loser* (1975), *Live Bullet* (1976), *Stranger in Town* (1978).

Paul Siebel

In 1970 singer-songwriter Paul Siebel recorded *Woodsmoke and Oranges*. He followed this with *Jack Knife Gypsy* (1971). He had come from Buffalo to the folk clubs of Greenwich Village in the 1960s. In 1969, he was brought to Elektra Records under the sponsorship of blues player David Bromberg. Siebel's songs were covered by Bonnie Raitt, Linda Ronstadt, Waylon Jennings, folksingers Kate Wolf and Mary McCaslin, and by Bromberg. His best-known song was "Louise," which is about the life and struggles of a prostitute. "She Made Me Lose My Blues" is a country-sounding tune that opens his first album. "My Town" is an anti-war song in which Miss Delia's jingoistic patriotism is questioned. His second album *Jack Knife Gypsy* (1971) was more produced and included string arrangements and some electric guitar. "Pinto and the Pony," "Jasper and the Miners," and "Jeremiah's Song" reflect his tendency to write toward a place in his songs where country music meets folk music. A drug habit, drinking, and depression likely contributed to his decline after 1971. His work was not being promoted or received by any substantial audience. Minus that recognition, Siebel drifted toward other pursuits, got a Maryland parks job, and took up sailing. Siebel's two albums were reissued in Britain in 2004. You can hear his song "Louise" on YouTube.

Woodsmoke and Oranges (1970), *Jack Knife Gypsy* (1971).

Judee Sill

A tragic figure who seems to have alternated between rebellion, sensitivity, and an almost religious sensibility, Judee Sill sang solo at a piano. Jim Pons of The Turtles had hired her to write songs. She was promoted by David Geffen and toured with Crosby and Nash, who were then working together as a duo. "The Kiss" (1971) is perhaps her most recorded song. One hears in this song about the sweet communion of a kiss. Her first album on which the song appeared received attention from listeners but not a lot of radio airplay. "Jesus Was a Cross-maker," produced by Graham Nash, was issued as a single from that album. *Heart Food* (1973) was orchestrated with strings and horns. Judee Sill worked oppositions, wistfulness, and meditation into some of her songs. She became trapped in an addiction and died of an overdose but left an enchanting, small catalog of songs.

Judee Sill (1971), *Heart Food* (1973).

See the *Rolling Stone* feature article on Judee Sill. There is a two-volume CD, *Dreams Come True* (2005), which gathers her demo recordings.

Carly Simon

Singing with her sister Lucy as the Simon Sisters brought Carly Simon into the 1970s and her debut album *Carly Simon* (1971). On "That's the Way I've Always Heard It Should Be" her "marry me" line seems to stand out. The tuneful melody and vocal rose to a top twenty single that year. She listened to Odetta and folk music and classical music as a child. Music was all around the Simon sisters. So were books. Their father Richard L. Simon played classical piano in their home in the Riverdale section of the Bronx. In New York, he was one of the founders, with Schuster, of the Simon and Schuster Publishing Company. After starting with crossword puzzle books, they had grown into one of the world's most important commercial publishing houses. Not long after Carly Simon's first album appeared, her song "Anticipation" shot up the Billboard charts. (It had some soul and tact before it later was transformed into a Heinz ketchup commercial.) Nothing was making her audience wait for her next album, *No Secrets*, and the smash hit single "You're So Vain." With its distinctive guitar line and Carly Simon's now familiar singing voice and assertive delivery, the song rose to #1. People wondered who the song might be about. Who was the narcissist at the song's center watching himself in a mirror from the corner of his eye? Who had been the speaker of this song years ago when she was just a naïve young woman? And was it teardrops that left clouds in her coffee? The song seemed to enter one's thoughts and to linger there as some of the best songs often do. Carly Simon married James Taylor and they recorded "Mockingbird" together. "The Right Thing to Do" (1973) also appeared as a Carly Simon single. "Nobody Does It Better" (1977) and "You Belong to Me" (1978) were hits that appeared later in the 1970s. With these songs she became one of the major recording artists of the decade. She contributed to the Burt Bacharach and the Houston Symphony program on November 2, 1978. She brought backing vocals to several albums by other artists, including John Hall's recording *Bold*

Face (1978), following his work with the band Orleans. Carly Simon is on record as reporting that she has felt some uneasiness about performing live concerts. Even so, one can hear a beautiful concert program on *Live from Martha's Vineyard* (1987).

Carly Simon (1970), *Anticipation* (1971), *No Secrets* (1972), *Hot Cakes* (1974), *Playing Possum* (1975), *Another Passenger* (1976), *Boys in the Trees* (1978), *Spy* (1979).

Paul Simon

One of America's most important songwriters and pop music craftsmen, Paul Simon has been a sure solo performer, folk music poet, recording artist, and experimenter with rhythms and sounds from across the world. Simon and Garfunkel parted ways in 1969. "Bridge Over Troubled Water" in 1970 seemed to bridge the decades. Paul Simon then focused on solo ventures with his self-titled album in 1970. Next came *There Goes Rhymin' Simon* (1973) and *Live Rhymin'*, a solo live concert recording.

On Paul Simon's first solo album was the energetic "Mother and Child Reunion" and the hit "Me and Julio Down by the Schoolyard." There were story-songs like "Duncan." He brought a gospel idiom to "Loves Me Like a Rock," cast some pop hooks and satire in "Kodachrome," and created the bright "Me and Julio Down by the Schoolyard." He played songs from the Simon and Garfunkel days, like "The Boxer" and "America" and he introduced listeners to his dream reverie of "American Tune," Paul Simon stretched across a variety of styles: reggae, gospel, Dixieland, jazz, calypso, and the blues. On *Live Rhymin'* (1974) the Latin American group Los Incas contributed to "El Condor Pasa" and to a new version of "Boxer." *Still Crazy After All These Years* (1975) won the Grammy for album of the year. It included the catchy "Fifty Ways to Leave Your Lover" and a duo with Art Garfunkel on "My Little Town." He began appearing as a guest on *Saturday Night Live* and acting in the film *Annie Hall* (1977). Paul Simon continued to perform and he wrote the songs that would appear on *One Trick Pony* (1980).

Still Crazy After All These Years (1976)

The title song opens this award-winning album. "Still Crazy After All These Years" is a tuneful reflection on life, career, and friends. A saxophone solo by Michael Brecker adds some further life to this track. It is followed by a one-song reunion of Simon and Garfunkel on "My Little Town." While this melodic song has the bright harmony vocals we remember from them, it is critical of conformity in the little town. After the reflective light jazziness of "I'd Do It for Your Love" comes the snare drum introduction to another of Paul Simon's hits, "Fifty Ways to Leave Your Lover." As Jack is advised to go out the back and Stan is encouraged to contrive a plan, an energetic vocal delivery lifts this song up over its rhythmic pulse into the freedom the lyrics suggest. The verses are conversational, and the chorus returns with some wit and urgency. Gus is leaving the bus and Lee's key is on the table and he's out of there. That's three hits among the first four songs on this album, co-produced by Paul Simon with Phil Ramone. Following "Night Game," Simon is joined by Phoebe Snow on the propulsive gospel energy of "Gone at Last." We hear "Some Folks Roll Easy," "Have a Good Time," which also gained considerable radio airplay, and the record concludes with "You're Kind" and "Silent Eyes."

This is a well-textured and crafted recording. When it won the Grammy Award, Paul Simon thanked Stevie Wonder for not putting out an album that year. (He won Album of the Year in 1974, 1975 and in 1977.) In *Rolling Stone* (December 4, 1975), Paul Nelson observed that the title song made a stylistic break from other Paul Simon songs. He commented on Simon's "slick professionalism." Throughout, Paul Simon's songs are melodic, carefully shaped and produced. Released October 6, 1975, the album went to #1. It followed Paul Simon's first two-solo album which included three hit singles.

Paul Simon (1972), *There Goes Rhymin' Simon* (1973), *Live Rhymin'* (1974), *Still Crazy After All These Years* (1975).

Nina Simone

Soul singer, pianist, and songwriter, Nina Simone had a long career before the 1970s. Gospel, jazz, blues, and folk met with rhythm and blues in her music. On piano she could play Bach counterpoint. From the piano came a variety of styles. "Don't Let Me Be Misunderstood" (covered by The Animals) and "I Put a Spell on You" stand among the classics she created. Elton John, David Bowie, Van Morrison, and Cat Stevens are among the popular 1970s acts who have publicly recognized the music of Nina Simone. Her song (written by Jay Hawkins) "I Put a Spell on You" lies behind The Beatles' "Michelle," according to a comment by John Lennon. She spoke at civil rights meetings in the 1960s. She reacted to civil rights abuses in the American South with "Mississippi Goddamn," a song she suggested affected her music career. Nina Simone was recognized as a black female artist rivaled by few others. Her album *Black Gold* (1970) was nominated for the top R&B album of 1970. Only Aretha Franklin could best that. She spent the end of 1970 and much of 1971 in Barbados. Singer and friend Miriam Makeba urged her to go to Liberia. *It is Finished* was her final RCA album. She recorded her album *Baltimore* (1978), including Hall and Oates son "Rich Girl" and gospel spirituals.

Black Gold (1970), *Here Comes the Sun* (1971), *Emergency Ward* (1972), *It Is Finished* (1974), *Baltimore* (1978).

Patti Smith

Poet Patti Smith wrote poetry and rock music reviews before she was at the center of a band that deeply influenced the new wave-punk edge of rock music from the mid–1970s on. She drew upon Arthur Rimbaud, Paul Verlaine, French symbolists and the Beats, contemporary art, and Robert Mapplethorpe's photography, as well as rock and roll, the MC5, Lou Reed and the Velvet Underground, and other resources. She does not fit easily into the singer-songwriter image. However, her 1970s album *Horses* (1975) merits mention here. Beginning with Van Morrison's "Gloria," the record moves across rock, story, and thoughtful spoken word poetry. *Horses* broke through to make a significant difference in mid–1970s rock. *Radio Ethiopia* (1976) was The Patti Smith Group's next album. Radio listeners will recall her vocal on "Because the Night" with Bruce Springsteen. The song appeared on her album *Easter* (1978). That was followed by *Wave* (1979). While she performed with a band, rather than solo, she did create songs, poetry, and memoir. While she became semi-retired from rock music in the 1980s, she has continued with creative work and occasional public readings of her work. So, singer-songwriter of a sort.

Horses (1975), *Radio Ethiopia* (1976), *Easter* (1978), *Wave* (1979).

See *The Patti Smith Masters* (1996) and *Land 1975–2002* (2002) and the Patti Smith memoirs *Just Kids* (2010) and *M Train* (2015).

Phoebe Snow

She may be remembered for "Poetry Man" and "Harpo's Blues" in 1975. Other listeners remember Phoebe Snow for her vocal on "Gone at Last" with Paul Simon. Out of Teaneck High School, off Route 4 in New Jersey, minutes from Manhattan, she came from a family in which she was surrounded by music. Her mother was a former Martha Graham dancer and a dance teacher. Phoebe sang at The Bitter End on Bleecker Street in Greenwich Village and was signed to a recording contract for her first album, *Phoebe Snow* (1974). The Persuasions, Teddy Wilson, Dave Bromberg, and Dave Mason all made guest appearances on the album. She toured with Jackson

Browne and with Paul Simon. With Valerie Simpson and Patti Austin, she sang background vocals on Paul Simon's recording of "Fifty Ways to Leave Your Lover." Phil Ramone produced her thoughtful and jazzy recording *Second Childhood* (1976) and the follow-up album, *It Looks Like Snow*, which brought a bit more rock edge to her work. She recorded Paul McCartney's "Every Night" in 1979 and she ended the decade with a U.S.-Canada tour.

Phoebe Snow (1974), *Second Childhood* (1976), *It Looks Like Snow* (1976), *Never Letting Go* (1977), *Against the Grain* (1978).

J.D. Souther

Songwriter J.D. Souther gave us his songs through The Eagles, with Souther, Hillman, Furay Band, and other collaborations as well as through his work as a solo artist. His songs contributed to The Eagles and what became known as the Southern California sound. Glenn Frey and J.D. Souther wrote "Heartache Tonight," to which Bob Seger added a chorus. Souther also wrote "New Kid in Town." On his album *Black Rose* (1976), which consists of ten songs, he was joined by Joe Walsh, drummer Jim Keltner, Andrew Gold, Art Garfunkel, and David Crosby, among others. His songs include "Faithless Love," previously recorded by Linda Ronstadt, and "Simple Man, Simple Dream."

J.D. Souther grew up with the music of his opera singing mother and big band playing father. The song "Run Like a Thief" was recorded by Bonnie Raitt. "How Long?" was later recorded by The Eagles on *Long Road Out of Eden* (2007). His hit song "Only the Lonely" (1979) concluded the 1970s. You can hear more a recent performance, live at the Tin Pan in Virginia, February 2020, on YouTube. In an interview with Dan Harrison of *Richmond Magazine* he described his first album as "kind of harsh, deliberately pure and clean." These days he is involved with adoption and dog rescue. He occasionally performs his music as a solo troubadour/ singer-songwriter.

J.D. Souther (1972), *Black Rose* (1976).

Bruce Springsteen

The early 1970s saw Bruce Springsteen in the guise of street poet, a Stratocaster-gigging working class musician—writing, and singing stories of urban characters with names like Rosalita, Mary, Sandy, Magic Rat, Bad Scooter, Spanish Johnny, Puerto Rican Jane, Kitty, Wendy. Images and internal rhymes filled his musical stories: a barefoot girl on a Dodge, the ocean rising, more cars, mansions of glory, an amusement park. Music was a road to freedom, if not also salvation.

Springsteen played within the context of the E Street Band. He did not step out to do many solo shows until later years. However, he belongs with these singer-songwriters. Rock, R&B, and folk all meet in his songs. *Greetings from Asbury Park* and *The Wild, the Innocent, and the E Street Shuffle* were filled with colorful, wordy, rock and R&B inflected songs. They were filled with grit and imagination. Some critics and fans compared the Jersey shore rock performer with Bob Dylan because he wrote literate, albeit sometimes obscure, lyrics and had also been signed to Columbia Records by John Hammond. "Blinded by the Light," a stream of consciousness lyric built upon rhymes, suggested youth spun by life and on the run. It became a hit for Manfred Mann. A young protagonist in a hard world is inspired by "Mary Queen of Arkansas." It was hard to be a saint in the city another song told us. The New Jersey shore appeared in the plaintive ballad "Sandy." "For You" declared hope despite adversity. "Rosalita" provided an energetic danceable chorus and rhythm that made it a good song to end shows with. Springsteen was an energetic performer who played shows for two or three hours at a time. (*Billboard* in 2020 observed a concert that lasted more than four hours.) On May 9, 1974, music critic Jon Landau stated that he had seen the future of rock music "and his name is Bruce Springsteen."

The breakthrough album was *Born to Run* (1975), with the rollicking "Tenth Avenue Freeze-Out," "Jungleland," "Thunder Road," and the title song. "Born to Run," while a studio creation, has an energy that underscores any live performance. The vocal is distinct and edgy, performed with a raspy power. The fiery pulse of drums and bass joins the chorded drive of Roy Bittan's piano, and the song is lifted to its heights by Clarence Clemons's saxophone. On the recording "Born to Run" has the layering of a dozen guitar tracks, a fullness of keyboards, the driving rhythm section and signature sax, and touches of bell-like glockenspiel. A declaration of freedom in the lyrics is the song's keynote. To Wendy, there is a request, a plea, the sound of reassurance, wrapped up in an embrace. Engine and flesh are fused in this sharp metaphor into passionate romantic abandonment. The speaker of the song wants to know wildness, to realize what is real. Our gaze rises with a picture of the horizon of the amusement park and the vivid image of kids huddled on the misty beach. One sees the distant curve of the park: rides above, beach below, where the kids huddle. With a declaration, then comes the kiss: like a firecracker, an exclamation point! We hear a drum hit, vocal punctuation, and we're off into the night. An explosive saxophone solo says the rest.

The protagonist of "Thunder Road," in gentler but perhaps desperate tones, seeks Mary and he seeks redemption. She has sent away boys with ghosts in their eyes and has a graduation gown tattered in rags. We see a dusty beach road with abandoned cars. We hear an emotional ache in the voice. Even so, this character has a guitar, and he can give it a voice. He proclaims possibility, determination, and hope; they can break out and win.

Springsteen's ability to record was stalled for a few years because of management contract issues. He remained involved with performing concerts. He then produced the forceful, sometimes new-wave rock sounding, *Darkness on the Edge of Town* (1978). The first song, "Badlands," immediately declares that there is trouble is in the heartland and a feeling is smashing in his guts. The album was filled with working man images, a character's memories of working in his father's garage. His father is at work in "Factory." In "Something in the Night" there is search for escape. Some kind of alienation and misery is lurking on the edge of town. Yet, hope and belief await in "Promised Land." Hope awaited in Springsteen's concerts and a growing audience identified with the songs, and embraced the drama and that hope.

Greetings from Asbury Park (1973), *The Wild, The Innocent, and the E Street Shuffle* (1973/1974), *Born to Run* (1975), *Darkness on the Edge of Town* (1978).

See the autobiography by Bruce Springsteen, *Born to Run*. New York: Simon and Schuster, 2016. Dave Marsh, *Bruce Springsteen: Two Hearts, The Story*. New York and London: Routledge, 2003. Donald L. Deardorf II, *Bruce Springsteen: American Poet and Prophet.* Lanham: Rowman and Littlefield/Scarecrow, 2014. David Izzo, ed. *Bruce Springsteen and the American Soul: Essays on the Songs and Influence of a Cultural Icon*, Jefferson, N.C.: McFarland, 2011. Kenneth Womack, Mark Bernhard, Jerry Zolten, eds. *Bruce Springsteen, Cultural Studies, and the Runaway American Dream*. Ashgate/Routledge, 2012. Monmouth University holds the Bruce Springsteen Archives.

Jim Stafford

A 1970s humorist and novelty act, Jim Stafford's song "Spiders and Snakes" rose up the charts. He followed this with the quirky story-song, "My Girl Bill," with its lyric turn providing a twist at the end. Stafford, from southern roots, soon was a national entertainer who could be seen on a 1975 summer replacement variety show. There were two albums in the 1970s, perhaps with more fun than depth. There were country music treatments, with guitar, banjo, harmonica. "Swamp Witch" was produced by the pop singer Lobo ("I'd Love You to Want Me"). Stafford also created movie soundtracks.

Jim Stafford (1974), *Not Just Another Pretty Foot* (1975).

Cat Stevens

Cat Stevens was one of the most popular singer-songwriter hit-makers of the early 1970s. Several of Cat Stevens' songs are about seeking the spiritual amid the material world. This reflects his gradual movement toward a Muslim commitment, his musical changes, his re-invention of self, and his shift of names from Steven Dimitri Georgiou to Cat Stevens to Yusef Islam. Paul Samuel Smith was Cat Stevens' selection to produce his reflective album five months after *Mona Bone Jakon*. "Lady D'Arbanville" reached #8 in the UK in 1970. Elton John played piano on some Cat Stevens demos. "Katmandu" and "Fill My Eyes" which come later in the first album are among the strongest cuts. The obscure "Longer Boats" was evidently about flying saucers envisioned in a waking dream. *Tea for the Tillerman* (1970) began Cat Stevens' streak of popular album successes. It featured his songs "Father and Son" and "Where Do the Children Play?" On the song "Sad Lisa" strings quiver behind the piano that leads the tune along. "Miles from Nowhere" and "On the Road to Find Out" suggest his spiritual quest.

Teaser and the Firecat (1971) was more extroverted. He moved closer to a rock sound on this album. This included the popular hit "Peace Train," which moves along in a jaunty rhythm. He is followed by a "Moon Shadow" and the singer reflects upon what he would do even if he were to lose all the body parts he has. This song was released to follow his hit single "Wild World." One of the key songs here was "Morning Has Broken," which was his setting of a traditional piece by Eleanor Farjeon. It was unusual for Cat Stevens to include any song other than his own songs on his albums. The recordings for *Catch Bull at Four* were held for about six months, after his tour of Australia and New Zealand. It was at this time that Cat Stevens recordings rose further to the top of the charts in Britain, the United States, Canada, and Australia and New Zealand. On these albums Alun Davies (guitar), Gerry Conway (drums), Jean Roussel (piano), and Alan Jones (bass) contributed greatly to the sound. Cat Stevens broke into a new phase, recasting his music. His 1970s music became increasingly part of a spiritual quest which led him to embrace Islam.

Foreigner (1973)

Cat Stevens' self-produced *Foreigner* is an extended suite, in which musical gestures from 1970s soul/rhythm and blues, pop, and folk are drawn together in an experimental fashion. Recorded mostly in Jamaica, the album takes its title from Cat Stevens' self-exile in Brazil where he went to elude taxation. This album appeared at the crest of the singer-songwriter's popularity following his breakout album *Tea for the Tillerman*, featuring the hit "Wild World" and *Teaser and the Firecat* and his singles "Peace Train" and "Morning Has Broken." *Foreigner* appears as a medley of fragments in the suite which comprises side one of the recording. After the strengths of the suite, which has some interesting instrumental sections, the rest of the album seems a falling off from the high ground of his recent hits.

By 1973, Cat Stevens had a strong fan base and could release most anything. This album is that most anything: an innovative first side followed by "The Hurt," one of his weaker singles, "How Many Times," "Later," and "100 I Dream." The album did not receive many favorable reviews. Some critics have remarked that the record is a bit overblown or excessive. It surely is not reserved in tone. It has all of the jaunty, syncopated qualities of Cat Stevens' previous work. However, the R&B and Stevie Wonder listening that Cat Stevens turned toward distinguishes this album from his previous ones. Cat Stevens converted to Islam in 1977. He took the name Yusef Islam and then retired.

Mona Bona Jakon. A&M April 1970. "Lady D'Arbanville," "Maybe You're Right," "Pop Star," "I Think I See the Light," "Trouble," "Mona Bona Jakon," "I Wish, I Wish," "Katmandu," "Time," "Fill My Eyes," "Lilywhite."

Tea for the Tillerman. A&M 4280 (U.S.) Island ILPS 9135 (UK) November 1970. "Where Do the Children Play," "Hard-Headed Woman," "Wild World," "Sad Lisa," "Miles from Nowhere," "But I Might Die Tonight," "Longer Boat," "Into White," "On the Road to Find Out," "Father and Son," "Tea for the Tillerman."

Singles: June 1970, "Lady D'Arbanville"/ "Time/Fill My Eyes"; February 1971, Wild World/ "Miles from Nowhere."

Teaser and the Firecat. A&M 4313 Island ILPS 9154. "The Wind," "Ruby Love," "If I Laugh," "Changes IV," "How Can I Tell You," "Tuesday's Dead," "Morning Has Broken," "Bitterblue," "Moon Shadow," "Peace Train."

Singles: June 1971, "Moon Shadow"/ "Father and Son"; September 1971, "Tuesday's Dead"/ "Miles from Nowhere"; September 1971, "Peace Train"/ "Where Do the Children Play?"; December 1971, "Morning Has Broken"/ "I Want to Live in a Wigwam."

Catch Bull at Four. A&M 4365 Island ILPS 9206. "Sitting," "The Boy with a Moon and a Star on His Head," "Angel Sea," "Silent Sunlight," "Can't Keep It In," "18th Avenue," "Freezing Steel," "O Caritas," "Sweet Scarlet," "Ruins."

Singles: November 1972, "Sitting"/ "Crab Dance."

Foreigner. A&M/Island, July 1973. "Foreigner Suite," "The Hurt," "How Many Times," "Later," "100 I Dream."

Buddah and the Chocolate Box. A&M/Island. March 1974. "Music," "Oh, Very Young," "Sun C79," "Ghost Town," "Jesus," "Ready," "King of Trees," "A Bad Penny," "Home in the Sky."

Greatest Hits. A&M/Island. June 1975.

Numbers: A Pythagorean Theory Tale. A&M/Island. November 1975. "Whistlestar," "Novim's Nightmare," "Majik's Majik," "Drywood," "Banapple Gas," "Lad o' Freelove and Goodbye," "Jzero," "Home," "Monad's Anthem."

Izitso. A&M/Island. May 1977. "(Remember) Old School Yard," "Life," "Killin' Time," "Kypros," "Bonfire," "(I Never Wanted) To Be a Star," "Crazy," "Sweet Jamaica," "Was Dog a Doughnut?," "Child for a Day."

[Yusuf Islam] *Back to Earth.* A&M/Island. December 1978. "Just Another Night," "Daytime," "Bad Brakes," "Randy," "The Artist," "Last Love Song," "Nascimento," "Father," "New York Times," "Never."

Ray Stevens

Comic songs, novelty songs, encouragements, country songs, and the 1970s hit "Everything Is Beautiful" are in the forefront of the song catalog of Ray Stevens (Harold Ray Ragsdale). The optimism, gospel sound, and sing-along chorus of "Everything is Beautiful" made it a classic of the era. A song like this was far more profound than the later "Bridget the Midget" or "The Streak" (about running naked across baseball fields and in other public places). He began 1970 as a studio musician, songwriter, and producer. Through the decade he wrote and produced some adult contemporary singles that reached the pop charts. He recorded songs by a variety of other artists including the classic standard "Misty" (music Erroll Garner [1954]/ lyrics Johnny Burke). Ranging from the sublime to the ridiculous, Ray Stevens gave the world Glenn Miller's "In the Mood" as a clucking chicken and also wrote things like "I Need Your Help Barry Manilow."

Everything is Beautiful (1970), *Unreal!* (1971), *Turn Your Radio On* (1972), *Losin' Streak* (1972), *Nashville* (1973), *Boogity Boogity* (1974), *Misty* (1975), *Just for the Record* (1976), *Feel the Music* (1977), *There is Something on Your Mind* (1977), *Be Your Own Best Friend* (1978).

Al Stewart

Can there be such a thing as a singer-songwriter-historian with a guitar? Many listeners are familiar with the popular recordings of "The

Year of the Cat" and "Time Passages," the Al Stewart hits in the 1970s. Beyond these orchestrated pop music creations are some strikingly good guitar-driven folk story songs. Al Stewart is steeped in modern history, Scottish legend, and British Isles folksongs. His first recording appeared in 1967 and were reissued as *Bedsitter Images* (1970). It was immediately preceded by *Love Chronicles* (1969) on which Jimmy Page and Richard Thompson played some guitar. He played at the Glastonbury Festival in 1970. Stewart's album *Zero She Flies* (1970) included some acoustic guitar and electric guitar. *Orange* (1972) was an album that recorded a relationship breakup. The album included "News from Spain" and Rick Wakeman on piano. His further return to history and stories in his songs came with *Past, Present, and Future* (1973) which draws together those historical stories and folk idioms. His album *Modern Times* (1975) brought story songs and was produced by Alan Parsons. The album included the song "Carol." The title tracks for "The Year of the Cat" and "Time Passages" were hits that made his music familiar to many listeners. However, those memorable pop hits represent only a sample of Al Stewart's songwriting, which includes story, history, and a unique depth of insight.

Bedsitter Images (1970), *Zero She Flies* (1970), *Orange* (1972), *Past, Present and Future* (1973), *Modern Times* (1975), *The Year of the Cat* (1976), *Time Passages* (1978).

Also see *To Whom It May Concern: 1966–1970*, a re-release of his first three albums.

Stephen Stills

Stephen Stills is best known for his involvement in Buffalo Springfield (and as writer of their hit "For What It's Worth") and Crosby, Stills, and Nash from 1969 into the 1970s. He spent much of the 1970s with bands, like Manassas. However, he also produced some solo efforts. He alternated styles on his rough edged first album with his acoustic guitar in the snow outside Gold Hill in the Colorado mountains. He opened with "Love the One You're With." This was followed by "Do for the Others," "Sit Yourself Down," "Black Queen," and "Cherokee." The record included appearances by Jimi Hendrix, Eric Clapton, Ringo Starr, John Sebastian, Rita Coolidge, Cass Elliott, and Crosby and Nash.

Stills' second album (1971) included "Changing Partners," "Sugar Babe," and "Marianne." The year 1972 brought along Chris Hillman and Al Perkins, as Stills created Manassas and recorded a live double album. Hillman adds much musically with mandolin and his vocal and instrumental skills. However, it is primarily Stills' band and album. *CSN* (1977) was reviewed at the same time as Stills' *Manassas* (May 25, 1972) by Bud Scoppa. This was the reunion of Crosby, Stills, and Nash.

Stephen Stills (1970), *Stephen Stills 2* (1971), *Stills* (1975), *Stephen Stills Live* (1975), *Illegal Stills* (1976).

Noel Paul Stookey

Along with being a singer-songwriter, Noel Paul Stookey, member of the trio Peter Paul and Mary, has been a committed Christian dedicated to social causes and to assisting special needs children. His solo albums in the 1970s were recorded in his home studio in Maine. Perhaps Noel Paul Stookey is best known for "The Wedding Song" (1971). It has likely been sung at hundreds of weddings. It even appears on an episode of the television show *Mike and Molly* where it is sung by actress Cleo King who plays Mike's police friend Carlton's grandma. The song is registered in the public domain for charitable causes.

One Night Stand (1973), *Real to Reel* (1977), *Something New and Fresh* (1977), *Band and Bodyworks* (1979).

Livingston Taylor

The first album by *Livingston Taylor* (1970) was produced by Jon Landau on Capricorn Records. Livingston Taylor was a folk music-based songwriter-performer, the brother of James Taylor, who was making a quite visible "splash" in media attention at the time. "Carolina Day" was the single from Livingston Taylor's album. There were ten original songs and one cover tune. *Liv* (1971) included the song "Get Out of Bed." James Taylor and Carly Simon contributed vocals on "Be My Horizon" on the next record, *Over the Rainbow* (1972). *Three Way Mirror* (1978) was on Epic Records and included his song "I Will Be in Love with You." "Going Round One More Time" was recorded in the 1980s by James Taylor on *That's Why I'm Here* (1985). *Echoes* (1979) gathered up recordings of songs from Livingston Taylor's first three albums.

Livingston Taylor has a light touch, a clear singing voice that is similar to that of his brother. There is a likeable, bright, and at ease quality to his performances.

Livingston Taylor (1970), *Liv* (1971), *Over the Rainbow* (1972), *Three Way Mirror* (1978), *Echoes* (1979).

James Taylor

It has sometimes been said that the singer-songwriter era of the early 1970s began with James Taylor. *Newsweek* featured him, drawing attention to his self-contained music performances and his "confessional" songwriting. James Taylor had been recognized by The Beatles and their Apple Records. His smooth singing voice and distinctive guitar playing, with his bright tone, hammer-ons, inside chords, and gentle style was the talk of pop music critics. There had not been a lot of comment when The Flying Machine released its set of songs some years before. However, now James Taylor was identified as a leading figure in a wave of mostly mellow, mostly acoustic guitar or piano playing singer-songwriters. Indeed, the label singer-songwriter was coined to support record company goals and talent agency marketing of James Taylor.

James Taylor was performing songs at the Newport Folk Festival on the day (July 20, 1969), that Neil Armstrong and Buzz Aldrin first walked on the moon. His set was interrupted. However, Rolling Stone provided a review that set James Taylor on a trajectory almost as expansive as that of the Apollo astronauts. "Those fifteen minutes set a standard for clarity, wit, and magnetism that was never equaled during the four days of the festival" (Thompson 140). Jon Landau, in that publication, had previously commented that Taylor was one who "sings with resonance and plays with grace" (*Rolling Stone*, April 1969).

Sweet Baby James was recorded before Christmas in 1969 and released in 1970. The album was produced to give shape and continuity to the selection of songs and trim away the rough edges of folk music guitar. James Taylor was melodic, and he was smooth. That smoothness in the vocals was complemented by his lyrics, filled with soft open vowels, and by his guitar-playing style. His friend from the Flying Machine, Danny Kortchmar, joined him on the recording. Russ Kunkel played the drums. The title song was dedicated to his brother's baby, named James.

At the center of this recording is the dark meditation of "Fire and Rain." It became one of Taylor's most familiar early songs. He picked up some pace and energy with the blues of "I'm a Steamroller." He played his version of Stephen Foster's "O Susanna." The rest of the album consisted of mostly mellow, laid-back, sometimes troubled, attitudinal songs aimed for the heart. Carole King would support James Taylor shows on the road. He would play her songs "You've Got a Friend" and "Up on the Roof." The song "You Can Close Your Eyes" was evidently directed toward Joni Mitchell. In March 1971 he was on the cover of *Time Magazine*. James Taylor had opened a lane in pop music for a long line of singer-songwriters. He was "The man who best sums up the new sound of rock…" (*Time*, March 1971).

Mudslide Slim and the New Horizon was a new horizon, a recording on which to set aside the persona that the media was constructing around him. The songs were honest and personal. On "Hey Mister, That's Me on the Jukebox," he could be self-critical and self-aware about the spin of fame and fortune and commercial demands that had been placed upon him. "Long Ago and Far Away," "Riding on a Railroad," and "You Can Close Your Eyes" define the calming tone of the album. The album's most enduring song was Carole King's "You've Got a Friend." It is curious that one of the most-lasting songs deeply associated with James Taylor was his interpretation of this song by his musical friend.

One Man Dog was more sparse, acoustic guitar, scattered songs, a title that dedicated his album to his sheepdog on Martha's Vineyard where some of the songs were written. There are funky band pieces, with Kootch, Kunkel, Craig Dorge, and Leland Sklar (bassist of the long beard) contributing musical ideas. "Don't Let Me Be Lonely Tonight," the album's closer, became its first single.

Walking Man followed with some lyrical reflectiveness. *Rolling Stone* reviewer Stephen Holden observed the apparent dichotomy between the private James Taylor and his public persona (*Rolling Stone*, August 15, 1974). Taylor's well-crafted harmonic structures surround his poetry, Holden wrote. He cited "Rock n' Roll is Music Now." Taylor's approach to rock is more a charitable nod than an embrace of rock's rebellious voice. The walking man travels, drifts, walks on by not bothering to stop and talk. "Migration" brings a drifting tune about the creative process and "Me and My Guitar" is a reflection on the instrument that aids his songwriting art. "Let It All Fall Down" is a lament for the waning of sixties idealism. "Daddy's Baby" is for daughter Sarah and his relationship with Carly Simon. "Hello, Old Friend" provides a pleasant gesture and the album concludes with "Fade Away," affirming that to fade away for now is "not so bad." He invites his listeners to join him as the album fades away. *Gorilla* popped things up again into a brighter commercial sound that also burst forth on *J.T.* in hit songs like "Smiling Face" and the cover tune "Handy Man."

Sweet Baby James (1970), *Mud Slide Slim and the Blue Horizon* (1971), *One Man Dog* (1972), *Walking Man* (1974), *Gorilla* (1975), *In the Pocket* (1976), *JT* (1977), *Flag* (1979).

Singles: "Sweet Baby James"/"Fire and Rain" 1970, "Country Road"/"You've Got a Friend" 1971, "Don't Let Me Be Lonely Tonight" 1972, "One Man Parade"/"Hymn" 1973, "Daddy's Baby"/"Walking Man" 1974, "How Sweet It Is (To Be Loved by You)"/ "Mexico" 1975, "Shower the People" "Everybody Has the Blues"/"You Make It Easy" 1976, "Handy Man"/"Your Smiling Face" 1977, "Honey, Don't Leave LA" 1978, "Up on the Roof" 1979.

Richard Thompson

Fairport Convention's guitarist and songwriter in the 1960s did not become a fully solo act until the 1980s. However, in the 1970s Richard Thompson emerged as a unique singer-songwriter in his own right. Several of his albums were completed in a duo with Linda Peters Thompson, his wife at this time. "I Want to See the Bright Lights Tonight" was among familiar songs. One could hear "Henry the Human Fly" (1972). Island Records held their album until 1974. They recorded *Hokey Pokey* (1975) and they moved to East Anglia. Thompson played on Sandy Denny's recording in 1977 and moved back to Hampstead. He recorded on his own *First Logic* and *Sunny Vista* (1979). Richard Thompson opened during Gerry Rafferty's 1980 tour. More solo efforts continued in the 1980s. Thompson's instrumental skills and talent with words support his songs. Paul Zollo has observed that the songs engage "elaborate meters and rhyme schemes" (524).

First Logic (1979), *Sunny Vista* (1979). Richard Thompson's autobiography is *Beeswing: Losing My Way and Finding My Voice*. New York: Algonquin Books, 2021.

Townes Van Zandt

Well-regarded songwriter Townes Van Zandt lived for a time outside Nashville in a simple, unadorned house. In his solo work he played small clubs and coffeehouse venues. He played fingerstyle guitar and followed up on Lightnin' Hopkins blues and Dylan influences. Kevin Eggers was his first manager. John Lomax III, grandson of the folklorist and folk-song collector, became his manager. His albums included *For the Sake of the Song* and *Flying Shoes* (1979). He wrote "Pancho and Lefty," recorded by Willie Nelson. His songs included "If I Needed You" and "To Live is to Fly," "Tecumseh Valley," "Rex's Bloom." He recorded the concert album *Live at the Old Quarter in Houston Texas* (1977).

Delta Momma Blues (1970), *High, Low and In Between* (1971), *The Late Great Townes Van Zandt* (1972), *Flyin' Shoes* (1978).

Loudon Wainwright III

This folksong humorist is the son of a *Life* magazine journalist father and a yoga instructor mother, brother to Sloan Wainwright, and father to three working musicians, Rufus, Martha, and Lucy. He was married to folksinger Kate McGarrigle. Loudon Wainwright can make you laugh.

He is an engaging solo performer. In 1970, he played in several folk music clubs, and this led to his first recording on Atlantic Records. He recorded his novelty song "Dead Skunk in the Middle of the Road" in 1972. He also began an acting career with a role on the television show *MASH*. He later appeared in several films. Wainwright is best known for his witty and perceptive songs of tongue-in-cheek humor.

Loudon Wainwright III (1970)

The year 1970 marked the release of the first solo acoustic recording of Loudon Wainwright III. Wainwright's albums consist of songs of wit, satire, irony, and play. There are some darker critiques here among his quirky observations of life. With this album, entirely on acoustic guitar and vocals, one might make some comparisons at times to the wry and curious perceptions of Bob Dylan, or of Randy Newman. On this recording we hear "School Days," "Hospital Lady," "Ode to Pittsburgh," "Glad to See You've Got Religion," "Uptown," "Black Uncle Remus," "Four is a Magic Number," "I Don't Care," "Central Square Song," "Movies Are a Mother to Me."

"School Days" begins with recollections of an "obscene" youth in Delaware, who remembers posing as Marlon Brando and James Dean for the girls, rowing on a lake, imaging himself as Keats and Blake, Buddha and Christ, and asking the Pharisees of the world to see the truth. "Hospital Lady" has a quiet, slowly paced guitar part accompanying the voice. We see a portrait of a woman with a pink hat, bobby pins, rouge. She's an older lady, but don't forget she was once a young girl. Now we are brought to reflect back upon her life. "Ode to Pittsburgh" gives us a bright pattern on guitar. This ode recalls the city of Carnegie, steel, and trolleys, Forbes, and "the hill." "I'm Glad to See You've Got Religion" begins with strongly played chords. This is spare, guitar and vocal. The lines begin with a declaration of feeling glad in addressing someone. "Uptown" focuses on New York City, its sites and venues of mid-town, those north of 14th Street. "Black Uncle Remus" is an up-tempo portrait of a man out of his rocking chair, having his whiskey, who cries the blues and rusts his banjo strings. He is left with a question of what to do if black and blue. "Four Is a Magic Number" encourages safety in a brisk guitar and almost passionate delivery. It sounds like a father sitting down a son or daughter to discuss the mysteries of the world. We hear that four and five are magic numbers. The cross and fish are symbols associated with the priest. "I Don't Care" begins on guitar and trades on the blues. He says he has changed and doesn't need her anymore. He exclaims that he doesn't care. So, she can go to San Francisco and have knots in her hair.

He asserts that when he wrote her a song it was a lousy one. "Central Square" begins with an echoed distant guitar and "wah-wah." We hear of Mary McGuire and Big Frank Clark. They are observed by the speaker who was waiting for a bus. Frank has beer. They cross the street and sit on the church steps. We are told that Mary grabbed Frank's hat. Then we are back to distant "wah-wah." Frank pulled her ponytail, poured beer over her, kissed her, she giggled, and they stumbled away into the dark. On "Movies Are a Mother to Me" that simple spare guitar welcomes us to the movies that bring sanity after a conflict in a relationship. The mother can calm her boys. When feeling like he is fighting with himself, the speaker can go to the movies.

Loudon Wainwright III (1970), *Album I* (1971), *Album II* (1972), *Attempted Moustache* (1973), *Unrequited* (1975), *T-Shirt* (1976), *Final Exam* (1978), *A Live One* (1979).

See his autobiography *Liner Notes: On Parents & Children, Exes & Excess, Death & Decay and a Few of My Other Favorite Things.*

Tom Waits

Singer of earthy blues and jazz-inflected songs in a gravelly voice, the unmistakable Tom Waits emerged from San Diego. His songs were filled with working class characters, the night, the poor, the criminal, and the down and out. Waits vocal delivery, piano sound, and grungy look caught attention and he was signed to Asylum Records in Los Angeles in 1972. On *Closing Time* (1973), his piano-jazz styled music leaned further into folk. He did an East coast tour with folksinger Tom Rush. In 1974 he performed along the West coast. The Eagles covered "Ol' 55." Waits performed on a U.S. tour in 1976. He acted in the film *Paradise Alley* (1978) created by Sylvester Stallone. There was a relationship with singer Rickie Lee Jones. The album *Blue Valentine* involved more guitar than piano. There was a soundtrack from Waits for film director Francis Ford Coppola's *One from the Heart.*

Closing Time (March 6, 1973) was folk-jazz-blues. "Ol' 55" which opened the record was the single released from the album. "I Hope I Don't Fall in Love with You" followed. "Old Shoes" was country rock-waltz. Stephen Holden commented that Waits was a bit like Randy Newman but "boozier, earthier." "Ol' 55" was covered by The Eagles for *On the Border* (1974). "Martha" was covered by Tim Buckley, Meatloaf, and Bette Midler. "Closing Time" closes the album with an instrumental.

Closing Time (1973), *Heart of Saturday Night* (1974), *Nighthawks at the Diner* (1975), *Foreign Affairs* (1977), *Blue Valentine* (1978).

Wendy Waldman

Growing up in Los Angeles in a musical household contributed to Wendy Waldman's songwriting. Her father Fred Steiner provided music for television, such as for the *Perry Mason* show. She performed in Bryndle with Karla Bonoff, Kenny Edwards, and Andrew Gold. Two songs from Waldman's debut album *Love Has Got Me* (1973) were recorded by Maria Muldaur. This was followed by *Gypsy Symphony* (1974). After three more albums she left Warner Brother Records and turned her attention to songwriting in the 1980s.

Love Has Got Me (1973), *Gypsy Symphony* (1974), *Maria Muldaur* (1975), *Main Refrain* (1976), *Strange Company* (1978).

Jimmy Webb

This master songwriter came from a gospel church background in Oklahoma. He created a string of hit songs recorded by Glen Campbell ("By the Time I Get to Phoenix," "Galveston," "Wichita Lineman"), The Fifth Dimension ("Up, Up, and Away"), Richard Harris ("MacArthur Park," "Didn't We"), Englebert Humperdinck, Frank Sinatra, Barbra Streisand ("Didn't We"), Art Garfunkel ("All I Know") and others. His songwriting was distinguished. His singing served the songs well, although some critics found his vocal skills a bit thin. His solo recordings were varied, tuneful, nicely produced, and always interesting. *Words and Music* (1970) appeared on Reprise. *And So: On* (1971) brought the songs "Met Her on a Plane," "All My Love's Laughter," and "Marionette."

Words and Music (1970)

Jimmy Webb's *Words and Music* is spare with Webb on piano-vocals and Fred Tackett contributing guitar, drums, and bass. There were overdubs of percussion and some trumpet. The production on Webb's 1960s songs was frequently built up to support the commercial releases of recording artists. Here Webb is expressive, placing his songs in simpler arrangements. He had begun writing about issues. Such songs were less likely to be commercial, or to be recorded by other artists. He would sing and play them himself. The hit songwriter thus joined the singer-songwriter era on Reprise Records, a subsidiary of Warner Brothers. Webb's song "P.F. Sloan" is the best-known song on this album. The song recalls the songwriter P.F. Sloan, who wrote "Eve of Destruction." The lyrics offer a reflection on creative effort. In 1971, The Association ("Windy," "Cherish") released their single of this song. P.F. Sloan, down on his luck and impoverished at the time was grateful. Webb's other work on his album with Fred Tackett included "Sleepin' in the Daytime," which moves through several tempo changes. The guitar-work and horns lift this piece into something quite interesting. This song may be the most developed composition and achievement on this album. Webb's best work is arguably those songs on which his skill as a composer and knowledge of songcraft bring together harmonically complex movements. While he entered the realm of the singer-songwriter following songwriting successes in the 1960s, he never quite caught on commercially. However, he remains one of the most respected and admired of contemporary songwriters.

Words and Music (1970), *And So: On* (1971), *Letters* (1972), *Land's End* (1974), *El Mirage* (1977).

Jim Weatherly

Jim Weatherly is a member of the Songwriter's Hall of Fame. A Mississippi native, he always considered himself a songwriter who was writing country songs. Yet, his output shows how the same song may be treated in a variety of ways. Weatherly may be best known for R&B hits by Gladys Knight and the Pips like "Midnight Train to Georgia."

Magnolias and Misfits (1975)

Piano drives the opening of this solo album. On "If That's All Love Means to You," touches of guitar touches are immediately followed by Weatherly's vocal. Did any of his former U. Miss football teammates know how well that man could sing? The song increases in intensity and the vocal is surrounded by strings. Subtle background vocals begin to come more forward. (The "doo-doo" backgrounds toward the end could even be sung by the Pips.) Weatherly then settles into "The Closest Thing to Love," a ballad with a gentle vocal and intimate address to someone. This song rests in plaintive feeling about a relationship. Acoustic guitar is joined by piano and then by steel guitar and strings. There is an almost Elvis-like climb with vocal chorus "ah's" behind it. The orchestration builds and then drops out, leaving the bare vocal to finish the final lines. The third track, "It Must Have Been the Rain," is more reflective, and the singer refers to the memories in his head. There is rain outside, a fireplace inside. The song settles into a classic country sound with steel guitar and chorus vocals. A gentle guitar is heard underneath, with some piano. We next hear "Old Muddy" and are in Mississippi country with dobro, guitar, and a 4/4-time up tempo driven along by the bass. We hear of Arkansas, and one expects a wailing harmonica down there in the Old Muddy. Side one ends with the light guitar joined by strings that sets an atmosphere for sadness and regret on "If I Could Just Find My Way." The singer says it's over, but it's not really over until he delivers a lament of loss which proceeds slowly and steadily. He muses, and strings rise over the top to accentuate how it hurts him too. The background vocals wash through in "ooo" and subtle like the strings, as the piano moves this song along. The piano and string build toward the end and an arpeggio from the piano guide us to the conclusion.

On the second side of this record, the first song, "Love Finds Its Own Way" is a pop song that contrasts sections. It begins at a steady pace and then suddenly shifts gears. It's like you are driving in a quiet suburb and suddenly hit the highway. One is jolted from the slower verse to the suddenly quicker rhythm. The song then sounds like it belongs to a 1970s TV show theme.

The second cut, "How'd We Ever Get This Way," begins on piano in a reflective manner. This is a breakup song: sad and pensive. The singer addresses someone with a sad attempt at recollection. The speaker does not recall what he did to cause the break in their relationship. The bridge part introduces a vocal chorus to underscore the first line and they recede with the strings. The relationship is over. A piano's strength guides us through this singer's moments of questioning. Breathing space is allowed for a reflective quality to the singer's sense of loss and puzzlement about the changed and lost relationship and how they ever got to be that way.

The next song, "What's One More Time," bursts out in 3/4 time with a chorus followed by only the solo vocal. This is traditional country, with guitar, bass, and drums and the pop-country feel of that late 1960s, early 1970s period. A country chorus opens up alongside a steel guitar, a piano playing the high keys, and full string accompaniment. There are mostly female backing vocals behind Weatherly's vocal. This well-constructed song relies on these vocal dynamics, a rising crescendo, that then drops off to leave Weatherly's vocal solo to repeat the song's final lines. The title inevitably comes around at the end of each section.

"Love Has Made a Woman Out of You," the fourth song on the side, adds a harmonica to a country-folk story. The speaker notices how a girl he has known has grown into womanhood. He realizes that she was attracted to him but that he was too busy to pay attention to her. Now he regrets his shortsightedness. She is a beautiful young woman and is now with someone else. As if to celebrate her, the song moves into a bouncing up-tempo movement.

Jim Weatherly ends his album with a stirring tribute to his home state of Mississippi. The song opens with an orchestral sound, a melody and arrangement akin to those of state songs. It is almost reverential, hinting of the solemnity of an orchestra treatment under the magnolias. Then it is a country song with nostalgic harmonica, piano, and strings. The vocal is like a caress and personifies the place as a lady, once great, whose splendor is now obscured. This little masterpiece, a Mississippi song, offers an utterly beautiful personal tribute to end this recording.

Weatherly (1972), *A Gentler Time* (1973), *Jim Weatherly* (1973), *The Songs of Jim Weatherly* (1974), *Magnolias and Misfits* (1975), *Pictures and Rhymes* (1976), *The People Some People Choose to Love* (1976).

Tony Joe White

The writer of "Rainy Night in Georgia" developed songs in the southern rock style. Jon Landau wrote in *Rolling Stone* (April 1, 1971): "They [the songs] all speak from a personal depth and naturalness that is missing from all but the best of the singer-songwriters." However, Tony Joe White did not break out as a solo artist into any significant mainstream notice. He wrote "Pork Salad Annie," recorded by Joe Dassin, Elvis Presley, and Tom Jones. In the 1980s, "Secret Agent for the Blues" and "Steamy Windows" were recorded by Tina Turner.

Tony Joe (1970), *Tony Joe White* (1971), *Best of Tony Joe White* (1971, 1976), *The Train I'm On* (1972), *Homemade Ice Cream* (1973), *Eyes* (1976).

Jesse Winchester

A singer-songwriter in the late 1960s could disagree with the war in Vietnam, avoid the draft, and move to Canada. That is what Jesse Winchester did. Upon receiving a draft notice, he moved to Montreal. This choice made him controversial. Curiously, he was born on an army base in Louisiana and was related on his father's side to the famed Lee family of Virginia. Jesse Winchester had carefully considered views concerning the Vietnam War. His music was produced by Robbie Robertson of The Band. He was unable to perform in the United States. Several Jesse Winchester songs were recorded by other artists. Those songs included "Yankee Lady," "Isn't That So," "Mississippi You're on My Mind," "A Showman's Life," "The Brand New Tennessee Waltz," "Biloxi," "That's a Touch I Like," "Every Word You Say." He went back to the United States after pardons were issued. Ed Ward in *Rolling Stone* (August 6, 1970) commented that Jesse Winchester's album was one that every patriotic American should listen to. Winchester died in Charlottesville, Virginia, in 2014.

His posthumous album *A Reasonable Amount of Trouble* (2014) had liner notes from Jimmy Buffett.

Jesse Winchester (1970), *Third Down, 110 to Go* (1972), *Learn to Love It* (1973), *Let the Rough Side Drag* (1974), *Nothing but A Breeze* (1977), *Live at the Bijou Café* (1977), *A Touch on the Rainy Side* (1978).

Edgar Winter

Multi-instrumentalist Edgar Winter plays guitar, keyboards, drums, and saxophone. His music crosses rock, pop, jazz, and electronic epics like his instrumental hit "Frankenstein." He has generally worked with bands, like his Edgar Winter Group (Dan Hartman, Chuck Ruff, Ronnie Montrose). The band can be heard on albums like *They Only Come Out at Night* (1972). However, Edgar Winter plays solo as well. Edgar Winter straps a small keyboard so he can carry it across stage and is free to change between instruments. Along with "Frankenstein," the song "Free Ride" written and sung by Hartman was a big hit. The band included guitarist and solo artist Rick Derringer on the *Shock Treatment* (1974) album and in 1975. Guitarist Johnny Winter was his brother. Edgar Winter is included here for his solo work, his blues-based performances, his rock compositions, and his capable musicianship on several instruments.

Entrance (1970), *Jasmine Nightdreams* (1975), *The Edgar Winter Album* (1979).

Bill Withers

The echo of singer-songwriter Bill Withers' songs endures (I know, I know, I know). There may be some sunshine even though he is now gone. For the assurances of "Lean on Me," the brightness of "Lovely Day," the bluesy lament of "Ain't No Sunshine," and the reminiscing tribute of "Grandma's Hands" continue to underscore aspects of life that are universal. Bill Withers wrote songs that touched that in people. "Lean on Me" is built on a simple step-pattern on the keyboard: C major, D minor, E minor, F major and back again. The recognition of pain and sorrow in life is immediately followed with the affirmation that the possibility of hope, healing, and recovery is up ahead tomorrow. He declares that he can be leaned on when feeling weak, or when one is needing a friend. One can "carry on" with that support.

In 1970, Bill Withers was working in industry. He worked for the Douglas Aircraft Corporation. He worked for IBM. He circulated his songs, like "Ain't No Sunshine." *Just as I Am* (1972) included "Ain't No Sunshine" and "Grandma's Hands." *Still Bill* (1972) had the single "Lean on Me," which went to #1 in early July 1972. The album *Use Me* (1972) followed, as well as a live recording of a concert that autumn at Carnegie Hall. His recording was stalled for a time because of matters with Sussex Records. His songs were also recorded by Gladys Knight and the Pips. Withers was signed by Columbia Records in 1975. He recorded *Making Music* (1976). His pop single "Lovely Day" was on his next recording *Menagerie* (1977). He worked on projects with other musicians, like Grover Washington, Jr., with whom he would record the hit single, "Just the Two of Us," which was released in 1980. He concluded the decade with *'Bout Love* (1978) and with those collaborative projects.

Just as I Am (1971), *Still Bill* (1972), *Use Me* (1972), *Live at Carnegie Hall* (1973), *+'Justments* (1974), *Making Music* (1976), *Menagerie* (1977) *'Bout Love* (1978).

Kate Wolf

Within folk music circles, Kate Wolf was a well-regarded singer-songwriter. Her contributions were many and she has been recognized with an award that is presented in her name. She was from San Francisco and was best known in that region. Among her songs were "The Great Divide," "Love Still Remains," "Give Yourself for Love," "These Times We're Living In," and "Here in California." You can Google "Kate Wolf Music" or "Kate Wolf folksongs" to find some of her music performances. These are available on YouTube.

Two albums of Kate Wolf with the Wildwood Flower are *Backroads* (1976), *Lines on the Paper* (1977). *Safe at Anchor* (1979) appears as a solo album. These recordings precede *Close to You* (1981). (See *https://www. katewolf.com/albums*.)

Backroads (1976), *Lines on the Paper* (1977), *Safe at Anchor* (1979).

Stevie Wonder

A musical gift of Motown excellence in the 1960s, Stevie Wonder developed into one the key pop music makers of the 1970s, combining soulfulness and edge with tunefulness and social commentary. *Songs in the Key of Life* might be called the central masterpiece of his 1970s output, if it were not for the strength of *Innervisions*. From Stevland Hardaway Morris at birth to Little Stevie Wonder with Motown, he began to make a difference in pop music while still a teenager, from "Fingertips" at age thirteen to "My Cherie Amour." Blindness never deterred him. Rather, he grew in insight, musicality, and spirit. The 1970s began with *Music of My Mind* and *Talking Book*, which included the keyboard driven "Superstition." (That's a Hohner Clavinet keyboard we hear percolating with funkiness and creating an atmosphere throughout the song.) It also included the hit "You Are the Sunshine of My Life." Stevie Wonder received the Grammy Award Album of the Year three times with *Innervisions* (1973) ("Higher Ground," "Living for the City," "Golden Lady," "All in Love is Fair"), *Fulfillingness' First Finale* (1974) and *Songs in the Key of Life* (1976). The double-album *Songs in the Key of Life* (1976) featured the song "Sir Duke," a tribute to Duke Ellington with a full horn section whose sound you could feel all over. This was a concept album which he produced, arranged, and wrote and sang the compositions for. It included the songs "I Wish" and "Isn't She Lovely" and is regarded as one of classic recordings of the 1970s and Stevie Wonder's finest achievement. He concluded the decade with a soundtrack album *Stevie Wonder's Journey Through the Secret Life of Plants* (1979).

Music of My Mind (1971), *Talking Book* (1972), *Innervisions* (1973), *Fulfillingness' First Finale* (1974), *Songs in the Key of Life* (1976/1977), *Stevie Wonder's Journey Through the Secret Life of Plants* (1979).

Peter Yarrow

Long a center of folk music, Peter Yarrow was a member of the popular trio Peter, Paul, and Mary. He participated in the Newport Folk Festival. Among his accomplishments is his initiation and support of the Kerrville Folk Festival, which has touched audiences and has brought some of the finest singer-songwriters in folk music to public attention. In the early 1960s he hung out at The Gaslight and The Bitter End in Greenwich Village, which began to thrive on the Folk Revival begun by Woody Guthrie, Pete Seeger, The Weavers, The Kingston Trio, and others. Peter Yarrow wrote "Puff, the Magic Dragon" and "Torn Between Two Lovers" recorded by Mary MacGregor. In the 1960s, Pete Seeger's "If I Had a Hammer," Bob Dylan's "Blowin' in the Wind" and John Denver's "Leaving on a Jet Place" were among Peter, Paul, and Mary's hits. Yarrow became increasingly engaged in the civil rights movement, the anti–Vietnam movement, and other social causes.

Peter (1972), *That's Enough for Me* (1973), *Hard Times* (1975), *Love Song* (1975).

Jesse Colin Young

In 1967, The Youngbloods urged people to get together and to try to love one another. Jesse Colin Young (born Perry Miller) was at the front of that band. He recorded some solo albums while that band was still intact. As the 1970s, began Jesse Colin Young's song "Sunlight" appeared on Three Dog Night's album *Naturally* (1970). He started the album *Together* (1972) in his home studio. In 1972, The Youngbloods disbanded. *Song for Juli* (1973) followed. Around the time of his album *Light Shine* (1974), he opened for Crosby, Stills and Nash. In 1975, Jesse Colin Young was a creator of the beautiful "Songbird." We hear his gliding tenor vocal singing "that's how she feels about you."

You can hear Jesse Colin Young on YouTube in concert at the Capitol Theatre, April 17, 1976. He is surely in good voice with "Songbird." You will hear a shuffle beat, smooth flute lines, percussion, bass, keyboard, and guitar, and following the lengthy instrumental opening of "Song for Juli." At 3:20 you can hear the instrumental tempo change and at 3:35 the vocal begins. There is another tempo shift at 4:10. This music flutters on flute, percussion, bass, and keyboards. "Songbird" is a breezy tune with a shuffle beat. It is clear evidence that it is possible for the human spirit in song to transform a now defunct music hall on grimy Monroe Street in Passaic into a place of harmony and audience connection.

Together (1972), *Song for Juli* (1973), *Light Shine* (1974), *Songbird* (1975), *On the Road* (1976), *Love on the Wing* (1977), *American Dreams* (1978).

Neil Young

Neil Young started out as a singer-songwriter in Winnipeg. There he wrote songs like "Sugar Mountain," played in small clubs, and he met Joni Mitchell and guitarist Randy Bachman (The Guess Who, Bachman-Turner Overdrive). Young moved to Los Angeles, traveling there with bass guitarist Bruce Palmer. They became members of Buffalo Springfield, with Richie Furay, Dewey Martin, and Stephen Stills. Later Neil Young was brought into a working relationship with Crosby, Stills, and Nash, although he stayed an independent solo artist as well. He continued to record and perform with the band Crazy Horse, with whom he had begun working in 1968–69.

For Neil Young biography see Jimmy McDonough, *Shakey* (New York: Anchor, 2003). Neil Young, *Waging Heavy Peace* (New York and London: Blue Rider Press/Penguin Books, 2012), an autobiography. The Neil Young Archives are being developed by the artist as a long-term project.

Listeners can gain access to his subscription website to hear some of this collection. There are Box Sets and Performance Series, Official Releases, and Soundtracks. The full album of *Harvest* is available on YouTube, as are individual songs from the album, and many other Neil Young songs.

Harvest (1972)

Neil Young's *Harvest* was among the best-selling albums of 1972. The single "Heart of Gold" was played regularly on FM stations. The album has a warmth and clarity, and songwriting is central to it. Young wanted to record live, with minimal overdubs. He engaged Nashville session players and a no-frills band to knock out his tunes. *Harvest* features Young's high, reedy voice, acoustic guitar with fingerpicking patterns and broken or partial chords, and the touches of Ben Keith's steel pedal sound. The songs sound spontaneous, effortlessly created, and the delivery conveys simplicity. The album cover, steel pedal guitar, Nashville musicians, and a song titled "Are You Ready for the Country?" may have led some listeners to expect a country sound. However, Neil Young does not create a country album. There are no country figures or clichés within the lyrics. Rather, this is a collection of Neil Young songs with his signature sound all over them. The music is not complex. The styles are varied. Yet, there is a consistent mood. The songs are drawn together as in a knitted quilt. Young's preceding album, *After the Gold Rush,* was direct, unadorned, in-your-face, and dry without reverb. *Harvest* is often softer, mellower, except for its band-jam rockers.

Harvest begins on a bassline following a drumbeat and we hear an acoustic guitar coming in from the distance. There is the longing cry of a harmonica and Young's distinctive trebly tenor voice. "Out on the Weekend" addresses a lost love and brings images of a brass bed, pictures on the wall, and a pickup truck to take him out of there. The verses seem to pull inward, and the chorus move outside the self. The lyric for the title song, "Harvest," is oblique. Yet, the music is rather direct, simple, driven by honky-tonk piano. There is no clear distinction between verse and chorus.

"A Man Needs a Maid" is a title that troubled some listeners in this period of ERA/NOW feminisms and calls for women's rights. However, the speaker appears to need someone's assistance because he is so ineffectual. He asks when he will see her again. The London Symphony backs the song, although it really does not need all of that orchestration.

"Heart of Gold" comes next, with its simple, choppy strumming, almost march-like backbeat, and plaintive harmonica. "Heart of Gold" presents the idea of a search for a heart that is true and authentic and the singer's observation that he is "getting old." It is a repetitious four-chord song. Kenny Buttrey adds rhythm with the high-hat. Linda Ronstadt and James Taylor contribute background vocals. Teddy Irwin adds a second guitar on the left channel. Keith's steel guitar makes descending runs alongside the lyric about getting old. The lyric is tight, the pattern insistent. We are given the contrast of the singer's recollections of having been to Hollywood and to Redwood. "Heart of Gold" has less than a dozen lines of a lyric seeking love, authenticity, and goodness.

"Are You Ready for the Country?" may be asking if one is ready to embrace the natural, the authentic, and that heart of gold. It may be asking listeners: are you ready to listen to this? The Stray Gators bang out the song in a California barn. There is a taste of the raw rock we will hear in later years from Neil Young. Tim Drummond, Jack Nitzsche, Kenny Buttrey (and later Johnny Barbata), and the drug-addicted Danny Whitten devise an unpretentious and ragged electric rock sound. Here the country is not such a welcoming place. Maybe the song relates to Neil Young's "Alabama" and "Southern Man," without the politics.

In "Old Man" Neil Young identifies with an older man, the rancher from whom he has bought his new rural home. The young singer is twenty-four with so much more to live. Yet, he feels that he is a lot like how the old man must have been when he was younger. This song received considerable airplay and became something of an album-oriented rock standard.

"There's a World" has an orchestral arrangement. Jack Nitzsche created a mini film score here. There is not otherwise a lot of strength to this three-minute song, but it adds another dimension to the album.

The stormy rock-edged "Alabama" follows, perhaps as a rewrite of "Southern Man." The state is derided. But this is not the work of a journalist or a close analytical examiner. It is a song that brings forth imagery: the broken glass of windows the banjos sound through, a stranded car in a ditch. Young plays a white Gretsch Falcon guitar.

"The Needle and the Damage Done" begins with the familiar pattern off a D chord that was picked by a generation of guitar players. Young wrote this song while on his Crazy Horse tour in 1970. This was before his band member Whitten's overdose. He recognizes a habit that turns one into a wreck and registers some frustration in his lament. Young's approach is more thoughtful and solemn than shrill, and his music emerges within a gentle melodic pattern.

"Words" rings out with drums and some electric guitar distortion but never settles into a groove. There is none of the rock energy of Young's later blustery fire, like in "Rocking in the Free World." The lyrical intent is unclear. There are shifting time signatures, from 6/8 to 5/8 at the start. Yet, there is something satisfying about the symbolic lyric as it leaps across present and past tense. The singer seems to ponder what it means to have this public attention and how he might just live a life out of the limelight. There is a chug-a-lug forward propulsion to the song that brings *Harvest* to a satisfying conclusion.

After the Gold Rush (1970), *Harvest* (1972), *Time Fades Away* (1973, live), *On the Beach* (1974), *Tonight's the Night* (1975), *Zuma with Crazy Horse* (1975), *Long May You Run with Stephen Stills* (1976), *American Stars 'n Bars* (1977), *Comes a Time* (1978), *Rust Never Sleeps* (with Crazy Horse) (1979, live).

Frank Zappa

With a stretch, one might call Frank Zappa a singer-songwriter. He certainly was a creative, innovative musician and composer. He was a composer of free-form musical innovation: a bit like surrealism set to music. One day Frank Zappa heard of the modernist classical music piece "Ionisation" by Edgard Varèse, and he had to get a copy. The anecdote underscores Frank Zappa's continual openness to modern music in many forms and his wit and experimental creativity. Of course, he always appeared with his band, the Mothers of Invention. One would not see Zappa solo apart from other musicians often enough to regard him in the same category as the solo singer-songwriter. However, the singer songwriter spectrum is not easy to classify. His pieces were satirical jokes, cutting critiques, ventures in musical expansiveness. Zappa's creations included the music of harmonic surprise, movements into the unexpected. From *Freak Out* (1966) through the 1970s, Frank Zappa pushed the edges with satire, musical complexity, and serious play.

Zappa moved into Laurel Canyon as the Mothers of Invention disbanded in 1969. He pursued some solo projects, and he created his *Hot Rats* (1970) album which included some lengthy guitar solos on his own compositions. In the 1970s he explored film. He created a new version of the Mothers of Invention with some musicians from Britain and added Mark Volman, Howard Kaylan, and Jim Pons from The Turtles. On December 4, 1971, their equipment was destroyed in a blaze at the Casino de Montreux in Switzerland that was recalled in Deep Purple's classic rock song "Smoke on the Water." Not long afterward in London, Zappa was pushed off the stage by a crazed fan and was injured. He was unable to perform until September 1972. However, the creativity of Frank Zappa bloomed into his most popular album of the period, *Apostrophe* (1974). Zappa was prolific and his production of music continued through all the changes of the 1970s. His solo work included *Zoot Allures* (1976) and his critically acclaimed *Joe's Garage I* (1978) and *Joe's Garage II and III* (1979).

Solo albums: *Chunga's Revenge* (1970), *Waka/Jawaka* (1972), *Apostrophe* (1974), *Zoot Allures* (1976), *Zappa in New York* (1978), *Studio Tan* (1978), *Sleep Dirt* (1979), *Orchestral Favorites* (1979), *Sheik Yerbouti* (1979), *Joe's Garage I* (1979), *Joe's Garage II and III* (1979).

Albums with the Mothers of Invention: *Burnt Weeny Sandwich* (1970), *Weasels Ripped My Flesh* (1970), *Fillmore East* (1971), *Just Another Band from L.A.* (1972), *The Grand Wazoo* (1972), *Over-Nite Sensation* (1973), *Roxy and Elsewhere* (1974), *One Size Fits All* (1975), *Bongo Fury* (1975).

Warren Zevon

One of the most clever, satirical, and iconoclastic singer-songwriters of the "L.A. sound" in folk-rock and pop-rock. His songs ranged across guitar-driven rock, quirky songs of wit, and searching soulful lyrics. His first album *Wanted Dead or Alive* (1969) preceded the 1970s. He worked as a session player and as a musical director for the Everly Brothers. He lived in Spain during the first half of 1975. In September 1975 he was living in a house with guitarist Lindsey Buckingham, who was entering Fleetwood Mac with Stevie Nicks. He associated with Linda Ronstadt, members of The Eagles, and Jackson Browne, who produced his 1976 album. The title song for Linda Ronstadt's album *Hasten Down the Wind* (1975) was written by Zevon and her album included Zevon's "Poor Pitiful Me." The album *Warren Zevon* (1976) appeared, produced by Jackson Browne. Songs seemed to tumble out from Zevon: "Carmelita," "Frank and Jesse James," "The French Inhaler," and "Desperado," recorded by both Linda Ronstadt and by The Eagles. He wrote "Desperado Under the Eaves" as he was sinking into alcoholism and addictions. He remained a prolific songwriter. On *Excitable Boy* (1978), produced by Jackson Bowne and Waddy Wachtel, are the songs like "Werewolves of London," "Lawyers, Guns, and Money," "Roland the Headless Thompson Gunner." Mick Fleetwood and John McVie played on his song "Werewolves of London." Rolling Stone's Paul Nelson called the album "[o]ne of the most significant releases of the 1970s."

There was a gap of seven years between *Wanted Dead or Alive* (1969) and Warren Zevon's follow-up album. His first recording of the 1970s was the self-titled *Warren Zevon* (1976). It was followed by *Excitable Boy* (1978). The *Warren Zevon* album was remastered in 2008 on Rhino Records. "Frank and Jesse James," "Mama Could Not Be Persuaded," "Backs Turned Looking Down the Path," "Hasten Down the Wind," "Poor, Poor Pitiful

Me," and "French Inhaler" comprise the first side. "Mohammed's Radio," "I'll Sleep When I'm Dead," "Carmelita," "Join Me in L.A." and "Desperados Under the Eaves" are on side two. Jackson Browne, Lindsay Buckingham, Stevie Nicks, Don Henley, Glenn Frey, Phil Everly, Carl Wilson, Bonnie Raitt, David Lindley, and J.D. Souther are among those on the album. YouTube videos of performance of "Excitable Boy" are available. On the album *Excitable Boy*, "Werewolves of London," the fourth cut on side one, is a radio favorite of listeners to Warren Zevon. While the optimistic "Johnny Strikes Up the Band" begins the album, Zevon turns to dark humor on "Werewolves," citing horror films to suggest contemporary horrors. Roland travels with mercenaries. The CIA blows his head off and he then haunts the world. The Thompson gunner's story reflects the horrors of genocide. "Excitable Boy" has energetic piano and Linda Ronstadt backing vocals. In "Accidentally Like a Martyr" when one is rejected it is like a martyrdom. Zevon ends the album with "Lawyers, Guns and Money," suggesting paranoia and foreign affairs. The song begins with reference to a waitress who was with the Russians. You can hear this on YouTube. You can also see a video of his performance on April 18, 1980, at the soon to be closed Capitol Theatre on Monroe Street in Passaic. Rick Derringer, Hank Williams, Jr., and The Wallflowers covered this song.

Warren Zevon (1976), *Excitable Boy* (1978).

See: Crystal Zevon, *I'll Sleep When I'm Dead, The Dirty Life and Times of Warren Zevon*, Echo Books, 2007. George Plasketes, *Warren Zevon: Desperado of Los Angeles*, Lanham: Rowman and Littlefield, 2016.

Charting the Wide Appeal
of Singer-Songwriters

Singer songwriters in the 1970s often had crossover appeal. Some of their songs were categorized as "easy listening." The year 1970 began with "Raindrops Keep Falling on My Head" by Burt Bacharach and Hal David at #1, with the vocal by B.J. Thomas. Bacharach and David also reached #1 in February with Dionne Warwick singing "I'll Never Fall in Love Again." Paul Simon and Art Garfunkel reached #1 with "Bridge Over Troubled Water" in March and The Beatles were at #1 with "Let It Be" in April. It was the week of February 20, 1971, that Gordon Lightfoot's "If You Could Read My Mind" reached #1 on the *Billboard* easy listening chart. He was the first singer songwriter to reach #1 with his own performance of his own song. The year 1971 had again begun with a Bacharach-David hit, "One Less Bell to Answer," recorded by The Fifth Dimension. Bobby Goldsboro followed at #1 with Mac Davis's song "Watching Scotty Grow." David Gates sang his #1 song "If" within his band, Bread. The Summer brought Carole King's "It's Too Late" and "You've Got a Friend," sung by James Taylor, to the #1 spot. "Baby I'm-a Want You" by Bread's David Gates rose gently to #1 also in November. The year was filled with singles sung by The Carpenters, The Fifth Dimension, Englebert Humperdinck, Andy Williams, Sonny and Cher, Olivia Newton John, and Chicago. Joan Baez sang "The Night They Drove Old Dixie Down."

Don McLean's "American Pie" was a lengthy breakthrough song that went to #1 in January and February of 1972. Harry Nilsson's vocal on "Without You" by Badfinger's Pete Hamm and Tom Evans secured #1 and was heard widely throughout February and March. Badfinger's own recording of "Day After Day" also received extensive airplay at this time. Cat Stevens' recording of "Morning Has Broken" went to #1 in May. "Song Sung Blue" by Neil Diamond was the summertime #1, holding that spot on the charts from June through July. Then came Gilbert O'Sullivan's "Alone Again (Naturally)" throughout August. David Gates "Guitar Man," performed with Bread, reached #1 next and Mac Davis's "Baby, Don't Get Hooked on Me" immediately followed at #1. Lobo's "I'd Love You to Want Me" went #1 at the beginning of December. O'Sullivan and Bread repeated in the #1 spot at the end of the year with "Claire" and "Sweet Surrender," respectively. The vocal group Three Dog Night scored two #1 singles during the year: "Old Fashioned Love Song" and "Black and White."

Singer songwriters were appearing regularly in the top twenty during this time. In January 1973, Carly Simon's "You're So Vain" intrigued listeners. (In a 2015 interview, Simon admitted the song was about Warren Beatty.) A one-hit wonder Edward Bear had held the #1 in March with the pleasant "The Last Song." Then Stevie Wonder, with "You Are the Sunshine of My Life," and Elton John, with "Daniel" soared to the #1 position. Paul McCartney and Wings gave listeners "My Love" which whoh-whoa-whoa-whoa'd its way to #1 in June. "Adult contemporary" was Anne Murray, Perry Como, Helen Reddy, Tony Orlando and Dawn. Paul Simon, now solo, reached #1 in September with "Loves Me Like a Rock." Art Garfunkel had his own #1 in the autumn with his soaring vocals on Jimmy Webb's song "All I Know." The year ended with Jim Croce's "Time in a Bottle."

The singer songwriter presence on the *Billboard* adult contemporary charts appears to have peaked in 1974–75. There was "Time in a Bottle" (January) and "I'll Have to Say I Love You in a Song" (April) by Jim Croce. There was John Denver's "Sunshine on My Shoulders" (March) and "Annie's Song" (July). Joni Mitchell's "Help Me" went to #1 at the end of May. Gordon Lightfoot had two songs reach #1: "Sundown" (June) and "Carefree Highway" (October). Dave Loggins sang "Please Come to Boston." Neil Diamond's "Longfellow Serenade" went to #1 in the autumn. Mac Davis encouraged people to "Stop and Smell the Roses" and Barry Manilow sang about "Mandy," lifting the chorus with dramatic modulations. During the year Anne Murray turned Kenny Loggins' "A Love Song" into a #1 hit. The mix of crossover music included everything from Barbra Streisand ("The Way We Were") to The Carpenters, and Helen Reddy, and Charlie Rich to Love Unlimited Orchestra. Marvin Hamlisch played "The Entertainer," which was based in Scott Joplin ragtime. Chicago scored two #1 hits, with "Call on Me" and "Wishing You Were Here."

In 1975, #1 adult contemporary songs included recordings by Carole King, Neil Diamond, Gordon Lightfoot, John Denver, Don McLean, Phoebe Snow, Barry Manilow, Michael Murphey, Janis Ian, and James Taylor. Simon and Garfunkel reunited for the #1 "My Little Town." Glen Campbell, The Eagles, The Carpenters, Neil Sedaka all reached the chart's top spot. John Denver had three #1 adult contemporary hits ("Fly Away," "Looking for Space," "Like a Sad Song"). (All of these do not appear on the *Greatest Hits* album, which was issued before this.) John Denver began 1976 with "Fly Away," reaching #1 in January and February. Vocalist Olivia Newton John had three different singles rise to the #1 position on the adult contemporary charts. Paul Simon advised on "Fifty Ways to Leave Your

Lover" while Carole King counseled that "Only Love is Real." James Taylor encouraged his listeners to "Shower the People" (with love, not water). John Denver was "Looking for Space" while John Sebastian was heard on the television theme song "Welcome Back." Neil Diamond reached #1 with "If You Know What I Mean." At the end of the year Mary MacGregor was "Torn Between Two Lovers" and Elton John was singing "Sorry Seems to Be the Hardest Word."

The commercial success of some of the most familiar singer-songwriters continued. James Taylor ("Handy Man") and Carly Simon ("Nobody Does It Better") had #1 adult contemporary hits. Just beyond the mid–1970s the disco phenomenon began. New wave punk staked its claim against slick production and what was now being called corporate rock. Country music was about to morph into more of a commercial pop sound. As 1977 began, Barbra Streisand was heard on "Evergreen," the theme for the film *A Star is Born*. Glen Campbell was singing about "Southern Nights" and Leo Sayer's tenor vocals sang the melodic "When I Need You." America celebrated Memorial Day with Jimmy Buffett's "Margaritaville" at #1. Barry Manilow had two chart toppers: "Weekend in New England" (Randy Edelman) and "Looks Like We Made It" (Will Jennings, Richard Kerr), neither of which he wrote. Pleasant female vocals from Barbra Streisand, Yvonne Ellman, Jennifer Warnes, Olivia Newton John, Rita Coolidge, and Debbie Boone, graced the charts at #1. The Bee Gees ended the year at #1 with "How Deep is Your Love?"

Billy Joel led off the next year at #1 with "Just the Way You Are." Neil Diamond's "Desiree" spent a week at #1 on the adult contemporary chart. Sam Cooke's "Wonderful World" was sung in a collaboration by Paul Simon, Art Garfunkel, and James Taylor. Barry Manilow couldn't smile without someone. The duo of England Dan and John Ford Coley held the #1 spot for the months of April. Chuck Mangione's horn-playing filled the air as May flowers bloomed. The Commodores sang "Three Times a Lady" and Roberta Flack and Barbra Streisand were again at #1. It seems as if singer songwriters began to fade from top chart positions. However, Gerry Rafferty scored a #1 hit with "Right Down the Line" and Al Stewart ended the year with "Time Passages."

Some sentimental country crossover emerged at the #1 spot in April and May of 1979. Randy Van Warmer's song "Just When I Needed You Most" was written to his father who had passed away when the songwriter was a child. Kenny Rogers reached #1 with "She Believes in Me," a songwriter's affirmation of the love of his significant other who sustained belief in him regardless of whether his songs sold or changed the world or not. Anne Murray also underscored this trend of the country/pop crossover song with three #1 hits that year. J.D. Souther was at #1 with "You're Only

Lonely" in November and in December. The year ended with Stevie Wonder's "Send One Your Love."

Of course, the *Billboard* adult contemporary charts are only one measure of the popularity of the singer-songwriter phenomenon in the 1970s. Yet, the charts appear to show that the phenomenon was strongest between 1971 and 1975. Let's expand this a bit. The overall *Billboard* charts for 1970 shows Neil Diamond's "Cracklin' Rosie" in the top twenty for the year. Melanie's "Lay Down (Candles in the Rain)," Steve Wonder's "Signed, Sealed, Delivered, I'm Yours" and John Lennon's "Instant Karma" are listed in the top forty. James Taylor's "Fire and Rain" is the only other singer-songwriter song in the top 100. "Bridge Over Troubled Water" was the chart's top single and Simon and Garfunkel also had "Cecilia" in these listings. The attention to singer songwriters grew in 1971. Carole King's album led the way, with "It's Too Late" among the top ten singles for the year. John Denver's "Take Me Home, Country Roads" was there and so was James Taylor's recording of Carole King's "You've Got a Friend." Marvin Gaye's "What's Going On," hovering near the top 20 for the year, is listed at #21. ("Mercy, Mercy" [The Ecology] is listed at #63.) Bill Withers' "Ain't No Sunshine" is listed by *Billboard* at #23. Former Beatles Paul McCartney ("Uncle Albert/Admiral Halsey") and George Harrison ("My Sweet Lord") appear in the top forty. So does Gordon Lightfoot's "If You Could Read My Mind" (at #38). Carly Simon's "That's the Way I've Always Heard It Should Be" is among the top fifty songs listed. Stevie Wonder's "If You Really Love Me" is listed in the top fifty. Ike and Tina Turner's version of "Proud Mary" by John Fogerty is here. Cat Stevens' "Wild World" and Neil Diamond's "I Am, I Said" are also in the top 100.

The *Billboard* top 100 in 1972 shows the rise of the singer songwriter even more clearly. The year's #1 was Roberta Flack's recording of "The First Time Ever I Saw Your Face," a song by Ewan McColl which emerged from the folk song tradition. This was also the year of "American Pie" by Don McLean. In the top ten songs for the year are Gilbert O'Sullivan's "Alone Again (Naturally)," McLean's "American Pie," Bill Withers' "Lean on Me," Mac Davis's "Baby, Don't Get Hooked on Me," and Melanie's "Band New Key." Neil Young's "Heart of Gold" was in the top twenty. Neil Diamond's "Song Sung Blue" was among the top popular songs. Jonathan Edwards's "Sunshine" was also in the top forty for the year, as was Elton John's "Rocket Man." Songs ranged from "If Loving You Is Wrong I Don't Want to Be Right," and The Stylistics' "Betcha by Golly, Wow" to Michael Jackson singing about a rat and a rocking robin that went "tweet, tweet." There were more animals at #1 with Robert John and Group singing "The Lion Sleeps Tonight." The O'Jays told us about "The Back Stabbers" and The Moody Blues sang "Nights in White Satin." America sang the puzzling lyrics of "A Horse with No Name" and Climax sang "Precious and Few." Harry Chapin sang "Taxi" and Jackson Browne had a top 100 hit with "Doctor My Eyes," This was the year of "Mother and Child Reunion" (Paul Simon), "Morning Has Broken" (Cat Stevens), "You Don't Mess Around with Jim" (Jim Croce), "I Saw the Light" (Todd Rundgren), and Arlo Guthrie's version of Steve Goodman's "City of New Orleans." Carly Simon sang "Anticipation." Bill Withers sang "Use Me." Curtis Mayfield sang "Freddie's Dead." All of them reached top positions on the *Billboard* charts. In all, the singer songwriters ascended the charts alongside artists as diverse as Alice Cooper, James Brown, Charley Pride, Yes, and Bobby Vinton.

"Tie a Yellow Ribbon Around the Old Oak Tree" told the story of a man returning home from prison hoping to see a ribbon telling him he was still loved and welcome. Upon arriving he saw dozens of yellow ribbons. "Killing Me Softly" was another beautiful vocal effort from Roberta Flack. In between those top-listed songs is Jim Croce's "Bad, Bad Leroy Brown" his amusing story about a very bad dude. Kris Kristofferson's "Why Me" and Carly Simon's "You're So Vain" were also in the top ten alongside Elton John ("Crocodile Rock") and Marvin Gaye ("Let's Get It On"), Billy Preston ("Will It Go Round in Circles") and McCartney and Wings ("My Love"). The Edgar Winter Group's instrumental "Frankenstein" figures into the *Billboard* list at #16. Stevie Wonder's "Superstition," John Denver's "Rocky Mountain High" and Paul Simon's "Loves Me Like a Rock" are all in the top forty of the most popular commercial songs of the year. It was a time when pop music could chart hits like "Diamond Girl" by Seals and Crofts alongside "Love Train" by the O'Jays. Grand Funk's "We're an American Band" and "Long Train Runnin'" by the Doobie Brothers were in the top forty for the year along with Maureen McGovern singing "The Morning After." Turn on a radio and there were: Elton John, Sly and the Family Stone, Three Dog Night, Diana Ross, Gladys Knight and the Pips, or "Little Wily (Won't Go Home)," in a bizarre and eclectic mix across genres. This was also the age of hits from hard rock bands like Deep Purple ("Smoke on the Water"), Mountain ("Mississippi Queen"), Bad Company ("Feel Like Making Love"), and progressive rock groups like Emerson, Lake and Palmer ("Lucky Man") and Yes ("Roundabout"). In this popular music context of David Bowie's "Space Oddity," the Allman Brothers playing "Ramblin' Man," and the Stylistics singing "Break Up to Make Up." The singer songwriters heard most widely in 1973 included Jim Croce, Carly Simon, John Denver, Kris Kristofferson, Elton John, Stevie Wonder, Paul Simon, James Taylor, Carole King, Joni Mitchell, and Neil Diamond.

The strength of the singer songwriter phenomenon is also indicated by the artists listed in the Billboard top 100 for 1974. John Denver, Gordon Lightfoot, Jim Croce, Joni Mitchell, Andy Kim, Dave Loggins, Cat Stevens,

Todd Rundgren, Stevie Wonder, and Elton John, all had songs in the top 100. The future awaited just beyond that chart: Billy Joel, Bruce Springsteen, Dan Fogelberg all had their first releases by this time. There was some taste for novelty songs in 1974, like Ray Stevens' "The Streak" and Jim Stafford's "Spiders and Snakes." Harry Chapin's "Cat's in the Cradle" reached #1 in December of that year and his song is listed in the Top 100 of 1975. We see there in the top 100: Janis Ian's "At Seventeen," Phoebe Snow's "Poetry Man," and Michael Martin Murphey's "Wildfire." James Taylor's cover of "How Sweet It Is (To Be Loved by You") and John Denver's "I'm Sorry" are also listed in the top 100 for 1975. If we take just that first half of the decade, we can see several artists whose songs appear in the top positions on the charts again and again. This is an indication of the popularity of these singer songwriters, audience interest in certain kinds of songs, and commercial marketing of the singer-songwriter genre. There is a distinct appeal of these songs and of these artists. Their cultural impact is unmistakable.

One thing that becomes clear from looking at the highest charting popular songs is that, except for the songs of Marvin Gaye, there was no social-political comment in them. Bob Dylan's protest songs were of 1962–63. Phil Ochs had few successors. P.F. Sloan's "The Eve of Destruction," "Society's Child" by Janis Ian, "People Get Ready" and "Keep on Pushing" by Curtis Mayfield were songs of the 1960s. The spirit of "the sixties" was still in the air in the "singer-songwriter era" of the early to mid–1970s. One could hear it in Melanie's "Lay Down (Candles in the Rain)," perhaps. It surfaced with fire and vitriol in Neil Young's "Ohio," recorded by Crosby, Stills, Nash, and Young after the tragedy at Kent State. However, that song was an exception. Harry Chapin was perhaps the most socially and politically active singer-songwriter of the 1970s, but his best-known songs are not political songs or social critiques. He dedicated his work to hunger awareness. Concerns with nuclear power brought forth the No Nukes movement. Neil Young and others were later involved with Farm Aid. Singer-songwriters like Jackson Browne and Bruce Cockburn would later become quite engaged in public causes and criticism of U.S.–Latin American policy. Hit songs dealt with personal issues some listeners could relate to. They were usually melodic songs, and they came to listeners from increasingly familiar singing voices. This book, of course includes many singer-songwriters on the margins of this. So, beyond the profiles provided here, a recommended listening listing might point you to recordings that will be helpful as you further explore their voices, ideas, creativity, and what their songs mean to you.

Recommended Listening

This is a listing of thirty of the most influential singer-songwriters of the 1970s with recommendations of key recordings for you to listen to.

Jackson Browne's songs were being recorded by several artists before Asylum Records put out his first record. That record carried the image of a wrapper on the cover that said: "Saturate Before Using." So, the Jackson Browne album came to be associated with that, as if it was the title of the album. "Doctor My Eyes" was the first hit single through which listeners came to know his music. *For Everyman* is representative of Jackson Browne's style during this period. *Late for the Sky* was called his "masterpiece" by Bruce Springsteen and it merits your attention. *The Pretender* features the title song and this album placed Jackson Browne in the center of popular music. *Running on Empty* secured that, along with the live performance of "The Load Out" and "Stay."

Harry Chapin proclaimed the importance of what man's life could be worth. A good entry-point into the music, lyrics, and social commitments of Harry Chapin is the recent documentary *Harry Chapin: When in Doubt Do Something* (2021). The greatest hits live album is also a good starting point. Harry Chapin was an engaging performer, surrounded by a fine band. Listen to his albums in sequence, beginning with *Heads and Tales* (1972), on which the song "Taxi" appears. You will find "Cats in the Cradle" on *Verities and Balderdash* (1974). Don't pass up *Short Stories*, or *Sniper and Other Love Songs*. The album *Living Room Suite* is also bright and entertaining.

Bruce Cockburn, while perhaps underestimated, is one of Canada's great singer-songwriters. He is an exceptional guitar player, a poetic lyricist, and a thoughtful social critic. His 1970s output of one album every year culminates in *Dancing in the Dragon's Jaws* (1979). The spare and intriguing *High Winds, White Sky* (1971) is a good starting place for exploring Bruce Cockburn's songwriting and guitar playing. *Anything, Anytime, Anywhere* (1979) collects sixteen singles from the 1970s. *The Best of Bruce Cockburn* appears on YouTube and includes his best-known socio-political songs.

Leonard Cohen's greatest hits collections include: *The Best of Leonard Cohen* (1975) and *Greatest Hits* (Sony 2009). There are live performances on *Live in London*. *The Essential Leonard Cohen* is available from Rhino records. "Bird on a Wire" is available on YouTube. So are several other Leonard Cohen performances of his songs, including "Happens to the Heart," "Hallelujah," and one of "I'm Your Man" live from Dublin. From November 9, 2018, through April 9, 2019, the Musée d'Art contemporain de Montréal ran a retrospective exhibit of Leonard Cohen's career. *Leonard Cohen: The Complete Albums Collection* (2011), with live and studio recordings from 1967 to 2009, is available from SONY. The box set consists of 17 albums. You can find information on *https://www.leonardcohen.com*. There is UK site Legacy of Leonard Cohen: *https://www.legacyrecordings. uk.com*.

Jim Croce's *Photographs and Memories* (1974), a 14 song greatest hits album, along with and *Faces I've Been* (1975), a career retrospective with 4-sides including some of his work with Ingrid Croce, provide an overview of his brief and significant career. Reviewing the posthumous *Photographs and Memories*, *Billboard* marveled about the "fountain" of excellent work produced "in barely two years." A *Greatest Songs* (1980) compilation also followed. In 1990, the Songwriter's Hall of Fame finally acknowledged Croce's songwriting and his impact. Rhino released *The Classic Hits of Jim Croce* (2006). The box set *Jim Croce: The 50th Anniversary* Collection makes that clear. This is one of the most comprehensive overviews of Jim Croce's songs. You can see some videos of Croce singing "Time in a Bottle" and "Operator." There is a video of Croce and Murray Muehleisen performing in Ireland in 1973. This is an intimate performance for a very polite and respectful audience. You can hear Croce introducing his songs.

When it comes to **John Denver**, there is probably no better way into the work of John Denver than to listen to his *Greatest Hits* album of 1973 and *Greatest Hits Volume II* from 1977. The first *Greatest Hits* album includes several songs that are not technically "hits" but that do provide a sense of John Denver's style, qualities, and themes. These themes expand into ecological concerns and other topics as one follows John Denver through the 1970s. One has to move through the post–1973 recordings to see the growing popularity and range of John Denver. One way to do this is to listen to *Greatest Hits, Volume II*. What is most interesting about these albums is that John Denver re-recorded his hits songs in new versions. A third *Greatest Hits* album was released in 1984. It is not clear what is meant by "greatest hits" at this point, although this is a good collection of John Denver songs. The *John Denver RCA Albums Collection* is a box set that brings together 24 John Denver albums from 1969 to 1970 through 1986. This is 17 hours of music. You will really have to like John Denver if you wish to order this one. Amazon lists this for $469.

Neil Diamond's *Hot August Night* double album of live performances stands as one of the milestones of his songwriting and performing in the 1970s. *Longfellow Serenade* is a central studio album in a decade that saw eight studio album recordings. "Cracklin' Rosie" was the first of his big 1970s hits. "Song Sung Blue," "I Am, I Said" were among the others. In the 1960s this was a rather fierce pop-rock writer who emerged as a star performer after his big hit "Sweet Caroline." He morphed into a middle-of-the-road vocalist, doing duets with Barbra Streisand. This suggested to Paul Simon at the Rock and Roll Hall of Fame induction ceremony one possible reason for the delay in admitting Neil Diamond. The first Neil Diamond *Greatest Hits* (1968) album recalls the early years with Bang Records. *Neil Diamond's All-Time Greatest Hits, Legend* can be heard on YouTube. You can also hear on YouTube *Neil Diamond's Greatest Hits* (2020).

Nick Drake only left us a few recordings. However, his recordings have been revived and represent a legacy. One may wish for more. He recorded *Five Leaves Left* (1969), *Bryter Layter* (1971) and *Pink Moon* (1972). A 1974 effort was abandoned. One might obtain *Way to Blue: An Introduction to Nick Drake* (1994) to gain a good overview of his music. There are several other compilations available for exploring his music. However, this one is most reflective of his work. *Time of No Reply* (1985) included previously unreleased material. *The John Peel Session* (2014) will give you a taste of a live performance of five songs. These BBC recordings provide different versions of the songs than those originally recorded for albums. Box sets have also been assembled: *Fruit Tree* (1979), *Tuck Box* (2013).

There are two **Bob Dylan** *Greatest Hits* albums from the 1970s and they might be places to begin the journey into Dylan's catalog of recordings. *Writings and Drawings* will give his song lyrics for you to read. *Highway 61 Revisited* and *Blonde on Blonde* are classic Dylan recordings from the 1960s. *Nashville Skyline* marks a turn to some country-sounding production. *Blood on the Tracks* is a pivotal album for Dylan's 1970s songwriting. *Desire* continues his emphasis on the story song, and includes some collaboration, some violin-fiddle. The Bob Dylan website is at *https://www.bobdylan.com*.

Dan Fogelberg's masterpiece is the double-album *The Innocent Age* (1980). *Souvenirs* might be a good starting place. Then one can either backtrack to *Home Free* and *Captured Angel* or jump ahead to the neo-classical *Netherlands* and the rockier *Phoenix*. *Twin Sons of Different Mothers* is a crisply recorded mostly instrumental collaboration with flutist Tim Weisberg. *Windows and Walls* is an album that includes some fine performances, along with the sentimental and poignant title song. There are several collections of Dan Fogelberg's songs: *Greatest Hits* (1982), *Love Songs* (1995), *The Very Best of Dan Fogelberg* (2001), *The Essential Dan Fogelberg* (2014). The finest collection of his work is *Portrait*, a 4 CD boxed set. There is also the live album, *Dan Fogelberg: Greetings from the West,* and his 1979 solo live performance, *Live at Carnegie Hall* (2017).

Richie Furay's career can be discovered through listening to Buffalo Springfield, Poco, and the two Souther, Hillman, Furay albums. *I've Got a Reason* well represents his 1970s solo work. However, you can also listen to *Dance a Little Light,* his next solo recording. The biography by Thomas Kitts covers Furay's life and music. Furay's Christian commitment is also a significant part of his life. *I've Got a Reason* is Christian inspired but not especially evangelical. The full album is available on YouTube.

Marvin Gaye was among the most engaged songwriters of public commentary in the first years of the 1970s. This became evident when listening to "What's Going On?" and "Mercy, Mercy (The Ecology)." By the mid–1970s Marvin Gaye had moved toward more sensual content in his songs and a further emphasis upon concert performances. You can hear that energy on eleven songs on a recording simply titled *Marvin Gaye* (Play 247). *What's Going On?* (1971) is a good starting point for taking in his 1970s music. *Marvin Gaye Collected* (2017) and *The Very Best of Marvin Gaye* (1994) each provide a more comprehensive overview. *Marvin Gaye Greatest Hits* full album has been posted on YouTube.

Carole King's *Tapestry* (1971) is one of the essential singer-songwriter albums of the early 1970s. You need not necessarily go beyond this one album of hers. However, if you do, the overall quality of the tapestry of this singer-songwriter's talent becomes increasingly clear. *Rhymes and Reasons* (1972) and *Fantasy* (1973) were gold albums. *Wrap Around Joy* (1974), with the hits "Jazzman" and "Nightingale," was also a popular gold album. *Pearls: The Songs of King and Goffin* (1980) recalled the older hits and some newer collaborations. Among the interesting albums you might listen to is Carole King's performance with James Taylor, *Live at the Troubadour* (2010). This has also been broadcast on video on PBS stations across the United States. *The Essential Carole King* includes her own performances and performances by artists singing her songs. *Beautiful: The Carole King Musical* opened in 2014 on Broadway.

Billy Joel's *Piano Man* is probably a good starting point for your listening. One can always backtrack to *Cold Spring Harbor. The Stranger,* produced with Phil Ramone, is his most complete and consistent album of the 1970s. It was something of a launching pad for his string of hits which followed. There are two collections of *Greatest Hits.*

Elton John filled the 1970s with hit songs. You might start with the first *Greatest Hits* (1974) album and with the film biopic "Rocket Man." Or, *Goodbye Yellow Brick Road* (1974), a classic double-album might be a good choice. However, turn back to 1969 also and get hold of the first album and the Troubadour performances. Work your way through

Tumbleweed Connection, Madman Across the Water, Honky Chateau, and *Don't Shoot Me I'm Only the Piano Player*. That will bring you to *Goodbye Yellow Brick Road* (1974) and to the *Greatest Hits* (1974) album. Of course, then comes the rest of an illustrious career and many more hit songs and performances.

Gordon Lightfoot was among the most popular, influential, and best-selling singer-songwriters of this decade. There were several hit songs: "If You Could Read My Mind," "Sundown," "Carefree Highway," "The Wreck of the Edmund Fitzgerald." *Gord's Gold* (1975) and *Gord's Gold II* (1988) would be a good starting point for a listener. *Songbook* (Rhino, 1999) is a box set collection for anyone who would like to hear the span of his career across the 1960s, 1970s, and later. It is available for about $40. Rhino has also produced *The Complete Singles 1970–1980*. United Artists put out a series of *Best of Lightfoot* albums in the early 1970s.

Don McLean's *American Pie* album is one movement in a series of albums you ought to listen to consecutively. *Tapestry*, with "Castles in the Air," gives us the emerging folk singer-songwriter. The *Don McLean* album, for all the starkness of its black and white cover, shows us the depth of his songwriting and his vocal abilities. *Homeless Brother* is perhaps the best produced of the Don McLean albums of this period. *Solo* is a terrific introduction to Don McLean in concert.

Joni Mitchell's *Blue* (1971) is one of her critically acclaimed albums. *For the Roses* (1972) stays mostly within folk music roots. However, *Court and Spark* (1974) brings folk music into play with jazz. This continues with *The Hissing of Summer Lawns (1975)* and *Hegira* (1976), which is itself an album that suggests and provides a sense of movement. *Don Juan's Reckless Daughter* (1977) moves ahead with further jazz experimentation. Joni Mitchell's jazz experiments with Charles Mingus led to *Mingus* (1979). For earlier material you might refer to *The World of Joni Mitchell* (1971). Listen to her collected songs and performances on *The Reprise Albums* (2021), *Greatest Hits, Joni Mitchell Anthology, Joni Mitchell: The Studio Albums 1968–1979* (2012). Two volumes of *The Joni Mitchell Archives*, currently in development, appeared in 2020 and 2021. *Live at Carnegie Hall*, 1969 was released on October 29, 2021.

Van Morrison's expansive career dates back into the 1960s and that is the most obvious place to begin if you wish to trace his emergence as a singer-songwriter. One could go back to his band Them and the single "Gloria." (Listen also to Patti Smith's version of this song.) "Domino," "Tupelo Honey," "Moondance," "Brown Eyed Girl" are among the hit singles he created. However, wider listening will include Morrison's path from *Astral Weeks* (1968) through *Moondance* (1970), *His Band and Street Choir* (1970) and *Tupelo Honey* (1971) to *St. Dominic's Preview* (1972) in the early 1970s. One might also explore his somewhat mystical-spiritual inquiries and expressions across his albums through the 1980s to *Hymns to the Silence* (1991). While Van Morrison is often an introspective writer, he has also produced many bright, extroverted hits. You can find some of his recordings and clips of Van Morrison performances on YouTube.

Laura Nyro's *Stoned Soul Picnic: The Best of Laura Nyro* provides some of "the best," or at least best-known of Laura Nyro's compositions. There are two discs, with 19 songs on the first disc and 15 on the second disc. This is a representative compilation and a good path for anyone entering into Laura Nyro's music. It is helpful to also listen to how her albums are sequenced and the performances she brought to them. Columbia/Legacy/Sony put out the album in 1997. Ten songs from Disc One may appear on your computer. The audio CD is available from Amazon for $16. Michael Kort's biography *Soul Picnic: The Music and Passion of Laura Nyro* will complement your listening. There are YouTube recordings of her performances of "Soul Stoned Picnic," "Wedding Bell Blues," "And When I Die," "Save the Country," and a 1970 cover of King and Goffin's "Up on the Roof." There is a live show recording of Laura Nyro in Pittsburgh. A 1971 Carnegie Hall show carries the note that that recording cannot be reproduced.

John Prine's first album offers a good entry into his songwriting and matter-of-fact delivery of his songs. *Prime Prine* (1976) is perhaps the best overview of his work in the 1970s. The Chicago songwriter spent some time in Nashville and this country-inflected sound appears on songs like "Angel from Montgomery." However, you can discover the roots of John Prine's songs on the albums of the early 1970s. And don't forget his fellow Chicago songwriter-performer Steve Goodman, an introduction to whom can be found on the double album *The Essential Steve Goodman* (1976).

Carly Simon as pop song hitmaker is to be found on *Reflections: The Greatest Hits of Carly Simon*, which has 20 tracks, 19 of which are hit songs. This is a fine overview of her music. There were previous greatest hits collections including *The Best of Carly Simon* (1975) and *Anthology* (2002). *The Greatest Hits of Carly Simon* can also be heard on YouTube. Her 1987 concert *Live from Martha's Vineyard* (1988) offers another interesting angle on her music.

Paul Simon's solo career took some new turns after "Bridge Over Troubled Water." *Live Rhymin'* (1974) features Paul Simon in performance and is one of the best places to go to gain a sense of his music in those first few years of his solo activity following Simon and Garfunkel. For a full picture, one should go back to the Simon and Garfunkel recordings of the 1960s and proceed through Paul Simon's first few solo albums. There were several hit singles: "Loves Me Like a Rock," "Mother and Child Reunion," "Me and Julio Down by the Schoolyard," "Kodachrome," "Fifty Ways to leave Your Lover" among them. Simon's solo story-song writing comes out in "Duncan" and "American Tune." *Paul Simon 1966–1993* is a wonderful 4 CD and booklet set of many of hit top singles through those years. *Paul Simon Live in New York City* is a recording of twenty songs at a concert on June 6, 2011.

Bruce Springsteen in the 1970s worked entirely from within the context of his E Street Band. While *Born to Run* is the breakthrough Springsteen album it is valuable to listen to the street-poet rocker of *Greetings from Asbury Park* and *The Wild, the Innocent, and the E Street Shuffle.* Then one should turn to *Darkness on the Edge of Town.* Following *Born in the U.S.A.*, the spare *Nebraska* album begins to show Springsteen as a solo singer-songwriter. Recorded, in part, at home, these are stripped down ballads that go straight to the heart and to stories. These six albums form a core for listening to Springsteen and his further output in the 1980s and after.

Cat Stevens' albums and singles of the 1970s are noted under his entry in this book. His popularity crested between 1971 and 1975. That is, he was a main figure in the center of the singer-songwriter era. From *Tea for the Tillerman* (1970), *Teaser and the Firecat* (1971), and *Catch Bull at Four* (1972), he rose to prominence with a series of top ten singles. By the time of *Buddah and the Chocolate Box* (1974) Cat Stevens was at his peak. You can listen through those albums. Or, if you just want to hear the Cat Stevens hits, turn to *Greatest Hits* (1975). You can also get this on YouTube.

James Taylor was originally cited as being at the center of the era of the singer-songwriter. The first *Greatest Hits* album features songs from 1970 through 1976. It has been one of his best-selling albums. *Greatest Hits II* was released in 2000 and has 16 songs. His albums across the decade introduced the hits "Fire and Rain," "You've Got a Friend," "Country Road" and ran through popular cover tunes like "Handy Man," "How Sweet It Is (To Be Loved by You)" and "Up on the Roof" on to his own songs like "Shower the People" and "Your Smiling Face." *Sweet Baby James* and *Mudslide Slim and the Blue Horizon* are important starting points. *One Man Dog* was recorded mostly in a home studio. Many critics and listeners seemed to want to walk on by *Walking Man. Gorilla* included the radio hit "How Sweet It Is." The *J.T.* album pops things up into more radio friendly hits. This album received a Grammy nomination for Album of the Year. *The Best of James Taylor* (2003) is a collection of his releases while recording with Warner Brothers Records. James Taylor's first Columbia Records release was *J.T.* (1977). Rhino Records provides a collection of the Warner Brothers albums 1970–1976.

Bill Withers' "Lean on Me" and "Ain't No Sunshine" continue to be played frequently. "Lean on Me" has provided many people with an uplifting message encouraging endurance and the power of friendship and mutual support. An overview of the career of Bill Withers, who died in 2020, is available on *Bill Withers: Greatest Hits* (1981). This album collects his top songs of the 1970s.

Stevie Wonder's albums of the 1970s included three recordings that were awarded Album of the Year. One may start with any of these: *Innervisions, Fulfillingness First Finale, Songs in the Key of Life.* The double-album *Songs in the Key of Life* is a favorite. A compact career retrospective of 21 songs is available on *Stevie Wonder: The Definitive Collection* (2002) from Motown Records.

Neil Young's *Harvest* was his best-selling album of the decade. For Neil Young the 1970s starts with *After the Gold Rush* (1970) ("Only Love Can Break Your Heart," "Tell Me Why," "Don't Let It Bring You Down"). This was his follow-up to *Everybody Knows This is Nowhere* (1969). This prolific singer-songwriter has created an archive. If you become a member the wide variety of Neil Young's songs and performances become available to you. For listeners who wish to focus on the 1970s, his work with Crazy Horse continues through the decade even as he moves in and out of his alliance with Crosby, Stills, and Nash. The live album *Four Way Street* (1971), *CSNY 1974*, and the compilation *So Far* will give you a taste of Crosby, Stills, Nash and Young. You might listen to "Ohio," "Southern Man," "Helpless," which have Neil Young vocals and are all available on performances on YouTube. *On the Beach* (1975) was a melodic mid-decade Neil Young recording. *Long May You Run* (1976) was an album developed and recorded with Stephen Stills. With *Comes a Time* (1978) he returned to the Nashville country sounding style of *Harvest*. However, the *Rust Never Sleeps* (1978) tour with "Hey Hey, My My (Into the Black)" was rock-oriented and new wave–punk influenced. To approach Neil Young in the 1970s is to explore the many sides and styles of this singer-songwriter.

Warren Zevon was highly regarded in the Los Angeles pop music community. Following *Wanted Dead or Alive* (1969) in the 1970s, he gave us two more solo albums, *Warren Zevon* (1976) and *Excitable Boy* (1978). "Werewolves of London" continues to get airplay on classic rock stations. However, the depth and range of Zevon's songwriting and performances is best explored through these three albums. There are a dozen subsequent recordings through 2003, one of which was recorded with members of R.E.M.

Singer Songwriters and Their Bands

Several singer-songwriters emerged from bands. You might listen to them within the context of those bands and then select a solo album.

These artists include Eric Clapton (The Yardbirds, John Mayall and Blues-breakers, Cream, Blind Faith), Gene Clark (The Byrds), David Crosby (The Byrds; Crosby, Stills and Nash), John Fogerty (Creedence Clearwater Revival), Peter Frampton (Humble Pie), Richie Furay (Buffalo Springfield, Poco), David Gates (Bread), Henry Gross (Sha Na Na), Chris Hillman (The Byrds, Flying Burrito Brothers), Iain Matthews (Fairport Convention), Van Morrison (Them), Graham Nash (The Hollies; Crosby, Stills and Nash), Gram Parsons (The Byrds), Gerry Rafferty (Stealer's Wheel), Todd Rundgren (The Nazz), Stephen Stills (Buffalo Springfield; Crosby, Stills and Nash; Manassas), Richard Thompson (Fairport Convention), Jesse Colin Young (The Youngbloods), Neil Young (Buffalo Springfield; Crosby, Stills, Nash and Young). Some, like Neil Young, Stephen Stills, Edgar Winter, and Elton John, also formed bands, although they also could play solo. Others were inseparable from their bands in the 1970s: Bruce Springsteen, Bob Seger, Steve Miller, Frank Zappa. (Springsteen's *Nebraska* [1982] was a departure from his involvement with the E Street Band, as is the case with some of his later work.) There are also duos, trios, like Loggins and Messina, or Souther, Hillman, Furay. Listening to their work together will complement any investigation of the music of each of the members.

The Time-Life Collection of Singer-Songwriters

The Time-Life series of Singer-Songwriters is the most complete overview of the decade's most popular singer-songwriters. The advantage of this series is that it brings together top songs into one place for easy access. Of course, that was before MP3s and IPods, when that one place would be on CDs. This series stretches the term singer-songwriter to include duos and bands. We hear songs that were commercially successful. This is a wonderful set but many of the songs are not those of singer songwriters. What we have is a mix of easy listening/adult contemporary hits with singer-songwriter material. Even so, with two CDs in each package this is a fine retrospective of the era. *Early 70s*, for example, includes The Doobie Brothers, B.J. Thomas, Bread, Aretha Franklin, Looking Glass, Three Dog Night, Vicki Lawrence, Anne Murray, and America—none of which would be called singer-songwriters. However, the same two CD set includes Jim Croce's "Operator," Todd Rundgren's "I Saw the Light," Harry Chapin's "Taxi," Lobo's "I'd Love You to Want Me," and Nilsson's "Coconut." The 1970–1971 CD brings you Carole King ("It's Too Late"), Marvin Gaye ("What's Going On?"), Bill Withers ("Ain't No Sunshine"), Richie Have's playing George Harrison's "Here Comes the Sun," Jonathan Edwards' "Sunshine," John Denver's "Take Me Home, Country Roads," Cat Stevens' "Peace Train," Carly Simon's "That's the What I've Always Heard It Should Be," James Taylor's "Fire and Rain," Melanie's "Lay Down (Candles in the Rain)," John Lennon's "Jealous Guy," Stephen Stills' "Love the One You're With," and Bread with David Gates singing "If." However, the Nitty Gritty Dirt Band, Janis Joplin, and The Hollies on this same CD are not singer-songwriters.

Singers and Songwriters. 19 volumes. (432 tracks) New York, Time-Life, 2000–2002. (29 volumes in United Kingdom and Europe) Topical releases followed 2003–2004.

Other Collections of Recordings:

Blue Beat Music Playlist. 111 artists. 3090 songs.www.bluebeatmusic.com
70s Singer Songwriter Essentials, Apple Music. Individual songs.
https://musicapple.com

These singer-songwriter songs are a cultural legacy. You can access many of these songs on your computer by entering the name of the artist or the title of the song. YouTube videos range from the "official" ones uploaded by artist managers, companies, artist's families, or artist's themselves and the unofficial ones placed on YouTube by fans. The "unofficial" ones could be taken down at the request of an artist or a company. However, many of these remain available and the artists, their families, or other copyright owners do not much care about this presence on the Internet. Consequently, YouTube offers many possibilities for exploring the singer-songwriters of the 1970s, including some real gems.

YouTube Videos

There are many YouTube videos that will provide you with performances, interviews, and recordings. Here are just a few of the many interesting ones. Note that some YouTube videos are "official" (posted by the artists or their management or record companies, or by broadcast stations) and others have been uploaded by fans. The latter could be taken down at the request of the recording artist, or a company affiliated with that artist. Those are the current digital copyright rules. The YouTube videos or audio recordings that you can access on your computer provide an excellent way to explore the singer songwriters listed in this book. This is a sample:

Jackson Browne: Home videos—"Some Bridges," "The Pretender" (2021) for Roger Brown of Berkley School of Music, "The Waiting" by Tom Petty. "Farther On." "I'll Do Anything" concert video (1:45:10), "Running on Empty" live in concert. "Take It Easy" with The Eagles. "Before the Deluge."

Harry Chapin: Capitol Theatre, Passaic, N.J. October 21, 1978. Actor-comedian Chevy Chase makes an appearance, joining Chapin onstage. Final Concert, 1981, Hamilton Place. "Remember When the Music" (audio only): Chapin discusses the activism connected with 1960s music and culture. Then he sings his song "Remember When the Music."

Jim Croce: *Jim Croce in Concert in Ireland.* This is a particularly good video of Croce in concert with his sideman Maury Muehleisen.

Neil Diamond: Interview on RTE Irish television *Late, Late Show* with a live audience. He speaks of his liking for science and thoughts of going into medicine before music took him in a different direction. He also talks about development of his songs as a young songwriter at the Brill Building in New York. His songs began reaching audiences when he wrote more personally about experiences or aspects of his life, he says. He plays "I'm a Believer" slowly and the audience sing-along is charming. He discusses "Sweet Caroline" and plays a bit of the song.

Bob Dylan: "Tangled Up in Blue" (1975 performance), "One More Cup of Coffee" (1975 concert). Dylan under a hat, wearing some facial makeup, can be seen in concert around the time of the *Desire* album. Portland concert 1990, audio only. "Blowing in the Wind" television performance, 1963. "Forever Young" with Bruce Springsteen at Rock and Roll Hall of Fame and "All Along the Watchtower" at Rock and Roll Hall of Fame.

David Gates: Television performances—"If" 1975, 1977 (A Sweet Surrender, Helter Skelter Publishing) "Never Let Her Go," UK television (1975), "It Don't Matter to Me," 1971. "Make It with You" Introduced by Gates, who says he wrote it for his wife and played it for her at home. Also, "Make It with You" with Bread on Midnight Special, 1977. See Bread-The Biography.

Steve Goodman: Capitol Theatre, Passaic, N.J. performance.

Don McLean: interview on the *Late, Late Show*, RTE, Irish television. He and the host have a conversation about his music before a live audience. He sings one verse of "Vincent" and explains where the song came from. He sings a verse of "Mountains of Mourne" and sings and discusses "And I Love You So." The audience happily sings along to some of "American Pie." There are several YouTube videos (most of them audio only) of "American Pie." A BBC performance of "American Pie" may be the best of these. There is a video of McLean performing "Castles in the Air." A 1972 performance of "Vincent" appears on Sounds for Saturday.

Patti Smith: Capitol Theatre, Passaic, N.J. May 11, 1979.

Bruce Springsteen: Born to Run, Dancing in the Dark, Hyde Park, 2009. Milan, July 3, 2016. A 1987 band documentary. Capital Centre, 1978 Darkness on the Edge of Town tour. Madison Square Garden, New York 2016.

Jesse Colin Young: Capitol Theatre, Passaic. N.J. concert.

Warren Zevon: Capitol Theatre, Passaic, N.J. April 18, 1980.

Selected Documentaries

General

Echo in the Canyon (2018). Laurel Canyon, Los Angeles music. Andrew Slater, director.
The Last Waltz (1978). The Band, Bob Dylan, Neil Young, Joni Mitchell, Eric Clapton, and others. Martin Scorsese, director.
No Nukes (1980). Jackson Browne, Bonnie Raitt, Graham Nash, Bruce Springsteen. Danny Goldberg, director.
Troubadours: Carole King/James Taylor and the Rise of the Singer Songwriters (2011). American Masters, PBS. Morgan Neville, director.
Woodstock (1970). Michael Wadleigh, director.

Singer-Songwriters

David Bowie: *David Bowie: Five Years* (2015). Francis Whately, director. *Ziggy Stardust and the Spiders from Mars* (1979). D. A. Pennebaker, director.
Jackson Browne: *Jackson Browne: Going Home* (1994). Janice Engel, director.
Johnny Cash: *The Johnny Cash Show: The Best of Johnny Cash, 1969–1971.* Michael B. Borofsky, director. ($25). *Johnny Cash's America* (2008). Robert Gordon, Morgan Neville, directors. *Live in Montreaux 1994* (2005).
Bruce Cockburn: *Rumours of Glory: Concert Film*, Music Hall, Toronto, 1982.
Leonard Cohen: *Bird on a Wire* (1974). Tony Palmer, director. *Leonard Cohen: Live at the Isle of Wight 1970* (2009). Murray Lerner, director.
Jim Croce: *Songman: The Untold Story of Jim Croce* (2016). Robert Langpaap, director.
David Crosby: *David Crosby: Remember My Name* (2019) A. J. Eaton, director.
John Denver: *John Denver Country Boy* (2013). Steve Freer, director.
Nick Drake: *A Skin Too Few: The Days of Nick Drake* (2002). Jeroen Berkvens, director.
Bob Dylan: *Don't Look Back* (1967). D. A. Pennebacker, director. *Renaldo and Clara* (1978) Bob Dylan, producer. *No Direction Home* (2005) Martin Scorsese, director. *Rolling Thunder Revue: A Bob Dylan Story* (2019). Martin Scorsese, director.
George Harrison: *George Harrison: Living in the Material World* (2011). Martin Scorsese, director. *The Concert for Bangladesh* (1972). Saul Swimmer, director. *Concert for George* (2003), David Leland, director.
Billy Joel: *Billy Joel: A Matter of Trust, The Bridge to Russia* (2014). Jim Brown, director. *Hired Gun: Billy Joel* (2016). Fran Strine, director. *The Last Play at Shea.* Narrated by Alec Baldwin, Paul Crowder and Greg Whitely, directors.
Carole King: *Carole King and James Taylor Live at the Troubadour.* PBS, 2021. *Carole King: Natural Woman* (2016). American Masters, PBS. George Scott, director.
John Lennon: *Lennon Legend: The Very Best of John Lennon* (2003). Simon Hilton, et. al. *Imagine: John Lennon* (1988). John Solt, director.
Gordon Lightfoot: *Gordon Lightfoot: If You Could Read My Mind* (2019). Martha Kehoe and M. Tesoni.
Kenny Loggins: *Kenny Loggins Alive. Kenny Loggins from the Grand Canyon. Kenny Loggins from Redwoods. Kenny Loggins Live from Soundstage.*
Bob Marley: *Marley* (2012). Kevin Macdonald, director.
Paul McCartney: *McCartney* (2021) 6 episodes, Hulu. Rick Rubin, producer.

Joni Mitchell: *Joni Mitchell: Woman of Heart and Mind* (2003). American Masters. Susan Lacy and Stephanie Bennett, directors.

Van Morrison: *Van Morrison in Ireland* (2008). Michael Radford, director. *Van Morrison: Under Review, 1964–1974* (2008).

Harry Nilsson: *Who Is Harry Nilsson (and Why Is Everyone Talking About Him)?* (2012) John Scheinfeld, director.

Nina Simone: *What Happened to Miss Simone?* (2015) Liz Garbus, director.

James Taylor: *Carole King and James Taylor Live at the Troubadour.* PBS, 2021. *The Making of James Taylor's Breakthrough Album Sweet Baby James* (13 minutes). https://albumism.com *Breakshot: My First 21 Years. An Audio Memoir* (2020) (audio only). (See the interview with Bill Flanagan, February 26, 2020, on YouTube.) *James Taylor, Everyday: Live at the Beacon Theatre* (1998), Beth McCarthy-Miller, director.

Townes Van Zandt: *Be Here to Love Me: Townes Van Zandt* (2004). Guy Clark, Willie Nelson, Kris Kristofferson. Margaret Brown, director.

Bill Withers: *Still Bill* (2008). Demani Baker, Alex Vlack, directors.

Neil Young: *Rust Never Sleeps* (1979). *Neil Young: The First Decade* (2019). *Neil Young Under Review, 1966–1975* (2007). *Neil Young: Heart of Gold* (2006). Jonathan Demme, director. *Neil Young Journeys* (2011), concert video. Jonathan Demme, director.

Frank Zappa: *Eat That Question: Frank Zappa* (2016). Thorstein Schutte, director. *Zappa* (2020) Alex Winter, director.

For Further Reading

Borshuck, Michael. "The Professional Singer-Songwriter of the 1970s," *Cambridge Companion to the Singer-Songwriter*. Cambridge University Press, 2016, 89-100.

Boyd, Jenny, and Holly George-Warren, *Musicians in Tune*. Fireside, Simon & Schuster, 1992.

Davis, Sheila. *The Craft of Lyric Writing*. Writer's Digest, 1984.

Dicaire, David. *The Folk Music Revival, 1958–1970*. McFarland, 2011.

Epstein, Lawrence J. *Political Folk Music in America from Its Origins to Bob Dylan*. McFarland, 2010.

Gioia, Ted. *Delta Blues: The Life and Times of the Mississippi Masters Who Revolutionized American Music*. W. W. Norton, 2008.

Hoskyns, Barney. *Hotel California: Singer Songwriters and Cocaine Cowboys of the LA Canyon, 1967–1976*. Fourth Estate, 2006.

Palmer, Robert. *Deep Blues: A Musical and Cultural History of the Mississippi Delta*. Penguin, 1992.

Pollock, Bruce. *In Their Own Words*. Collier, 1975.

Riggio, Ronald. "Why Do Young People Listen to Old Music?" *Psychology Today* (August 2018).

Roszak, Theodore. *The Making of the Counterculture*. Faber & Faber, 1970.

Sarlin, Bob. *Turn It Up, I Can't Hear the Words*. Coronet, 1975.

Shepherd, John. *Tin Pan Alley*. Routledge, Kegan Paul, 1982.

Walker, Luke. "Tangled Up in Blake: The Triangular Relationship among Dylan, Blake, and the Beats" (1–18), in *Rock and Romanticism*, James Rovira, ed. Lexington Books, 2018.

Walker, Michael. *Laurel Canyon: The Inside Story of Rock and Roll's Legendary Neighborhood*. Farrar, Straus, and Giroux, 2003.

Webb, Jimmy. *Tunesmith: Inside the Art of Songwriting*. Hachette, 1999.

Williams, Katherine, and Justin A. Williams. *The Cambridge Companion to the Singer-Songwriter*. Cambridge University Press, 2016.

Yagoda, Ben. *The B Side: The Death of Tin Pan Alley and the Rebirth of the Great American Song*. Penguin, 2015.

Zollo, Paul. *Songwriters on Songwriting*. 4th ed. Da Capo, 2003.

Individual Artist Biographies and Autobiographies

Bego, Mark. *Bonnie Raitt: Still in the Nick of Time*. Carol Publishing, 1995.

_____. *Jackson Browne: His Life and His Music*. Citadel, 2005.

Bennighof, James. *The Words and Music of Paul Simon*. Praeger, 2007.

Bielen, Ken. *The Words and Music of Neil Young*. Praeger, 2008.

_____. *The Words and Music of Billy Joel*. Praeger, 2011.

Bonca, Cornell. *Paul Simon: An American Tune*. Rowman and Littlefield, 2014.

Borodowitz, Hank. *Billy Joel: The Life and Times of an Angry Young Man*. Hal Leonard, 2011.

Bowie, David, and Mick Rock. *Moonage Daydream: The Life and Times of Ziggy Stardust*. Universe, 2005.

Buffett, Jimmy. *A Pirate Looks at Fifty*. Random House, 1998.

Butler, Patricia. *Barry Manilow: The Biography*. Omnibus, 2009.

Carlin, Peter Ames. *Homeward Bound: The Life of Paul Simon.* St. Martin's-Griffin, 2017.

Cash, Johnny. *Cash: An Autobiography.* Harper, 2003.

Clapton, Eric. *Clapton: The Autobiography.* Broadway Books, 2008.

Cockburn, Bruce. *Rumours of Glory: A Memoir.* Harper, 2014.

Collis, John. *John Denver: Mother Nature's Son.* Mainstream, 2003.

_____. *Van Morrison: Inarticulate Speech of the Heart.* Little, Brown, 2010.

Costello, Elvis. *Unfaithful Music and Disappearing Ink.* Blue Rider Press, 2016.

Croce, Ingrid, and Jimmy Rock. *I've Got a Name: The Jim Croce Story.* Da Capo, 2015.

Crosby, David, and Carl Gottlieb. *Long Time Gone: The Autobiography of David Crosby.* rpt. David Crosby & Carl Gottlieb, 2007.

_____. *Since Then: How I Survived Everything and Lived to Tell About It.* G.P. Putnam's Sons, 2006.

Curtis, Jim. *Decoding Dylan: Making Sense of the Songs That Changed Modern Culture.* McFarland, 2019.

Denver, John. *Take Me Home: An Autobiography.* Crown Archetype, 1994.

Dushan, Joshua. *Billy Joel: America's Piano Man.* Rowman and Littlefield, 2017.

Dushan, Joshua, and Ryan Raul Benegale. *We Didn't Start the Fire: Billy Joel and Popular Music Studies.* Lexington, 2020.

Dylan, Bob. *Chronicles I.* Simon & Schuster, 2005.

_____. *Writings and Drawings.* Random House, 1973.

Dyson, Michael Eric. *Mercy, Mercy Me: The Art, Loves, and Demons of Marvin Gaye.* Civitas, 2005.

Egan, Sean, ed. *Bowie on Bowie: Interviews and Encounters with David Bowie.* Chicago Review Press, 2015.

Elliott, Michael. *Have a Little Faith: The John Hiatt Story.* Chicago Review Press, 2021.

Eng, Steve. *Jimmy Buffett: The Man from Margaritaville Revealed.* St. Martin-Griffin, 1997.

Fong-Torres, Ben. *Hickory Wind: The Life and Times of Gram Parsons.* Pocket Books,

Frampton, Peter. *Do You Feel Like We Do?: A Memoir.* Hachette, 2020.

Goldman, Albert. *The Lives of John Lennon* (1988). Chicago Review Press, 2001.

Greene, Jackson M. *Here Comes the Sun: The Spiritual and Musical Journey of George Harrison.* Bantam, 2010.

Halperin, Ian. *Fire and Rain: The James Taylor Story.* Citadel, 2000.

Harrison, George. *I Me Mine.* Chronicle Books, 1980.

Harrison, Olivia, and Mark Holborn. *George Harrison: Living in the Material World.* Abrams, 2011.

Hilburn, Robert. *Paul Simon: The Life.* Simon & Schuster, 2018.

_____. *Johnny Cash: The Life.* Little Brown, 2013.

Humphries, Pat. *Nick Drake: The Biography.* Bloomsbury, 1998.

Huntley, Eliot J. *Mystical One: George Harrison After the Breakup of The Beatles.* Guernica, 2004.

Inglis, Ian. *The Words and Music of George Harrison.* Praeger, 2010.

Inglis, Sam. *Harvest.* 33⅓. Continuum, 2003.

Izzo, David, ed. *Bruce Springsteen and the American Soul: Essays on the Music and Influence of a Cultural Icon.* McFarland, 2011.

Jackson, Laura. *Neil Diamond: His Life, His Music, His Passion.* ECW, 2005.

Jennings, Nicholas. *Lightfoot.* Viking, 2016.

Kantor, Ira. *Hello, Honey It's Me: The Story of Harry Chapin.* Independently published, 2020.

Kessel, Corrine. *The Words and Music of Tom Waits.* Praeger, 2008.

King, Carole. *Carole King: A Natural Woman, A Memoir.* Grand Central, 2013.

Kitts, Thomas M. *Finding Fogerty: Interdisciplinary Readings of John Fogerty and Creedence Clearwater Revival.* Lexington Books, 2013.

_____. *John Fogerty: American Son.* Routledge, 2016.

_____. *Richie Furay.* New York and London: Routledge, 2022.

Kort, Michelle. *Soul Picnic: The Music and Passion of Laura Nyro.* St. Martin's Griffin, 2002.

Laurie, Greg. *Johnny Cash: The Redemption of an American Icon.* Salem Books, 2019.

Light, Alan. *The Holy or the Broken: Leonard Cohen, Jeff Buckley, and the Unlikely Ascent of Hallelujah*. Atria, 2013.

Lundy, Zeth. *Songs in the Key of Life*. 33⅓. Continuum.

Madden, Caroline. *The Springsteen Soundtrack: The Sound of the Boss in Film and Television*. McFarland, 2020.

Marcus, Greil. *When That Rough God Goes Riding: Listening to Van Morrison*. Public Affairs, 2011.

Marsh, Dave. *Two Hearts: The Bruce Springsteen Story*. Routledge, 2003.

McCartney, Paul. *McCartney, The Lyrics* (2 vols.). Liveright, 2021.

McDonough, Jimmy. *Shakey: Neil Young's Biography*. Anchor, 2002.

McParland, Robert. *Crosby, Stills, Nash, and Young's 50 Year Quest*. McFarland, 2019.

_____. "Into the Slipstream" (Van Morrison, Bob Dylan, George Harrison), *Finding God in the Devil's Music*. Edited by Alex Di Blasi and Robert McParland. McFarland, 2019.

Mercer, Michelle. *Will You Take Me as I Am? Joni Mitchell's Blue Period*. Free Press, 2009.

Miller, Stephen. *Kris Kristofferson: The Wild American*. Omnibus, 2010.

Mills, Peter. *Hymns to the Silence: Inside the Words and Music of Van Morrison*. Continuum/Bloomsbury, 2010.

Montgomery, Ted. *The Paul McCartney Catalog: A Complete Annotated Discography of Solo Works, 1967–2019*. McFarland, 2020.

Moscowitz, David. *The Words and Music of Bob Marley*. Praeger, 2007.

Myers, Paul. *Todd Rundgren: A Wizard, True Star*. Jawbone, 2010.

Nash, Graham. *Wild Tales: A Rock and Roll Life*. Crown, 2013.

Nelson, Sean. *Court and Spark*. 33⅓. Continuum, 2007.

Nelson, Willie. *It's a Long Story: My Life*. Back Bay Books, 2016.

Nogowski, John. *Bob Dylan: A Descriptive Discography and Filmography, 1961–2020*. McFarland, 2021.

Norman, Philip. *John Lennon: The Life*. Ecco, 2009.

_____. *Paul McCartney: The Life*. Little Brown, 2016.

_____. *The Life and Music of Eric Clapton*. Little Brown, 2018.

Parton, Dolly. *Dolly Parton, Songteller: My Life in Lyrics*. Chronicle Books, 2020.

Pegg, Nicholas. *The Complete David Bowie*. London: Titan, 2011.

Perone, James E. *The Words and Music of James Taylor*. Praeger Books, 2017.

Plasketes, George. *Warren Zevon: Desperado of Los Angeles*. Rowman and Littlefield, 2016.

Ricks, Christopher. *Dylan's Visions of Sin*. Ecco, 2004.

Ritz, David. *Divided Soul: The Life of Marvin Gaye*. Da Capo, 2003.

Rogovny, Seth. *Bob Dylan: Prophet, Mystic, Poet*. Scribner's, 2009.

Schruers, Fred. *Billy Joel: The Definitive Biography*. Crown, 2015.

Schuck, Raymond J., and Ray Schuck. *Do You Believe in Rock and Roll? Essays on Don McLean's American Pie*. McFarland, 2012.

Searles, Malcolm C. *A Sweet Surrender: The Musical Journey of Bread, David Gates, James Griffin and Co*. Helter Skelter, 2015.

Shapiro, Marc. *Behind Sad Eyes: The Life of George Harrison*. St. Martin's Press, Griffin, 2003.

Shipton, Alan. *Nilsson: The Life of a Singer Songwriter*. Oxford University Press, 2015.

Shelton, Robert. *No Direction Home: The Life and Music of Bob Dylan* (1986), rpt. Backbeat Books, 2011.

Simmons, Sylvie. *I'm Your Man: The Life of Leonard Cohen*. Ecco, 2011.

Simon, Carly. *Boys in the Trees: A Memoir*. Flatiron, 2015.

Smith, Patti. *Just Kids*. Ecco, 2010.

Snow, Mat. *Beatles Solo: The Illustrated John, Paul, George, and Ringo After the Beatles*. Race Point, 2013.

Spitz, Marc. *Bowie*. Crown, 2010.

Springsteen, Bruce. *Born to Run: An Autobiography*. Simon & Schuster, 2016.

Stafford, David, and Carolyn Stafford. *Maybe I'm Doing It Wrong: The Life and Music of Randy Newman*. Omnibus, 2016.

Streissguth, Michael. *Johnny Cash: The Biography*. Da Capo, 2007.

Tarr, Joe. *The Words and Music of Patti Smith*. Praeger, 2008.

Taylor, Michael Francis. *Harry Chapin: The Music Behind the Man*. New Haven Publishing, 2019.

Thompson, Dave. *Hearts of Darkness: James Taylor, Jackson Browne, Cat Stevens, and the Unlikely Rise of the Singer Songwriter*. Backbeat, 2012.

Thompson, Richard, and Scott Timberg. *Beeswing: Losing My Way and Finding My Voice*. Algonquin Books, 2021.

Underwood, Lee. *Blue Melody: Tim Buckley Remembered*. Backbeat, 2002.

Urish, Ben, and Ken Bielen, *The Words and Music of John Lennon*. Praeger, 2007.

Wainwright, Loudon. *Liner Notes: On Parents and Children, Exes and Excess, Death and Decay and a Few of My Other Favorite Things*. Blue Rider Press, 2017.

Walsh, Brian J. *Kicking at the Darkness: Bruce Cockburn and the Christian Imagination*. Brazos Press, 2011.

Weller, Sheila. *Girls Like Us: Carole King, Joni Mitchell, and Carly Simon and the Journey of a Generation*. Atria, 2008.

White, Ryan. *Jimmy Buffett: A Good Life*. Atria, 2017.

White, Timothy. *James Taylor: Long Ago and Far Away*. Omnibus, 2001.

Womack, Kenneth, and Jason Kropps. *All Things Must Pass Away: Harrison, Clapton, and Other Assorted Love Songs*. Chicago Review Press, 2020.

Yaffe, David. *Reckless Daughter: A Portrait of Joni Mitchell*. Sarah Crichton Books, 2015.

Young, Neil. *Waging Heavy Peace: A Hippie Dream*. Plume, 2013.

Zevon, Crystal. *I'll Sleep When I'm Dead: The Dirty Life and Times of Warren Zevon*. Echo Books, 2007.

*Most biographers have written credible accounts of singer-songwriters based upon interviews and research. However, personality and perspective are involved. Paul McCartney and other associates of John Lennon regarded Albert Goldman's 1988 book as pure slander and fabrication. It may be best to listen to the singer-songwriter's recordings and to read interviews as well as to read more than one biography to gain a rounded picture of that individual.

Overviews on the Web

On the Records, Phil Bausch (May 30, 2020). Bausch lists some 1970s singer-songwriter albums. https://www.ontherecords.net/2020/05/singer-songwriters-of-the-70s.

"70+ Obscure Singer Songwriters Who Were Better Than James Taylor." They weren't all better than James Taylor, but the title is provocative. https://www.rateyourmusic.com.

Female Singer-Songwriters in the Early 1970s. A brief overview of some female singer songwriters from the 1970s with the intention of teaching students about them. https://teachrock.com.

World Café Looks Back, 70s Songwriters (April 2012). A brief overview of Joni Mitchell, James Taylor, Randy Newman, and Jackson Browne. https://www.npr.

The Ten Best Singer-Songwriter Albums. Sean Llewellen selects a few singer-songwriter albums. He lists Bob Dylan's *Blood on the Tracks*, Neil Young's *Harvest*, Joni Mitchell's *Blue*, Carole King's *Tapestry*, Don McLean's *American Pie*, Jackson Browne's *Late for the Sky*, Tom Waits' *Closing Time*, and Elton John's *Madman Across the Water*. He includes Bruce Springsteen's *Born to Run*, although Springsteen only became fully solo with *Nebraska,* and he includes Tom Petty, who was always with his band, the Heartbreakers. https://www.loudersound.com

Singer Songwriters of the 70s is offered on https://youtube.com. Dig a little deeper than this. There are many YouTube videos downloaded both officially by companies and unofficially by fans.

Rolling Stone's Best 100 Albums of the 1970s. https://www.listchallenges.com/rollingstone.

A listing of 70 top 1970s albums selected by the Paste Magazine staff: https://www.pastemagazine.com.

Index

197